MARGARET DALEY

A Family for Tory

&

A Mother for Cindy

Steeple
Hill®

Published by Steeple Hill Books™

STEEPLE HILL BOOKS

Steeple
Hill®

Recycling programs
for this product may
not exist in your area.

ISBN-13: 978-0-373-65129-0

A FAMILY FOR TORY AND A MOTHER FOR CINDY

A FAMILY FOR TORY
Copyright © 2004 by Margaret Daley

A MOTHER FOR CINDY
Copyright © 2005 by Margaret Daley

Printed in U.S.A.

CONTENTS

Books by Margaret Daley

Love Inspired

The Power of Love
Family for Keeps
Sadie's Hero
The Courage to Dream
What the Heart Knows
A Family for Tory
*Gold in the Fire
*A Mother for Cindy
*Light in the Storm
The Cinderella Plan
*When Dreams Come True
*Tidings of Joy
**Once Upon a Family
**Heart of the Family
**Family Ever After

Love Inspired Suspense

Hearts on the Line
Heart of the Amazon
So Dark the Night
Vanished
Buried Secrets
Don't Look Back
Forsaken Canyon
What Sarah Saw
Poisoned Secrets

*The Ladies of Sweetwater Lake
**Fostered by Love

MARGARET DALEY

feels she has been blessed. She has been married more than thirty years to her husband, Mike, whom she met in college. He is a terrific support and her best friend. They have one son, Shaun.

Margaret has been writing for many years and loves to tell a story. When she was a little girl, she would play with her dolls and make up stories about their lives. Now she writes these stories down. She especially enjoys weaving stories about families and how faith in God can sustain a person when things get tough. When she isn't writing, she is fortunate to be a teacher for students with special needs. Margaret has taught for over twenty years and loves working with her students. She has also been a Special Olympics coach and participated in many sports with her students.

A FAMILY FOR TORY

So that we may boldly say, The Lord is my helper, and I will not fear what man shall do unto me.

—*Hebrews* 13:6

To the people I work with,
especially Terri, Rene, Katie, Becky, Anne, Laurie,
Naomai, Mike, Lila, Stacie, Debbie, Lisa—
you all make coming to work each day special.

Chapter One

Slade Donaldson switched off the engine and glanced toward his eight-year-old daughter. "Ready, Mindy? Are you sure you want to do this? I'll be gone for about an hour."

Mindy nodded, her face brightening with a huge grin. "Tor-ee needs—my—uh—help, Dad-dy."

Every time he heard his daughter struggle to say something, his heart twisted into a knot that he feared would never unravel. "Then I'd better meet this Tory Alexander." Since his housekeeper had taken Mindy to her physical therapy for the past few months, he'd never met the woman who had brought her pony into the hospital to cheer up the children and captured his daughter's interest.

Mindy pointed toward a petite woman emerging from a barn, leading a horse on a rein. "Th—ere." Her grin widened, her brown eyes sparkling.

"Then let's go. I need to be at the bank in twenty minutes for my meeting." He thrust open his car door, then hurried around to help his daughter.

"I can—do—this." Mindy pulled herself to a standing position using the door.

The tightness in his chest made his breathing difficult. He offered his daughter his arm. She clasped it to steady herself, then began to make her way toward the woman by the opening into the barn. Two weeks ago his daughter had declared she didn't want to use her walker anymore. Each day since, Mindy had leaned less and less on him as she'd walked. Progress, Slade thought, due partly to this woman before him. She and her pony, Mirabelle, have been the reasons Mindy tolerated her physical therapy at the hospital over the past few months. He was in Tory Alexander's debt.

Tory saw Mindy approaching and tied the reins to the fence of the riding ring. Then she strode toward the girl with a smile of greeting. Slade was surprised by how small the woman was. The horse she'd been leading was at least seventeen hands tall, towering over her. Her long auburn hair was swept back in a ponytail with a few stray strands curling around her oval face. Freckles sprinkled her turned-up nose and her large brown eyes drew a person to her. Fringed in dark lashes, Slade felt their pull as she came to a stop only a few feet from Mindy and him.

Tory looked at his daughter. "I'm so glad you didn't have to cancel, Mindy." Then she turned those large brown eyes on him. "I'm sorry to hear about Mrs. Watson's emergency. Will her niece be okay?"

"She just went into labor a little early. My house-keeper assures me everything will be all right and she'll be back in a week or so."

"That's good to hear. I know she was excited about her niece's pregnancy. First in the family." Tory lifted her arm toward Mindy to take over being her support if she needed. "Come on, Mindy. Let's show your father the barn."

"I have a meeting I need to go to."

"Dad-dy, just—" Mindy swallowed several times "—see Bel-le."

Slade stared at his daughter's face, lit with hope and eagerness, and he couldn't refuse the invitation even though it would make him late. After all, she was the reason he worked fourteen-hour days. He wanted only the best care for Mindy, and that cost money. "Lead the way." Sweeping his arm toward the barn, he followed the pair.

As he entered, surprisingly the only scents to assail him were hay and leather. Scanning the darker interior, he noticed how clean the barn was. A few stalls had horses in them but most were empty. "Where are your horses?"

"In the pastures."

"How many do you have?"

"Fifteen and one pony, Mirabelle, or, as Mindy loves to call her, Belle."

"Th-ere," Mindy said, gesturing toward the last stall. She hurried her pace, her left foot dragging in the dirt.

Mindy stumbled. Slade lurched forward to catch her, but Tory had already steadied her. Mindy continued her fast pace toward Mirabelle, towing Tory behind her.

Tory quickened her step to keep up. "Whoa. Mirabelle isn't going anywhere."

"Haven't seen—her in—lo-ong time."

Slade scooped Mindy up in his arms and continued toward the stall at the very end of the barn. "It's only been five days, sweetie."

"Too lo-ong."

While Tory swung the stall door open, he went inside with Mindy. She squirmed.

"Dad-dy, put me down."

He settled his daughter in front of Mirabelle and kept his hands on her shoulders so she wouldn't fall as she found her balance. Even though her surgery had been eight months before, it was still hard for her to keep her equilibrium at times.

She bent forward and threw her arms around the pony's neck. Nuzzling the animal, Mindy giggled. "Isn't she ugly? No—" she shook her head "—pret-ty?"

Slade inspected the pony's golden brown coat and big brown eyes that suddenly reminded him of Mirabelle's owner. "Very pretty."

"You know Mirabelle has been waiting just for you so you could give her a good brushing. No one does it better." Tory produced a curry comb and passed it to Mindy.

Tory helped Mindy position herself so she could start on the pony's left side. With one hand clutching the mane, Mindy began her task. Tory stepped back toward the entrance, motioning for Slade to follow. Outside the stall she paused. Reluctantly Mindy's dad joined her.

"Do you think we should leave her alone like that?" he asked, a frown creasing his brow.

"She'll be fine. She's done that half a dozen times now and loves to. It's her private time with Mirabelle." A giggle drifted to her, and Tory smiled. "See. I think she tells Belle her secrets."

"What secrets?" Panic laced his question.

"All little girls have them. Who's her favorite movie star? What songs does she like? Who's her best friend at school?"

"She didn't go to school this year. She's being tutored at home."

"Is she going to attend in the fall?"

Slade opened his mouth to answer, then clamped it shut. He glanced away. "I don't know. It depends on her therapy and how fast she recovers."

"Mindy's so good with the other children who come for riding lessons. She misses her friends."

Slade straightened, his jaw clenched. "I won't have her go to school and be teased because she talks too slow and walks funny."

"Kids can be very accepting."

"And kids can be very cruel. Mindy's gone through so much this past year because of the car accident that took her mother and caused her epilepsy."

"But didn't the surgery make the epilepsy better?"

"She hasn't had a seizure, but at what cost?" Slade waved his hand toward the stall where his daughter was talking to the pony, frustration in every taut line of his body.

"Do you regret agreeing to the surgery?"

Slade plowed his fingers through his hair. "Yes—no. The doctors told me this was best for Mindy, that given time she would recover most of her speech and physical abilities. A few years from now we'll hardly know she had part of her brain removed."

"But it doesn't make it any easier right now?"

"No," he clipped out.

"I didn't mean to intrude, but Mindy has become very important to me. I was hoping she could come more often to the stables to help out. She asked me to talk to you about it."

"She did? When?"

"She called me this morning and asked."

"So that's who she was talking to on the phone. I thought it was one of her girlfriends. When I made that assumption, she didn't correct me."

"She wants to be my assistant and go with me to the hospital when I take Mirabelle next time."

Slade relaxed the tensed set to his shoulders. "It's hard for me to say no when Mirabelle is the reason my daughter would cheerfully go to the hospital for her physical therapy. Before Mirabelle, Mrs. Watson and I had a horrible time getting Mindy to go. Now with the promise of seeing the pony, she'll do just about anything."

"Animals can be great therapy for people. That's why I started my riding stable for people in need, especially children. So what do you say about Mindy helping me out?"

"Let me think about it. That's asking you to do a lot for Mindy."

"I don't mind. If I didn't want her to be my helper, I wouldn't have asked."

"Still…" Slade checked his watch. "I'd better get going. I'm already late as it is. I'll be back in an hour."

"We'll be in the riding ring."

Slade strode toward his car, feeling the touch of Tory's gaze on his back. It took a supreme effort not to turn around and look at her. She was an attractive lady who obviously loved animals and children. Very appealing qualities in a woman, he thought, then shook his head. What in the world was he thinking? After this past twenty-two months piecing his life back together, he didn't think he could deal with anything that required his emotions be involved. He had all he could handle with Mindy and her recovery. But first, he had to secure the loan for the second phase of the expansion of his company.

"You're doing great, Mindy. Sit up straight. Take command." Tory watched the young girl walk her horse around the riding ring. The child's face glowed, her proud expression attesting to one of the reasons Tory spent so much time and money on her Bright Star Stables—the looks on her riders' faces when they were successful. "Okay, Mindy, that's it for today. You need to cool Paint down now."

"Dad-dy say yes?"

Tory assisted Mindy in dismounting, then handed the

child the reins. "He's going to think about you helping me at the hospital with Mirabelle."

The girl's lower lip stuck out in a pout. "Why?"

"Because your day is full as it is. With your schooling and therapies, Mindy, you don't have a lot of extra time."

The sudden sound of Slade's voice made Tory stiffen. The erratic beat of her heart crashed against her chest. With her attention totally focused on Mindy, Tory hadn't heard him approaching. She didn't like being caught unaware. It emphasized her vulnerability. Swinging around toward him, she took in his tall height, over six feet, and muscular frame that even his suit couldn't conceal. She stamped down her alarm. This was Mindy's father.

The little girl gripped Tory's arm and twisted about to face her father who stopped a few feet from her. "Summer—is al-most—here. No sch-ool then."

One of Slade's dark brows arched. "Who said that?"

"No va-va-ca-tion?"

"You'll have one, a short one. But you have some catching up to do, young lady."

Mindy sighed heavily. "I can't—" The young girl paused and swallowed several times "—help Tor-ee?"

"No, I didn't say that."

A bright gleam shone in Mindy's eyes. "I can!"

"I didn't say that, either. I'm still thinking about it."

Instantly the child's expression crumbled and her shoulders sagged.

"Take care of your horse and let me talk with Tory for a minute. I won't be long."

Mindy led Paint toward the barn, her left foot leaving

a drag mark in the dirt. The little girl's head was lifted. Tory had been working the past month on instilling confidence into the child, something that had suffered after her operation.

The second Mindy disappeared into the barn, Tory swung around, prepared to defend her reasons for wanting the girl to work with her. Slade cut her off with "Mindy won't make her next lesson."

His words took the steam out of her. Surprised, she grappled for something to say. "Why?" was all she could manage to think of.

"With Mrs. Watson gone I don't have the time to bring her out here next Tuesday. As it is, I'm having a hard time getting help to take care of Mindy while my housekeeper's away. I thought today I had everything arranged, but my arrangements fell through."

"I can help," Tory said without really thinking through the consequences. But she adored the child and didn't want her to miss her twice-weekly riding lessons.

"I couldn't ask you—"

"You didn't. I volunteered to help. Mindy wants to spend more time here. I could use her help and watch her at the same time. It's perfect for everyone."

Slade shook his head, deep lines in his forehead. "But—"

Tory held up her hand to stop his flow of words. "Who are you going to get to sit with Mindy? Someone from a baby-sitting organization? Mindy and I are buddies. I would love to help her out. I wouldn't offer if I didn't mean it."

"I don't know how long Mrs. Watson is going to be gone. Everything happened so suddenly. She said a week or maybe longer."

"One thing I've learned taking care of animals is to go with the flow. One day at a time. Don't worry. The future will take care of itself." At least that was what she was counting on. Because right now she wasn't sure how long she could keep Bright Star Stables operational.

"Not without a lot of help from me." He took a deep breath and blew it out between pursed lips. "Okay. If you're sure."

"I am."

"Then I'll bring her first thing Monday morning."

"What time?"

Slade peered toward the barn, his eyes narrowing as though he were trying to see into the dark shadows. "I'm afraid seven. I have an eight o'clock meeting I need to attend."

"That's fine by me. I'm usually up by five. I'll have the stalls clean by that time." Mindy's presence reinforced all the reasons she worked long hours to keep Bright Star Stables going.

"That's mighty ambitious."

"There's nothing ambitious about it. I'm usually the only one to do it. I depend on volunteers to help. Otherwise, this is a one man—or rather, woman—show."

"Thanks. You're a lifesaver." Slade stuck his hand out.

Tory stared at it for a brief moment, then fit her hand

within his and quickly shook it before pulling back, taking a step away as she did.

"Hopefully Mrs. Watson will only be gone for a week."

"Don't worry about how long it will be."

The tense set to his shoulders relaxed. "Now that only leaves rearranging her speech and physical therapies next week."

"When are they?"

"Mindy has speech Monday afternoon at four and physical therapy Tuesday and Friday mornings."

"I need to come into town Monday. I can take her and you can pick her up there."

"I can't—"

"Didn't we just go through this? I know how important her therapies are for her and how hard it can be to rearrange. It's no big deal."

"Tor-ee, I'm fin-ished."

Tory swung around to watch as Mindy made her way toward them. Dirt dusted her cheeks with some bits of hay sticking out of her hair. "Are you all right?" she asked while Slade rushed toward Mindy.

The little girl waved her father away. "I'm o-kay. Just—fell, that's—all."

Slade looped his arm about Mindy's shoulders. "Are you hurt?"

Mindy shook her head, dislodging a piece of hay that floated to the ground.

"We should have brought your walker. This uneven surface—"

"No! I—I—hate it!"

"Your dad agreed to you helping me. In fact, you're going to be my assistant all next week while Mrs. Watson is gone."

"I am!" Mindy brushed the rest of the hay from her hair, a huge grin revealing a missing tooth. "Thanks, Dad-dy."

"You're welcome, sweetie."

"I get—to—miss—sch-ool?" The child's eagerness peppered the air with her enthusiasm.

"No way. I'll have your homebound teacher come out here for the week."

Some of Mindy's enthusiasm evaporated, a slump to her stance. "I hate—sch-ool—too."

"Mindy, we've had this discussion. School and your lessons are important." Slade held his arm out for his daughter to take, then he led her toward his car.

Tory followed, wishing she had the right to step in. She remembered when she was struggling to learn to read in elementary school. She'd hated school, too, until she had mastered her problem. Mindy had to fight hard to regain everything she'd once taken for granted, such as walking, talking, taking care of herself. It would be normal for her to feel that way about her lessons when she was still trying to recoup what she'd lost after the operation.

After securing Mindy into the front seat and closing the door, Slade moved toward the back of the car where Tory stood. "We've had this argument every week since the homebound teacher started. She remembers what she used to be able to do with ease. Now those things are so hard for her that she often becomes very frustrated."

There was a part of Tory that wanted to reach out and

touch this man in pain, but there was a part that held her frozen in place. "She's come a long way in a short time."

Dark shadows clouded his blue eyes. "If I could trade places with Mindy, I would in a heartbeat. The worse thing for me is to have to stand by and watch her suffer."

His whispered words held anguish in them. Tory lifted her hand toward him, her fingers trembling as they lay on his arm for a brief moment before slipping away. "Prayer has always helped me through the difficult times."

"Mindy was innocent. This should never have happened to her in the first place. She was perfectly normal until the car wreck. Why would God do this to her?"

The pain in his voice robbed Tory of her breath. The heaviness in her chest threatened to squeeze the air completely from her lungs.

He started to turn away, then swung back toward her. "It's been a long week. I didn't mean to burden you with this. I'll bring Mindy out Monday morning." He offered her a fleeting smile, said, "Thanks for all your help," then strode to the driver's side and slid behind the wheel.

As his car pulled out, Tory fought the tears quickly filling her eyes. *Lord, help this man find his path back to You. He is hurting and needs Your comfort.*

"Wh-ere's—Dad-dy?" Mindy asked, worry furrowing her brow.

Tory glanced at her watch for the third time in ten

minutes. "His meeting probably ran over. That's all. We'd better wait here for him."

"Ba-th-ro-om." Mindy labored over the word, the lines in her face deepening.

"I'll wait out here in the reception area for your dad while you're gone."

"Be back." Mindy made her way across the room and disappeared through the door where clients went for their speech therapy.

Picking up a magazine, Tory began flipping through it, not really seeing the words on the page. Slade was fifteen minutes late. Why hadn't he called? What was wrong? She chewed on her lower lip, her own worry coming to the foreground. Finally she gave up trying to read the magazine and tossed it back on the table in front of her.

The outside door swung open, and Slade entered. He was all right, Tory thought, her gaze skimming down his length. Relief shimmered through her.

When he caught sight of her in the corner, he hurried to her and sat next to her. For just a second Tory's heart sped. She pressed her lips together to still her usual reaction to someone invading her space.

"I'm so sorry I was late. My cell phone is dead so I couldn't call you to tell you that I was sitting in traffic waiting for them to clear up an accident."

"Anyone hurt?"

He frowned, his blue eyes dark. "Yes. It was a mess. They're still working on it."

"Dad-dy!"

Slade looked toward Mindy who stood a few feet away. The little girl launched herself at her father, throwing her arms around him.

"You oo-kay?" Mindy plastered herself against her father. "What—" She couldn't finish her sentence. Tears shone in her eyes and one slipped down her cheeks.

Slade smoothed his daughter's hair back from her face and kissed the top of her head. "I'm fine. Just delayed. I couldn't call. Sorry about that. I know how you are when I'm late."

"Su-re—okay?" Mindy sniffed.

He squeezed her to him. "Yes, sweetie."

"He just got stuck in traffic," Tory said as she rose and gathered up her purse.

"What—was—a mess?" Mindy leaned back to peer at her father.

Slade paled. "Nothing important."

"Dad-dy, what?"

He forced a laugh. "My day, sweetie, but not now. How about us taking Tory out to dinner? I think she deserves our thanks for helping us out."

"Yes!"

Mindy's excitement touched Tory. She'd always wanted children—lots of them—but didn't see how that goal was possible now. Slade was so lucky to have a daughter like Mindy. "How can I refuse?"

"You—can't." Mindy scooted off her father's lap and took Tory's hand, pulling her toward the door.

"I guess my daughter is hungry, even though it's not much after five. Do you mind an early dinner?"

Laughing at Mindy's eagerness to leave, Tory tossed back over her shoulder while the child was dragging her through the opened door, "I'm always hungry, so I can eat early or late or both. Where are we going? I can follow you in my truck."

"Leave your truck here and I'll bring you back for it afterward."

"I can follow—"

"Plee-ze," Mindy said, stopping in the middle of the parking lot.

"You make it hard to say no, young lady." Tory forced a scolding tone to her voice, but she was sure the smile that accompanied her words wiped out any threat.

"You—will?"

Tory looked toward Slade for help. He shrugged and shook his head. She was on her own. "I guess so. But wouldn't it be easier if I—"

At Slade's car while opening the back door, Mindy announced, "You—can—sit—" she paused, searching for her words "—in the front."

"No, that's—" Tory watched as the little girl hopped into the back seat faster than she had seen her move since she had known her.

Over the top of the car Tory spied Slade looking at her. "I guess I'll sit in front."

"Please. I draw the line at being a chauffeur."

When Slade started the engine and pulled out of the parking space, he asked, "Any favorite place you would like to go?"

"I'm not picky. Wherever you two like."

The second he maneuvered the car into the flow of traffic Mindy said, "Music—plee-ze."

Tory switched on the radio. She'd found Mindy loved to listen to it even while working in the barn.

The end of a popular song sounded over the radio, then the announcer came on. "Now for a traffic update. There has been a multicar wreck on—"

Slade switched the dial to Off. Surprised, Tory glanced at him. Then she heard the scream from the back seat.

Chapter Two

"Nooo!" Mindy screamed over and over.

Slade crossed two lanes of traffic to pull into an almost-deserted office parking lot. Before Tory had time to react to the situation, he was out of the car and thrusting open the back door.

He hauled his daughter into his arms and held her tightly to him, whispering, "It's okay, sweetheart. You're all right. I'm here. Nothing's going to hurt you ever again. I promise."

Tory twisted around, desperately wanting to help Mindy. She had come to love the child in the short time she'd known her. The child's sobs filled the air with her pain, a pain Tory wished she could wipe away.

"Mom-my," Mindy cried, her voice muffled by the blue cotton of Slade's shirt.

But Tory heard the pitiful wail and knew the announcer had triggered a memory of Mindy's own wreck that had changed the little girl's life forever. Tory's heart pounded against her chest in slow, anguish-filled throbs, mirroring the distress in Mindy. Tory knew more than most how quickly life could change; one split second could make all the difference. If only she hadn't gone out…. Tory pushed the memory away, refusing to allow it into her mind. She couldn't alter the past, but with God's guidance, she could protect herself.

She caught Slade's attention and mouthed, "Can I help?"

He shook his head, stroking his daughter's back. "Sweetie, Mommy's gone. But I'm here for you."

"It—it—" Mindy struggled for her words. "It—hurt."

"I know, baby. But you're safe now."

Slade's eyes slid closed, but not before Tory saw their glistening sheen. Tears clogged Tory's throat and misted her own eyes. She blinked, trying to get a grip on her emotions that careened out of control.

Mindy shuddered and Slade clutched her tighter. "Mommy's watching over you, baby. Taking care of you. She'll always be with you in here." He laid his hand over his daughter's heart.

Helpless, Tory drew in deep breaths after deep breaths but still she ached for the pair. She felt as if she had intruded on a private family moment and should disappear. She would give anything to take the child's pain away, but from experience knew that was something another couldn't do.

Mindy pulled back, sniffing and wiping her nose.

"I—" she sucked in a huge gulp of air "—know, Dad-dy."

He cupped his daughter's face in his large hands. "I love you, sweetie."

She sniffled again. "I know."

Slade brushed the pads of his thumbs across Mindy's cheeks, erasing all evidence of her tears. "Are you ready to show Tory a good time?" Tenderness marked his expression as he peered at his daughter with eyes a soft azure. "I thought we would go to your favorite restaurant."

"Goldie's?"

"Of course. Is there another?"

"No!" A grin split Mindy's face.

Slade kissed his daughter, then slipped from the back seat. When he settled behind the steering wheel and started the engine, he threw Tory a glance that caused her heart to flip over. Sadness mixed with a look of appeal for understanding. She slid her hand across the console, almost touching Slade in reassurance. At the last second she pulled back and smiled at him instead.

"I love Goldie's hamburgers and onion rings," Tory said to Mindy, trying to ignore the heat of a blush she felt creep up her face at Slade's intense regard.

"Me, too." Mindy clapped, her left hand curled so that her palms didn't meet.

"With everything on it, even onions."

Tory caught Slade's look. The smile that glinted in his eyes warmed her. Her blush deepened. Aware his gaze was still riveted to her, she shifted in the leather seat, crossing and uncrossing her ankles. Uncomfortable under his intense scrutiny, she searched for something to say. Silence dominated the small confines of the car. Nothing she thought seemed appropriate so she let the quiet reign.

Fifteen minutes later Slade drove into the parking lot next to Goldie's. After he assisted Mindy from the back seat, they all headed into the restaurant, decorated in homespun décor, reminiscent of a farmhouse, with the scent of baking bread and coffee saturating the air.

Tory sat across from Mindy and Slade in the booth along the large front window that overlooked a pond. Geese and ducks swam in the water, which drew the little girl's attention.

"Look—" Mindy frowned, her brow wrinkled in thought "—bab-ies."

The fluency of the little girl's speech had improved over the months since Tory had known her, but still the child labored to put her words together, to find the correct word to say. Tory wanted to hug her for her perseverance.

"The last time Mindy and I were here, the geese were sitting on their nests. They're three couples and it looks like they have all had their babies. Now she'll want to come back every week to keep track of them."

"I have a pond, Mindy, on my property. We'll have to ride there one day and have a picnic."

"Dad-dy, too?"

Tory's gaze slid to Slade's. "Do you ride?"

He laughed. "Sort of."

Tory arched one brow in question.

"The last time was in high school, so it's been years since I've been on a horse. Is it like riding a bicycle?"

"Sort of." Tory downed a large swallow of ice water, her throat suddenly parched.

"Well, then, yes, I do ride—or let's just say I know how to fall gracefully when the horse bolts."

"Now you've piqued my curiosity. What happened the last time you rode?"

"I had leaned over to open the gate into the pasture when my horse got spooked by a rabbit darting in front of him. He decided to take off, leaving me dangling from the gate."

Mindy giggled. "Oh, Dad-dy."

"I've fallen a few times, too, and I can't always say they were graceful falls." Tory took another long sip of her water, relishing the cool liquid.

Slade started to say something when the waitress approached to take their orders. After she left, he grinned. "When I fell, I landed in a mud puddle and was covered from head to toe. It was a *big* mud puddle."

"When can—we—do it?" Mindy asked, eagerness giving her face a radiant glow.

"How about this weekend? I'm free after church on Sunday." Tory glanced from the little girl to Slade.

"Only if you allow me to bring the picnic."

"This is my treat. I invited you."

"Then let me bring the dessert." Determination marked his expression.

Tory shrugged. "Fine."

"What do you like?"

"Oh, just about anything with chocolate. Surprise me."

"I've gotten the impression you weren't someone who liked to be surprised."

"Not usually." Tory clasped her hands in her lap to still their trembling. Control and order were so important in her life, the threads that held it together. "I don't like to take risks, either, but I think I'll be safe with you bringing the dessert."

"Isn't your Bright Star Stables a financial risk?"

"Yes, but then some things are important enough to risk. I saw a need and wanted to do something about it."

"And this parent is grateful. If I can help you with anything, please let me know."

Tory thought about her low bank account, but pride kept her from saying anything. For many years she had done everything on her own. She was used to that and would somehow make the therapeutic riding program a success. When her aunt's inheritance had allowed her to fulfill a dream, she'd known in her heart this was what God had wanted her to do with her life. God would provide the means to keep Bright Star Stables going.

Slade's gaze bore into her as if he could reach into her mind and read it. "It's okay to ask for help when you need it."

"Look—Dad-dy." Mindy jostled her father's arm, then pointed out the window at the baby geese swimming in a line behind one of their parents with the other bringing up the rear.

If it wouldn't have raised more questions at Mindy's timely interruption, Tory would have gladly hugged and kissed the child. The conversation was getting too personal for her. Keeping people at a distance had become such a habit for her that any probing into her feelings or past proved highly uncomfortable. She swiped the film of perspiration from her upper lip, then finished off her cold water.

After watching the geese with his daughter for a few minutes, Slade returned his attention to Tory. "I'll drop the subject for now, but it's in my best interest to see Bright Star Stables continue."

Mindy swung her gaze to her father, a deep line across her forehead. "What's—wrong?"

With his regard trained on Tory, Slade answered, "Nothing, sweetheart. I just wanted Tory to know how much we both appreciate the work she does."

Mindy bounced up and down. "Yeah!"

Heat scorched her cheeks. She noticed a few patrons looking their way. Breaking eye contact with Slade, she studied her place mat. "Thank you," she whispered, relieved that the waitress brought them their food, taking the focus off her. She preferred being in the background, having had more than her share of the limelight in the past—something she never wanted to relive again.

Tory bit into her thick, juicy hamburger and sighed. "I'd forgotten how great this tasted." She popped a small onion ring into her mouth. "And this. Of course, this will go straight to my hips."

"I don't think that'll hurt you." Slade dumped several sugar packets into his iced tea.

"It will if I had to buy a whole new wardrobe. About all I can afford is a flour sack." The second she'd said it, she regretted the reference to her financial state.

Slade's eyes gleamed, but his lips remained pressed together.

Tory blew out a breath of air, thankful he wasn't going to pursue the topic. "Have you lived in Cimarron City long?"

"All my life. How about you?"

"Just a few years. I moved here from Dallas."

"What made you leave Dallas for Oklahoma?"

She should have expected the question, but still it took her by surprise. "The weather."

"We have the same beastly heat in the summer as Dallas."

"Actually, my aunt died and left me her small ranch. I came to sell it and decided to stay."

"You don't miss the big city."

"Cimarron City is big enough for me. Besides, I'm a country gal at heart, and even though there are eighty thousand living here, it doesn't seem that way when I'm out on my ranch."

"But it's still a far cry from Dallas."

And for that Tory was thankful, but didn't say it out loud. Her memories of her hometown of Dallas were laden with sorrow, which had nothing to do with the city itself. But if she never went back, that would suit her just fine. "Do you have any other family here?" She wanted to take the focus off her and Dallas.

"I have an uncle in a retirement home in Tulsa. His

son moved away when he went to college and hasn't returned except to visit a few times. My younger brother lives in Chicago and loves the big city. My father died ten years ago and Mom decided to live in the southern-most tip of Florida where it's warm all the time. So I'm the last Donaldson here in Cimarron City."

Mindy tugged on his arm. "Me—too."

"How right you are. Mindy and I are the last Donald-sons here. How about your family?"

Tory finished another huge onion ring, then washed it down with a swallow of raspberry-flavored tea. "All my family lives in Texas."

"Do you see them much?"

"They visit the ranch every summer for the Fourth of July."

"You don't go home?"

"It's hard for me to get away because of the horses. Someone has to look after them and I can't afford help. I'm stuck, but I don't mind."

"Are all the horses at the ranch yours?" Slade took a bite of his hamburger.

"No, I stable some. That brings me some needed income to do what I love."

"The therapeutic riding program?"

Tory nodded. "I'll need to get back to the ranch before dark. I still have some chores to do."

"Are you through, Mindy?" Slade tossed his napkin on the table.

The little girl gulped down the rest of her choco-late milk.

"Yep," she said, displaying a creamy brown mustache.

Slade took her napkin and wiped her mouth. "We'd better go. You have a big day tomorrow. You've got physical therapy in the morning."

Mindy pouted. "Do—I—have to?"

"It won't be long, sweetie, before you won't have to. But for now, yes."

After paying for the dinner, Slade escorted Mindy and Tory to his car. Twenty minutes later, he pulled into the parking lot at the speech therapist's office.

He glanced at Mindy in the back seat and smiled. "She still falls asleep riding in the car when she's exhausted."

"She worked hard today at the barn. She also rode." Tory pushed her door open and was surprised when she saw Slade get out of the car, too. "I'm only parked a few feet away."

"I know," he said, coming around the front of his car. "But I felt I owed you an explanation about what happened earlier with Mindy. And I don't want her waking up and overhearing."

The spring air cooled Tory's cheeks and the soft wind blew stray strands of her hair about her face. She brushed them behind her ears, the scent of freshly mowed grass lacing the breeze. "You don't need to explain anything." She moved the few feet to her truck door, aware of Slade's presence in every fiber of her being. She clutched the handle.

"After the accident, I couldn't get Mindy to ride in a car for months. Finally she does, now, but any mention of a car wreck and she falls apart. I try to shelter her from hearing about any accidents, but sometimes I can't."

"Like today when she was listening to the radio."

"She loves to listen to music. She usually listens to CDs."

"But I turned the radio on before you could put a CD in. I'm so sorry. I didn't know. I was just trying to help since you were focused on driving."

He took a step toward her. Her heart skipped a beat. She plastered her back against her door, her hands tightening into fists.

"We've always listened to the radio while doing the chores in the barn," she said, needing to talk to take her mind off his nearness.

"I'm not telling you to make you upset. I just wanted you to know some of the things that Mindy is still coping with."

"Is there anything else? I don't want to be the cause of any more anxiety."

"She still wakes up from nightmares. Thankfully not lately. I'm hoping those are behind her." He raked both hands through his hair, a look of anguish on his face. "Because frankly I have a hard time coping with seeing my daughter like that."

"From what I saw back there, you did a wonderful job of reassuring her. That's all you can do." The hammering of her heart eased as the conversation centered on Mindy.

"Is it? There should be something else I can do to make things better for Mindy." Rubbing one hand along the back of his neck, he rolled his shoulders to relax the tension gripping him.

But Tory saw its continual grasp on him in his taut stance and the grim lines craving his expression. "Being there for Mindy is the most important thing you can do."

"The wreck should never have happened. If only—"

Instantly, without thought, Tory started to lay her fingers over his mouth to still his words. She froze in midaction, her eyes widening. His gaze riveted to hers. For a few seconds everything came to a standstill.

Dropping her arm to her side, she said in a strained voice, "It doesn't do us any good to think about the what-ifs. We can't change the past. We can only influence the present."

"Live for today? Forget about the past?"

"Right." If only she could heed her own advice. She was trying, but there were times it was so difficult.

"Have you been successful doing that?"

She forced a smile. "I'm working on it."

"In other words, no."

Tory yanked open her truck door. "I'd better be going. I still have a lot of things to do before dark." She escaped into the quiet of her pickup, determined to keep her eyes trained forward. But even though she didn't look at Slade, she felt his probing observation delve deep inside, seeking answers about her past, something she guarded closely and never wanted to relive. And above all, certainly didn't want to share with anyone.

Quickly she backed out of the parking space, and as she pulled out into traffic, she chanced a glance at Slade.

He stood where she had left him, a bewildered look on his face. After that evasive move, she wondered if he would bring Mindy tomorrow to the ranch.

Out on her front porch Tory eased herself into the old rocker and raised her glass of iced tea to press it against her heated face. The coldness felt wonderful after Tory had spent most of the day doing the work of two people. She needed to hire someone to help her, but that just wasn't possible at the moment, especially after the notice she'd received from the bank today.

Resting her head, she closed her eyes and continued to roll the glass over her flushed skin. At least Slade brought Mindy out late this morning. The child's cheerful attitude was a balm that soothed those long hours of work and her fretting over where the money for the loan was going to come from. With Mindy next to her, she repaired the fence in one pasture and even had time for the child to ride this afternoon after the three o'clock lesson. Every day Mindy was improving, self-confident when she handled the new mare.

When Tory thought about the little girl eagerly handing her the nails for the fence, Tory's heart swelled. She wanted children so badly—her niece and nephew weren't enough. Even the children she taught didn't fulfill the void in her heart. It was that simple and that complex. She released a long sigh and finally took a sip of her drink.

A scream rent the air. Tory bolted to her feet, the glass crashing to the wooden planks of the porch.

Leaping over the mess, she rushed for the door and wrenched it open as another scream vibrated down her length.

In the living room Mindy sat ramrod straight on the couch with her eyes so huge that was all Tory could focus on. She was at the child's side in an instant that seemed to take forever.

Hugging Mindy to her, she murmured, "What's wrong, baby?"

"I—I—" The child tried to drag air into her lungs, but she couldn't seem to get a decent breath.

"Take it easy. Relax. One breath at a time, Mindy." Tory willed her voice to stay calm while inside she quaked, the beat of her pulse roaring in her ears.

Finally Mindy managed to inhale and exhale a deep breath, then another. But the fright remained in her eyes as the little girl looked at Tory.

"I—I—heard—" Mindy started to hyperventilate.

"Nice and easy, baby. Heard what?"

"Mom-my—cry."

Tory wanted to say the right thing. Her mind went blank. *Oh, Lord, please give me the strength to help her, to soothe her pain.* "Did you have a bad dream?"

Tears welled in Mindy's eyes as she nodded. Tory framed the child's face and tugged her toward her, laying her head on her chest and pressing her close.

"It was only a dream, baby. Not real."

"I—know." Mindy hiccuped. "Still—" A shudder rippled down the child's length.

"It seemed real to you?"

Mindy nodded, her breath catching. "I didn't—" Again the child fought for her next words. "Say—bye."

Tory wrapped her arms tighter about the little girl, wanting to hold her and never let her go. "Did you go to the funeral?"

Mindy shook her head. "In hosp-it—" She didn't finish the word.

"I'm sorry, baby. Have you talked to your dad about this?"

"No." Her muffled reply came out on the end of a sob.

"He should know. Do you want me to talk to him for you?"

Mindy pulled back, tears still shining in her eyes. "Plee-ze."

"Are you sure?"

"I—can't make—him sad."

Mindy's own sadness tore at Tory's composure, leaving it shredded. In that moment she would do anything for the child. Was this how mothers felt about their children? "Then I'll talk to him."

Mindy's stomach rumbled.

"I think a certain little girl is hungry. You did a lot today. Why don't you help me with dinner? When your father comes to pick you up, I'll see if he would like to stay and eat."

Mindy labored to her feet with her good hand reaching out to grasp Tory's. "Good. Dad-dy—doesn't—uh—cook."

"What have you two been eating since Mrs. Watson left?"

"Piz-za—take—" frustration pinched Mindy's features into a frown "—out."

"Well, then tonight you two will have a home-cooked dinner. I pride myself on my cooking skills."

Tory rose and walked with Mindy into the kitchen, a large, cheerful room with plenty of sunlight and floor-to-ceiling windows that overlooked the pasture behind the house. Blue, yellow and orange wildflowers littered the meadow as though a painter's palette had been dumped there. A huge oak tree with a tire swing stood sentinel over the backyard.

"Do you like spaghetti?" Tory asked, going to the sink to wash her hands.

"Yes!" Mindy followed suit and used a paper towel to dry them.

"Then that's what we'll have. I'll chop up the onions while you man the skillet and brown the ground beef."

"I'm—the cook? I've—never."

"You're eight. It's about time you started. I can teach you." The second Tory said the last sentence she realized she might not be able to carry through with her promise. She was assuming more than she should and wished that were different. Since Mindy came into her life, she'd found an added purpose that had been lacking before.

"Wait—till—Dad-dy sees—this." Wearing an apron, Mindy stood on a stool to brown the meat using a wooden spoon and a gloved hot pad.

An hour later the doorbell rang. Tory left Mindy to finish setting the table while she hurried into the entry hall. She opened the screen door to admit Slade, looking tired but with a smile of greeting on his face. Stepping into the house, he drew in a lungful of air, peppered with the scents of onion, ground beef and baking bread, and licked his lips.

"What do I have to do to wrangle an invitation to dinner out of you?" he asked as he made his way back to the kitchen where Mindy was seated at the large oak table in front of the bay window.

"I—picked—these." Mindy pointed to a glass vase full of multicolored wildflowers from the meadow behind the house.

"Does this mean we are staying?" Slade asked, eagerness replacing the lines of exhaustion on his face.

"Unless you have somewhere else you need to be." Tory removed the loaf of French bread from the oven and placed it in the center of the table. "Mindy didn't think you would mind since you're probably sick of take-out."

Slade walked to the stove and peered into the large pot of simmering spaghetti sauce. "I must have done something right today. This smells divine."

"You'd probably say that about anything you didn't have to fix or order at a fast-food place."

"True. But this exceeds anything I could have imagined."

Heat scored her cheeks. She was always uncomfortable with compliments. "Have a seat next to Mindy," Tory said, and dished up the food.

After placing the bowls on the table, she sat across from Slade and said, "Mindy, do you want to say the prayer?"

The little girl clasped her hands and bowed her head. "Thank—you, Lord, for—" Mindy lifted her head, her brow wrinkled in thought "—for this."

The simple but effective prayer brought a lump to Tory's throat. Every day, Mindy's bravery was a wonderful example to her. The child had to relearn so many things, but not much got her down. Tory was sure the girl's frame of mind was part of the reason for her fast recovery.

After dishing up his food, Slade slid his forkful of spaghetti covered in the thick meat sauce into his mouth. He closed his eyes, a look of contentment on his face. "I can't believe it, but it tastes even better than it smells."

"Mindy was the best little helper I could have."

The eight-year-old straightened her shoulders and announced, "I put—spa—this—in the water." Mindy gestured toward the spaghetti. "Salt—too."

"I didn't realize you could cook, sweetheart. I'll have to get you to fix something for me."

"Real-ly?" Mindy's eyes grew big and round.

"Yeah. Maybe Mrs. Watson will let you help her in the kitchen and teach you some dishes."

"Have you heard from Mrs. Watson?" Tory asked while breaking off a slice of buttered bread from the warm loaf.

"She called last night to tell me her niece and baby boy are doing fine. She'll probably be back by the first of next week. She's going to stay a few days longer than planned."

"Well, if you need me to watch Mindy at the first of next week, that'll be fine with me."

"Yip-pee!" Mindy clapped and bounced in her chair. "We—could—cook—again."

"That would be great," Tory said, her regard resting on Slade, waiting for his answer to her offer.

"How can I say no, especially if I can get another dinner out of it?"

"Are you wrangling for another invitation to dinner?" Tory grinned, responding to the teasing light in his blue eyes.

"You're a sharp lady."

"I have my moments. What do you like to eat?"

"Anything that doesn't move."

"My, that leaves the door wide-open. Are you sure you don't want to narrow it down some?"

"I'll put myself in you two ladies' hands. After all, you're doing me a favor so I can't be too demanding."

The word *demanding* sent a chill down Tory's spine. She clenched her fork and dropped her gaze to her half-empty plate. "Mindy and I will come up with something."

"Our—uh—secret," Mindy said with a giggle.

For the next few minutes while everyone finished their dinner, silence dominated the large kitchen except for the ticking of the clock over the desk by the phone. Mindy finished first, dragging the napkin across her face.

"Can I—swing—on the—tire?" the little girl asked Tory.

"Sure, if it's okay with your father."

"I'll walk you out there." Slade rose.

"No, Dad-dy—I can—do it—by my-self." Mindy pushed to her feet and started for the back door.

Slade took a step toward his daughter.

"She'll be all right. She went by herself to pick the flowers for the table. She wanted to surprise you with them."

Slade peered at Tory, worry in his gaze. The door opened and closed, its sound emphasizing Mindy's need for independence.

"I'm letting her do some things alone. It's important to her."

"But she still falls sometimes."

"All children fall. In fact, earlier today she fell in the barn, but she picked herself up and continued with what she was doing."

Slade stared out the large window that afforded him a good view of the oak tree with the tire hanging from it. He watched his daughter wiggle her body through the hole and lie on her stomach. He scrubbed his hands down his face and forced his attention away from Mindy. "Can I help you clean up?"

"I'll get—" Tory saw Slade's need to keep busy and said instead, "Sure. I'll rinse. You put the dishes in the dishwasher."

"I think I can manage that."

While Tory put the leftover food in the refrigerator,

Slade cleared the dirty dishes from the table and stacked them beside the sink. A couple of times his gaze strayed toward the window, his mouth pinched in a frown.

"It's hard letting go." Tory turned the water on to rinse off the worst of the food before handing the dish to Slade.

"Yes. Mindy's been through her share of pain and then some. I don't want her to have to suffer anymore."

"All parents feel that way, but suffering is part of life. In fact, it probably makes us stronger people." At least, that's what I keep telling myself while going through my own ordeal, Tory thought.

"She's eight years old. Enough is enough."

"She's done a wonderful job of bouncing back."

"She still has a ways to go."

"But she will make it. I predict this time next year you won't be able to keep up with her and she'll talk your ear off."

"I look forward to that prediction coming true." Slade closed the door to the dishwasher and leaned back on the counter, his arms folded over his chest. "You really think she's doing okay?"

Tory smiled. "Yes. You should see her with the young riders. I have a class of three-, four- and five-year-olds and she's great with them. Like a pro."

"Speaking of classes, Mindy tells me about how hard you work to keep this operation up and running. You could use some help around here."

"Don't I know it. But that costs money, money I don't have."

"After Mrs. Watson returns and things settle down,

I could take a look at your books and see if I can help in any way. Even though I'm not an accountant, I've taken a few classes in order to help me with my business."

Tory lifted her shoulders in a shrug. "Sure. With the stable, I've learned to accept help where given." She wiped down the sink, then draped the washcloth over the edge. "I told Mindy I would talk to you about something that happened earlier today."

"This doesn't sound good."

"She had a bad dream this afternoon while she was taking a nap. She told me she remembers her mother crying the last time she saw her."

Tension whipped down Slade's length, his expression unreadable.

"She said she didn't get to go to the funeral for her mother."

"She was still in the hospital." The defensive tone in Slade's voice spoke of the emotions he was holding in check.

"She didn't get to say goodbye to her mother and I think that's bothering her."

His eyes became diamond hard and his jaw clenched.

Tory cleared her throat, its dryness making it difficult to speak. "I thought I would take her to her mother's grave site and let her say goodbye, unless you would like to. I think she needs to for closure."

A nerve in his cheek twitched. He walked toward the window that overlooked the backyard. "No. I will when everything settles down with Mrs. Watson."

"I'll go with you, if you want."

"I—" Glancing outside, Slade went rigid, then spun toward the door and yanked it open.

Chapter Three

Slade rushed out the back door toward Mindy who lay on the ground by the tire swing. Tory quickly followed. As he approached, his daughter pushed herself to her knees and struggled to stand. All he saw was the scraped skin on her shin and blood beading around the wound. The heaviness in his chest made his breaths shorten.

He scooped up Mindy into his arms. "Are you all right, baby?"

She squirmed. "Dad-dy—oo-kay."

Slade started for the house.

"No! Swing!" Mindy continued to wiggle until he put her down. She headed for the tire.

"But your leg—"

Tory touched his arm, stopping his progress toward his daughter. "She'll be fine. I'll take care of the scrape later."

He swung his attention from his daughter to the petite woman who stood a foot from him. The physical contact was so brief that Slade wondered if Tory's fingers had grazed him. Now her hands were laced together so tightly that her knuckles were white and tension lined her features.

"Why don't you push her while I go get a Band-Aid and something to clean up her shin?"

Slade watched the woman, who had been a part of his daughter's life for months, who was becoming very important to Mindy. Tory walked toward the back door with a grace and confidence Slade had seen when she dealt with her horses. But beneath that layer of assurance was a vulnerability that drew him to her. She had been so good with Mindy. He wanted to help her as she had helped him. But he didn't know what the problem was.

"Dad-dy."

He twisted toward Mindy. "Do you want me to push you?"

"Yes!" Mindy began to worm her way through the hole in the tire.

Slade grasped her around the waist and situated her safely on the swing with her arms looped around the rubber and her legs dangling in front. He gripped the tire and brought it back a few feet, then let go. His daughter's squeals of laughter erased his earlier concerns. In the past twenty-two months he hadn't heard that sound nearly enough. Tory was not only good *with* Mindy but *for* her, as well.

The back door slamming shut indicated Tory's return. Slade peered over his shoulder as she approached him, noting the shadows of dusk settling over the yard, obscuring her expression. He gave his daughter a few more pushes, then let the swing come to a slow stop.

"I hate to cut this evening short, Mindy, but it's getting late and we have to get up early tomorrow and come back out here."

Mindy squirmed through the hole, resisting any help from him. She stood patiently while Tory dabbed some hydrogen peroxide on the scrape, then covered it with a Band-Aid.

Tory straightened. "Why don't you let Mindy spend the night with me? That way she'll get to bed on time and you won't have to drive all the way back out here tomorrow morning."

"Yes!" Mindy clapped her hands. "Plee-ze."

"She doesn't have her pajamas or toothbrush."

"I have a T-shirt she can wear and I have an extra toothbrush. She can wear the extra clothes she has out here and you can bring another set tomorrow evening."

Slade took in his daughter's eager face and said, "Okay, if you're sure."

"I wouldn't have asked if I wasn't."

"Goo-dy." Mindy started for the tire swing.

"No, young lady. You need to get ready for bed."

His daughter's lips puckered into a pout. "But— Dad—"

"Mindy, your father's right. We'll need to get up early to take care of the horses."

"Oh yeah." Mindy's pout disappeared as she began

her trek toward the house without another thought to the tire swing.

"I don't think I've ever gotten that quick of a turn-around about bedtime."

Tory grinned. "It's all in what you can offer them."

"And you have the advantage. You've given her something to look forward to. Thank you."

"It's been my pleasure."

Two red patches graced Tory's cheeks, heightening her quiet beauty. She veiled the expression in her large brown eyes and started to follow Mindy into the house. The woman's every motion was economical, nothing wasted, Slade thought as he observed her mount the steps to her deck. He inhaled deeply of the spring air, laden with the scent of wildflowers and earth. Scanning the backyard surrounded by fenced pastures, he decided that he liked the country and its seemingly slower pace.

"Again, thank you for letting Mindy stay over. I hope she goes to sleep. She was so excited when I said good-night." Slade stepped out onto the front porch.

Tory came out, closing the screen door but leaving the wooden one open. "I'll check on her in a few minutes and see if she fell asleep."

"Don't let her talk you into staying up. She's quite good at that."

"Then she's met her match." Tory leaned into the wooden railing and scanned the darkness that blanketed the landscape. A firefly flew near. She observed its pro-gression across her yard and into the trees that lined the west side of her house. When the blackness swallowed up the insect, reminding her of the lateness of the hour, her tension grew at the isolation and night surrounding them.

"You do have a way with Mindy. You're a natural with children."

The compliment washed over Tory, easing some of the distress trying to weave its way through her. "I love children. That's one of the reasons I started the riding program."

"You'll be a wonderful mother someday."

This compliment bore a hole into her heart, and she felt as though the rupture bled. She didn't see herself having children anytime soon, and yet according to her doctor, her time was running out. An uncomfortable silence fell between them, one that compelled Tory to say, "In order to be a mother you have to have a husband. I don't see that happening."

Slade tilted his head and stared at her. "Why not? You're an attractive, intelligent woman." The intensity in his eyes pierced through the layers of her reserve.

"My life revolves around my stable and my work" was the only answer she could find.

"The right man could change that."

"And disappoint all the children?" Her voice husky, Tory shook her head. "I don't think so."

He chuckled. "I guess I shouldn't argue with that. After all, my daughter is benefiting from your work and the Bright Star Stables." He reached out and squeezed her hand. "I'd better be going. Long day tomorrow."

Even though his casual touch lasted only a second, an eternity passed while Tory fought for her composure. The feel of his fingers around hers had burned into her skin. It had taken all her willpower not to yank her hand from his and flee into the house.

"Good night," she murmured as he left. Trembling, she brought her arms behind her back and laced her fingers together.

For a short time tonight she had glimpsed what it would be like to have a family. The yearning had blossomed in her heart. Then her fears returned and latched on to her, making any thoughts of having her own children an impossibility.

The children's giggles danced on the light breeze. Eyes closed, Tory threw back her head and let the sunlight bathe her face in warmth. The gentle lapping of the water against the shore and the serenade of a mockingbird nearby mingled with the continual laughter from Mindy and her best friend.

After spending the morning at church, this was a perfect way to spend the afternoon, Tory thought, opening her eyes to her bright surroundings by the pond. A family of geese swam from the other side toward the little girls who tossed bread crumbs on the ground by their feet.

"I'm glad Mindy's friend could come," Tory said, shifting on the blanket spread over the thick, lush grass by the water.

"So am I. She hasn't gotten to see Laurie much this

past year. Thank you for making the suggestion that Mindy bring a friend." Slade sat by a tree.

With her arms propping her up, Tory leaned back, watching the children with the geese all around their feet. "Being with friends can be an important part of the healing process."

"And I've isolated her too much?"

Tory peered at Slade with his back against the large oak tree, one leg drawn up with his arm resting on it. The vulnerability in his voice matched the look in his eyes. "She's been pretty busy this past year recovering from the operation and the accident."

"Now it's time to move on?"

"Yes. She told me the other day she wants to go back to school in the fall. She misses her friends."

Slade flexed his hand, then curled his fingers into a tight fist.

"What are you waiting for? For everything to be perfect? That's a tall order. When is any situation perfect?" Tory knew she was pushing, but this was important to Mindy, so therefore important to her.

Slade blinked rapidly several times as though he hadn't realized the implication of his actions for Mindy. "I just don't want her hurt anymore. Last month we went to the mall for some new clothes and a couple of children laughed at Mindy when she walked by. She acted as if she didn't hear them, but there were tears in her eyes. I don't want that to happen to her at school. She'll hate going."

"God only gives us what we can handle."

Slade shoved to his feet, a scowl creeping into his features. "Mindy has handled enough for an eight-year-old."

"She has said something about going to church with me some Sunday. I would love for her to come. She said she used to go with you and your wife, but not since the accident." Tory rose, feeling at a disadvantage with Slade hovering over her. She moved back a few paces into the warmth of the sunshine.

"Things have been so hectic and—" He paused, inhaled a deep breath and continued. "No, that's not quite true. I feel God has let my family down. He took away Mindy's mother. He took away who my daughter was. She's had to start over, relearning the simplest things. What kind of God puts a child through that? Why couldn't it have been me?"

The anguish that marked his words settled heavily over her. She needed to soothe his pain away. "We don't always know why God does what He does, but He has reasons we don't always see at first. What Mindy is going through now will shape the type of person she becomes. That may be a good thing in the long run."

"So suffering makes a person better?"

"Sometimes. It can open a person up to other possibilities, more life-affirming ones." Tory thought of her own change in the direction her life had been heading. Right now she could still be working for that large manufacturing firm in Dallas, never knowing the power of God's healing through animals, never having seen the joy on the children's faces when they rode a horse.

Slade turned his back on Tory and stared at his daughter retreating from the horde of geese demanding more bread, her giggles attesting to her happiness. "I'm sorry, I don't buy that."

"Time has a way of changing a person's perspective."

"Not all the time in the world would ever change how I feel about this."

"But fighting what has already happened won't make it go away."

He spun toward her, a frown descending. "I should go with the flow?"

"Accept the changes and make the best of them."

"No!"

The anger in his voice, the slashing scowl, caused Tory to tense and step away from him. Every nerve ending sharpened to full alertness.

His gaze drilled into her for a long moment, myriad emotions flickering deep within. Suddenly his frown collapsed, any anger he had evaporating. He plunged his fingers through his hair once, twice. "I'm sorry. I get so frustrated when I think of all that Mindy has gone through and still has to go through. All I want to do is make things better for her." He rubbed his hands down his face. "It should have been me, not Mindy. Don't you see that? She had nothing to do with the accident. She was an innocent bystander who happened to be sitting in the back seat of the car."

The defeated look in his eyes impaled Tory's heart, reminding her of how much pain had already been suffered by this man and his daughter. She moved toward him, wanting to comfort him. "Were you driving the car?"

His fingers delved into the black thickness of his hair over and over as though he wasn't sure what to do with his hand. "Yes."

That one word, full of guilt, hung in the air between them. Anguish etched deep lines into his face. Her heart twisted in a huge knot that seemed to lodge in her throat.

"A young man late for an appointment ran a red light. I didn't see…" His husky whisper trailed off into the silence.

"So you blame yourself for the accident. You didn't run the red light. It wasn't your fault."

"But if only I had seen the car in time, I could have done something. By the time I slammed on the brakes and swerved, it was too late." He stared off into the distance as though he were reliving the nightmare all over again, his eyes dull with the memories.

"Sometimes things happen that we have no control over." Control was always the issue, Tory thought, fighting her own sudden tightness about her chest. She struggled for a breath of air. Up until lately she had done so well keeping her own demons at bay. Why now, when she had a new life, must she be reminded of her own past pain?

"I know life can throw us a curve at any moment."

Tory swallowed the lump in her throat and asked, "How will you blaming yourself help Mindy?"

He stabbed her with narrowed eyes. "Don't talk to me about blame until you've walked in my shoes."

Tory dropped her gaze from his unrelenting one,

looking beyond his shoulder toward the pond. She took a moment to gather her frayed composure before saying, "True, I haven't walked in your shoes, but I've done my share of blaming myself when I really had no control over the situation. I've discovered it does no good and doesn't change a thing for the better."

"I need to check on Mindy. I don't want those geese to attack her."

"I think we would have heard—" Tory didn't finish her statement because Slade had left, striding toward his daughter, his arms stiff at his sides, his hands opening and closing.

Tory's muscles released the tension gripping them, and she sank down onto the blanket. Shivering, she drew her legs up and hugged them to her chest while she watched Slade place his hand on Mindy's shoulder and listen to his daughter and Laurie talk about the geese, their voices drifting to Tory. Mindy pointed to one of the adult geese herding the rest of them toward the pond. A baby, trying to scurry to catch up with the group heading back to the water, brought a huge grin to the little girl's face, emphasizing the power animals had over people.

"Hey, is anyone hungry?" Tory called out to the trio by the water.

"Yes," both girls answered.

Slade took Mindy's hand and led the group to the blanket under the tree. "Are you kidding? We've worked up quite an appetite watching those geese gobble up all that bread."

"Oh, Dad-dy—you're—al-ways—hun-gry."

"And I know what a good cook Tory is. I've been saving room for this picnic lunch since she asked us. I could eat a bear."

Mindy put her hand over her mouth and giggled.

"Well, I'm fresh out of bears today, but I have fried chicken. Will that be all right?" Tory asked the group.

The girls nodded while Slade licked his lips, his eyes dancing with merriment.

"Bring it on," he said while settling on the blanket across from Tory.

Mindy sat next to Tory with Laurie on her other side. The picnic basket was in the middle of the circle, every eye on it as Tory slowly opened the lid, releasing tantalizing aromas. She made a production out of delving into the basket and slowly bringing the contents out for everyone's view. Next to the chicken she placed a plate of chocolate-chip cookies, Slade's contribution to the lunch, a bowl of coleslaw and a container of sliced strawberries, pineapple and bananas.

After saying a brief prayer to bless the food, Tory said, "I prefer not to have to take any of this back with us so dig in."

"If we can't finish this off, I volunteer to take the leftovers home with Mindy and me." Slade raised his hand as though he were in school and he was waiting for the teacher to pick him.

"You've got yourself a deal," Tory said, laughing. "But of course, if Mindy and Laurie keep piling it on, there won't be any left for either of us *today,* let alone any leftovers."

Slade tried to sneak a chicken leg from Mindy's plate. She captured his hand and pried it out of his grasp. Then he turned to Laurie who hid her goodies behind her back.

"I think you're gonna have to fend for yourself. It really isn't very hard to fill your plate with food. Here, let me show you." Tory demonstrated how, by putting a piece of chicken on her paper plate, followed by a scoop of coleslaw then fruit salad.

"How about a cookie? Dessert is the most important food here, in my opinion. That's why I volunteered to bring it. I know a bakery that makes the best cookies I've ever eaten." Slade inched his hand toward the plate.

Tory gently tapped him on the knuckles with a plastic spoon. "You're supposed to be setting an example."

Slade grinned. "I thought I was supposed to be eating lunch."

"Is your dad always this ornery?" Tory exaggerated a stern look.

Mindy bent over in laughter.

He quirked a brow. "I don't believe that's a compliment."

"Well, at least you're astute."

"Mindy, come to your dad's defense," Slade said while plucking up the last chicken leg and waving it like a sword.

Mindy and Laurie continued to giggle.

"No help there," he muttered, and dumped the last of the coleslaw onto his plate. When he took a bite of the chicken, he smacked his lips and said, "Mmm. This is better than my mother can fix."

Tory nodded, saying, "Thank you. I'll take that as a compliment."

"Of course," he continued as though she hadn't spoken, "my mother has never fried a chicken in her whole life." He looked innocently at Tory while putting a spoonful of coleslaw into his mouth. "And this is as good as Aunt—"

Tory held up her hand to stop him. "I think I've had enough of your *compliments* for the day."

For the next ten minutes everyone ate their lunch to the sounds of the geese honking across the pond. Mindy craned her neck to see what was going on while cramming a cookie into her mouth, then snatching up another one.

Laurie stood and moved toward the water. "They're chasing away a beaver."

Mindy struggled to her feet. "Bea-ver?"

"There's a family on the other side. They dammed the stream that feeds into the pond and have built their home there."

"Can we go look?" Laurie asked.

"Can we?" Mindy stood next to her friend, observing the commotion across the pond.

"Let me finish eating and I'll go—"

"Dad-dy, I can—go a-lone." Mindy straightened her shoulders and lifted her head.

Slade threw a glance toward Tory, one brow arched in question.

"Stay away from the edge of the pond and stay on the path," Tory said.

When the girls started toward the other side, Slade came to his feet to keep an eye on their progress. "Are you sure they'll be all right?"

"They'll be fine. The path is wide, worn and level."

Slade bent and picked up his paper plate to finish eating his lunch while he observed Mindy. "You probably think I'm being overprotective, but I don't want anything else to happen to my daughter."

"You're doing what you think is right."

"It's the parents' job to protect their children. I let her down once. I won't do it again." Slade popped the last bit of food into his mouth.

"Mindy doesn't feel that way. She thinks you're terrific."

"She talks about me?" Slade dropped his empty plate into the trash bag, then lounged against the tree, his arms folded over his chest, his legs crossed.

"All the time."

Both of his brows rose, his sky-blue eyes growing round. "And?"

"She wishes you didn't have to work all the time."

"So do I, but all her doctor bills and therapy cost a lot of money. I want the very best for Mindy. Hopefully after my company's expansion is complete, I'll have more time for my daughter."

There was so much Tory wanted to say to Slade, but his look didn't encourage further discussion. She didn't have the right to interfere, even if she had come to love Mindy like a daughter. "Have you heard from Mrs. Watson? Will she be back soon?"

A scowl darkened the expression on his face. "No."

"Is there a problem with her niece or the baby?"

"Everyone's fine. The problem is she now wants to stay and take care of her niece's baby. She feels her family has to come first and her niece can't find good arrangements for the baby. I know she's right, but still—" He clamped his mouth closed on the rest of his words.

Tory pushed to her feet. "What are you going to do now?"

Slade stared at his daughter on the other side of the pond, his brows slashing downward. "I don't know. I have to find another housekeeper, which I know won't be easy. I felt so lucky when I found Mrs. Watson."

"I'll be glad to watch Mindy until you get a new one."

"I can't—" He stopped midsentence and looked back at Tory. "Are you sure you don't mind? Because frankly, if you do, I'm not sure what I'm going to do."

"This past week with Mindy has been great. I enjoy the company and she loves working with the animals. She's even taken to the cat and her new litter that lives in the barn."

"No wonder she's been pestering me about getting a cat."

"She's named all the kittens, and after feeding and grooming Mirabelle, that's where she goes next to check up on them."

"I just found out yesterday about Mrs. Watson not returning. I haven't had a chance to get in touch with the agency yet, but I will first thing tomorrow. I promise I'll get someone as soon as possible. In the meantime, I'll pay you for taking care of Mindy."

She could use the money, but for some reason she couldn't find herself accepting payment for something she wanted to do. Taking care of Mindy was important to her—an act of love. "No. Mindy is giving me as much as I'm giving her."

"But—"

A shout from across the pond snatched the rest of Slade's protest. He whipped about, every line in his body taut.

Chapter Four

Slade sprinted forward. Tory whirled around, her heart thumping against her chest. Mindy had fallen at the edge of the pond and now sat waist-deep in the water. Her scream of surprise turned to giggles as Laurie plopped down beside her and began splashing her.

Slade slowed to a jog. The tension in his body eased. Tory scooped up two kitchen towels she'd brought, the only thing she had to dry off the girls with, and hurried after Slade, thanking God the whole way that the children were all right.

When Slade halted near Mindy, she paused in her water fight with Laurie, looked at her friend, then they both began pelting Slade. The astonishment on his face made Tory laugh. She stood back from the girls, out of their reach, trying to contain her laughter. She couldn't.

Slade stepped back, tossing a glance over his shoulder at Tory. "I'm glad you're enjoying yourself,

Miss Alexander." Water dripped from his face and hair, soaking his shirt. Beneath his mocked exasperation his eyes danced with amusement.

"Yes, I am." Tory brought her hand up to cover her mouth, but her laughter still leaked out.

Slade huffed. "Melinda Marie Donaldson, you need to get out of that pond right this minute."

"Oh, Mindy, you're in *big* trouble. Your dad used your full name." Laurie stood.

Mindy flung her hand across the water one last time, sending it spewing up toward her father. "I'm—stuck—Dad-dy."

While the last spray of water rolled in rivulets down his face, Slade's mocking scowl crumbled into a look of concern. He hurried forward to pick up Mindy.

The little girl held up her hand. "Help—me—st-and."

The water lapped over Slade's tennis shoes as he took his daughter's arm and assisted her to her feet. He whispered something into Mindy's ear, then she said something to Laurie.

When they all faced Tory at the side of the pond, soaking wet while she was dry, her laughter died on her lips. "Okay, what are you all up to?"

"Nothing," Slade said, all three of them heading toward Tory with determination in their expressions.

She backed up, her heart beginning to race. The feeling of being cornered suddenly swamped her. "Stop right there."

No one did. Sweat popped out on Tory's forehead. Her heartbeat accelerated even more. She continued to step away from the trio while trying to tamp down her fear. But she couldn't control the trembling that shook her body, nor the perspiration rolling down her face. Tory's gaze flitted from the group to the area around her. That was when she realized she was standing at the edge of the pond in some tall weeds, her tennis shoes stuck in the mud.

Slade stopped, putting his arm out to halt Mindy and Laurie. "Girls, she's our ticket back to the barn. We'd better take mercy on her." He clasped Mindy's shoulder. "And speaking of the barn, we need to gather everything up. Laurie has to be home by five and we'll need to take care of our horses before we leave."

"Aw, Dad-dy."

"Scoot." He turned Mindy toward the blanket and prodded her gently forward. When the children were halfway to the blanket and out of earshot, he asked, "Are you all right?"

His questioning probe drilled through Tory's defenses she'd thrown up. The beat of her heart slowed as she brought the gripped towel up to wipe her face. "Other than my shoes caked with mud, yes."

He took a step toward her.

She tensed.

He halted, his gaze softening. "Thank you for inviting us this afternoon."

Tory blinked at the sudden shift in the conversation. Relieved by it, she offered a tentative smile and said, "You're welcome. Maybe Mindy can bring Laurie out some other time to ride with her."

"May I use one of those towels?" He held his hand out to her but didn't move any closer.

She looked down at the towels each crushed into a ball in her hands. A blush heated her cheeks. "Yes." After tossing one to him, she released her death grip on the other one and relaxed her tense muscles.

Slade wiped his face, then slung the towel over his shoulder and started back toward the blanket at a slow pace. Tory pulled her feet from the mud and followed behind him, her shoes making a squishing sound that announced her arrival. The two girls giggled when they saw her.

She put her hands on her waist. "At least I don't look like two drowned rats. Here. Use this to clean up." Grinning, Tory flung the towel toward Mindy, then sank down by the basket to repack it.

She'd overreacted at the edge of the pond. The children and Slade were only trying to include her in their playfulness. Mindy was important to her and Slade was important to the little girl. She would have to learn to relax better around him because if she was truthful with herself, she'd enjoyed herself today. For a brief time she'd experienced again what it must be like to have a family.

"Glad—Dad-dy out—of town." Mindy took a big lick of her chocolate ice cream.

Tory sat next to the little girl on the porch swing, taking her own lick of her single-scoop ice-cream cone. "You are? Why?"

"Miss—you."

Her simple words tugged at Tory's heart, making her eyes glisten. "I missed you, too. I'm glad you got to spend last night with me." She bit into her cone, the crunching sound filling the silence.

Mindy shifted so she could look up at Tory. "Me—too."

"How's Mrs. Davies? You haven't said anything about your new housekeeper."

The little girl pinched her mouth together. "Don't—like."

"How come?"

"Mean." Mindy twisted back around and licked her ice cream, her shoulders hunched, her gaze intent on a spot on the ground.

"Why do you say she's mean?" Her stomach knotted with concern, Tory placed her ice-cream cone on the glass table next to the swing.

Mindy wouldn't look at her. She continued to eat her ice cream, her head down, her shoulders scrunched even more as though she were drawing in on herself.

"Mindy?" Tory slid from the swing and knelt in front of the girl. Lifting the child's chin, Tory asked, "What's happened?"

Tears welled in Mindy's eyes. "She—doesn't—like me."

Desperate to keep her voice calm, Tory took the child's napkin and wiped the chocolate from her face. "Why do you say that?"

"She—likes—to—uh—yell." Her tears fell onto

her lap. "Told—some—one on—phone—I'm—a cri-crip-pled—uh—re-tard."

Tory pried the ice cream cone from Mindy's trembling fingers and laid it alongside hers on the glass table, then she scooped the child into her arms and held her tight against her. "You aren't, sweetie. You're a precious little girl who I admire and think is remarkable."

"You—do?" Mindy mumbled against Tory's chest.

Tory pulled back and cupped the child's tear-stained face. "You're such a courageous person. Not many people could have done what you've done as well. Look how far you've come in such a short amount of time."

Another tear slipped from Mindy's eye, then another. "I—love—you."

Tory's heart stopped beating for a split second, then began to pound a quick beat against her chest. Her own tears rose and filled her eyes. "I love you, too." She drew the child to her, kissing the top of her head, the apple-fresh scent of Mindy's shampoo permeating the air. "Have you told your father about Mrs. Davies?"

Mindy shook her head.

"He needs to know how you feel."

"She—was—the six-th—one—he—talked to. Hard—to find."

"Still, he needs to know. I can say something to him if you want."

Mindy straightened, knuckling away the tears. "Yes!" She covered her mouth with her hand, her eyes round. "Look." Pointing to the table, she giggled.

Melted chocolate ice cream pooled on the glass surface, nearly blanketing the whole table. Tory laughed, too. "I think we made a mess. I'll go get something to clean it up with."

Tory hurried into the house and unrolled some paper towels, then retrieved a bottle of glass cleaner from under the sink. She started for the porch. The phone ringing halted her steps.

Snatching up the receiver, she said, "Hello."

"Tory, this is Slade. How's it going?"

The warm sound of his deep, baritone voice flowed through her. Trying to ignore the slight racing of her heart, she answered, "Fine. Are you back?"

"Yes. I thought I would pick up some pizzas for dinner. What do you think?"

"Pizzas as in plural?"

"Yep. Since we all like different kinds."

The implication of his words struck her. Over the past month she and Slade had gotten to know each other well— their likes and dislikes. She was even able to relax around him. "Sure. Mindy will be glad you're home early."

"Tell her I'll be there in thirty minutes."

When Tory hung up, her hand lingered on the receiver. When had Slade Donaldson become such a good friend? The question took her by surprise. Their relationship had changed quickly, something that further surprised her. She hadn't let someone get this close, this fast, in a long time. She knew they both loved and cared for Mindy, but there was something else about their time together that went beyond the little girl.

When Tory returned to the front porch, she found Mindy standing by the rail, staring down at the flower bed. Tory put down the glass cleaner and towels on the swing and came up beside the child.

Mindy angled her head, glancing up at Tory. "Some-thing—big—went—under—house. Uh—dark." The child waved her hand toward the area behind a large azalea bush that had just lost its last red bloom. "What—is it?"

"It's not the cat?" Tory bent over the rail to glimpse into a black hole that led to the crawl space under the house.

"No-oo."

Straightening, Tory shook her head. "I don't know, then. Maybe a raccoon. Two summers ago I had a family move in under the house."

"With—bab-ies?"

"Yep."

Mindy tried to stretch over the railing to get a better look. Tory had to hold her and pull her back when she nearly tumbled into the bush below.

"I want—to see." Mindy pouted, tiny lines crin-kling her brow.

"Not right now. Maybe some other time. Your dad is on his way with dinner and we have a mess to clean up."

"He is?"

"He's bringing us pizza."

Mindy's whole face brightened with a big grin. She moved toward the table, her foot dragging behind her more than usual, an indication the child was tired.

"Maybe you should rest before he comes," Tory said while sopping up the melted ice cream with the paper towels.

Mindy grabbed the glass cleaner and sprayed it on the table. "I'm—oo-kay."

The way the child held her left hand curled against her body told Tory otherwise. "Sit. I'll see to this."

Mindy fought a yawn. "Dad-dy—will be—here."

"He still has twenty minutes."

The child backed up against the swing and eased down onto its yellow cushion. She masked a big yawn while leaning back to rest her head. Her eyelids drooped, then snapped open. Tory finished cleaning the table, and by the time she gathered up the dirty paper towels to take back into the house, Mindy's eyes were closed and her head was cocked to the side.

Tory moved the child so she lay on the cushion. Brushing back Mindy's dark brown hair from her face, Tory stared at the little girl who had become so important to her. The child had gotten up with her at dawn to help her take care of the horses and she hadn't stopped the whole day. She'd been by her side while she'd cleaned out the stalls and fed the horses. She'd ridden with her and helped her fix lunch. Mindy filled her life with a renewed purpose.

She'd missed Mindy this past week when Mrs. Davies had started to work for Slade. She'd only seen her when she had her two lessons. When Slade had asked her if Mindy could spend the night since Mrs. Davies couldn't stay with her, she had jumped at the chance to have the girl with her for a full twenty-four hours. It had seemed like Christmas in June.

One of Mindy's legs began to slip off the swing. Tory caught it and tucked it back under her. The child stirred but continued to sleep.

Again Tory brushed a stray strand of hair that had fallen forward behind Mindy's ear. "I wish I was your mother," she whispered. Tears crammed her throat. She wasn't Mindy's mother, would never be. The thought pierced her heart like a red-hot poker.

Slade pulled up in front of Tory's small, one-story white house surrounded by large oaks and maples and felt as though he had come home. Tory rose from a white wicker chair on the porch and waved. Peace rippled through him. Clasping the steering wheel, he closed his eyes for a few seconds to relish that feeling. He could imagine her fragrance of lilacs, the light in her eyes when she smiled, and he held on to that serenity for a couple of seconds longer. Then reality blanketed him in a heavy cloak of guilt. Exhaustion cleaved to him, sharpening the sensation there wasn't enough time in a day to correct what had happened to his daughter.

The aroma of the pizza wafted to him, reminding him that he'd brought dinner and he was hungry. Sliding from the car, he grabbed the three boxes and headed for the porch.

Tory's eyes lit with that sparkle that always made him feel special. He responded with his own grin, saying, "I hope you two are hungry. I got medium ones for everyone."

"Medium! Who else is coming?" Tory stepped to the swing and nudged his daughter who lay curled on the yellow cushion, sleeping.

Mindy's eyes blinked open. She rubbed them as she propped herself up. "Dad-dy!"

She started to get to her feet, but Slade motioned for her to remain sitting. He brought her pizza box to her and opened it on the seat next to her.

"Why don't we eat out here? I'll go get some lemonade for us to drink." Tory rushed inside, the screen door banging closed.

Mindy stared at her pizza but didn't pick up a piece.

"Aren't you gonna dig in? I thought half of it would be gone by now." Slade sat in a chair across from his daughter.

"Can't. Wait—for Tor-ee. We always—say a—" Mindy squinted "—prayer be-fore eat-ing."

"Oh, right," he murmured, remembering a time when he, Carol and Mindy used to do that—before the accident, before his world had been turned upside down and inside out. "How was your day?"

"The—best!" His daughter's expression came alive. "I—helped. I got—to—ride."

"You're becoming quite the rider."

Mindy straightened her shoulders, her chin tilting at a proud angle. "Yep."

Tory pushed the screen door open with her foot. Slade rose and quickly took the pitcher of lemonade from her. After the drinks were served, she sat in the chair next to Slade's, across from Mindy.

"We—wait-ed," Mindy said, carefully putting her glass on the table next to the swing.

Tory bowed her head with Mindy following suit. Slade stared at them for a few seconds, then lowered his. The words of the simple prayer weaved their way through his mind. Had he given up on God too soon? Had he been wrong to stop going to church, to keep Mindy at home? Tory seemed to draw comfort from the Lord. But then she hadn't been responsible for her child struggling each day—

"Dad-dy!"

Mindy's voice penetrated his thoughts. He looked up to find both of them were staring at him as though he were an alien from outer space. His daughter had a piece of pizza in her hand, one bite taken from its end. Tory had nothing. Then he realized he still held the other two boxes in his lap. He quickly passed Tory's to her and opened his own.

"I'll share if you're that hungry," Tory said in a teasing tone.

"Even though I forgot to eat lunch, that one is all yours. The least I can do is provide dinner for you after you watched Mindy for me."

"Looks like I got the better end of the deal. You shouldn't work so hard that you forget to eat."

"Had a flight to catch and a gal to get back to. A mighty pretty gal if I do say so myself." His gaze strayed to his daughter.

Mindy giggled, her mouth stuffed with food. She started to say, "Da—"

"Nope. No words from the peanut gallery, especially when a certain pretty gal's mouth is still full of pizza."

Giggling some more, Mindy covered her mouth.

Tory watched the exchange between father and daughter, the love deep in their eyes. Mindy washed her food down with a big gulp of lemonade.

Slade leaned over and handed his daughter a napkin, pointing to her chin. "You have a red beard."

Father and daughter's shared laughter pricked Tory with longing. She wanted that with a child. She wanted a family. And time was running out for her. She didn't see any way she was going to accomplish that goal. Too many obstacles.

"Was your business trip successful?" Tory settled back in her chair, her stomach knotted.

Picking up his pizza laden with everything but the kitchen sink, Slade said, "Things are proceeding according to my plans. Hopefully I won't have to travel as much in the future."

Mindy clapped. "Goo-dy!"

"I figured you would like that," Slade said, taking a bite of his food.

The little girl popped the last piece of her third slice into her mouth, then took a large swallow of lemonade. Pushing herself to her feet, she said, "Save—for—later?"

"Sure, but I thought you were hungry?" Slade's brow knitted in question.

"My—show—is on." She started for the door.

"Show? What show?" Slade asked as his daughter banged the screen door closed behind her.

Tory shrugged. "Beats me. She doesn't watch much TV when she's here."

"She's always been a fast eater, but she beat her record this time."

"I think she wanted to leave us alone so I could talk to you."

The frown lines deepened as he shifted his blue gaze to her. "This doesn't sound good. What happened?"

Her stomach muscles constricted even more, tension taking a firm grip on her. "Mindy doesn't like Mrs. Davies."

"Why?"

"She overheard the woman calling her a crippled retard to someone on the phone. She doesn't think Mrs. Davies likes her."

Anger slashed across his face. He flexed his hands then balled them. "A crippled retard?"

Her own indignation stiffened her spine. She remembered the hurt in Mindy's voice and expression when she had told her earlier and wanted to demand Slade do something about it.

He tossed the pizza box he held onto the swing and surged to his feet. Every line in his body spoke of his rage. "She came highly recommended. Her references were excellent. How can—?" He paused, opening and closing his hands again, took a deep breath and continued. "How can anyone say that?"

"I don't know," Tory said, having a hard time herself understanding why Mrs. Davies would say that about Mindy, even if the woman didn't know the child was listening.

Slade scrubbed his hands down his face, then plopped down onto the swing, facing Tory. "What do I do now? I can't have someone like her taking care of Mindy, but I need someone to watch my daughter. Mrs. Davies was the best applicant from the batch I had. I—" He snapped his mouth closed and stared at a place behind Tory. When he reestablished eye contact with her, a bleak look was in his expression.

Tory resisted the urge to toss the pizza box to the floor and slip into the place next to him on the swing, taking his hands within hers. It was tempting, but she sat frozen in her chair, watching a play of emotions flit across his features.

A hopeful gleam appeared in his blue eyes. "Unless you'd like to take the job."

For a moment Tory forgot about her ranch and the horses, her dream, and thought about accepting the offer, turning her back on the past four years. She loved Mindy and didn't want someone else looking after her. But she couldn't walk away from her dream and the people who depended on her, Mindy being one of them. "I've grown to love your daughter. I'd be glad to have Mindy come out here, but that's a short-term solution. We could do that until you find someone else."

"But you're perfect for Mindy. She's always talking about you. She's so comfortable at your place. Isn't there a way we could work this out?"

"It doesn't seem practical." Regret tinged her voice. She thought of the long hours she had to spend taking care of the ranch as it was right now. She could manage to help for a while, but without assistance with the ranch, everything would catch up with her. She could only do so much. "There's so much I have to do around here. Going back and forth to town would be very time-consuming."

"What if I moved out here?"

Surprise widened her eyes. "Where?"

He shrugged. "Here?"

"Here!" Her mouth went dry and perspiration cloaked her forehead.

"Yes." Slade rose. "There's got to be something that could work." He began to pace as though he needed to keep moving in order to gather momentum. "Maybe we could get married? For Mindy." The second he said those words, he halted, his eyes huge with shock.

"Married?" Stunned, Tory watched him begin walking again from the swing to one end of the porch, then back.

Chapter Five

"Yes, married," Slade said, moving toward her. He came to sit across from her, pulling his chair closer so that his knees were only inches from hers, the shock replaced with enthusiasm. "I could help you with this ranch. You could hire someone to assist you. You've been worried about money. With my expansion nearly completed, my company's going to be doing well. Money won't be a problem. We could help each other."

Still stunned, Tory listened to his words as though she were a bystander observing the scene from above. She had a hard time getting past the word *married*. "But—" Nothing else came to mind.

"Don't answer me right now. Think about it. We're friends. We both care for Mindy. You would be a terrific mother for her. In fact, I can't think of anyone better for that role. Mindy needs someone like you in her life on a permanent basis. This could be a good partnership." The eagerness in his voice made his words rush together.

Marriage? Partnership? Was that a possibility? She'd given up hope of ever getting married, even though she wasn't quite thirty. She'd given up hope of ever trusting enough to have a real marriage. Desperate, Tory grasped on to a sane rational reason not to go through with his proposal. "Marriage is a serious step. There're so many things involved."

Leaning forward, he clasped her hands. "I know. That's why I don't want you to give me an answer right away. Think about it."

"You should, too." The intensity in his gaze burned heat into her cheeks. "I mean we aren't in l—" She couldn't seem to say the word. It lumped together in her throat and refused to come out.

"We aren't in love?" One brow quirked. "No, but we are good friends. I can tell you things I haven't told another. I trust you one hundred percent with my daughter."

The last sentence produced a surge of pride. For a moment she relished that feeling, but then reality took over, bringing her back to the problem at hand. "But what if you find someone later who you fall in love with and want to marry? To me, marriage is forever."

A shadow crossed over his face, darkening his eyes as if a storm gathered in them. He pulled away and stood. "I won't. I had that once in my life." He paused, angled his head and asked, "But have you?"

Tension constricted her muscles until she had to force herself to relax. The drill of his gaze prodded her to answer by shaking her head. She didn't think she could ever trust someone that completely that she could let down her guard and fall in love. To be in love was to give more of herself than she thought possible.

"Then perhaps you'll fall in love one day and want to marry?"

She came to her feet, face-to-face with him, only a yard separating them. "No, I won't."

"Why not? You have so much to offer any man."

But not you, came unbidden into her mind, and she wondered why her heart contracted with that thought. She knew she needed to say something, but what? Silence stretched between them; the only sound drifting to her was from the people talking on the television show Mindy was watching.

Slade took one step closer. "Why not, Tory? You're a warm, generous person. You would be a perfect mother. I've seen you with Mindy and the other children you work with."

She wanted to back away, but the chair was behind her. For a few seconds she felt trapped, her heart quickening its pace, her breathing becoming shallow. No, this is Slade. A friend. Mindy's father. Someone she'd been alone with many times. She forced deep breaths into her lungs and said, "I was badly hurt once."

"What happened?"

The question, spoken low, the words laced with compassion, focused all of Tory's attention on the man before her. Painful memories, buried deep, threatened to swamp her. She shoved them back into the dark recesses of her mind, where she was determined they would remain. "Not important now."

He covered the small space between them and took her hands. "I'm a good listener."

The warm, comforting wrap of his fingers about hers attested to the man she had come to know, a man who loved his daughter so much he would marry Tory to give Mindy a mother. "I know."

"When you're ready, I'll be here for you."

His quiet statement mesmerized her. She found herself leaning closer, the scent of his lime aftershave enveloping her in a protective cocoon. He released one hand and cupped her face. She stared into the blue depths of his eyes, no longer stormy but gleaming like diamonds on water. She felt herself become lost, drawn toward his kindness. Was it possible to be more than friends? The honking sound of a flock of geese flying overhead broke Tory's trance.

She pulled back and to the side, forcing a smile to her dry lips. "I appreciate your offer, but to me what has happened in the past is best left in the past." When several feet separated them, Tory turned toward him.

Slade picked up the boxes of pizza. "I'd better get Mindy home. I need to call Mrs. Davies and tell her I no longer need her services."

"Bring Mindy out here tomorrow morning. I'd love to watch her until—"

"Until you decide about my proposal?"

She nodded. "Or, you find someone to take care of Mindy."

His gaze linked with hers. "I've already found someone."

Moonlight streamed through the window in the living room and pooled on the floor near Tory's feet. Darkness cloaking her, she stared at the circle of light as though there was an answer to Slade's question written in it. But for hours she had fought the demons of her past and still she was no closer to an answer now than she was when she had tried to go to sleep at midnight.

Silence surrounded her. Usually she liked the quiet that reminded her she was alone. But not this evening. She wanted the silence to be filled with the laughter of children, with the voices of daughters and sons. Slade had dangled a dream in front of her—to be a mother. And she couldn't think of a more beautiful child to be her daughter than Mindy.

Pushing herself to her feet, Tory navigated around the coffee table and headed for the kitchen. She flipped on the overhead light and brightness flooded the room, causing her to blink. She put a pot of water on to boil, then sat at the table and waited.

Should she risk marriage to Slade to fulfill her dream? She folded her hands together and bowed her head. *Dear Heavenly Father, please help me make the right decision. There's a part of me that thinks this is the right thing to do. But then my fear takes over and I*

*don't know what to do anymore. I care for Slade. He's
a good man. And I love Mindy like she is my own child.
Please give me a sign showing me the way.*

A high-pitch whistle disturbed the quiet, startling
Tory. She leaped to her feet and hurried to the stove to
remove the kettle. After fixing herself a cup of herbal
tea, she sat again at the table, her elbows resting on its
wooden top.

What to do? The second hand on the wall clock
sounded—tick, tick, tick. Seconds merged into minutes
and still no answer.

Nibbling at the back of her mind was the one thing
that was stopping her. Being a true wife in every sense
for Slade. Could she do that? They hadn't discussed that
part of a marriage, but she wasn't naive. She knew he
was a man in every sense of the word and would want
more from her than she might ever be able to give.

With her eyes closed, she sipped at her tea and tried
to imagine life as Slade's wife, as Mindy's mother. The
child's laughter, her smile, filled Tory's mind. Mindy's
need for a mother sliced through her defenses, urging
her to take the risk and deal with the consequences
later. If only she could—

Slade prowled his dimly lit den, too restless even to
sit. Beyond the picture window he saw that night had
lightened to a dark gray. Soon dawn would color the
eastern sky with oranges and pinks. Soon his daughter
would be up and ready to go to Tory's for the day, eager
to spend time with the woman she had grown to love

like a mother over the past few months. Soon he would see Tory again.

What would she tell him today?

That question had plagued him all night to the point he hadn't been able to sleep. One part of him was so stunned he had asked Tory to marry him, but the other felt as though it was the answer to all his problems and the best thing for his daughter. And he would do anything for his daughter. The most important was righting what his child had gone through these past couple of years, giving her back as normal a life as possible.

He could still see the flash of red out of the corner of his eye as the truck ran the light. He could still hear the crunch of metal as the pickup plowed into the passenger's side of his car where his wife sat. And he could still hear his daughter's screams and his wife's moans—the last sounds she made before slipping away. There were times when he imagined the scent of blood and gasoline still hung in the air and the wail of sirens shrieked closer.

If only— He buried his face in his hands and tried to block the images from his mind. He wanted to leave the past in the past as Tory had. But every time he looked at Mindy he was reminded that he had survived with only a few bruises and cuts while his family had suffered.

What had Mindy done to deserve this kind of punishment? What had he done? All he had ever wanted was to love and protect his family. He had failed his daughter once. He wasn't going to again. Tory was the best thing for Mindy, and he was determined to persuade her to marry him and give his daughter the family she deserved.

Standing at the fence watching a mother and colt frolicking in the pasture left of the barn, Tory heard the sound of a car approaching on the gravel road that led to her house. She didn't have to glance over her shoulder to know it was Mindy and Slade. She cradled the cup of tea and brought it to her lips, taking several sips of the now-lukewarm brew. Coldness cloaked her even though the temperature was quickly rising into the mid-seventies. Her eyes stung from lack of sleep, but her jittery nerves kept her moving.

A car door slammed shut, then another one. Mindy called out to her. Tory turned and leaned back against the wooden fence, waving at the little girl as she headed into the barn to see Mirabelle. Dressed in dark blue dress slacks, Slade strode toward her, tired lines marking his features. He hadn't slept much the night before, either. Good, she thought, since his surprise proposal certainly had robbed her of any rest.

Finishing her tea, she placed the mug on the post, more brown than the white it was supposed to be. "When will you be picking Mindy up?"

"I have a late-afternoon meeting with a contractor about the additions to the plant. When I'm through with him, I'll come straight here. It should be by six."

"Mindy and I can have dinner ready for you."

A smile curved his mouth. "I'd like that." He

started to say something else but stopped before the first word was out.

"I don't have an answer, if that's what you want to know."

"I figured as much. Did you get any sleep last night?"

She gestured toward her face, sure the circles under her eyes were still evident. "What do you think?"

"No. Neither did I."

"So, I should probably have an answer soon if either one of us wants to get any sleep?"

"Yep, that about sums it up."

His crooked grin melted any defenses she had automatically erected. She pushed away from the post and rolled her shoulders. "I'm not as young as I used to be. There was a time I could stay up all night and keep going strong the next day. That's not the case anymore. I'm hoping Mindy will want to take a nap later this afternoon."

"Since she was up bright and early this morning, I'd say she probably will. She was so excited to be coming out here and not having to stay with Mrs. Davies."

"I'm glad." She started past Slade, making her way toward the barn. "Why don't you let her spend the night? Bring some clothes for her this evening, and when she goes to sleep, you and I can have a talk." She hadn't realized until the words were out of her mouth that she would give Slade an answer that evening. But she would. Now she just had to figure out what that answer would be.

"Then I'll swing by the house and pick up some of Mindy's clothes." Slade stopped at his car and opened the door, throwing Tory a heart-stopping look.

From the entrance into the barn Tory watched Mindy's father drive away, her time running out. Twelve hours to go.

"Tor-ee, can—I ride?"

She turned toward the little girl standing in the middle of the barn. "Sure, just as soon as I finish mucking out two stalls."

"I'll—help."

"I was counting on that." Tory approached Mindy and clasped her on the shoulder.

The little girl threw her arms around Tory's waist. "I'm—so glad—no—Mrs. Davies. Thank—you."

"You're welcome." Tory leaned back, staring down at Mindy. This child was the reason the answer wasn't a simple no.

"I'm—a good—uh—helper." Mindy puffed out her chest. "You—need—help."

"I tell you what. I need to feed the cat and her kittens. Can you do that for me while I take care of the last two stalls?"

"Sure." Mindy's blue eyes gleamed, big and round.

"You know where their food is?"

The girl nodded.

"I'll come get you then when I'm through."

Mindy started for the tack room while Tory hurried toward the last stall on the left. Twenty minutes later, her muscles shaking with fatigue, Tory went in search of Mindy. She heard the child before she saw her. Mindy was outside the back entrance, talking to the kittens.

She held one in her lap, stroking it and saying, "Maybe—I'll—get to—stay—here. I see—you— every—day. Wouldn't—that be—nice?" The child buried her face in the kitten's fur, rubbing it back and forth across her cheek. "Tor-ee—needs—me."

Tory's throat jammed with emotions of love. She did need Mindy. More than she realized. Tory closed her eyes for a few seconds. *Thank you, Lord, for showing me the answer.*

Swallowing several times, Tory stepped from the shadows into the light. "Are you ready to ride, Mindy?"

Dusk blanketed the farm, cooling the air slightly. The dark clouds to the south hinted at a chance of rain. Crickets trilled and frogs croaked. Tory brushed a stray strand of hair, fallen from her ponytail, behind her ear. Taking a deep breath, she relished the scents of grass and earth that mingled with the fragrance of the honeysuckle she'd planted along the fence to the west.

She needed to paint the fences, the barn and the house. Each year more of the white flaked off and yet she neither had the time nor the money to do that. There weren't enough hours in the day.

The screen door banged closed behind her. The sound of even footsteps approached her. She remained by the porch railing, her fingers grasping it a little tighter.

"I finally got Mindy to go to sleep. All she wanted to talk about was the kittens and Belle. She told me when she grows up she wants to work with animals like you, Tory." Next to her Slade settled himself back against the railing, his arms folded over his chest, and faced her. "See what kind of influence you have on Mindy?"

She looked away from the intensity in his gaze, warmed by his compliment and a bit afraid she could never live up to what Mindy needed. "It's going to rain tonight. How is Mindy in a thunderstorm?"

"Fine. Unless the thunder gets too loud."

"I love rain. A good storm cleanses the earth."

"So long as it doesn't set in for days at a time."

Tory turned away from the yard and half sat, half leaned on the railing next to Slade, their arms almost touching. "Rain is important to a farmer."

"How long are we going to discuss the weather before we talk about what I asked you last night?"

She slanted a look toward him, her head cocked. "Impatient?"

"Yes, I was patient all the way through that delicious dinner. How did you know I love pot roast?"

"Mindy mentioned it to me."

"I guess I'm a meat-and-potatoes kind of guy."

She suspected he was as nervous as she was about their impending discussion. "Also, according to your daughter, a dessert kind of guy, too."

"Is that why we had blackberry cobbler?"

"Yes."

"Did you and Mindy make that today?"

"Yes, but the ice cream was store-bought. I only have so much time to cook."

"But you enjoy cooking?"

"Yes. I wish I had more time to do that."

"Which brings me to why I am here. I can give you more time to do those kinds of things. Will you marry me, Tory Alexander?"

The question hovered between them, its implication vibrating the air as though a hundred hummingbird wings beat against each other. She took a deep, fortifying breath and opened her mouth to reply. No words would come out. They lodged in her throat. Swallowing several times, she tried again. "First, we should talk about—" Still she couldn't say what she needed to.

"About what?"

The mere thought flamed her cheeks. She palmed them, feeling the searing heat. "What kind of marriage will we have?"

A dawning light shone in his eyes. "Do you mean, will we have a real marriage in every sense of the word?"

Her heart paused in its frantic beating, then resumed its crash against her chest. Its thundering roar in her ears drowned out all other sounds. Perspiration beaded on her forehead. "Yes," she finally said in a voice stronger than she thought possible.

He shifted so he fully faced her. "I hope so, but, Tory, you will call the shots. It will be up to you."

She veiled her expression. She could accept those terms, but could he? What if she couldn't ever take that step? What if—

No, she would deal with it one day at a time. The Lord would show her the way. She lifted her gaze to his. "Yes, I will marry you."

* * *

Tory stood back from the one-story farmhouse and surveyed the freshly painted wood. White with hunter-green trim gleamed in the sunlight, rejuvenating the old structure. Even the swing and wicker furniture on the porch had been painted to match the trim. Turning toward the horse barn, she watched the three painters putting the finishing touches to its hunter-green trim. Then the fences would be painted white. Satisfaction and pride welled up in her.

Eight days ago she had accepted Slade's proposal and the next day he'd had painters out here to discuss painting whatever needed to be done. The following day they'd started and had been working nonstop since then. Slade wanted the work done by the time of their wedding in four days. It would be close.

A blue Honda, at least ten years old, pulled into the drive leading to the house. She waited by the gravel road while the man parked and climbed from his vehicle. Approaching him, she extended her hand. "You must be Gus Morris."

The older man with a full head of white hair pumped her arm. "Yes, ma'am. I sure am. It's a pleasure to meet you."

"Let's talk while I show you the operation." Tory started for the barn.

Gus, who was no more than two inches taller than Tory, fell into step next to her. "It looks like you're sprucing up the place."

"Yes." Tory gestured for Gus to enter the barn first.

"I have fifteen horses—five of them mine and one pony. I offer classes, usually in the afternoon. The people who stable their horses here come out and ride, some more than others. I make sure the horses are fed and taken care of each day." Tory paused in the middle of the barn. "Also, I keep the stalls clean and keep an eye on the various horses. I'll inform the owner if a problem is developing. As you saw, I have several riding rings and also paddocks and trails for people to use."

"What will my duties be?"

"Cleaning out the stalls, feeding and watering the horses, keeping the tack in good shape. You'll be assisting me with whatever needs to be done."

"Hours?"

"From six in the morning until three in the afternoon. You'll have an hour off for lunch."

The short man grinned, his brown eyes twinkling. "As I told you over the phone, I miss my ranch. I miss working with horses. My kids wanted me to move here, but they neglected to give me anything to do. I found retirement isn't for me."

"Do you think you can manage the duties?" Tory took in Gus's wiry frame.

"Been doing that kind of stuff all my life. Don't you worry about me. I am all muscles, no fat. I'm in good health and driving my daughter bananas. She's actually the one who saw the advertisement in the paper and showed it to me."

"Then, Mr. Morris, you've got yourself a job and you can start tomorrow if you want."

"Please, call me Gus. Mr. Morris just makes me seem older than I care to be."

"Tor-ee—I'm—done." Mindy came to the entrance of Belle's stall, holding a curry comb in one hand, hay sticking to her T-shirt.

"Who's this little lady?" Gus asked.

"This is my helper, Mindy. This is Gus, Mindy. He'll be working here and helping us."

Gus covered the distance between Mindy and himself in three strides. "Let me see what you've done." He looked inside the stall and whistled. "That's a mighty fine job, if I do say so myself."

Mindy beamed. "Thanks! Belle—is—my—resp—" Her brow knitted as she glanced toward Tory.

"Responsibility," Tory said for her.

"Belle is one lucky pony then." Gus turned toward Tory. "I'll be here tomorrow at six straight up."

As the old man left, Mindy shut the stall door and made sure the latch was hooked, then she walked toward the tack room to put up her curry comb. "Dad-dy be here—soon?"

"Soon. But you're staying for dinner again. Your father and I still have to talk about the wedding plans."

"Four—days. Can't—wait."

"Ready to help me with dinner?"

Nodding, Mindy took Tory's hand.

"I thought we would have hamburgers tonight. What do you think?"

"Yes."

When a black Taurus headed toward her house, Tory

stopped for a moment, trying to make out who was behind the wheel. Judy? She was early.

"Who's—that?"

"My older sister. She wasn't supposed to come for the wedding until Thursday."

"Sis-ter!" Mindy quickened her pace, nearly falling in her haste.

Tory steadied her. "Slow down. After the day we put in, I don't have that kind of energy. Judy isn't going anywhere."

"Will—she—be my—aunt—when—you—mar-ry—Dad-dy?"

"You bet."

"Neat!"

Judy slid from the car and stretched. "I know I'm early. But Brad told me to come and he'll bring the kids with him in a few days. How can I pass up a minivacation without the children?"

Tory studied her sister's face, her expression innocent, and wondered about Judy's motives behind her early arrival. Her older sister was always trying to protect her. She was sure Judy was here to scout out the situation for Mom and Dad and make a report before they came. "Judy, I want you to meet Mindy. She's Slade's daughter."

Mindy lifted her hand to shake Judy's. "I—help—Tor-ee."

"That's what she said to me. She's lucky to have such a good helper."

Mindy preened, a big grin on her face.

"Pop the trunk and I'll help you with your luggage." Tory moved around to the back of the car. When she saw the jammed trunk, she laughed. "I should have known you'd bring your whole closet with you."

Judy bent down and whispered into Mindy's ear, "Ignore Tory. She likes to make fun of me and what I pack for a trip. My motto is to always be prepared and in order to do that I have to bring choices."

Mindy giggled.

"And of course, Mom had me bring some wedding gifts for you."

"Gifts?" Mindy's eyes grew round. "I'll—help—open?"

"I wouldn't ask anyone but you. Come on, we'd better get started or we'll be out here all night unloading the car."

"Well, Mindy, I think you did a superb job with the baked beans." Judy wiped her mouth on her napkin and laid it on the side of her empty dinner plate. "And the hamburgers were great, Slade. Grilled to perfection."

"Yes—Dad-dy." Mindy finished off her chocolate milk.

Slade pointed to his mouth and waited until his daughter had used her napkin to clean hers before saying, "With compliments like that, I could get used to cooking."

Judy rose and began taking the dishes to the sink. "My contribution to this dinner is to clean up."

"I'll help." Tory stacked several plates on top of each other.

"While you two are doing that, Mindy and I will take a walk down to the barn. I wanted to check out how the painters are coming along."

Tory put the plates into the sink. "If it doesn't rain, I think they'll get finished by the wedding."

When Slade and Mindy left the kitchen, Judy brought a platter and bowl over to the counter. "She's every bit as cute as you said."

"And?"

"What do you mean 'and'?" her sister asked, again that innocent expression on her face.

"I know you, Judy. Is Mom watching the kids so you could come early and pump me for information?"

"Why, Victoria Alexander, I don't know what you're talking about. Brad—"

"You haven't suddenly changed. You're dying to know what in the world has gotten into me. Don't deny it."

Judy placed one fisted hand on her waist. "Okay. I'll admit Mom and I were curious."

Tory barked a laugh. "Merely curious?"

"You weren't even dating anyone the last time I talked to you, what, a week before you made this grand announcement that you were getting married. What's going on?"

"I've known Slade for some time. I don't tell you and Mom everything."

Judy's expression sobered. "Have *you* told Slade everything? Does he know what happened?"

Chapter Six

Tory started rinsing the dishes off to put into the dishwasher, but her hands shook so badly she nearly dropped a plate. Judy reached around her and turned the water off.

"Tory, you can't keep running from the truth."

A band about Tory's chest tautened, constricting the air in her lungs. She drew in a deep breath, then blew it out through pursed lips. Once. Twice. Still she felt as though she were suffocating. Clasping her wet hands together to still their trembling, she closed her eyes, wishing she could block the world out as easily as flipping off a switch. Life wasn't like that. She'd learned that painfully. There were times she felt as though she were running as fast as she could and going nowhere.

She focused on the feel of Judy's arms around her as she said, "The truth? You don't think I've faced it? I have every day for the past four years. As much as I want to forget, I can't. I've tried. Believe me, I've tried."

Tears, from the depth of her bruised soul, filled her eyes and coursed down her cheeks.

"Does Slade know about you being raped?"

The question struck Tory with the force of a sledgehammer. Even though she didn't move, she felt as though she had been knocked back against a brick wall. "No, I don't see why I should share my past with him. It's in my past. It has nothing to do with my future." Shame and humiliation nibbled at the edges of her mind. She shut down, refusing them entry.

Judy's arm tightened about Tory. "Who are you trying to kid? Our past has everything to do with our future."

Tory wrenched herself from her big sister's embrace and put several feet between them, anger surging to the surface. "If I tell Slade, it will be when I want to."

Judy held up her hands. "I agree, Tory. I won't say a word to him. But that doesn't mean I don't think he has a right to know."

"Why? Because you think I'm tainted?" She remembered the looks she'd gotten, the whispers behind her back after she'd brought charges against Brandon Clayton. Cold fingers spread out from her heart to encompass her whole body. She'd felt as if she were the one who had done something wrong, not Brandon.

Horror replaced the concern in her sister's expression. "No! Never! You know better than to say that. Who held you when you came home that night? Who wept with you? Took you to the hospital? Stood by you through the trial?"

"Why are you doing this now, right before my wedding?"

Judy covered the short distance and clasped Tory's upper arms. "Because I'm worried about you. Because I want you to be happy. And if that means with Slade, then great. But I know a marriage must be based on the truth."

"I haven't lied to him."

"But you aren't telling him everything."

"I doubt I know everything about him. Who does until they have lived with someone for years, if even then?"

"That's a cop-out, Tory."

"No, what I'm doing is what I must do to survive." Tory yanked away from Judy, sucking in deep breaths of air, her heart pounding against her chest.

"Survive? You—"

The sound of Mindy's and Slade's voices drifted to Tory. The slam of the front door followed by footsteps nearing the kitchen prompted Tory to swipe her hands across her cheeks. She spun about, her back to the entrance while she tried to compose her shattered nerves.

She wasn't the same person she'd been four years ago. She had a right to put that life behind her and move forward. To forget the pain. To grasp on to what happiness she could.

"Tor-ee, I—heard—the ani-mal under—the—house—a-gain."

Forcing a smile, Tory turned toward Mindy. "You did? She must be making her home there."

"Yep. I—showed—Dad-dy."

The questioning probe of Slade's gaze skimmed over

her features. Tory concentrated her attention on the little girl, praying he couldn't see beneath her false facade. "Was everything all right at the barn?"

Mindy nodded. "You—aren't—done?" She glanced at the dishes still stacked at the side of the sink.

"Nope. Judy and I got to catching up and forgot to work."

"I—can—help."

Tory clasped her shoulders, wanting to drag the child against her and hold on to her forever. "You've done enough. I don't want to tire my best worker out."

"Besides, honey, it's time for you and I to get home. The next few days are gonna be plenty busy."

"Dad-dy—do we—have to?" Mindy straightened her slumped shoulders. "I'm—not—tired."

Tory brushed her finger under the child's eye, following the line of a dark circle beginning to form. "Is that so?"

"Well—may-be—a little." Mindy held up her fingers to indicate less than an inch.

"I need you rested. We have to go for our last fitting for our dresses tomorrow."

"Oh—" the child's eyes grew round "—yes!" She grabbed her father's hand and began to tug him toward the door. "We—better—go."

Slade hung back and said over his shoulder, "Judy, now you see why I think Tory is perfect for Mindy. She works miracles with my daughter. See you tomorrow bright and early."

When the sound of the front door closing drifted to

Tory, she stiffened, curling her hands into tight balls at her sides. The silence of the house eroded her composure. The seconds ticked into a full minute. She knew her sister behind her was trying to decide how best to pursue their earlier topic of conversation.

Tory whirled about. "I'm through discussing my past, Judy. If you want to stay and enjoy my wedding, then I expect you to respect my decision to put my past behind me and not talk about it. Understood?"

"You've made yourself very clear, but—"

"Don't, Judy. I want you to stay, but I'll ask you to leave if you continue."

Judy blew out a huff of air, a frown marring her pleasant features. "Okay, but that won't stop me from worrying about you."

"I didn't think it would. But I'm a big girl now. I know what I'm doing."

"Do you?"

No! But with God's help I'll figure it out. Because I have to. For Mindy's sake. For Slade's sake. And most of all, for my own sake.

His wedding ring gleamed in the sunlight. Slade spread his fingers wide and stared at the simple gold band. Married for an hour. He'd never thought he would ever marry again—not after the way his life had fallen apart with Carol's death.

On the light breeze his child's laughter floated to him. He glimpsed his daughter playing with Judy's children, such joy on his child's face. He'd done it for

Mindy. He wanted her to have as normal a life as possible. He wanted a mother for her.

Searching the small crowd who'd gathered for his wedding reception, he found Tory talking with her parents and his brother, the only member of his immediate family able to make his wedding since his mother was unable to travel due to poor health. Like flames of a fire, her long, straight auburn hair fell about her shoulders, catching the rays of the sun. The soft folds of her white dress swirled about her knees as she moved with her parents toward her sister and brother-in-law. The tailored bodice and delicate beadwork along the scooped neckline emphasized Tory's petite frame.

She caught him looking at her and smiled. Even across the lawn he saw the sparkle in her gaze as though golden honey mingled with the chocolate of her eyes. Behind that smile there lay a vulnerability that he suspected went deep. It was that very vulnerability that spoke to him and touched his own wounded soul. For a fleeting moment he wondered if it was possible to heal each other's hurts.

He looked away, his gaze dropping to his left hand again. The wedding ring felt heavy and tight. He twisted the band around, a momentary sense of panic attacking. What had he done? He wasn't a whole man. All he could offer Tory was loyalty and friendship. There wasn't anything else left inside.

"It's a little late to be having second thoughts," Paul, his friend, said.

"I'm not. This was a good decision. Tory is right for Mindy and me."

"I have to admit I was surprised by this sudden move. Frankly, I wasn't even aware you were dating." Paul peered toward Tory. "Sandy and I want to have you all over for dinner sometime soon. Maybe after the honeymoon."

"We aren't going on a honeymoon."

"Don't let work keep you from going away."

"You know I'm in the middle of my plant's expansion. I'm putting in a new assembly line to make plastic containers for Wellco. Besides that, I've got several new contracts starting that I need to oversee." Slade wouldn't even tell his friend that the real reason he wasn't going on a honeymoon was his marriage wasn't a normal one. Maybe one day, but not now. Paul had already worried enough about him.

"And how does your new wife feel about all this work?"

"She understands."

"Then you have a special woman because Sandy certainly wouldn't."

"We'll have a honeymoon later."

"When that happens, we'd love for Mindy to stay with us. Laurie misses her and all she talks about is that picnic at the pond you all invited her to. She thinks Mindy is one lucky girl to live on a horse ranch."

"Laurie is welcome to visit anytime," Slade said, realizing he was already beginning to feel the ranch was his home.

That took him by surprise, but as he let his gaze travel over the backyard, the feeling of having come home grew. Already Mindy's toys were evident with a new swing set near the freshly painted white fence separating the yard from the horse pasture. On the deck sat his grill from his house and several blue-and-green pieces of his patio furniture, including a round glass table shaded by an umbrella with big blue flowers on it.

He was selling his house in town even though it was bigger. He had made a commitment to Tory and that involved making her riding stable a success. His home was here now.

"Mom, you should sit down. You've been on your feet too long." Tory took a hold of her mother's arm to guide her to the nearest chair. The pale cast to her mother's features worried her. Eleanor Alexander's weak heart had curtailed her activities in the past few years, and today she had overdone it. "Are you taking your medicine?"

"Yes, dear. I'm just fine." Eleanor patted her daughter's arm. "You worry too much." She eased onto the folding chair and indicated Tory sit next to her. "We haven't had much time to talk these past few days. I never thought you'd be able to put together a wedding so fast, but you did. I wish I could have helped more."

"You being here is all I need."

"Well, of course, I'd come to my daughter's wedding, dear." A tiny frown furrowed her brow. "Are you sure, Tory?"

"Now look who's worrying. I'm sure. Slade Donaldson is a good man. I'm lucky to have found him." As she said those words to her mother, Tory felt the right-ness in every one of them. Slade was an excellent choice for a husband. They were friends. Wasn't that a good reason to marry someone? Much better than passion and love. Ever since her rape, she didn't see her life filled with either of those emotions. When the man she had been dating had forced himself on her, he had taken not only her virginity but her trust in her judgment in men. Slade made her realize not all men were like Brandon Clayton.

Her mother sighed. "I won't lie to you. I've been worried about you ever since—" Her mother couldn't voice aloud what had happened to Tory. She never had. Eleanor pinched her lips together, her frown deepening.

Tory laid her hand over her mother's. "I know. But I'm getting better with each day." *Some days I don't even think about what happened four years ago.* For all her declarations to Slade and Judy about putting the past behind her, she knew in her heart it was always there, just waiting for when she let down her guard. It would have been so much easier if she had lost her memory of the rape. Then she wouldn't wonder if her life would ever be normal again.

"I'm glad, dear. I think this marriage is a good step in the right direction. I like your young man and Mindy is adorable. A ready-made family. I know how impor-tant a family is to you."

And her time for starting her own was running out. Tory had never told her mother that she had been diagnosed with endometriosis. Her mother had been upset enough about the rape. Tory hadn't wanted to add to her mother's worries. She knew how much her mother wanted lots of grandchildren. She'd gotten her love for a large family from her mother.

"Mindy is fitting right in with Ashley and Jamie."

Tory looked toward Mindy playing with her new cousins. "Yes, they hit it off right away. It's nice they are all about the same age."

"Has Judy told you the good news yet?"

"No."

"Oh, dear. I thought she would have told you the first night."

"Told me what, Mom?"

"She's going to have another baby in seven months. But don't say anything. She hasn't told the kids yet. She just found out the day she came up here."

Tory knew the reason her big sister hadn't said anything. She hadn't wanted to put a damper on the festivities. She was happy for Judy and she would let her know as soon as possible. Her sister needed to stop trying to protect her. She'd learned to deal with disappointments, and never having her own children was a very real possibility. "That's great, Mom. Judy probably didn't want to take away from my day."

"Knowing your sister, you're probably right." Her mother peered over Tory's shoulder. "I think Maude is trying to get your attention."

Tory shifted in the chair and found her aunt standing by the long table laden with food. Aunt Maude waved to Tory to come cut the cake she'd baked the happy couple.

Her mother's color still hadn't returned. Her eyes dull, she attempted a smile. "I think it's time to cut the cake, dear. I'll watch from here."

"Mom, maybe you should go into the house and lie down."

"No—" she fluttered her hand in the air "—I'm fine, dear."

"Mother?"

"Go. I see your young man has already been roped by Maude into participating. The groom has to have a bride by his side when he's cutting the cake."

Tory pushed to her feet, her legs suddenly weak. Her gaze linked with Slade's. For a few seconds the rest of the people faded, and she and Slade were the only two who existed. Earlier that day in her church she'd married him for better or worse, forever. She was now part of Slade and Mindy's family. The implication of what had transpired made her falter as she walked toward her *husband.* Doubts took hold of her heart and squeezed. Had she done the right thing for everyone?

Slade took her trembling hand and clasped it, conveying his support in his gaze and touch. "Is your mother all right?"

"She says yes, but I think she's overdone it. She'll be the last person to complain if she isn't feeling well."

"Are you two ready to cut the cake?" Aunt Maude asked, snatching the knife off the table and presenting it to Tory.

She grasped it with Slade's hand over hers. The warmth in his palm seared into her. For a second she felt branded, panic swimming toward the surface. She shoved it back down and smiled for the photographer.

Slicing the knife into the bottom layer of the two-tiered carrot cake, her favorite, she prepared the first piece to feed Slade. Her fingers quivered as she lifted the cake to his mouth. His lips closed over the dessert, nipping the tips of her fingers. A tingling awareness chilled her. Dropping her hand away, she entwined her fingers, trying not to shake.

Slade's eyes sparkled like blue fire as he brought her morsel toward her. When she opened her mouth, his finger grazed her bottom lip, again sending a current of sensations zipping through her. She swallowed too soon and nearly choked. Coughing, tears springing to her eyes, she desperately tried to draw air into her lungs and couldn't quite succeed.

Slade patted her on her back. "Tory, are you okay?"

Finally taking a shallow breath, she nodded, unable to speak.

Slade gave her a glass of water that Aunt Maude handed him. Concern etched his features and gave him an endearing appeal.

"It—went down—the wrong way," Tory said.

"When you told me your favorite cake was carrot, I didn't realize you would try to inhale your piece. There will be plenty left for you, I promise."

Tory laughed, all tension fleeing. Slade made her laugh. Slade cared about her. Slade was a loving father.

Those were three things she needed to remember as they learned to live together.

"Toast. Toast," Brad, her brother-in-law, called out.

Aunt Maude thrust a glass of lemonade into each of their hands.

Slade faced Tory and lifted his high, his gaze connected to hers. "To a wonderful woman who has opened her home and heart to my family."

The sweet words washed over her in warming waves. Her mind went blank as she took a sip of her drink. Then it was her turn and still she didn't know how to express her churning emotions. The crowd fell silent, every pair of eyes on her.

She ran her tongue over her dry lips and said, "To a man any woman would be lucky to have as a husband."

"Hear, hear," someone shouted from the back.

Heat flamed her cheeks as she sipped some more of her lemonade, soothing her parched throat. Tory moved away from the table to allow Aunt Maude and Judy to cut the rest of the cake and pass it out to the guests.

"How are you holding up?" Slade asked, leaning close to her ear.

His whispered words feathered the nape of her neck and sent a cascade of goose bumps down her spine. She shivered, again a mass of jittery nerves. "Fine. I will say the past few weeks have been a whirlwind, but the ranch looks nice. And all thanks to you."

"This is my home now. We are partners."

His gaze robbed her of rational thought. She felt lost in the swirling blue depths as though she were drowning in a lake, a whirlpool dragging her under for the third time. "Yes," she managed to say even though her mouth felt dry as an August day in Oklahoma.

"How's Gus working out?"

Tory spied the old man talking to her father and grinned. "He has been a blessing. He may be sixty-eight, but he works like he's years younger. And he knows his way around horses."

"Mindy has taken a liking to him."

"If I'm busy with book work, she's out helping him. He's good with her."

Slade took her hand and brought it up between them, his gaze fastened to hers. "You're good with her."

There was little more than a few inches separating them and Tory should have been afraid. Always before when a man got too close, all her alarm bells rang and sent her flying back. But slowly Slade had insinuated himself into her life until she wasn't scared of his nearness. She even enjoyed his touches. Maybe everything would work out. Hope planted itself in her heart. She wanted her life back. Like Mindy, she was struggling for normalcy.

"Time for you to throw the bouquet."

Her sister's words broke the spell Slade had woven about her. Tory stepped back, her hands dropping away from his. And for a few seconds she felt deprived.

"I've got all the single women lined up below the deck. All you have to do is toss it into the crowd."

"Crowd?" Tory spied the three women by the deck. One was eighteen, another in her thirties and the last in her seventies.

"I can't help it that you know mostly married women. I thought about having Mindy and Ashley join the group, but I don't think either Slade nor I want to deal with two young girls dreaming of getting married just yet."

"You've got that right," Slade said with a chuckle.

"So it's our cousin and two ladies from your church." Judy pushed the bouquet of white roses into Tory's hand.

Tory felt all eyes on her as she strode to the steps that led to the back deck. Perspiration popped out on her forehead. She didn't like being the center of attention, but the day of the wedding the bride always was. She should have eloped. Of course, then her family would never have forgiven her and she suspected Mindy wouldn't have been happy, either. The little girl had been all smiles as she walked down the aisle to the altar earlier that day.

With her back to her guests, Tory tossed the bouquet over her head, then spun about to see Mrs. Seitz nearly shove her eighteen-year-old cousin out of the way to grab the flowers. The seventy-year-old proudly waved the bouquet in the air, catching sight of Mr. Weaver by the punch bowl. He colored a deep red.

After that the guests started to leave, surrounding Tory and Slade to say their goodbyes. Slade by her side felt right. Maybe this could work. *Please, Lord, give me the strength to do what I need to be a good wife and mother.*

The bellow of a bullfrog and the occasional neigh from a horse in the paddock vied with the chorus of insects. The nearly full moon lit the darkness, creating shadows that danced in the warm breeze. Tory, dressed now in shorts and a T-shirt, sat on the porch swing with her legs drawn up and her arms clasping them to her chest. Resting her head on her knees, she listened to the night sounds and thought back over her wedding day.

She was no longer Tory Alexander, but Tory Donaldson. That realization produced a constriction in her chest. She was responsible for more than herself now. Her arms around her legs tightened. Everyone was gone, even her family who were staying at a motel in town and Slade's brother. It was just Mindy, Slade and her. She no longer heard nature's background noise. The lack of voices isolated her, sharpening her senses.

She knew Slade was there before she saw him standing by the steps. She'd heard the soft shuffle of his feet moving across the yard; she'd thought she'd smelled his lime-scented aftershave wafting to her. Lifting her head, she asked, "Did you find it?"

Slade produced the stuffed pony. "By the swing set."

"Good. I know how important favorite toys are."

"I'll be right back." Slade mounted the steps and went into the house.

Minutes later he returned and folded his long length into the chair next to the swing. "She was still awake, waiting for me to bring Belle. After the excitement of today, I'd have thought she would have been asleep the second her head hit the pillow."

"Belle is special to Mindy."

"The stuffed one as well as the real one." He stretched

his legs out in front and crossed them at the ankles. "I don't know about you, but when my head hits the pillow, I'll be asleep."

Sleep? She didn't know if she could right now with Slade only a wall away from her. When she had accepted his proposal, she hadn't really thought about the sleeping arrangement. Even though he didn't share her bedroom, they shared a small house. She'd avoided any kind of level of intimacy for so long she wasn't sure how to share one bathroom, the same living quarters, even the kitchen first thing in the morning.

"It has been a long day," she finally said, his silence indicating he expected her to say something. She unfolded her legs and swung them to the floor. Standing, she rolled her shoulders and worked out the kinks.

When he rose, too, the small porch suddenly became smaller. She could definitely smell his aftershave as the scent surrounded her. The distance between them was less than an arm's length. If she wanted, she could reach out and touch him easily. In the dim light from inside the house she could see his handsome features, marked with uncertainty and tenderness.

He quirked a smile. "I realize this is a bit awkward."

"A little." When his smile grew, she said, "Okay, a lot."

He shifted closer, linking his hand with hers. "We'll make this work."

"For Mindy."

"For us, Tory."

His voice, pitched low, flowed over her. She shivered

in the warm, June night. His hand slid up her arm, sending a cascade of chills down it. He moved even closer until there was only a breath between them. Cupping her face with his other hand, he stared into her eyes as though trying to read what was in her soul.

Exhausted from the long day and the emotional treadmill she'd been on, Tory melted against him, her legs giving out. He tilted her chin up, pausing for a few seconds before bringing his mouth down on hers. The mating of their lips wasn't like the quick peck at the end of the wedding ceremony; it was a blending of breaths and parrying of tongues. Weak with sensations foreign to her, Tory welcomed the taste of him—until he wound his arms about her, pressing her closer.

Suddenly she couldn't breathe. Panic eroded her composure, prodding her heart to crash against her rib cage. She shoved him away, gasping for air. His startled expression rendered her speechless. She pushed past him, taking the steps two at a time.

The pounding of her bare feet on the cool grass matched the pounding of her pulse. She saw the one light on in the barn and headed for it. Inside she stopped, bending over and drawing gulps of air into her burning lungs.

How in the world had she thought she was ready for this?

What must Slade think? Her husband had kissed her and she had fallen apart. She wrapped her arms around herself and walked toward the back of the barn. Opening the door, she stood staring at the pasture beyond, the moonlight streaming down in a crystal clear sky. The scent of hay and horses saturated the air, a familiar scent that usually comforted her. Except that her heart beat rapidly and she couldn't get a decent breath.

"Tory, what just happened back there?"

Chapter Seven

She tensed, her back to Slade.

"Tory?"

She bit the inside of her mouth, wishing she had an easy answer to his question. Staring at the ribbon of moonlight pooling in the meadow, she whispered, "I'm not ready to take our relationship to the next level."

"Is that what you thought that kiss was? The beginning of a seduction?"

She shrugged, nothing casual about the gesture. "It is our wedding night. I thought—"

"We're friends. I wouldn't rush you like that."

He was only a few feet behind her now. She sensed his puzzled gaze drilling into her back, trying to discern what had panicked her. This would be a perfect time to tell him as her sister had encouraged her. Then she remembered some of the whispers said behind her back— *Maybe she had asked for it. Maybe she'd led him on.*

They had been dating. She knew in her heart she hadn't asked to be raped, but the shame of the act clung to her as though it were a second skin. Could she have done something differently to prevent it? Why couldn't she have seen it coming? She had dated the man for several weeks, known him much longer, or so she'd thought.

"Tory, we talked about our marriage one day—being real in every sense. Have you changed your mind?"

Yes. No! How could she answer him when she was so torn up inside? She didn't know what she wanted. What a mess!

"Have you, Tory?"

She wheeled around and faced him, praying her expression was neutral, that none of the anguish twisting her stomach was visible. She never wanted to hurt this special man, but she was afraid she would. "No—one day." She looked toward Mirabelle's stall, then back into his eyes. "Please be patient. We haven't known each other long. Give me time."

One corner of his mouth lifted in a grin. "I had intended to do that very thing. A kiss isn't making love, Tory."

She sucked in a deep breath and held it for a few seconds before releasing it. "I know. It's just that I haven't dated much. I've been so busy and…" She let her words trail off into the silence, hoping he drew the conclusion she'd led a sheltered life, which was true for the past four years, and even before that.

"I understand."

You do? She almost said the words out loud but stopped herself before she revealed her doubts. Instead she said, "I think these past few weeks are finally catching up with me. I'm overreacting. I'm sorry, Slade."

"You have nothing to be sorry for. It will take a while for us to adjust to living under the same roof. And I agree. It has been a long few weeks. I think I'm gonna turn in now."

"I'll be up to the house soon."

She watched him stride toward the entrance, his bearing suggesting the same weariness she felt. No matter how much she wanted to deny it, there had been a hurt expression in his eyes she'd glimpsed for a brief moment before he had managed to mask it. He didn't really understand. How could he when there were times she didn't?

She spun about to stare out the back door, looking toward the heavens. *Dear God, I hurt Slade tonight. Please help me to make this marriage work. I'm in over my head. I don't want to fail.*

Bright light pricked her eyelids. Tory slowly opened her eyes to find not only sunlight flooding her bedroom but Mindy sitting on her bed with a huge grin on her face.

"What time is it?" Tory raised herself up on her elbows, the fog of sleep clouding her mind.

"Se-ven."

"Seven!" Tory bolted straight up and peered at the clock on her beside table. "I overslept."

Mindy surveyed the room. "Where's—Dad-dy?"

"Uh—"

"Right here, hon." Slade lounged against the doorjamb, cradling a mug in his hand.

The scent of coffee teased Tory, steam wafting to the ceiling. She could use a big cup— Oh, my gosh! One hand went to smooth her hair while the other pulled the sheet up nearly to her chin. Her face felt as hot as the steaming cup of coffee.

Mindy eased herself down off the bed and trudged toward her father. "Go-ing—to see—Belle."

"Hold it, young lady," Slade said as his daughter squeezed past him. "We're going to breakfast in town in—" he checked his watch "—forty-five minutes. You need to be back here and cleaned up."

"I—wi-ll." Mindy disappeared from sight.

Tory clutched the sheet to her chest, wishing she had on her flannel nightgown she wore in the winter. Instead, she was dressed in a flimsy pair of short pajamas whose top had thin straps. She would have to remember in the future that she now shared a house with a man.

"Why didn't you get me up earlier?" she asked, the hard edge to her voice she attributed to her nerves. It wasn't every day she had a handsome man standing in her bedroom doorway, looking very appealing in a pair of tan slacks and navy blue Polo shirt that brought out the blue of his eyes. His conservatively cut hair was still damp from a shower, taken she realized in her bathroom. The thought again emphasized the awkward situation she found herself in.

"Because you didn't come back to the house until after one. I thought you could use the sleep. You've been working nonstop for the past few weeks."

Tory scanned the room for her robe. Where was it? When she spied it, it lay on a chair by the window. Too far for her to leap to and slip on without him noticing a few bare spots of skin. She had lived alone too long. She gestured toward the sky-blue cotton robe. "Would you get that for me, please?" The last word came out on a husky whisper, barely audible across the room.

One brow rose, his eyes locked with hers. Then he shrugged away from the door, strode to the chair and snatched up the short robe. When he brought her the garment, a smile was deep in his expression.

She grabbed the robe and slipped it on. When she stood on trembling legs to belt it, she noticed that the blue material didn't cover nearly enough of her legs. But it would have to do until she could get rid of her... *husband.* The word swirled in her mind.

When she faced Slade, she felt better prepared to carry on a conversation. He moved back to the doorway, his left shoulder cushioned again against the wooden frame. Slowly he lifted the mug to his lips and sipped, his gaze never leaving hers.

She swallowed several times, sure that if she spoke, her voice would come out a squeak. "I hope you made a large pot of that," she finally said, and was pleased to note the strength in her words.

"Yes. I can get you some."

"No, I'll get dressed and be in the kitchen in a few minutes."

When he left, he pulled the door closed and Tory

hurried to throw on her new black jeans and a white blouse. After stuffing her feet into her tennis shoes, she headed for the bathroom to brush her teeth and wash her face. She entered the kitchen ten minutes later.

Slade had a cup of coffee poured for her and sitting on the table next to him. He tossed aside the newspaper and watched her cross the kitchen and sit in the chair opposite him. She slid the mug toward her, cupping her hands around it and bringing it to her lips. The strong brew slipped down her throat, giving her system a jolt of needed caffeine.

When she felt fortified with coffee, she rested her elbows on the table and said, "We need to discuss what we're going to say to Mindy about our situation. I gather by her question this morning you haven't said anything to her about why we got married."

"I told her we wanted to create a home for her, which is the truth."

"Yes, but she thinks we share a bedroom." Tory took another sip of her coffee. "She wasn't here when you moved in your things."

"I suppose you're right." His brow furrowed. "I hadn't thought to say anything to her. I don't want her to worry about us being a family."

"Still we need to say something to her about why we aren't sleeping in the same bedroom."

"I could always say I snore."

"Do you?"

He lifted his shoulders in a shrug. "I don't know. Carol never said anything about it."

"After our breakfast with my family, maybe we'll be able to talk with Mindy, together."

"Okay, together."

The smile he sent her doubled her heartbeat. He made the word *together* sound like a promise of things to come. She downed the rest of the coffee. "I'd better check on the horses before we leave."

"I was down there a while ago. Gus has everything under control. He came early so you wouldn't have to do anything today."

"But—"

"Tory, he wanted to do something special for you since you got married yesterday, so he's putting in some extra time."

She couldn't remember when she hadn't needed to go to the barn and take care of the horses. She wasn't sure she knew what to do with the leisure time.

"Relax. We'll be leaving for town in a few minutes anyway. Why don't you read the paper?" Slade slid a section toward her.

"When did I start getting the newspaper? I never have time to read it."

"I started its delivery today."

"Oh" was all she could manage to say. She wondered what else in her life would change because of this man.

"Gus—spect-ing—me." Mindy stuffed the rest of her turkey sandwich into her mouth, her cheeks ballooning.

"You aren't going anywhere, young lady, until we're finished with lunch." Slade downed the last of his iced tea.

Putting her hand to her mouth, Mindy mumbled something and pointed to the sack with Tory's lunch inside.

"Tory can wait a few minutes while you chew your food properly."

His daughter picked up her glass of milk and took several gulps. "I—told—Tor-ee—I'd—bring—uh—lunch."

"And you will, after you and I have a little talk."

"But—Dad-dy—" A pout formed on her mouth.

"What?"

"Can't—we—la-ter?"

"When? I can't seem to get you to sit long enough even to eat."

Mindy pushed away her empty plate and leaned one elbow on the table, resting her chin in her palm. Her pout grew.

He really was tickled his daughter had a renewed interest in life, but she hardly stopped long enough to say hi to him. He'd been trying for the past few days to have a heart-to-heart with her about his marriage to Tory ever since he and Tory had discussed it on Saturday. He'd come home today from work just so he could before the afternoon riding lessons began. And now he felt as though he needed to hog-tie his daughter to get her to listen. Maybe he and Tory could make sure they rose before Mindy and went to bed after her. Usually that wouldn't be a problem, but every once in a while his daughter got up in the middle of the night.

"I wanted to explain why Tory and I aren't slee—" *Hold it! That isn't the way I want to tell Mindy.* Heat suffused his face as he thought of all the potential questions he could get from Mindy if he had continued. He wasn't ready for a discussion with his daughter of how babies were made. Truth be told, he never would be. *Isn't that what mommies do?* Sweat beaded his brow. "I mean why we aren't sharing a bedroom."

"That's—kay."

He sagged against the back of the chair. "It is?"

"Tor-ee—plain."

"She did?" Couldn't he come up with more than two-word questions?

Mindy grinned. "She—hogs—the bed."

He almost said, "She does?" but thankfully stopped himself before the first word came out. Sweat rolled down his face. He brushed away the salty trail. This father-daughter talk wasn't going the way he'd planned. But then he'd really not had this planned out. He'd come into this discussion with one thing on his mind: to get it over with as quickly as possible. He didn't want his daughter to know the real reasons Tory and he had married. It would worry and upset Mindy, which were two things he was determined not to do.

"When did Tory tell you?" he asked, deciding he and Tory needed to work on their communications better.

"To-day." Mindy struggled to her feet. "Can—I—go?"

"Sure." He watched his daughter slowly make her way to the back door, her left foot still dragging behind her. The sight, as always, wrenched his heart. If only he had been able to avoid the accident. If nothing else, he should be the one recovering, not Mindy.

After taking the dishes to the sink and rinsing them off, he headed for the barn to start that communicating he and Tory needed to do. He found her finishing up with the blacksmith. Tory, even in hot weather, wore long jeans and riding boots with a short-sleeve plaid shirt and a beautifully designed leather belt her father had given her at Christmas. Her hair was pulled back in its usual ponytail with auburn wisps framing her face, void of any makeup but with a healthy glow to her cheeks and a smattering of freckles across the bridge of her nose. The way she looked amplified the woman he was getting to know—honest, caring, down-to-earth.

He waited to approach her until after the man left. When she saw him, her face lit with a smile that warmed him. He liked that she was glad to see him.

"Did you and Mindy have a nice lunch?"

"Yes, and it was informative."

"How so?"

"My daughter informs me that you hog the bed."

"Oh, that." The color in her cheeks deepened to a nice scarlet shade. "I know we talked about discussing it together, but we could never seem to find the right time. So when Mindy and I got to talking and I realized you hadn't said anything, I did. Was that why you came home in the middle of the day?"

"Yep." He stepped a little closer and lowered his voice so Gus and Mindy who were down at the other end of the barn didn't hear, "Well, do you?"

"What?"

"Hog the bed?"

Her brown eyes grew round before she veiled them and turned away to pick up a wooden box at her feet. "I guess so."

"You don't know."

She cradled the box to her chest and stabbed him with an exasperated look. "It's not like I watch myself sleep. I do sometimes find myself waking up at odd angles across the middle of the bed. Why?"

"Just curious. I want to know the little and big things about my wife."

Wife. The word seemed to jolt Tory if the widening of her eyes meant anything. She still wasn't used to it or the fact that she was married to him. If truth be known, neither was he.

She started walking toward the tack room. He followed. At the door she twisted around and eyed him.

"I thought with the expansion, you'd need to get back to work."

He leaned one shoulder against the wall by the tack room and crossed his ankles. "Tired of me already?" He glanced at his watch. "We've only been married three days, one hour and fifteen minutes."

"You want to spend time with me?"

Beneath the question Slade noted the hint of vulnerability that crept into Tory's voice. He wanted her to trust him enough to tell him what had happened in her past that made her unsure, especially of men. Several things came to mind, but until she confided in him, it was only speculation on his part.

"You're my wife. Isn't that what husbands and wives do?"

"You tell me. I've never been married." The corners of her mouth began to twitch as she took up his playful mood.

He folded his arms across his chest as though he would be hanging around for a long time. "Well, I don't have a vast knowledge, but I think so."

"You can always help me muck out a stall."

"I'm thinking more along the lines of a date."

"Don't you have it all backward? You're supposed to date a woman, *then* marry her." Laughter tinged her voice.

He liked seeing her smile and laugh. "What can I say? I'm an unconventional kind of guy."

"So you want me to go out on a date with you."

He nodded. "Without Mindy. Just you and me." The second he made the suggestion, a wariness entered her expression, which she quickly covered. But he'd seen it. "Don't get me wrong. I love my daughter and like spending time with her, but I want our marriage to work. That means we need to get to know each other well, keep the communication lines open."

"Who'd stay with Mindy?"

"Gus."

"Gus?" She said the name loud enough that the older man at the back of the barn with Mindy perked up and called out to Tory.

"Do you need something?" Gus stepped toward them.

"Uh—" She shot Slade a "help me" look.

Slade pivoted toward the older man. "We were just discussing your offer to baby-sit Mindy one evening so Tory and I could go out."

"When?" Mindy came out of Belle's stall.

"We're not sure yet, sweetheart. Would you be okay with that?"

"Yes!" His daughter pumped her arm in the air.

Slade turned back to Tory who stood slightly to the side and behind him. "So?"

"When did you and Gus make this arrangement? He's gone when you arrive home."

Home. The word had come so naturally from her that its implication made Slade pause for a few seconds. The farm was becoming his home and it was definitely Mindy's. "At the wedding. It was another one of his gifts to us. Perfect if you ask me. Mindy adores him, thinks of him as a grandfather."

"But—" Her protest died on her lips.

Slade wanted to take her into his arms and smooth away the tiny frown lines on her forehead. Remembering the kiss they had shared only reinforced his desire to embrace her. But he didn't. He resumed lounging against the wall, waiting for her to say something.

"I guess we could go out to dinner sometime this week. I'll have to ask Gus when he's available."

"Wednesday, Thursday and Friday nights."

"You know already?"

"Yep. He told me those were the nights he's usually free. Monday night is his book club and Tuesday he goes bowling."

"My gosh, you know more about Gus than I do, and I work with him every day."

"See. That's what I want to avoid with us. I want to know what your favorite color is. What movies you like to see. Do you read?"

"Yellow. What is your favorite color?"

"Green."

"I like comedies and I love to read when I can find the time."

He pushed away from the wall. "This is good. It's a start. But there is so much more, and since we're sharing living space, I figure we should get to know each other."

"Okay. How about Thursday night? My riding lessons are over with by five that evening."

"Then it's a date. I'll tell Gus to stay late on Thursday. Where would you like to go?"

"To tell you the truth I haven't been to too many places in Cimarron City. I'll let you pick."

"Surprise you?"

"So long as I know what to wear. I'll let Gus know for you."

"Great. I need to get back to work before my secretary files a missing-person report." As he strode away, he whistled some tune he'd heard earlier on the radio, a lightness in his heart.

Humming a song she'd heard at church last Sunday, Tory appraised her outfit in the full-length mirror on her closet door. The soft pastel-blue rayon dress emphasized her narrow waist with a wide belt of the same material adorned in sequins and beadwork in flower designs. Along the scooped neckline and hem were the same flower decorations. She drew the white shawl about her shoulders and turned one final time to make sure she looked all right, the full skirt billowing out, then falling to below her knees when she stopped and faced the mirror again. Fortifying herself with a deep gulp of oxygen, she checked her hair, styled in a French braid that hung down her back. A few wisps framed her face, devoid of most makeup except pink lipstick and dark mascara.

A knock sounded at her door. She jumped. "Yes?"

"Are you ready?" Slade asked without opening the door.

"Yes, I'll be out in a sec." Tory glanced back at herself. Was she ready to go out on her first date in over four years? Even though Slade was her husband, she felt as though this was their first date. Her nerves were jittery, her mouth dry—just as if she'd never shared a house with the man.

When she entered the living room, Gus whistled and Mindy clapped, bouncing up and down on the couch.

Tory scanned the room. "Where's Slade?"

"Right here."

She whirled toward the sound of his deep voice. He stood in the doorway into the kitchen, his gaze traveling slowly up the length of her.

He let out his own whistle. "You look great. Ready?"

The male appreciation she saw in his eyes robbed her of the ability to speak. She swallowed several times and finally managed, "Yes."

"I left the information of where we're going, by the phone, Gus."

"You two go out and have fun. Miss Mindy and I are going to have our own fun. I've got some movies we're gonna watch, and some popcorn."

"Bedtime is nine, Mindy. Don't give Gus any trouble about going to bed."

Mindy beamed, her hands folded in her lap. "I won't."

Slade gave Mindy a kiss, then Tory did.

As she and Slade walked toward the front door, she heard Mindy ask Gus, "Can—I have—a soda?"

Slade paused, said, "Just a minute," and went back to the living room. "No caffeine, Mindy, or you'll never get to sleep."

"But—Dad-dy—"

Slade held up his hand. "Fruit juice, young lady."

"Oo-kay."

Tory could imagine the pout on Mindy's mouth as she agreed. If they let the little girl, Mindy would drink sodas all day long. She definitely had a sweet tooth. The thought of Mindy settled her nerves. When Slade returned to her side, Tory sent him a smile, grateful for his laid-back ways and his innate understanding.

When she slid into the passenger's side of Slade's car, she followed his progress around to the driver's side, admiring his self-confidence conveyed in how he carried himself, the pride he took in his appearance. He looked dynamite tonight, dressed in a charcoal-gray suit with a white shirt and a red tie.

"I'm guessing from the way we're dressed that we're going to a nice restaurant tonight," Tory said as Slade pulled out onto the main highway into town.

"It's the new one out on Old Baker's Road."

"The restaurant they made out of the Whitney's Flour Mill?"

He nodded. "I hear the food is delicious. I thought we could check it out before your parents and sister's family come back to town during the Fourth of July weekend."

"You don't have to take them out to dinner. They don't expect that."

"I want to get to know them, too. Gus has already agreed to baby-sit one of those evenings so just the adults can go out."

"I know my sister will be thrilled."

"It's good for a couple to go out by themselves every once in a while. I want us to at least once a month."

A couple! Once a month! Oh, my. She knew that what Slade thought was right. Each day she was married to him made it seem more real than the day before. Sometimes she found herself wanting to pinch herself to see if she would wake up from a dream. Just a month ago she wouldn't have thought of herself as someone's wife or mother and certainly not half of a couple.

At the new restaurant the sound of the stream behind the old mill lent a tranquil quality to the evening. The sun dipped behind the tall maples and oaks along the west side, creating shadows as night grew closer. The fresh scent of earth and forest saturated the warm air and the coolness of the surrounding towering trees chased away some of the heat of a June day.

The atmosphere was romantic and further enhanced by the quaintness of the restaurant, its decor rustic.

It was as though they had stepped back into the 1800s. Inside, Tory took in the candlelit tables with white tablecloths covered with crystal, china and silver. Each place setting gleamed with the flames from the candles.

Slade assisted Tory into her chair at a table for two in a corner alcove. The picture window afforded her a view of the small stream rippling over rocks. Perfect. She could tell Slade had taken care in selecting the place to eat for their first date. The idea pleased her.

After placing their orders, Tory relaxed in her chair. "I have to admit I don't eat filets too often. Too expensive on my budget."

"That's all changed now, Tory. We're married. What is mine is yours."

Half of a couple, she reminded herself, still not used to that concept. After the incident four years ago she hadn't thought that would ever happen. Of course, her marriage wasn't the normal kind.

Next to her he leaned forward. "What kind of expansion plans do you have for the Bright Star Stables?"

"Expansion? None. All I've ever wanted to do was pay my bills. I've never thought beyond that."

"What if you could dream? What would you like to do with the stables?"

Tory blew out a breath of air, all the possibilities

she'd pushed to the back of her mind flooding her now. "I'd like to have an indoor riding ring so I could have lessons all year long."

"Done."

"Done? What do you mean?"

"I want you to start making plans to build one. I think that's an excellent way for me to invest my money."

"But—" Stunned, Tory couldn't think of anything else to say.

"Don't forget, Mindy will benefit more than anyone if you have an indoor riding ring."

Her shock still firmly gripped her. "You have that kind of money?" Again she realized she really didn't know that much about Slade—except that he was a kind, loving father and a good friend.

"I haven't had a chance to tell you yet, but my company was just awarded a big contract I've been pushing for this past year. An international food company has contracted us to make all their plastic containers."

"Then this is a celebration tonight."

He raised his water glass. "To both of our dreams."

What were his dreams? she wondered, taking a sip of her ice water, her gaze bound to Slade's. Thankfully the liquid was cold to chase away the heat that permeated her.

"I do mean it, Tory, about making plans for the indoor ring. I'd like it built by next winter. That way, Mindy can continue with her riding therapy."

"I'm not even sure where to begin."

"How about with contacting some contractors about bidding on the indoor ring? The company that did my expansion work was excellent and reasonable." He covered her hand on the table. "It's about time your dreams come true."

The feel of his hand over hers riveted her senses to the roughness of his fingertips and the warmth of his flesh. "What are your dreams?" she murmured, her shock slowly wearing off to be replaced with a reality, a reality that centered around Slade and his daughter. They were an intricate part of her life now. Her family. If only she could take the next step. Time was running out on her dream to have a child of her own, if she was ever able to.

"I want Mindy to be whole again."

Before he withdrew his hand, Tory felt the tension in his touch. "Is that all?"

"That's the only one I can afford right now."

Puzzled, she tilted her head to the side. "Why?"

"My life is on hold until Mindy is well."

"She is well. She's no longer having seizures."

He gritted his teeth, the line of his jaw hard. "She struggles every day. I don't call that well."

"She doesn't see it as struggling."

His eyes became pinpoints, his lips pressing together. He remained silent, the atmosphere at the table suddenly frosty. Tory fought the strong urge to touch his arm, instinctively knowing he would pull away. He didn't see his daughter in the same light as she did.

Tory unfolded her napkin and placed it in her lap,

needing to do something with her hands. "Mindy wanted me to ask you to come to church with us this Sunday. Will you?" She hoped the topic change would ease the strain that sprang up between them.

He cloaked his expression, releasing a deep sigh. "I don't know. I may have to work on Sunday."

"Work?"

"Yes, with that new contract I'll have some things I'll need to iron out."

"You have an open invitation to come with us any Sunday you can. Mindy has made some friends she wants you to meet."

The tense set to his shoulders relaxed. He lifted his gaze to hers. "To be truthful, I don't know if church is for me."

"Because of the accident?"

He nodded, taking a deep swallow of his water.

"God hasn't let you down. He just may have a different plan for you."

"Don't you understand? It's never been about me. It's about Mindy and—" He clamped his mouth shut and looked away.

About his deceased wife. He'd walked away from the accident. She hadn't. Mindy hadn't. Tory reached out and laid her hand on his arm, praying he wouldn't pull away. He stiffened for a few seconds. When the tension melted from his expression, his posture, Tory felt a connection to him that went straight to her heart and bound them together for several beats.

Maybe she had been brought into his life not only to help Mindy but to help him. Slade's hurt went deeper than she suspected he realized. *Lord, show me the way to help Slade heal, to forgive himself for surviving.*

Shaking his head, he stared at her hand on his arm. "This was supposed to be a celebration, a beginning for us. How did everything get so turned around?"

Tory smiled. "I think we were talking about our dreams."

Placing his hand over hers, he linked gazes. "I want to help make yours come true."

And I want to help make yours come true. But Tory wouldn't voice her wish out loud.

"So I want you to start right away on the indoor riding ring."

Tory thought about her other wish and wondered if Slade could help her with that one. Her fear had been with her for so long she was afraid it wasn't possible.

Chapter Eight

"Do you—think—Dad-dy—will—let me go to—" Mindy scrunched up her face and thought for a few seconds "—sch-ool?"

Tory shifted the bag of clothes from one hand to the other in order to open the truck door for Mindy. The child pushed her walker away and lifted herself into the front seat. "Do you want to go back when school starts?"

Mindy screwed her face up into another thoughtful expression. After a minute, she nodded. "I—miss my—" she searched for the right word "—friends."

Tory closed the door and folded up the walker to put in the bed of the truck. Remembering the battle she'd had that morning to get Mindy to use the walker brought a smile to her mouth. By the end of their trek through the mall the little girl had been leaning heavily on the walker. Even though she doubted Mindy would say she was glad she'd insisted they take the walker, Tory was sure Mindy was thankful. She hated admitting she still needed occasional help, especially if she was going to be doing a lot. She still tired easily and didn't want to take a nap when she needed to. Gus had changed that. He'd declared one day how important his catnaps were to him each afternoon. Since then Mindy had taken her "catnaps" without complaint. Slade and his daughter were a lot alike, Tory was discovering. Slade didn't think he needed any help, either. But he was hurting, and she intended to help him any way she could.

After stowing the walker, Tory slipped behind the steering wheel and started the truck. "Then we'll just have to convince your father how important going to school is to you."

"Let's—go see—him—now," Mindy said, in all the eagerness she was known for.

Tory checked the clock on the dashboard. "It's close to lunchtime. We could take him out to eat."

"Yeah! Sur-sur—" Mindy struggled for the word and ended up frowning.

"Does your dad like surprises?"

"Yes! Sur-prise—him."

"Then that's our next stop before we go to speech therapy."

Mindy smiled, displaying the new gaping hole where her loose tooth had been the evening before. She dug into her purse and produced her five-dollar bill from the tooth fairy. "I'll—buy."

Tory headed toward the company headquarters about

a mile from the mall. "I've got a better idea. Let's get your dad to treat us."

"Oo-kay. I—can—get—can-dy—la-ter."

"I was thinking more along the lines of ice cream before we head back to the ranch."

"Yes!" Mindy clapped.

When they arrived at Donaldson Corporation, Mindy hurried ahead, her fatigue forgotten in her haste to see her father. Tory quickly followed, never having been to Slade's headquarters. She glanced up at the four-story building and had visions of running around lost in the large place. One of the security guards waved at Mindy as she made her way toward the hallway off to the left.

"I'm with Mindy," Tory said to the guard.

"You must be Mrs. Donaldson."

Hearing her new name sent a rush of excitement through her. She really hadn't thought much about her being Tory Donaldson. It had only been two weeks since their marriage. "Yes, I am."

Mindy disappeared through a door at the end of the corridor. Tory quickened her pace, eager to see Slade in his work environment. The company was so much a part of him as her riding stable was a part of her.

When Tory entered the outer office, the secretary behind the desk smiled at her. "Mindy's inside with her father, Mrs. Donaldson." The older woman stood and extended her hand. "I'm Mrs. Hardmeyer. I'm sorry I couldn't make your wedding."

After greeting Slade's secretary, Tory approached the double doors that led to his office. When she stepped inside, she found Mindy sitting on his lap, giggling. "We came to steal you away for lunch."

"Lunch? Already?" Slade glanced down at a gold clock on his desk. "I've been so busy I'd forgotten the time."

"Then you'll let us take you out." Tory scanned the large office with a bank of windows behind Slade's massive oak desk, littered with stacks of files and papers. Off to the left sat a cozy area for conversations with a long brown leather couch and two comfortable-looking plaid chairs. Bookcases were along the other side of the room. The office reflected Slade's personality.

"Plee-ze, Dad-dy."

He grinned, his eyes gleaming. "How can I refuse an invitation from two lovely ladies?"

"You—can't." Gripping the desk, Mindy slid off her father's lap and stood next to him. "Rea-dy."

"I guess I am." Laughter laced his voice as he rose.

"One day when we have more time I'd like a tour of your company."

"Just let me know and I'll set aside some time."

"Me—too."

Slade ruffled his daughter's hair. "You, too, sweetheart. We'll make it a family outing."

"Like—uh—lun-ch."

Walking toward the exit with Slade and Mindy reinforced the feeling of family that was growing in Tory. She settled into Slade's car, parked near the entrance, and let him pick the restaurant while Mindy told her father about their shopping trip. With Gus at the stables, she could afford to take some time off and enjoy this outing with Mindy and Slade. She didn't have to worry like she used to about what she had to do at the ranch.

"I—got—new—dress—for—chur-ch."

"I bet you look pretty in it."

"Will—you—come? In play—Sun-day."

Slade shot Tory a narrowed look. She raised her eyebrows and shrugged.

"I'll see, sweetheart."

"Plee-ze," Mindy said from the back seat.

With tiny lines creasing his forehead, Slade maneuvered his car into a parking space next to a hamburger joint. "I'll be there to see you. What part are you playing?"

"Hor-se."

"Horse! What's the play about?"

"Noah's Ark. Mindy's representing the two horses. She wanted to since she rides them. Different pairs of animals are being played by one child since we don't have enough children to do two of every animal."

"Are you wearing a costume?" Slade asked, opening the door for Mindy to slide out of the back seat.

The little girl nodded. "Mrs. Pl-ank's—do-ing—it."

"Because I don't know how to sew other than sewing on a button in an emergency." Tory fell into step next to Mindy with Slade on his daughter's other side.

"That's okay. If you ask me to do anything other than change a light bulb around the house, I'd have to hire someone to do it."

While Mindy went ahead of them and stood in line behind a young boy and his mother, Tory hung back with Slade. "Are you okay about church on Sunday? The play isn't that big a deal. Some of the Sunday school classes have been working on it the past few weeks. They're going to perform in the rec hall on the stage after the nine o'clock service."

"I'm fine. It's a big deal to Mindy. I'll be there. Are you sure she'll be okay in front of an audience?"

"Yes. Will you come to the church service, too?"

He blew out a breath of air. "You're a very determined woman."

"Yes."

"We'll make it a family outing, then."

"Good." The pleasant warmth that coursed through her veins at Slade's mention of the word *family* caused a sharpening of her awareness of the man beside her. He might not be handy around the house, but she was beginning to depend on him, and that frightened her. Her emotions had been locked up so tight for a long time. She was afraid to release them and feel again, afraid her judgment somehow would be wrong again. Or that Slade wouldn't be able to accept her for whom she really was.

Tory started for Mindy. Slade placed a hand on her arm to halt her movements.

"Thanks for making this easy, Tory. I do feel we're becoming a family and Mindy thinks so. She told me last night while I was putting her to bed."

A tightness jammed her throat. She felt it, too. She might never have the children she wanted, but Mindy was like a daughter to her and this man was responsible.

She owed him a lot, but she didn't know if she could ever totally be free of her past to unconditionally give of herself in a marriage. Slade deserved that.

"Thank you again for agreeing to go to church Sunday with us." Tory tore the fresh spinach and placed it in the large wooden salad bowl. "Mindy talked all day about you coming to see her be a horse in the play."

"Does she have a speaking part?" Slade opened the cabinet door and extracted the dinner plates.

"Yes." Pausing in chopping up a tomato, Tory glanced at her husband setting the table as though they had been working side by side in the kitchen for years instead of weeks. "Just a small part."

"But still, she's speaking in front of an audience." He shook his head. "I don't know if that's wise. What if someone laughs at how slow she speaks? What if she forgets her lines?"

Tory put her balled hands on her waist. "They won't, Slade Donaldson. And even if they did, we're here to help her get through it. You can't constantly protect Mindy from life."

Looking up, he frowned. "Frankly, I don't know that I've done such a great job of protecting my daughter from life so far."

"She wanted to do this play. I'm not sorry I told her yes."

"You should have checked with me."

"Then come to church with us each week and you'll know what's going on. If I'm going to be responsible for taking care of Mindy when you aren't here, then you'll have to trust my judgment about what is good for her." Her fingernails dug into her palms, remembering her own qualms earlier about her judgment.

"I do trust you."

"Then quit acting like you don't. Mindy has enjoyed rehearsing with the others. No one has made fun of her. Not everyone is like those children in the mall."

The tense set to his shoulders relaxed. The hard lines of his face smoothed. "Did we just have our first fight?"

Tory dropped her hands to her sides. "I guess we did."

"Just like an old married couple."

"Speak for yourself. I'm not old," she said with a laugh, needing to lighten the mood before she began to dream of them as a real old married couple.

"Seriously, I don't know if I'll ever stop worrying about Mindy and how people will receive her."

"I know. That's part of being a parent. I worry, too."

Slade finished setting the eating utensils on each bamboo place mat. Tory continued cutting the rest of the tomatoes, listening to him moving around the table. There were still times that it seemed strange to wake up in the morning and find Slade in the kitchen fixing the coffee or coming out of the only bathroom in the house after having taken a shower, his hair wet, dressed in a robe. When she had been in college, she'd shared an apartment her last two years. It was like that but of course different since Slade was a male.

"I'll get the barbecued chicken. It should be done by now."

Slade stood right behind her and the sudden sound of his voice so near her ear caused her to jump and gasp. Laying a hand against her chest, she drew in deep breaths and twisted about to look at him. "You scared me. I didn't hear you approach." The rapid beat of her heart still pounded against her rib cage. His lime-scented aftershave swamped her senses.

"Sorry." He offered her a smile. "I didn't know making a salad could be so absorbing."

"Just thinking," she said, turning back to complete the task. The hand that held the knife trembled.

"Anything you'd like to share with me?"

No way. "You know Dave Patterson is meeting with me on Monday about the plans for the indoor riding ring."

"He's a good man. I think you'll be impressed with his work."

"Mindy can't wait. She told me once we have the indoor ring she can ride every day even when it's raining or snowing."

Slade picked up the large platter and walked to the back door. "That's the whole idea."

"I'll go find Mindy and have her wash up."

As Slade disappeared outside, Tory put the salad bowl in the middle of the table then headed toward the front porch where she'd left Mindy earlier to play. The heat of a summer day blasted her when she stepped out onto the porch. A breeze ruffled the stray strands of her ponytail but did nothing to relieve the warmth.

She scanned the area. "Mindy." Walking to the edge of the porch, she searched the yard. Mindy knelt by a bush along the front of the house, her face pressed down as she looked beneath the shrubbery. "Mindy, what are you doing?"

"A ba-by." Mindy scooted closer to whatever she was looking at.

One of the kittens? Tory hurried down the steps to where Mindy was. Standing a few feet behind her and to the left, she stooped down to see what the child was so fascinated by. Curled in a ball was a small black fluffy animal with white markings.

Mindy started to reach for the animal. Tory shouted, "No."

The fluffy ball uncurled, his dark eyes opening. It hissed, arching its back, its raised tail pointed toward Mindy. Before Tory could grab the child and yank her away, the baby skunk sprayed the arm still reaching toward it. Mindy jumped back, landing on her bottom. The skunk scurried away, disappearing under the house, its horrible odor left behind.

"Ph-ew!" Mindy waved her arm around, the pungent smell quickly spreading.

Tory covered her mouth and nose, her eyes blinking from the intense odor emanating from Mindy.

"I—thought—it was—a new—kit-ten." Tears welled in the little girl's eyes. "I—uh—stink."

"I guess we found out what's living under the house. A family of skunks." With tears streaming down Mindy's face, Tory couldn't resist hugging the child, keeping her sprayed arm away from her. "We'll take care of this."

"The—play!"

"By Sunday. I promise."

"Mindy, Tory, what's going on?" Slade sniffed the air. "I smell a skunk."

"Those raccoons under the house are really skunks."

"We have a problem."

"That's an understatement." Tory gestured toward Mindy. "She got just a little too close."

He made his way toward them, a grimace forming on his face. "What should we do about the smell?"

Tory started walking with Mindy toward the house. "I'll need you to go into town and buy several bottles of hydrogen peroxide. I have one bottle but I don't know if it will do the trick."

"Hydrogen peroxide?"

Tory waved her hand. "Go. I'll explain later."

Inside she had Mindy remove her shirt. "I'll put this outside until I can get rid of it."

After that Mindy sat on the lip of the tub while Tory went about mixing up a homemade remedy. Using the hydrogen peroxide she had on hand, she combined it with baking soda and liquid dishwashing soap. While foaming, she spread it on Mindy's sprayed arm and hoped for the best.

Thirty minutes later, Slade hurried into the house with five bottles of hydrogen peroxide, ready to do battle with the odor. He stopped when he saw Mindy, dressed and smiling. He sniffed the air. The skunk scent still lingered but definitely not as strong as before.

"What happened?"

"I had enough hydrogen peroxide to take care of it this time. Thankfully the skunk sprayed Mindy's arm. Not too large an area. We'll treat the area again. The odor should wear off completely by Sunday. The more important question is what are we going to do about the family living under the house?"

"Good question. Skunks are definitely out of my expertise."

"I'm not sure, either. We could try loud noises or bright lights. It may not be easy."

"Well, we need to do something. I don't want a repeat of today." Slade's nose wrinkled up, trying to get used to the faint odor that peppered the air as a reminder of their guests under the house.

"I—won't—bo-ther—again. Prom-ise."

"I know, honey. But I don't think it's wise to have a family of skunks living under the house. Do you think a loud noise will work?"

Tory shrugged.

Slade retrieved the stereo from the kitchen and placed it on the bench on the deck. He switched on a radio station with rock-and-roll music and turned it up loud.

"If that doesn't drive them away, it sure will take care of me," he shouted over the din.

Back inside the house the noise was marginally softer. At least they didn't have to yell at each other to hear. But the sound of the bass vibrated the house and dinner was eaten in quiet to the background music of the eighties and nineties.

Afterward Tory began clearing the dishes. "Why don't I ask around and find out what might work? I don't think I can take much more of this noise."

"Just our luck. We'll drive ourselves nuts while the skunks have a good old time." Slade went outside and switched off the radio.

Silence blissfully filled the air. Tory released a long sigh. Then she suddenly heard a crash and ran toward the back door. Slade flew over the railing and jogged toward the hose. He turned it on and pointed it toward a large skunk scurrying across the grass. From the safety of the other side of the yard Slade tried to drive the animal away. Instead, he ended up drenching the ground and forming several mud puddles.

The skunk disappeared into the meadow, out of reach of the water spray. Slade set his face in determination and stretched the hose as far as he could. It didn't do any good. The water fell short of its target.

Mindy and Tory stood on the deck, watching the battle. Tory covered her mouth, trying to contain her laughter. Because the nozzle wasn't on tight enough, it leaked water from the hose connection and ran down Slade's arm and onto his pants and tennis shoes.

"Dad-dy—fun-ny."

"Yes, very."

He dropped the hose and strode to the deck. "This is war. She has to come back and I'm gonna be ready for her."

"I'll get you a towel. Don't forget I can make some calls and see what we can do about the skunks."

"I think she was actually mocking me," Slade

grumbled while heading back to the hose with a lawn chair in his hands.

Mindy giggled.

"I know, Mindy. No one will believe he is standing guard waiting for a skunk to return home."

Tory went into the house and grabbed a large towel. When she walked through the kitchen to the back door, she noted the stacked dishes by the sink. She shook her head and stepped outside to the sight of Slade bolting out of the lawn chair, switching on the hose, and running toward the returning skunk. His feet hit one of the mud puddles and flew up into the air. Slade landed on his back, staring at the sky, with the hose in his hand, squirting water upward like a fountain. It fell in sheets onto his prone body, thoroughly soaking him.

Mindy doubled over laughing while Slade pushed himself to his elbows, water dripping off him. The skunk disappeared under the house. The hose continued to drench the ground around Slade.

Tory hurried to the faucet and twisted it off. "Stay there. I'll get some more towels."

"Oh—Dad-dy—you're—too—much." Mindy started toward the stairs to the backyard.

"I agree, Mindy, but I think you'd better stay here. It looks pretty slippery out there." Tory waited until Mindy stopped by the railing before she headed back inside for some more towels.

She knew there was a competitive edge to Slade, but with a skunk? He was too much, Tory thought, her own laughter bubbling to the surface as she recalled his soaked, muddy body. When she returned to the deck, Mindy held the hose and was spraying her father clean. He pirouetted slowly, allowing her to reach his back, as well. When he was rinsed off, he took a towel from Tory and turned the faucet off. The sounds of two animals fighting came from under the house.

He arched one brow, a frown marring his features.

"It's catching."

"Like—a cold?" Mindy asked with a giggle.

Slade shivered, hugging his arms to him. "If I don't get inside and changed, I'll get a cold," he grumbled.

"It's ninety degrees out here. I don't think so."

Slade sloshed up the steps. "It could happen. I've heard of summer colds."

"Hold it. Where do you think you're going? You're still dripping wet. And those shoes!"

He held up his hands. "I'll take them off. Promise." He bent down and removed his tennis shoes and socks, then draped them over the chair to dry. Taking another towel, he ran it down his body one more time. "Okay?" He spread his arms wide and turned in a full circle.

"Fine."

When Slade disappeared into the house, Mindy looked over the railing at the crawl space where the skunks lived. "They—don't—sound—hap-py."

"If your father has anything to do about it, they won't be until they move on."

"The—ba-by was—cute."

"Melinda Donaldson, you better not try to hold one again."

Mindy stuck her lower lip out. "I—won't."

"Good." Tory clasped the child's shoulder and started for the back door. "Now, we have a dinner to clean up. Do you think you can help me while your daddy is changing?"

"Yes!"

Together they entered the kitchen and began rinsing the dishes to put in the dishwasher. Tory thought back to the past few hours and even though nothing had gone according to plans, she had enjoyed herself. Combating the skunk problem had made them seem even more like a family. She relished that feeling.

Slade sat down next to Tory in the audience and leaned close. "Are you sure about this?"

"Yes, Mindy will be fine. I got her in her horse costume and she knows her line."

"Still—"

"Slade, stop worrying. You saw the children with Mindy. They have accepted her and she feels part of the group."

Sighing, he settled back and crossed his arms as though steeling himself for the next twenty minutes.

The lights in the recreational hall dimmed and the audience of parents and friends quieted. The curtain on the stage opened, revealing a boy playing Noah standing in front of what was supposed to be the newly built ark, even though it was a cardboard cutout. Soon the children appeared who represented the various animals of the world. When Mindy came on stage, dressed in brown

burlap, a long tail of twined rope fastened to the back,
Slade tensed, clasping Tory's hand and holding it hostage.

Mindy trudged toward Noah and stopped. "We—
want—to—join—you."

Tory heard the swoosh of air leave Slade when
Mindy finished her line. He squeezed her hand, but
instead of releasing his grasp, he kept it clasped. His
hand surrounding hers felt right. He didn't let it go until
the end when everyone clapped as the children took
their bows.

He rose and stretched. "I'm glad that is over."

"Why?" Tory came to her feet.

"It's not easy holding your breath until your
daughter makes her appearance." His mouth quirked
in a lopsided grin.

"Holding your breath?"

"Not exactly the whole time, but it was hard to breathe
properly when all I could do was worry if she would
remember what to say. I definitely hope she doesn't want
to go on stage as an actress. I don't think I could take it."

"Knowing you, you'll support anything Mindy
wants to do."

"Dad-dy," Mindy called out a few feet from them.
She weaved among the adults until she was standing
next to Slade. "I—did—it!"

"Yes, you did, sweetheart. You're braver than I would
be. I don't think I could get up in front of a group of
people and recite lines."

"I—didn't—for-get one—word." Mindy's chest
swelled, her chin lifted.

"Nope."

"I'm—get-ting—bread." Mindy crunched her face into a frown. "I mean—cake." She headed off into the crowd toward the table at the back of the recreational hall that had a large sheet cake on it with fruit punch next to it.

"Mmm. Chocolate cake sounds good." Slade eyed the pieces being sliced.

"I'm sure there'll be enough for the adults, too."

"You know I have a weakness for chocolate." He watched Mindy take a plate and a cup and walk toward a group of children sitting at a table.

"Is that your only weakness?"

"I do like ice cream and French fries. Both probably aren't too good for you."

"Oh, my, with weaknesses like those, you're in big trouble." Tory splayed her hand over her chest in mock shock.

A serious expression descended on Slade's face. "I wish that was all."

"What deep, dark secrets could you possibly have?" Tory asked, thinking of her own that she kept close to her heart.

"We all have secrets we want to protect."

"Not from God."

Slade's frown evolved into a scowl, his lips clamped together. When Reverend Nelson joined them, Slade relaxed his expression into a neutral one, but Tory saw the slight stiffening to his shoulders that indicated his tension. When had she come to know Slade so well?

They had been married only a few weeks, and yet she knew his moods even when he was trying to mask them.

"It's good to see you at church, Slade." Reverend Nelson shook his hand. "I hope this means you'll be coming more often with Tory and Mindy."

"Possibly, when work permits."

"We could use someone with your expertise on our budget committee."

"I don't know if I have that kind of time."

"I hope you'll think about it. Tory, I like your idea about using your horses for the summer carnival. The kids will enjoy riding."

When the reverend left, Slade asked, "What summer carnival?"

"The one we'll be hosting over the Fourth of July weekend."

"Hosting!"

Tory automatically took a step back. "I know I should have said something sooner, but it was just decided yesterday. Once I volunteered the horses, the committee liked the idea of moving the carnival to the ranch. There's more room and I won't have to transport the horses. It's good advertisement for the riding stable especially now that it's being fixed up."

"But the Fourth is a week away."

"I know. Mindy will be excited."

"You mean she doesn't know yet?" His frown returned.

Tory closed the space between them, placing her hand on his arm. "I haven't had a chance to tell her, either."

"Sometimes I think I'm the last to know what's

going on," he grumbled. "How many people come to this carnival?"

"Probably over a hundred. The church uses it as a fund-raiser."

"Have you volunteered me for any jobs?"

"Of course not. I hope you'll help me with the rides, but you don't have to do anything if you don't want to. In fact, you can spend the day at work if you want to escape."

Slade snorted. "Not if I want to come home to two ladies who will be speaking to me."

"I'd better tell you also that my family has definitely decided to visit over that weekend. They come every year and believe me, this one will be no different."

"Checking me out?"

Tory nodded.

"I can live with that. Thank goodness I didn't make any plans for the holiday."

"I'm not used to running my plans by someone. I haven't had to before."

"We're a family, Tory. Don't forget that."

She inhaled a calming breath and braced herself. "I also think we should go to Carol's grave site today after church. I know the past month or so has been hectic with you looking for a housekeeper then us getting married so suddenly."

Slade closed his eyes for a few seconds, and when he opened them again, Tory saw the anguish in his gaze.

"Mindy needs to say goodbye to her mother."

"I know. We'll go."

"Do you want me to go, too?"

"Do you want to?"

"Yes, we're a family, Slade. And don't forget that."

"Then let's get Mindy and go now."

The ride to the cemetery was done in silence with a quick stop at a grocery store for some fresh flowers. Slade pulled up to the grave site and helped Mindy from the back seat. Tory followed the pair to the marble headstone with Carol Marie Donaldson's name. Mindy put the assorted flowers in the vase at the base of the headstone, then stood back.

"They—die—with-out—wa-ter."

Tory scanned the area and found an outdoor faucet nearby. "We can fill the vase with some water before we leave."

With a somber expression, Slade placed his hands on Mindy's shoulders and stood behind her. "Mommy's buried here."

"She's—with—God—now."

"Yes, sweetheart."

"Can—she—hear—me?"

"I believe she can. I'm sure she's watching over you. She loved you very much."

Mindy leaned her head back until she stared at the sky above her. "Mom-my, I—love—you." Tears roughened her voice. "Tell—God—hi—for me. Good-bye, Mom-my."

Tory fought to keep her own tears at bay. *Carol, I promise I'll look out for Mindy and love her as you would,* Tory vowed, brushing the back of her hand across her cheeks.

Chapter Nine

The sun dipped below the tree line as Tory approached Slade by the fence. With his forearms propped on the top of the railing, he stared at the horses eating grass in the field. For the past three days he distanced himself from her until he hardly said a word tonight at dinner. Even Mindy had noticed and said something to her while she was putting her to bed.

"Are we having our second fight?" she asked, stopping only an arm's length away from him.

He threw her a glance, then resumed watching the horses. "No. What makes you think that?"

She shrugged. "Oh, I don't know. Maybe the fact today we have exchanged no more than a handful of words."

"Got things on my mind."

"About the church carnival in a couple of days? I'm sorry I didn't consult you first. I—"

"I'm not upset about the carnival, Tory."

She shifted so she faced him. "Then what are you upset about?"

He didn't look at her, but tension vibrated the air between them. The silence stretched to a full minute, and Tory began to wonder if he'd even heard her question.

"It's really not a secret. Today is the second anniversary of the car wreck." He leaned into the fence, his gaze still trained forward on the animals in the field.

The tension sharpened, cutting through Tory's defenses that were always erected. "And?"

He stabbed her with his narrowed gaze. "And what?"

"Anniversaries are for marriages, things like that, not a car wreck. It's not productive to look back like that."

"So you never look back and wonder what your life would be like if something didn't happen?"

His question caused Tory to suck in a deep breath. "Not if I can help it. Is that what you're doing? Wondering what your life would be like if the wreck had never happened?" She hadn't wanted the wreck ever to happen, either, but she couldn't keep the hurt from lacing her words.

"I was thinking about how different Mindy's life would be if she hadn't been in the wreck, if I had paid more attention and been able to avoid the truck."

"No matter how much you beat yourself up over this, accidents happen."

He turned toward her, lines creasing his brow. "You don't understand! I was arguing with Carol about her going back to work. I should have been paying better attention. The last words my wife and I exchanged were said in anger."

Until Slade came to terms with his wife's death and the wreck, there was no chance for their marriage to work. She saw it in the pain that shadowed his eyes. She heard it in the anguish reflected in each of his words. She wanted to take him into her embrace and hold him close to her heart. She wanted to erase the ache he felt and replace it with hope. "She knows how you really felt."

"I broke my own rule. I never fought with Carol in front of Mindy. That day I did. I was tired, having put in a long day of negotiations with the union." He pivoted away, staring again at the horses. "I don't think my daughter remembers much about that day. But if she ever remembers the argument I was having with Carol, she'll blame me."

The torment in his voice shredded her composure. Tears clogged her throat. She stepped toward him and laid her hand on his shoulder. The muscles beneath her palm bunched. "Mindy loves you. Nothing is going to change that, Slade."

"I was driving and I walked away. No one else did."

She placed her other hand on his other shoulder. "Let God into your heart. Let Him heal you."

"What if you're too broken?"

As though they had a will of their own, her arms wound about him and she laid her head on his back. Too broken? She'd thought that at one time, lying in the hospital bed after her date had assaulted her physically and emotionally.

"No one's too broken for God to fix."

He straightened away from the fence, cupping her clasped hands. The quick rise and fall of his chest underscored the emotions churning inside him. Turning within the circle of her arms, he lifted her chin so his glittering gaze could seek hers. "I can't ask Carol for her forgiveness."

"Then ask God."

"I've forgotten how."

The sound of his voice, heavy with emotions, filled her with sorrow. Tory splayed her hand over his chest, feeling the rapid beating beneath her palm. "It's simple. Ask from the heart."

He plunged his fingers into her hair, loose and about her shoulders the way he liked it, and cradled her face between his hands. "You're an amazing woman."

"Slade, you are not to blame for what happened. Carol wouldn't want you to waste your life agonizing over something you can't change."

"Ah, your motto. Forget the past."

"Learn from the past but move on. You can't change what's happened, but you might have some control over what is to happen."

One corner of his mouth lifted. "That's why I'm focusing all my energy into making sure Mindy recovers." His hands fell away from her face.

She missed the warmth of his palms against her cheeks. For a few moments she'd felt connected to

Slade. Now she felt the distance as he stepped back against the fence. "Mindy is recovering." But was he? He might not have been physically hurt in the wreck but he was emotionally. Would he ever heal? The brightness and hope of their future as a married couple dimmed.

"I know. I just want it to have happened yesterday. Patience has never been my strong suit." He took her hand and started for the house. "I could learn some from you. I've seen you with your students, with Mindy, with your horses. You have a great deal of patience. Want to share some with me?"

"I'm gonna need all I have to get through this carnival. I forgot what a big deal it was. The next few days will be hectic and I still have to see to my horses."

"Not to mention your family coming tomorrow."

"You don't mind, do you?"

He stopped at the bottom of the steps up to the front porch. "The question is, will your family mind? It's gonna be crowded here."

"Don't worry about them. Judy has a camper. The kids are going to stay out there while the adults are staying in the house."

"There are only three bedrooms, Tory."

"Oh."

With all that had been happening, she hadn't stopped to think about the sleeping arrangements. Three couples. Three bedrooms. That should be simple and it would be if she was sharing a bedroom with her husband.

"How do you want to deal with the situation?"

His question brought her anxiety to the surface. Share a bedroom—a bed with Slade. Or, tell her family about her arranged marriage. "I don't know," she finally said, searching the dark shadows of his face for some kind of answer. In his blue eyes she saw support and comfort and drew strength from that.

"Ju-dy! Tor-ee!"

"I think the children found us." Judy brought the glass of lemonade to her lips and took a long drink.

Three heads appeared around the corner of the barn followed by three bodies. Ashley, Jamie and Mindy surrounded Judy and Tory. She and her sister were sitting in the shade of the barn, but it was still hot, the sun still up in the western sky.

Ashley placed her hand on her waist. "We've been looking all over for you two."

Judy's daughter reminded Tory so much of her big sister even down to the straight long blond hair and hazel eyes. "We thought we would let the men prepare dinner."

"Dad-dy—is."

Tory pressed the ice-cold drink to her forehead, thinking about Slade's expertise in the kitchen, which consisted of boiling water and opening cans. "He is?"

"Uncle Slade is getting pizza for dinner," Jamie piped in. "Daddy and him are driving into town right now."

"Where's Grandma and Grandpa?" Judy asked, finishing the last of her lemonade.

"Grandma is still taking a nap. Grandpa is watching

the news." Ashley grabbed her mother's arm. "Come on. Daddy will be back soon with dinner. We were supposed to find you."

Judy threw a helpless look toward Tory. "I knew it was too good to last."

Tory checked her watch. "I guess thirty minutes is better than none."

Mindy followed Ashley's lead and took hold of Tory's arm, pulling on her. "Come—on."

Tory blew a long sigh out between pursed lips. She'd wanted to explain to her sister about the sleeping arrangements but hadn't found the right words. They had sipped their drinks, stared at the horses in the paddock and hadn't said more than a few words in the past thirty minutes, relishing the silence instead.

"I believe our quiet time is up, sis," Judy said, laughing as her daughter tugged her toward the house almost at a jog.

Mindy and Tory took up the rear at a much slower pace. "Jam-ee—calls—Dad-dy—Un-cle—Slade. Do—you—uh—" she paused for a few seconds "—think I—could—call—Ju-dy—Aunt?"

"She'd be flattered. We're all family now."

"I've—been—think-ing. Can—I—call—you—Mom?"

Stunned, Tory halted in her tracks, tears springing to her eyes. She opened her mouth to say something but nothing came out. The question, spoken so casually, robbed her of coherent thought.

"If—you—don't—want—"

Tory swallowed several times. "I would love for you

to call me Mom," she said, tears streaming down her face.

"Why—are—you—cry-ing?"

Tory smoothed back Mindy's hair, then swiped at the wet tracks running down her cheeks. "Because you've made me so happy."

"Do you—think—Dad-dy—will—care?"

Would he? Slade still had so much guilt over the car wreck that had taken his wife's life. Yes, he wanted Tory to help him raise Mindy, but even though they were married, she really didn't feel like his wife. They were housemates with a license declaring them husband and wife. That piece of paper was only one small part of it.

"Honey, you'll have to ask your father that. I can't answer for him."

Mindy took her hand. "Then—I will." She started for the house again.

Tory reached out to open the screen door when she heard a car coming down the lane toward the house. Slanting a look over her shoulder, she saw Slade and Brad pull up in front and climb out of the silver sedan. "Dinner has arrived."

"I—love—piz-za."

"So do I. It's just never on any diet that I know of."

"Diet?" Slade carried five large boxes. "What diet?"

"The diet I need to start after this weekend."

Slade's gaze traveled slowly down Tory's length before reestablishing eye contact with her. "Why? I don't see the need."

Heat, having nothing to do with the ninety-degree

temperature, flamed her cheeks. "I've been fixing more full-course meals than I usually eat. Trust me. I need to cut back."

"I like you just the way you are."

Slade's impish grin that curved his mouth curled her toes. "Pleasantly plump?" For a few seconds she'd forgotten that Brad and Mindy were standing close, listening to every word said.

"The pleasant part is right." Slade's grin grew to encompass his whole face, down to the twinkle in his eye.

Brad cleared his throat. "If we don't get these inside, they will be stone-cold."

"I—like—cold—piz-za, Uncle—Brad."

Everyone looked at Mindy, surprise on Brad's and Slade's faces. Tory watched Slade's reaction to what Mindy had said. His surprise quickly transformed into acceptance.

He thrust open the door, holding it for Mindy and Tory to enter the house first. "You might like cold pizza, but I don't."

"We probably should reheat them anyway. That's a fifteen-minute drive."

When Tory came into the kitchen, she immediately turned the oven on to four hundred degrees. Slade and Brad laid the five boxes down on the counter and quickly escaped to the back deck while the women reheated the pizza.

Outside, the house shaded the wooden deck, offering some relief from the temperature while a light breeze stirred the hot air, making it bearable. Jamie darted down the steps to the yard and dashed across to the tire swing. He conned Ashley into pushing him by promising he would do the same for her. Mindy stayed on the deck watching them from the railing.

Slade folded himself into a cedar lounge chair, stretching his legs out in front of him. "Are you okay with Mindy calling you Uncle?"

"You bet." Brad sat next to him. "You have a wonderful daughter."

Slade's attention shifted to Mindy who braced herself against the railing. She was tired. He could tell by her drooping shoulders and the fact she hadn't joined the other two at the swing. Ever since Tory's family had arrived, his daughter had been going a mile a minute, trying to keep up with everyone. He longed for the day when she would race across the yard, leading the pack, instead of following slowly behind.

"I don't think I'll have any trouble getting her to go to bed tonight, especially with the kids camping outside. She's so excited about that."

"Saturday after the carnival Judy and I are heading to Grand Lake to camp for a few days before we head home. Tory's parents are going back to Dallas. We would love to take Mindy along."

"Camping? If she wants to go, that'll be fine with me. I can rearrange her therapy sessions if need be."

"Ashley will be thrilled. She's been talking about taking Mindy with us. Jamie, too, even though she's just a girl, he said."

The way Tory's family had taken Mindy into their

hearts only reconfirmed he'd made the right decision in marrying Tory. "Sweetheart?"

Mindy twisted around, looking at Slade.

"Would you like to go camping with Ashley and Jamie? They're going to Grand Lake for a few days."

A smile lit his daughter's face. "Yes!"

"Just as I thought," Slade said to Brad.

"It's my turn. Get off," Ashley shouted.

Brad surged to his feet. "Better take care of this before war is declared."

Slade patted the chair that Brad had vacated. "Come sit by me. Are you enjoying Ashley and Jamie's visit?"

Mindy came toward the lounge chair, her foot dragging more than usual. "Yes. They—are—uh—fun." She scooted back until her feet dangled over the edge. "Dad-dy, can—I ask—you—some-thing?"

"Sure, anything."

She clasped her hands together in her lap and studied them. "I—want—to—" she drew in a gulp of air "—call Tor-ee—Mom. Is—that—kay?" She swung her large gaze to his.

Okay? There was a part of him that was thrilled she wanted to call Tory Mom. But there was a part—where his guilt lay buried—that wanted to say no. Words crowded his throat, closing it.

Mindy's eyes grew round. "I—won't—if—you—don't—want me to."

Slade fought to keep his expression neutral while he brought his reeling emotions under control. His guilt affected so many aspects of his life. He needed to come to terms with it before it destroyed what was good in his life—Mindy and Tory. He wanted them to be a family. There was nothing else he could say but, "Honey, whatever you want is fine with me."

"I—love—Mom-my. But—I—love—Tor-ee, too."

He clasped his daughter's hands between his. "I know. You can love more than one person. Your life is always richer with people you care in it."

"Is—that—why—you—uh—uh—" Mindy pinched her lips together "—mar-ried—Tor-ee?"

"Tory is important to us both," he said, aware that Brad and his two children were walking toward them. When they came up the steps, Slade stood. "Tell Tory I needed to check on something down at the barn."

"But the pizza is—"

Slade strode from the deck and around the house, re- alizing his sudden disappearance would seem strange. But he had to be alone, at least for a few minutes while he put himself back together. His emotions lay frayed, the past few days having taken their toll on him.

He sought the quiet and coolness of the barn, walking to the far end. Leaning against the opening, he stared at the pasture beyond. One chestnut mare with her colt chewed on the grass on the other side of the fence. The sun had vanished behind the line of trees, bringing shadows to the landscape. The scent of earth, hay and horses swirled about him. A cardinal and its mate flew overhead and perched in the maple tree near the building. Serenity was all around him, and yet inside his emotions roiled, churning his stomach.

Tory was right. His guilt was ruling his life. That had to change if their marriage would ever have a chance. Was the Lord the answer? He'd never been good at praying, asking for what he needed. Was that why his prayers after the accident had gone unanswered?

"Slade, is there something wrong?"

He pivoted toward the sound of Tory's worried voice. She walked toward him, concern in her eyes. "No," he answered. But when he continued to look at her, he said, "Yes. Why are you here?"

"I know how much you like pizza, and when you didn't come in for dinner, I knew something was wrong. Brad told me you came down here. I thought maybe something happened that I needed to check on, too."

He gestured to the area around him. "Everything's fine."

She came within a few feet of him. "Then Mindy must have asked you."

Surprised at how perceptive Tory could be, Slade turned away from her, not wanting her to read all his doubts in his expression. "Yes, she did."

"Is it okay?"

"I should ask you that question."

"Of course, it's okay. I love Mindy like a daughter."

The muscles in his shoulders and neck ached from holding himself so tense. "Then it's okay with me. I told Mindy it was up to her."

"But it bothers you?"

The waver in her question pierced his armor. He whirled about, needing to clarify his feelings not only to

Tory but himself. "I was a little surprised, that's all. When I married you, I wanted us to become a family, but—"

"But you feel as though you've betrayed Carol?"

He nodded, his throat so tight he didn't think he could say one word.

"One of the things I like about you is your loyalty. Carol was your wife for seven years. You loved her. I don't expect those feelings to go away. We entered into this marriage for Mindy. We both love her." She took a step toward him. "It's okay, Slade, to continue living, to enjoy life. I'll keep some pizza for you. Come up whenever you're ready. I'll make sure no one bothers you until then."

He watched her walk away, her head held high, her shoulders back. He'd hurt her. Even though her expression hadn't shown it, he could tell by the dullness in her eyes. That had been the last thing he'd wanted to do. He couldn't continue like this.

Turning toward the pasture, he strode to the fence and climbed over it. In the field among the wildflowers, he slowly went around in a circle, taking in all the marvels of nature. God was everywhere. He needed God back in his life. He needed peace again.

He fell to his knees and bowed his head. *Dear Lord, please help me to overcome this guilt I feel for surviving when Carol didn't, when Mindy came away hurt. Please help me to move on in my life and to put the past behind me. I need to for Mindy's and Tory's sakes, but mostly for my own. In Jesus Christ, amen.*

* * *

"What's that sound?" Judy asked as she placed the last plate into the dishwasher.

"We have skunks under the house. They're fighting. Probably the male wants to move and the female wants to stay put." Tory dried her hands on the towel looped around the handle on the refrigerator.

"Skunks! When did this happen?"

"I'm not sure. Sometime in the spring. We thought we had a family of raccoons. We found out the hard way we didn't."

"You say 'we' so easily. Married life agrees with you."

Tory remembered her conversation with Slade earlier that evening in the barn. She thought it could, but how was she going to compete with a woman who was dead? She wanted her marriage to work, but she wasn't sure how to make that happen.

"Have you told him yet?"

"No. Why do you keep bringing it up? I want to forget about that part of my life."

"If it were that simple, you would have long ago. The very fact you haven't said anything to Slade about being raped tells me you haven't dealt with it." Her sister shut the dishwasher and turned it on. "Do you trust him?"

"If I didn't trust him, I wouldn't have married him."

"Then tell him."

"I will when the time is right." Whenever that would be. She almost said something to him earlier in the barn, but the words wouldn't come out. Her past was as much a barrier to their marriage as his. What a pair they made!

"Do you think the men have gotten the children down yet?"

"In other words, do I think it's safe for us to come out of the kitchen?"

"Yep. Notice how fast I jumped at the chance to let them take care of the kids tonight? It's been a long day."

"Tell me about it. And tomorrow will be longer with setting up for the carnival on top of everything else." Tory headed for the living room. "Let's join Mom and Dad. I'm sure Slade and Brad have everything under control."

"I can tell you haven't been a mother for long or you wouldn't have said that."

When Tory entered the living room, her mother was cradled against her father's side on the couch, her eyes drifting closed. "Is she okay, Dad?"

He put his forefinger up to his lips, a plea in his eyes. "You two through with cleaning up?"

"Yep, and we got the easier of the two chores," Judy said as she settled into a chair across from the couch.

"Tsk, tsk. Putting children down to bed isn't a chore." The teasing light in their father's eyes dimmed when their mother murmured something and nestled closer to him.

"Dad?" Tory noticed the dark circles under her mother's eyes. It looked as if she wasn't sleeping well, but since she'd gotten here early this afternoon, that was about all she'd done.

Eleanor's head sagged even more, her chest rising and falling slowly as she sank into sleep. Tory's dad watched her for a few minutes before answering, "She hasn't been feeling well for the past couple of months. Tires easily. She goes to the doctor again next week when we get back. I'm afraid it's her heart."

"Why didn't you tell me?" Tory asked. "I knew she wasn't feeling well at the wedding, but I didn't know it had been going on for so long."

"I didn't want to worry you."

"Where my family is concerned, I don't want to be kept in the dark."

Her father's gaze drilled into her. "The same goes for you. Both your mother and I have wondered about this sudden marriage. We get a call one day inviting us to your wedding with no warning that you were even dating someone."

"I guess we all have our secrets."

"That's not what families do."

Her father pinned her with a probing look as though he could reach into her mind and see all her doubts about a good man marrying someone who might not be able to give him what he deserved. She started to tell her father the reasons behind her marrying Slade, but taking a look at her mother firmed her determination to keep quiet. He had enough to worry about without adding to his problems. All his married life he'd had a deep love for his wife. He wouldn't understand why she'd married Slade without that same kind of deep love.

The sound of the front door opening and closing alerted Tory to the men's return. She focused on the entrance, hoping her father didn't pursue the conversation, especially with Slade in the room.

When he and Brad entered, Tory laughed. "You two look like you wrestled a bear."

While tucking in his shirt, Slade exchanged a glance with Brad. "Three children who didn't want to go to bed are worse than a hungry bear." He ran a hand through his disheveled hair.

"Next time we'll let you ladies put the little darlings down while Slade and I clean up the kitchen."

"What took you all so long?" Judy asked, trying to contain her laughter behind her hand.

"First, I had to tell a story, then Slade. Then they wanted us to act our stories out. I'm exhausted." Brad plopped down onto the couch next to his father-in-law.

"If you think you're exhausted now, wait until the carnival." Tory shifted so that Slade could sit on the footrest to the chair she was using.

"So it doesn't look like there's any rest and relaxation with this vacation." Brad took a handkerchief from his pocket and wiped his brow.

"Who said vacations were for resting and relaxing?" Tory's father gently shook her mother awake.

"Obviously no one who knows the Alexander family," Brad grumbled, assisting his mother-in-law in standing.

"We're going to bed. It has been a long day for us." Her father cradled her mother against him and walked toward the hall.

"That's our cue to turn in, too." Judy stood, offering her hand to Brad.

In under two minutes the living room was cleared except for Tory and Slade. Her gaze caught his, then dropped to her lap. The only place for him to sleep was on the living room couch or in her bedroom. Tomorrow morning she didn't want to explain to her family why Slade had slept on the couch. And yet, could she share a bed with him—her husband?

"I guess we should go to bed, too," she murmured, twisting her hands together.

Slade covered them. "Tory, nothing will happen you don't want to happen. That's a promise."

She believed him, but there was still a small part of her that would automatically panic. Closing her eyes, she prayed for strength to make it over this hurdle. It was important for their marriage.

She rose and extended her hand to him. He clasped hers and came to his feet. She faced him with only inches between them, so close their breaths merged.

"Why don't you get ready for bed first? I'll be along later. I want to check on the kids. Mindy's never camped out before."

Another stone in the wall around her heart crumbled. Sometimes she felt as though he could read her mind. The connection was disconcerting. "She'll be fine. Ashley will look out for her."

While she made her way to the bathroom, Slade left the house. She prepared for bed in less than fifteen minutes. By the time Slade came into the room, she was under the covers with the sheet pulled up to her chin. Since they had moved his clothing into her bedroom, he gathered his pajamas and headed for the bathroom, switching off the overhead light as he exited. All that lit the room were the slits of moonlight streaming through the slats in the blinds.

Tory clutched the sheet and stared at the dark ceiling. Her heart hammered against her chest while her pulse raced through her. An eternity later Slade reentered the bedroom, obviously feeling his way to the bed. She heard him crash into the nightstand and started to turn on the lamp on the table by her. Before she could, Slade eased down onto the mattress next to her.

"Good night, Tory." He rolled over onto his side away from her.

"Night," she managed to say.

Slade was her husband.

Slade was a good man and a wonderful father.

She trusted Slade.

Slowly her heartbeat returned to its normal pace and she released her death grip on the sheet. Slowly her muscles relaxed and her eyelids drooped. Sleep crept over her and she sank into the world of dreams.

Something hit his arm. A moan pierced his sleep-drenched mind. Slade's eyes bolted open.

Another moan sounded in the silence of the house. Tory twisted, kicking out at him. Pain shot up his leg. He scrambled away from her and came off the bed, reaching for the lamp.

"Don't. Please."

For a few seconds he halted his movements, thinking she was awake and knew he was going to turn on the light. But looking at Tory thrashing on the bed confirmed what he'd originally thought. She was asleep, caught in a nightmare. Flicking on the lamp, he blinked at the sudden brightness while Tory bolted straight up in bed, terror on her face.

Chapter Ten

Tory jerked the sheet up, gripping it in her fists. The sound of her heartbeat thundered in her ears. She knew Slade was speaking because his mouth moved, but for a few seconds she couldn't hear what he was saying. The suffocating compression around her chest threatened her next breaths. Pulling air into her lungs, she scooted back against the headboard.

"Tory? Are you all right?" Slade sat on the mattress, reaching out toward her.

She nodded, evading his touch to stand on the other side of the bed. Snatching up her robe, she stuffed her arms into the terry-cloth sleeves and belted it. The double-size mattress separated them, but it wasn't far enough away for Tory.

Flashes of her nightmare clung to her mind. The fear. The pain. The humiliation. Her body shook with the memories of four years ago—of the nightmare that plagued her when she allowed her fear to grow.

The concern on Slade's face tore further at her fragile composure. She wanted to reassure him she was all right, but she couldn't get words past the constriction in her throat. Again she forced herself to inhale deeply until the crashing of her heart against her rib cage subsided.

When he started to round the end of the bed, she held up her hand and managed to say, "I'm okay."

Thankfully he stopped and studied her. If he had touched her, she was afraid she would have come unglued. She could still remember her assailant's hands on her, and the memory left her feeling unclean. She needed to shower.

Glancing at the bedside clock, she sighed when she saw it was nearly five in the morning. "I'm getting up. It's nearly time and I might as well get started on today's chores before the carnival committee comes out here to set up for tomorrow." Without waiting for him to say anything, she went to her closet and withdrew her clothes for the day.

As she crossed the room to the door, he finally said, "Tory, something frightened you. Do you want to talk about it?"

"No." She opened the door and escaped out into the hall.

The click of the door as Tory closed it reverberated through the bedroom, the sound bouncing off the walls and striking him with its finality. Slade stared at the wooden barrier between him and his wife. Until just a few minutes ago he'd thought they had made progress in their relationship. The nightmare was the answer, but she had locked the door and thrown the key away.

Exhaustion cleaved to every part of her. Tory took a moment to sit and regroup before the next set of children arrived to ride the horses. Perspiration plastered strands of her hair to her face and neck. She ran a towel across her forehead and around her neck but that did little to relieve the heat of a summer's day.

"Another hour and the carnival will be over," Judy said as she sat down beside her on the bale of hay in the shade of the barn. "This has been a roaring success. Everyone says so. They particularly like the horse rides for the children and young at heart."

The words her sister spoke barely registered on her numb mind. Tory closed her eyes and wished she could keep them closed for the next twenty-four hours. Sleep. She needed it badly. The night before she had lain next to Slade, listening to his even breathing and trying desperately not to fall asleep, not to dream again. She'd managed to stay awake most of the night and gotten up early again to do her chores before everyone else got up. Now, however, the lack of sleep the past forty-eight hours had caught up with her. She couldn't even lift her arms to brush a horsefly away.

"Tory? Are you with me?" Her sister waved her hand in front of Tory's eyes.

She blinked and offered her sister a smile. "Yes, barely. This has been a *really* long day."

"And it's not even three o'clock yet." Judy angled

around to face her. "Mom and Dad have decided to leave this evening, too. Dad wants to get Mom back home."

"Yeah, he's worried about her. I'm worried about her."

"He's going to take her to the doctor as soon as he can."

"Good."

"And we'll leave right after them. We can get to Grand Lake before dark and set up camp. The kids want to go fishing first thing tomorrow morning. You two newlyweds will finally have the house all to yourself. You'll have peace and quiet for three days. Consider this one of my wedding presents to you, sister dear."

"Peace and quiet. I won't know what to do with myself."

"Do I need to give you a lecture on the birds and the bees?"

Tory hadn't thought beyond the fact she would have her bedroom to herself again and would be able to get a good night's sleep. But without Mindy in the house, she and Slade would be alone as husband and wife for the first time. He hadn't said anything to her about the nightmare, but he had kept his distance as though he weren't quite sure what to make of the situation.

That makes two of us, she thought, and shoved to her feet. "I think I hear the next group of kids. Ready?"

For the next hour Tory, with Judy's help, assisted children onto the saddle and led them around the riding ring. Some of them had been on horses before and rode without assistance. The laughs and smiles on the children's faces made the work worth it for Tory. When the last one left and the cleanup crew went about dismantling the carnival booths and picking up the trash, Tory eased down on her front porch steps for a break.

Slade came out of the house and sat next to her. "Okay?"

"I'm not sure my feet are attached to my legs. But other than that, I'm fine."

"Mindy is almost packed and ready to go on her adventure, as she calls it."

"Has she ever been camping?"

"No, so I guess it is an adventure for her. She hasn't been fishing, either."

"She'll have a good time with Ashley and Jamie."

"You don't know how much it means to me that those two have taken a liking to my daughter."

"I think my niece and nephew are pretty lucky to have a friend and cousin like Mindy."

"The cleanup crew have promised me two more hours and no one will know we had a carnival here with a hundred visitors."

"It was a success. I think I'll offer again next year."

"Reverend Nelson was hoping you would."

Tory slanted a look at Slade, shielding her eyes from the glare of the sun. "You talked with Reverend Nelson?"

He nodded. "I told him I would be on the budget committee."

Tory's mouth fell open. "You did?"

"Yes. I've decided to start going with you and Mindy to church."

"When?"

"After our talk the other evening at the barn, I've been thinking. I was wrong to turn away from God just because something didn't happen the way I thought it should. I want to give Him another chance and hope He hasn't abandoned me."

Tory took his hand. "He hasn't. He doesn't work that way."

"I hope you're right because I can't do it alone. I realize my guilt has been getting in my way and I need to learn to deal with it. I hope He will help."

"He will." She squeezed his hand, then released it and rose. "I'd better go see if Dad and Mom need any help."

As she climbed the steps to the porch, his news lightened her heart and gave her hope. After the emotional turmoil of the past few days, she was glad for some good news.

Inside the air-conditioned house she relished the cool air while she made her way to the bedroom her parents had used. Her father slammed the suitcase closed as she entered the room. Her mother sat in the chair by the window, staring out at the workers cleaning up the grounds.

"Can I help with anything?"

"No, honey. I've got everything packed and ready to go." Her father placed the suitcase on the floor by the bed.

"I'm sorry, Tory, I haven't been feeling very well." Her mother turned her attention toward her.

She went to her mother and knelt in front of her. "You never have to apologize for anything, Mom. I'm so glad you came to visit."

Her mother brushed back Tory's stray strands from her ponytail. "I know how much you hate coming home. This is the least I can do for you. The carnival was lovely again this year."

Her father came over to help her mother to her feet. She leaned heavily into him as he started for the door. Tory picked up the suitcase and followed them out to the car. Her throat tightened at the frail picture of her mother as her father helped her into the front seat.

While he stowed the suitcase in the trunk, Tory said, "Let me know what the doctor says."

"Of course, honey." He hugged her and kissed her on the forehead. "You have a good husband, Tory. I can rest easier now."

Slade approached her and stood at her side while her father started the engine, waved, then drove from the ranch. Tears misted her eyes. One fell and rolled down her cheek.

"Are you okay?" Slade wiped away the tear with his finger.

"Yes, but I just realized my parents are getting old."

"It's hard to watch the people we love becoming ill."

And he would know better than most, Tory thought as her father's car turned onto the highway and disappeared from view.

The sounds of children's voices followed by her sister's filled the air. The rest of her houseguests came down the steps, lugging their duffel bags. Brad carried Mindy's for her.

"Well, we're heading out now," Judy said as she tossed her bag into the back of the camper. "You have my cell number?"

"Yes."

"We're only two and a half hours away."

"I know."

"I'm not telling you but Slade."

The paleness beneath his dark features emphasized how hard this would be for him to let Mindy go. Tory clasped his hand to convey her support as he watched his daughter climb into the camper.

He leaned toward her and whispered, "Except for spending the night occasionally with you, I haven't been away from her since the accident. Three days is a long time."

"You can always stop her from going."

"Oh, yeah. That would be great. I'd never hear the end of that. Nope, I can do this."

"Letting go is hard."

"More than I thought. But she keeps telling me she's growing up."

As the camper headed for the highway, Mindy waved, a huge grin on her face.

"This will be good for her."

"I'll keep telling myself that over the next few days." Slade scanned the area where the carnival had been. "They're almost done cleaning up. The place will be back to normal in no time."

Normal? What was normal? A couple of months ago sharing a house with a man would have been so far from normal for her. She knew more than most how quickly life could change.

"I'll give the crew a hand. You need to rest, Tory. Take a nap. I know you haven't slept well the past few nights. Things will be back to normal in the house this evening, too. I'll take care of everything. I'll have my things moved back to my old bedroom."

It was hard for her to turn over the care of her ranch and animals to anyone, but she was too tired to argue. Besides, she had gotten good practice with Gus. "I think I'll lie down for a while or I won't make it to dinner."

"You didn't get enough junk food at the carnival?"

"Actually, except for the hamburger you brought me, I haven't had anything else to eat. Too busy with the horse rides."

"I should have helped you."

"If I'm not mistaken, Reverend Nelson had you supervising the races. When were you gonna help me? In between the sack race or the three-legged one?"

He turned her toward the house and nudged her forward. "Go. Take a nap. I'll fix something for dinner."

"I know I should be worried about that comment, but I don't have the energy to."

As she climbed the steps, she heard him say, "I can open a can of soup and fix a sandwich. I'm not that inept in the kitchen."

"I won't comment on that statement." She entered

the coolness of her house and made her way toward her bedroom.

In the room her gaze fell on Slade's pajama bottoms folded on the chair, an instant reminder of the past few nights sleeping in the same double bed as he. She'd known every time he had turned over or even moved a little. She'd listened to his soft breathing, surrounded by his scent that she'd come to know so well, and had yearned for things to be different.

She walked to the bed, its softness beckoning. As she sat, she caught a glimpse of Slade's Palm Pilot on the nightstand. Another sign of how much he'd become a part of her life in a short time. Easing back onto the pillow, she rolled onto her side and the second she closed her eyes, sleep descended…

The suffocating pressure of his weight squeezed the breath from her. Her ears rang from the blow to her head. Pain tore through her, wave after wave. Nausea rose to clog her throat.

In the dim light, his hideous face loomed over hers. "You know you want it." His maniacal laughter rang out, underscoring how trapped she was.

"Please. Don't!" she whispered through swollen lips, tasting the blood that pooled in her mouth.

A scream ripped from the depth of her soul…

Tory shot up. Darkness greeted her. Where was she? She could still hear the laughing taunt echoing in her mind. Arms came about her, drawing her against a hard body. Another scream welled up in her as she shoved away from the hard body.

"Tory!"

"Get away from me!" She scrambled off the bed and across the room, gasping for oxygen.

Lamplight flooded the room, revealing Slade on the other side of the bed, his expression a mixture of shock and concern. "You had another nightmare."

Inhale. Exhale. One breath at a time. She rubbed her temples as if that could rid her mind of the terror she'd lived with for four years, revisited each time she had her nightmare.

"Is it the same one?"

She looked up at Slade who thankfully kept his distance. Inhale. Exhale. She wasn't being raped. She was in her house, in her bedroom.

"Tory, I want to help you."

The soft plea in his voice unraveled the little control she was gaining over her composure. "You can't help." She crossed her arms over her chest, her hands sliding up and down her arms. But nothing she did warded off the chill burrowing into the marrow of her bones. She was so cold.

"What happened to you? What's behind these nightmares?"

She shook so much, she groped for the stuffed chair she knew was behind her and sat before she collapsed. She huddled back against the cushions, seeking some warmth from the cotton fabric.

He took a step toward her. Then another.

"Please. Don't!"

The words—the same she uttered in her nightmare—halted him. "Why won't you go home to Dallas?"

Tears flooded her eyes as suddenly as the light had the room only moments before. "I can't. Too many memories of what happened."

"What, Tory?"

Through the sheen of tears she stared at him. In her mind she knew she should tell him what happened, but in her heart she couldn't find the words. She couldn't bear it if he—

"In God's eyes we are partners. What affects you affects me."

Sniffing, she brushed at her tears. "I know. I just have a difficult time talking about it."

"Did someone hurt you?"

In the depth of his eyes she saw compassion, understanding, and the dam on her memories broke. "I was raped four years ago. I was beaten up and put in the hospital by someone I knew and dated for a month. I never saw it coming until it was too late." She hunched forward, trying to draw in on herself, wishing she could make herself invisible.

"Where is he now?"

The steel thread in his voice caused her to look up at him. A nerve in his jaw twitched; his pupils were pinpoints. "In prison."

"Good. You pressed charges?"

She nodded, the pain and humiliation of the trial inundating her all over again. By the time it had been over she'd felt as if she'd been raped a second time but this time in public. After that she'd fled to Oklahoma and had never gone back to Dallas.

"Tory, you did nothing wrong."

"I went out with him. I thought I liked him. How could I have been so wrong?"

"Some people are quite good at putting up a front for others."

"Don't you understand? This makes me doubt my judgment about people."

"I know. But you must trust me on some level or you wouldn't have told me. That's a start."

"Is it? I don't know anymore. I'm so tired. I thought the nightmares were over. I hadn't had one in a long time."

"Until we had to share a bed?"

"Yes."

"I will never do anything you don't want me to."

"He kept telling me that I wanted it." The tears returned to blur her vision. She squeezed her eyes closed, trying to control her reeling emotions. She'd shed too many tears over that man, lost so much time because of the emotional scars his assault left on her.

"I almost have dinner ready. I was about to stir the soup when I heard you scream." He picked up his Palm Pilot. "I'm going to gather my things and move them back to the other bedroom now." When his arms were full of his clothing, he started for the door, saying, "I'll put these up and get the rest later. Why don't you come on into the kitchen and eat something?"

Tory drew in a deep breath. "What temperature did you put the soup on?"

"That burnt smell is from the toast for the sandwiches. The toaster was on too high and the first batch came out a little charred."

"I don't think that's it." She lumbered to her feet. "You put your clothing up while I check the soup."

Hot soup actually sounded good right now, she thought, walking toward the kitchen. The coldness was still embedded in her bones, and she hoped the soup would warm her up some. When she entered the room, her gaze went immediately to the stove where the contents of the pan were boiling all over the range top. Wisps of smoke drifted upward. She hurried across the kitchen and switched the burner off, shaking her head at the high setting Slade had put the soup on.

"Is the soup ruined?"

She spun about at the sound of his husky voice. "Yes."

"I knew you would be hungry. I thought high would get the soup done faster."

"There's some logic in that thinking, and it would have worked if you had been standing over the pan, watching it."

"And I would have, but I got sidetracked by a beautiful, caring lady."

The heat from a blush seared her cheeks. She busied herself by taking the pan to the sink and filling it with warm water. Then she used a sponge to wipe off as much of the burnt soup from the top of the stove as possible, considering the burner was still hot.

"I do appreciate you coming to my rescue." She sat at the table where the sandwiches were. She picked up the ham and cheese. "I thought you were toasting the bread."

"I decided against it and went with plain bread." He slipped into the chair across from her as though he knew instinctively to keep his distance still.

"I'm gonna really have to give you some cooking lessons."

"That's okay. There are some things better left to the experts."

"It's not difficult."

"And I believe you, but—" He shrugged as though that gesture said it all.

"But you'd rather not learn."

"I just feel there are some things in life better off a mystery. Cooking is one of those things for me."

Tory laughed. "You're hopeless."

"I like that."

"That you're hopeless?"

"No, your laugh."

For a long moment her attention was totally focused on him to the exclusion of everything else. He was the one who made her laugh. He was the one who had given her a chance at a family. She owed him and wasn't sure how in the world to pay him back.

Chapter Eleven

Slade leaned against the railing of the deck, sipping his coffee. The hot summer air was still bearable at seven in the morning. The quiet would soon be disturbed by the sound of a bulldozer preparing the ground for the new indoor riding ring. But for the time being all Slade heard was an occasional bird, and he relished the silence.

Peace. He'd first moved out to the ranch because it had made sense because of Tory's work with the riding stable. Now he couldn't think of any other place he'd rather live. The sounds in the country were nature's sounds. And the best part was he only had to go twenty minutes to town. Not a long commute, and well worth it since Mindy loved living here.

A month had passed since Tory had told him about her past—a month in which he'd tried to court her and alleviate her concerns. In that time he'd realized he wanted their marriage to work on all levels. He was falling in love with her. That realization robbed him of his next breath. After Carol's death, he hadn't thought that would be possible. He hadn't wanted to open himself up to the kind of pain he'd suffered when she'd died. Now he knew it was too late. If Tory and he couldn't work through their problems, he wouldn't be able to avoid being hurt.

There were so many times he wanted to hold her, kiss her, and yet he held himself back, remembering that evening a month ago. She'd come unglued when he'd tried to comfort her after the nightmare. The terror on her face had scared him. Thank goodness the man responsible for putting that look on his wife's face was behind bars.

The bang of the back door alerted him to the fact that Tory had returned from the barn. He turned, fixed a smile of greeting on his face and handed her the cup of coffee he'd poured for her. "Everything okay with the horses?"

"Yes. Gus is worth his weight in gold. I can leave the ranch and not worry about it. I never felt that way before."

"Well, then maybe we should pay your parents a visit some long weekend."

She tensed, her hand bringing her cup to her mouth halting in midair. "I'm not ready to do that yet."

Until she was, he wasn't sure where their marriage stood. He took a long sip of his lukewarm coffee and saw the apprehension enter Tory's brown eyes. "Are you sure about Mindy returning to school?" he asked, deciding to change the topic of conversation before

Tory retreated. They were good friends, but there still was a part of herself that she kept from him.

"I'm positive. You see how she is at church. She gets along with the other kids. Some of them will be at the same elementary school."

"But what if—"

She placed two fingers over his lips. "Shh. No buts. She's talking faster and is getting around well without any help. Right now she's at the barn talking Gus's ear off and helping him muck out a stall. I'm impressed with her progress."

When Tory removed her fingers from his mouth, he missed her touch. "So are her therapists and doctor. She's come a long way and part of the reason is you."

"Oh, my, you're gonna make my head swell if you keep saying things like that."

"I'm only telling the truth. Your riding program has been great for her. She's a pro on a horse now and so proud of it. She's talking about showing horses later down the line."

"I know. She's mentioned it to me a few thousand times."

"That's my girl. When she gets something in her head, she doesn't let it go."

"Which leads me back to the school issue. She wants to go very much. She loves being around people."

Slade threw up his hand. "Okay. You've convinced me. I know when I'm outnumbered."

"Good, because we need to go to school today and meet her teacher. I have an appointment for us."

"You do? You were awfully sure of yourself."

Tory grinned and finally sipped some of her coffee. "I've gotten to know you well these past few months. I was pretty sure I could talk you into it since it was so important to Mindy." One corner of her mouth hitched up even more. "Besides, I could always cancel if I had to."

"So you had all your bases covered."

"You know that Mindy will continue to need some special education services for a while?"

"Yes. Is the special education teacher who we're going to meet?"

"Actually, the woman will be her homeroom teacher. I think the special education teacher will be there, too."

He filled his lungs with air. "I guess I'm ready for this. Even with her tutor this year, she's behind."

"But gaining every day." She came to him, balancing her mug on the railing. "I promise you this will work. If there's a problem, we'll figure it out together."

He couldn't resist her nearness. He cupped her face, searching her features he dreamed about at night. "You don't know how much your support means to me."

"I could say the same thing. You've been more than understanding and I appreciate that, Slade."

Slowly he bent toward her, giving her plenty of time to pull away. She remained where she was only inches from him, her scent of lilacs mingling with the smells of the outdoors—earth, grass and the roses along the back of the house. He brushed his lips across hers, once, twice. Still she stayed put. That was all the encouragement he needed.

He wound his arms around her and brought her up against him, slanting his mouth over hers. Deepening the kiss, he became lost in her embrace, drowning in sensations he'd thought never to experience again.

When he parted, putting her at arm's length, he struggled to get his breathing under control. Her chest rose and fell rapidly, too. Pleased by her reaction to his kiss, he smiled, noticing how bright and blue the sky was, not a cloud visible.

"Lately I've been thinking, what do you say about adding on to the house?" He retrieved his now-cold coffee from the railing and finished the last few swallows.

"What?"

"Oh, another bedroom and bathroom. Maybe a den and a dining room."

"That would double the size of the house."

"Probably. What do you think?"

"We don't need another bedroom. We have three."

"But they are small. I was thinking about a master suite."

Tory's eyes widened. Her hand shook as she reached for her mug and brought it to her lips.

"I'm being optimistic, Tory. When we share a bedroom, the one you are in now is way too small. And I do believe the day will come when that will happen." After the kiss they shared, he knew it was only a matter of time. She responded to him. That had to mean something.

"I must admit the house is small. Better suited for one or two people, not three."

"Or, we could build a new house and leave this one for guests."

"A new house?" She pondered the concept, her brow creasing. "That might be better than trying to add on to this one."

"Think about it. In a few months I'll have more time and could help oversee its construction."

"Until the indoor riding ring is finished, I wouldn't want to take on another project."

"Mom—Dad-dy."

Mindy's voice sounded in the house, causing both of them to turn toward the back door. She rushed out onto the deck, dirt smudges on her cheeks, hay in her pigtails and something Slade didn't even want to know, on her tennis shoes.

"Is it time to go to school?" Mindy came to a halt in front of them.

"If it was, we'd have to wait until you took a shower. No way, young lady, will you go to school looking like that." Tory's nose wrinkled. "And smelling like that. What have you been doing? Rolling around in the hay?"

"Help-ing, Gus."

"I know, but—oh, never mind. Just go in and take a shower. Our appointment is at eight-thirty."

"Mom—I have—plenty—of time."

"Scoot." Tory waved her hands toward the door.

With a pout on her face, Mindy trudged back into the house.

"I've noticed she calls you Mom a lot."

Tory blushed. "I think she's just trying to get used to it."

"I don't think that's why."

She slanted a glance toward him, one brow quirked.

"She feels you're like a mother to her."

Tory beamed, her dark eyes shining. "And I feel like she's my daughter."

"We haven't talked about having more children. How do you feel about that?"

"I—I—" she swallowed several times "—I've always wanted a large family."

"So have I. Carol couldn't have any more children after Mindy was born. We wanted more and were thinking of adopting when the accident occurred."

The color drained from Tory's face. She twisted away and walked past him to the railing to stare in the distance. When Slade came up to her side, he could tell by the look in her eyes that she was wrestling with something. He waited, wondering if she would trust him with whatever was bothering her. Since she'd told him about the rape, she had opened up more to him. But there was still part of her held in reserve.

"I want children of my own. I just don't know how long I have. A few years ago the doctor said I would probably have to have a hysterectomy in my not-too-distant future. I have endometriosis and every year it gets worse."

"I see."

She spun about. "Do you really understand?"

"I think so. We both want a family, and if we are gonna have that family, it needs to be soon. But you don't totally trust me yet. You're still not hundred percent sure about this marriage. Does that about sum it up?"

Tory nodded. "I'm trying. Really, I am."

The heavy thickness to her voice attested to the truth behind her words. Slade knew when it came to emotions a person couldn't always control things. He was still working through his own problems concerning the accident and Carol's death. How could he expect Tory to be over her ordeal and ready to settle down to be his wife in every sense of the word? No matter how much he wished she could get over what happened to her four years ago, it wasn't going to occur on his timetable, but on hers.

"I know you are, Tory." He took her hand. "You don't flinch from my touch or run from me. I believe that's a good sign." He forced a lightness into his voice that he wished he felt.

"It was my lucky day when you brought Mindy out for her riding lesson." She inched closer, her face tilted up toward his.

Their gaze connected and everything around Slade faded from his awareness except the vibrant woman in front of him. His fingers delved into the rich thickness of her hair, for once loose about her shoulders.

"We—need—to leave."

Tory jumped back as though caught doing something she shouldn't have. Her face became scarlet red and she busied herself by gathering up the two mugs and starting for the kitchen. "I need to change shoes and get my purse."

Slade looked at his daughter. He needed to talk to her about her timing.

"What are we going to do? We have a whole afternoon to ourselves." Slade switched on the engine to his car and pulled out of the church's parking lot.

"And you were worried about Mindy with the other kids."

"I guess I'll always worry about her. That's part of being a father."

"I have an idea what we can do."

"Nothing?"

"Nope. That does sound tempting, but I thought we might go for a ride."

"In the car?"

"No, you know very well I'm talking about riding a horse."

"That's what I was afraid of."

The laughter in his voice belied his words. She gave him an exasperated look. "I want to ride the new mare on the trail to the pond. Get her used to the terrain."

"Sure. You just want to see me ride again in all my glory." Slade came to a four-way stop sign and braked.

"You aren't bad."

"Yeah, I guess not. I can stay on the horse—as long as it goes at a sedate pace."

"So no racing across the meadow?"

"No way. Definitely out of my comfort zone."

"You know that needs to change. After all, I own a riding stable and you are my husband. People will expect you to know how to ride well."

His laughter rang in the car. "I hate to be a disappointment to all those people."

He started to ease out into the intersection when a car to his right sailed through the stop sign without coming to a halt. Slade slammed on his brakes, his eyes round as he watched the young teenager barrel down the road, not pausing in his haste to get wherever he was going.

Slade's grip on the steering wheel was white knuckled. His jaw clenched and he drew in calming breaths. "Are you all right?"

"Are you?" Tory touched his arm. Beneath her fingers, his muscles were bunched as though locked in place. "I'm fine. The seat belt works great."

He angled his head toward her, the darkness in his eyes reaching out to her. Then he firmed his mouth into a grim line and eased across the intersection. He didn't release his tight grip until he pulled into the lane leading to the ranch house. When he'd parked, he sank back, cushioning his head on the headrest. His hands shook as he removed them from the steering wheel.

"Thank goodness Mindy wasn't in the car," he whispered, his voice raw. "She's doing so well, I'm afraid..." His voice faded into the silence.

Tory's heart broke. She slid across the seat and took him into her embrace. "That was an example of how precarious life can be. In a blink of an eye, everything can change."

He pulled back to look at her. "I'm glad not this time. But you're right, which means we need to make the most of what we have."

"Live for the moment?"

"To a certain extent, but we should always have our thoughts on the future."

"Well, with that in mind, get changed and let's go for a ride. I still need to check out the new mare." She scooted back to her side of the car, aware of their close proximity that did strange things to her insides. She thrust open the door and tossed over her shoulder, "You have five minutes to change. The last one ready gets to cool down the horses."

With the challenge thrown down, Tory raced for the house, taking the steps two at a time. Slade pounded up to the porch and pushed past her once she'd unlocked the door. When she entered the coolness of the entry hall, he was nowhere to be seen. She heard the slamming of drawers and a closet door and quickened her own pace.

Four minutes, twenty seconds later, a knock sounded at her bedroom door. She threw it open, dressed in jeans, T-shirt and riding boots, and found Slade on the other side, similarly dressed.

His grin was lopsided. "I guess this means I won."

"You cheated."

"I did not."

"I had to open the door."

"Because you were the first one there. I can't help it if the key was hard to get out."

"I should have left it in the door," Tory muttered, and came out of her bedroom.

"Do you want to race to the barn?" He waggled his eyebrows. "Double or nothing."

"I think I'll cut my losses. Your legs are definitely quite a bit longer than mine."

"I'll give you a head start."

"How much?" She paused in the entry hall.

"Out the door and down the steps."

Tory dug into her jeans pocket and fingered the house key. "Okay."

She hurried out the door and quickly locked the dead bolt before Slade realized what she was doing. She heard his shouts as she ran down the steps and across the yard.

When Slade finally arrived in the barn a moment later, he said, "You play dirty, Tory Donaldson."

"You didn't say I couldn't lock the door."

"I had to go out the back door and around the house," he grumbled, but the frown on his face was a pretense if the twinkle in his eyes was any indication.

She clasped her hand over her heart. "Poor Slade. I feel for you."

"I get no sympathy." He scanned the barn. "Which horse do I ride?"

"Black Charger."

"I don't like that name. Isn't he the one you don't use with the children?"

Tory laughed. "Only because he is so big. Perfect for you but for small kids he's too tall."

"Sure. This from the woman who locks me in the house in order to win the race."

"You have a key to the dead bolt."

He exaggerated his frown and mumbled something under his breath. "Bring on Black Charger. I have something to prove today."

Tory saddled her new mare while Slade followed suit with his gelding. Then she led Buttercup out of the barn and mounted her. When Slade was on his horse, she started for the trail that led to the pond. The sun was high in the sky, bright and hot. A light, warm breeze cooled her cheeks and made the ride bearable until they got to the trees. In the shade of the woods Tory stopped and twisted around to see how Slade was doing.

He bounced along, his gelding doing a fast trot. He clutched his reins too tight and he sat too far back in the saddle. Halting the horse beside Tory's, he sagged forward.

"I think every bone in my body has been jarred."

"Remind me to give you some riding lessons."

"Now you tell me, when I still have to go all the way back to the barn."

"Relax. You need to loosen your hold on the reins. The horse can't move his head. Sit forward some in the saddle. You're too far back. The more in tune with the horse, the better the ride."

"Can I just hold on to the horn if he decides to bolt?"

"He won't. This is a pleasure ride."

"Pleasure ride? Your idea of pleasure is very different from mine."

"Come on. I'll go slow and easy the rest of the way to the pond. We'll let the horses graze a while before heading back."

"If I get off this horse, I don't know if I'll ever get back on."

Tory laughed, loving the teasing tone in his voice. He was enjoying himself as much as she was. She loved to ride, to be one with a horse. What would Slade do if she set her mare into a gallop? Probably panic.

One day she and Slade would race across the meadow. That picture popped into her mind with such clarity that she was surprised. And yet, the vision felt right. She now saw her life with Slade by her side. Maybe those children she wanted wasn't that far-fetched an idea.

She threw a glance over her shoulder to check on Slade. The grimace on his face made her smile. "Relax. We're almost there."

"We still have to go all the way back."

"I can't believe a man who was determined to fight a family of skunks would feel that way."

"If I remember correctly, I didn't win that battle. It wasn't until you had a professional come out that we got rid of the skunk family."

"But you gave it your best shot."

"All I can say is I hope they're enjoying their new home miles from us."

"Skunks are so cute looking. It's a shame people feel that way about them being around."

"You have to admit they have a wonderful defense."

"It sure makes me pause going near one." Again she

looked back toward Slade. "But you on the other hand went toe-to-toe with the mama."

"Hey, I had a hose in my hand and yards and yards of ground between me and her."

"Did you know a skunk's spray can reach across yards and yards?"

He rolled his eyes. "Now you tell me."

Tory left the trees behind. The glittering water beckoned. She nudged her mare a little faster, relishing the bright sunlight that bathed her face. It was a beautiful day, not a care to disturb her thoughts. When she neared the edge of the pond, she halted Buttercup and swung off her.

Slade came to a stop next to Tory. "I thought you weren't going to go faster than a walk."

"I couldn't resist." She smiled up at him and the world came to a grinding halt.

The sparkle in his eyes and the grin on his face sent her heart beating at a rapid pace. This man was important to her. He was offering her a second chance at the things she wanted in life. His patience with Mindy and her was unbelievable. Could she trust him with her heart, enough to be a wife in every sense?

His gaze left hers for a few seconds as he dismounted. When he reestablished eye contact, his reins fell toward the ground. He reached out and brushed her loose hair behind her ear, then cradled her cheek.

"You're beautiful, Tory."

She wanted to say something, but her throat seemed to close. He moved nearer. The feel of his palm against her skin, the blue gleam in his eyes, meant only for her, riveted her to the ground.

"I want you."

The husky words didn't send her into a panic. Instead, they caused her stomach to flip-flop. Was she ready to put the past completely behind her? To forget about her fears and surrender totally and willingly to another? When he touched her, she didn't feel dirty, used.

His other hand came up to frame her face. He inched forward and leaned toward her. When his mouth grazed hers, the last thing she wanted to do was push away. She went completely into his embrace while his lips settled over hers. This felt so right. He wouldn't hurt her. He wouldn't force her to give more than she wanted.

She stood locked in his arms, her head lying on his chest, for a long time. The quick tempo of his heartbeat matched hers. The warmth of his embrace went beyond comforting. She cuddled closer, enjoying the protective ring of his arms.

"I'm perfectly content to stay here all afternoon," Slade murmured against the top of her head. "But we need to pick Mindy up in an hour from Laurie's."

"Yes, and we still have the slow ride back to the barn and you'll have to cool down two horses." She leaned back.

"I protest that bet." His brow furrowed.

She smoothed the lines away. "Tell you what. I'll take care of Buttercup while you take care of Black Charger."

"And I'll take you and Mindy out to eat tonight. We'll celebrate."

"What?"

He waved his hand in the air. "Oh, I don't know. How about what a beautiful day this is?"

"Sounds good to me. Race you to the barn?" She started toward her mare.

He halted her progress with a hand on her arm. "No way, Mrs. Donaldson. Remember, slow and easy. I'm a beginner. Maybe one day we can race back. But this isn't the day."

"Chicken."

"And proud of it. I know my limits."

Tory waited until Slade mounted his gelding before getting up onto Buttercup. "I'm impressed. It only took two attempts to mount him."

"I'm a quick learner."

The ride back was done in silence. Tory savored the quiet, letting her thoughts wander to what happened at the pond. He had told her she would decide, set the pace, and he'd been true to his word. Maybe this evening they could explore more of their relationship.

After taking care of the horses, Tory headed toward the house with Slade beside her. "I need a shower before we pick up Mindy."

"I could use one, too."

His words, spoken casually, doubled her heartbeat. She slanted a look at him and realized his remark was an innocent one.

"I get dibs first."

"Of course, beauty before brains."

"I'm not even gonna touch that line."

His laughter echoed through the house as Tory hurried toward her bedroom, grabbed her robe and disappeared into the bathroom. For four years she'd gotten used to being by herself. Now she couldn't imagine this house without others in it. But Slade was right. This place was too small, especially if their family ever grew. That thought brought a smile to her mouth as she stepped into the shower and quickly washed the smell of horse and sweat off her body.

After toweling dry, Tory slipped on her terry-cloth robe and belted it. She ran a brush through her long hair, remembering Slade once telling her he liked it down about her shoulders. Was that why she was wearing it like that more? The realization she wanted to please Slade gave her pause. She was falling in love. When had that sneaked up on her? If she was truthful with herself, it had started from the very beginning with his concern and passion for his daughter.

A knock at the door startled her out of her musing. "Yes?"

"There's a phone call for you from Judy."

"Tell her I'll call her back in a few minutes."

"You'd better answer it now."

His tone of voice warned her something was wrong. She thrust open the door, aware she was only wearing her robe, and took the portable phone from him. "Judy?"

"It's Mom. The ambulance just left. She's been taken to the hospital. She had a heart attack. You need to come to Dallas."

Chapter Twelve

Tory stood framed in the picture window at her parents' house, staring at the street where she'd grown up. Dusk settled over the landscape, forcing some of the neighbors to switch on their lights. She remained in the dark, needing its comfort and shield.

Dallas. When she'd left four years before, she'd never wanted to return, hoped she would never have to. Her mother's heart attack had changed all that, and now she was faced with the past. Across the street and two doors down was Brandon Clayton's parents' house. They had thought their son had done nothing wrong, that she had lied about the rape. They had been so vocal in their protest, even though she had ended up in the hospital overnight from a concussion and cracked ribs.

"Tory?"

She pivoted toward the sound of Slade's voice.

"I got the overnight bag down. You'll need to pack what your mother needs."

She'd promised her father she would get some things for her mother, but she hadn't realized how difficult it would be coming back to this street. "I'm gonna stay at the hospital tonight. You and Mindy can stay here or at Judy's." She walked toward her parents' bedroom, her hands trembling, her legs weak.

"Brad said something about taking Mindy home with him so she could see Ashley and Jamie. I'll stay with you."

"No, you don't have to," she said in a rush. At his raised brow, she continued in a slower voice. "Mindy's upset. She'll need you." She knew that argument would persuade him as no other.

"I guess then I'll stay with her."

"You should be with her as much as possible."

"Are you sure you don't want me to stay?"

No! I'm not sure about anything right now. "Yes." The wounds of the past lay open, festering with the memories she tried to forget.

Only the day before she'd thrown aside her defenses and had contemplated making her marriage real in every sense. But all the fear and doubts had resurfaced the minute Slade had turned his car down this street—actually, when she'd seen the skyline of Dallas in the distance.

Tory hurriedly stuffed into the overnight bag what her mother would need. She needed to get out of the house before she fell apart. She didn't to have time for that. Her mother needed her and she was determined to be there for her. She ran four years ago. She wouldn't now no matter what turmoil she experienced.

Tory took the bag and left the bedroom to return to the living room where Slade was waiting. The worry and concern she'd seen in his eyes on more than one occasion was evident as he rose and reached for the suitcase. His fingers brushed hers. She snatched her hand away, interlocking her fingers to still their trembling.

The doorbell rang. Tory gasped at the intrusion. She looked toward the door but didn't move. Slade strode to it and pulled it open.

"May I help you?"

"How's Eleanor? I saw the car in the driveway and we all want to know how she's doing." The gray-haired woman gestured toward the houses on the street.

Mrs. Johnston. Tory closed her eyes for a few seconds before filling her lungs with a deep breath and heading for the door. "Mom's holding her own. They want to do triple bypass surgery on her as soon as she is stable and her condition is good."

"Oh, dear me. I was so worried when I saw the ambulance leave here yesterday afternoon." Mrs. Johnston peered around Slade, her gaze directed at Tory. "I didn't know if you would come home."

The censure in the woman's voice shredded Tory's composure. She dug her fingernails into her palms and counted to ten. Mrs. Johnston had been one of the doubters. She lived next door to Brandon's parents and let it be known she didn't believe Tory's version of the events. She schooled her features into a neutral expression and said, "Of course, I'd come home. Mom had a heart attack. She'll have surgery tomorrow or the next day. I wouldn't be any other place but beside her. Thank you, Mrs. Johnston, for inquiring about her health. I'll tell her when I see her in a little while."

"She can receive visitors?"

"Just family."

Mrs. Johnston's sharp gaze shifted to Slade, her mouth pinched into a frown. She stuck out her hand toward him. "I'm a neighbor from across the street."

"I'm Tory's husband." He shook the woman's hand.

"Ah, I remember your mother saying something about going to a wedding a few months ago."

"That would have been mine."

"You didn't send out any invitations?"

"No, Mrs. Johnston. It was a quiet wedding with a few friends and family."

The woman snorted. "Tell your mother I'll be up to see her when she can receive visitors."

Slade closed the front door as Mrs. Johnston stomped down the porch steps. Tory went to the picture window and watched the older woman make her way across the street and to Brandon's parents' house. She clenched her teeth and sucked in several deep breaths.

"A charming neighbor. Did I detect an undertone there?"

"I always said you were intuitive. She doubted my story about being raped and voiced her opinion to whoever would listen. She only came over to check out who was here. Mom and she hadn't been on the friendliest terms since—" Tory swallowed the rest of her words. She didn't want to go into the dynamics of the neighborhood right now.

"We've got everything. Let's get going. I'll drop you off at the hospital, make sure your mother is doing okay and go see how Mindy is doing."

"Give Mindy a kiss for me."

"I'll bring her to the hospital tomorrow morning. If I don't, she'll pester me until I do."

Slade locked the door to her parents' house while she carried the overnight bag to the car. When he joined her, Tory noticed Mrs. Clayton out on her porch talking with Mrs. Johnston. Both women turned and stared at her as she slid into Slade's car. A shudder shivered up her spine. She had done nothing wrong, but they made her feel as though she had. When would she be able to put the rape behind her?

"Where's Slade?" Judy asked, handing Tory another cup of coffee.

Tory watched Slade and Brad walk across the parking lot and climb into her brother-in-law's white SUV. "He went to your house with Brad. I thought it best he stay there tonight with Mindy. I don't want her any more upset than she already is, and hospitals remind her too much of what she went through." The lights of Dallas shone in the dark hours of night. She turned from the large window in the waiting room, suddenly needing to sit down.

"You're a good mother, Tory. I hope you can have children before it's too late."

Tory rolled her aching shoulders. It might already be too late. Coming back here brought forth all those feelings she had run from four years ago. She wouldn't be able to give her husband what she had dreamed of all her life. While her girlfriends in high school and college had had sex, she'd saved herself. And for what? For Brandon to take it by force—all those years obliterated in a single moment.

"I saw Mrs. Clayton today at the house."

Judy came to sit next to her. She took her hand. "Oh, sweetie, I'm sorry. I should have gone to get Mom's things. I wasn't thinking."

"Ashley and Jamie needed you. Besides, I should be able to go home and not worry about it."

"Did she say anything to you?"

"No, but Mrs. Johnston came over to see how Mom was doing. I think she really wanted to see how I was doing and to put in her barbs—again."

"Does Slade know?"

Tory hunched her shoulders, staring down at their clasped hands. "Yes. I told him when you took Mindy camping."

"Good. He had a right to know."

Tory jerked her head up and stabbed her sister with a look. "Why? It happened to me four years ago. Before I knew him."

"Frankly, Tory, because it has such power over you."

As close as she was to her sister, Judy didn't know the half of it. Tory withdrew her hand and bolted to her feet, restless, wanting just to forget everything. Why couldn't it be that simple? She didn't like what was happening to her all over again. The doubts. The fears.

"Tory, you've married a good man. Let him help you."

She wanted to shout, "He deserves better than me," but she kept the words deep inside, where they festered. "I don't want to talk about me. It's Mom I'm worried about."

"We'll know more in the morning. Hopefully the doctor will be able to operate on her and she can begin recovering."

"Let's pray." Tory bowed her head and folded her hands.

Tory stopped pacing and scanned the waiting room. She never wanted to see this place again. She'd lived here for the past few days, sleeping when she could on the hard blue sofa in the corner. She had never thought of herself as an impatient person until now. She felt like screaming in frustration.

Plowing her hand through her hair, she resumed her pacing. "When do you think we'll hear anything?"

Judy glanced at her watch. "It shouldn't be too much longer." She turned to her father. "Dad, do you want some coffee?"

He nodded, his face pale and deeply lined with exhaustion.

"Come on, Tory. You can help me bring some drinks back." Judy tugged on her arm to get her moving toward the door.

"But what if the doctor comes back soon?" Tory asked as she stepped out into the hospital corridor.

"A few minutes won't make any difference, and I think you need to get out of that room. You're driving everyone crazy with your pacing."

"Sorry, I'm restless."

"Personally, I don't know how you have any energy to put one foot in front of the other. We've all been up most of the past forty-eight hours."

"Can't sleep until I know Mom will make it through the surgery."

"Hence the reason I'm making you go with me. Did you see the looks that other family sent us?"

"I usually ride to get rid of this nervous energy, but I'm fresh out of any horses at the moment." Tory attempted a grin that immediately faded.

"Is Gus taking care of the ranch?"

"Yes, thank goodness for him. He's staying at the house and, from talking with him earlier today, loving every minute of it. He feels like he's on vacation from his daughter."

Judy entered the coffee shop and ordered hot coffee for herself, their father and Tory. Taking the tray, she started for the door.

"At least let me carry my own coffee," Tory said, plucking her cup from the tray, "since you wanted my help in getting the drinks."

"Slade and Brad should be back in a little while with the kids."

"I don't know if it's such a good idea for Mindy to be at the hospital. She has been upset ever since she heard about Mom."

"The kids will need to see for themselves Mom's okay."

"I know. But she has bad memories about the hospital."

"Honey, I know you want to protect her, but I think Slade's doing the right thing."

In the waiting room the surgeon who had operated on their mother stood with their father, speaking in low murmurs. The tension in her father's face had relaxed, sparking hope in Tory.

She hurried to the pair. "Dad? Is everything okay?"

Her father smiled, his blue eyes lighting. "She's going to be all right. The operation went well. Thank you, Dr. Richards." He shook the man's hand.

After the doctor left, her father collapsed into a chair, his shoulders sagging. "Thank you, Lord, for bringing my Eleanor through safely."

"Amen," both Tory and Judy said.

Tory sat on one side of her father while Judy took the other chair next to him and gave him his cup of coffee. His hand shook as he brought it to his lips.

"She made it. She made it," he murmured between sips.

"Dad, when can we see her?" Tory set her coffee on the table in front of her, too edgy to drink any more caffeine.

"Not too long. The nurse will let us know."

"Tor-ee?"

Tory glanced toward the door and smiled. Mindy hurried into the room and threw herself into Tory's arms. She kissed the top of the child's head and hugged her.

"Miss—you."

"And I missed you, young lady. How are you doing?" Tory pulled back to look into the child's face, smoothing her hair back.

"How's—Grand-ma?"

"She's gonna be fine. The operation was a success."

"Not—gonna—uh—die?"

Mindy's large eyes appealed to her, causing her chest to tighten. "No, baby. Grandma's going to be one hundred percent better." She hoped.

"Can—I see—her?"

"Soon." Tory caught sight of Slade standing back watching their exchange. She offered him a smile, her exhaustion beginning to take over. Her eyelids felt heavy, her movements slow, all the nervous energy drained from her.

"I'm glad to hear your mother is okay." Slade took the chair next to her, stretching his long legs out and crossing them at the ankle.

"Thank you," she murmured, then hugged Mindy to her, taking solace in the feel of the child in her arms.

There was a part of her that wanted to throw herself into his comforting embrace as Mindy had her, but her trip home had raised all her doubts and fears she'd begun to put to rest. Over the last month she'd thought she had moved past her memories to forge a new future. She'd been fooling herself.

When the nurse came into the room, she directed Tory's father to where her mother was. Time moved slowly as Tory waited her turn to see her mother. Weariness had a strong grip on her now.

Mindy scooted over to sit where Tory's father had been. Swinging her legs, she asked, "Do you—think—Belle—misses me?"

"Gus is taking good care of her. It won't be long before you see her again. What have you, Ashley and Jamie been doing?"

"Watch-ing—movies." The child shrugged. "Play-ing—games. Not much." She looked up at Tory. "Been—uh—uh—worried."

"You don't need to worry anymore. Things will be back to normal in no time," Tory said with more conviction than she felt. She'd finally thought her life was on track, but this derailment made her wonder if she was heading in the right direction. Slade deserved more than she was afraid she could give him.

When Mindy wandered over to Ashley and Jamie and they began to play a card game, Tory shifted around to Slade. With his head back on the cushion, his eyes closed, she studied his strong features, relaxed for the moment. A lock of his hair curled on his forehead. Her fingers itched to brush it back into place. She balled her hands and refrained from touching him. She twisted around, trying to find a comfortable position in the hard chair.

When she peered at Slade again, his eyes were open and watching her. She swallowed several times, but her throat remained parched. For a few seconds she glimpsed a yearning in his gaze that nearly undid her. He cloaked his expression and straightened.

"Did you call your office this morning?"

He nodded, his gaze fixed on her.

"How's everything in Cimarron City? Okay?"

"Fine. I've been informed by my secretary that I have done such a good job of hiring a great team that they can manage without me for a while." He angled so his knees touched her leg, and he took her hands within his. "I will be here for you for as long as you need me. Everything back home will take care of itself. You only have to worry about your mother."

The concern in his expression struck at her composure. She wanted to fall apart in his arms, to cry for her mother, for her lost innocence. But the sounds of the others held her rigid, especially the voices of the children. She pulled her hands from his and stood on shaky legs. If she stayed near him, she would fall apart, and Mindy didn't need to see that.

Tory paced from one end of the room to the other. With his fingers steepled in front of his face and his elbows resting on the arms of the chair, Slade observed her flexing her hands then curling them into fists. He wanted to help, but every time he'd tried, she'd shut the door in his face. He wasn't sure what to do anymore.

He shoved himself to his feet and said to Mindy, "I'll be back in a minute, sweetheart."

"Sure Dad-dy." She glanced up from her cards, giving him a smile that showed her missing tooth.

When he left the waiting room, he headed straight for the chapel, not wanting to be gone long. But he needed a quiet place to talk with God, a place free of distractions.

In the small chapel Slade sat on the front pew, bowed

his head and clasped his hands together. This was still
so new to him. He had been out of practice for so long.
Where to begin?

Suddenly the words filled his mind. *Lord, please help
me to be there for Tory. I don't know what she needs
anymore. I know what happened to her, but I still feel she
is holding something back from me, keeping something
buried deep inside her that is a barrier to any lasting relationship between us. Please show me what to do. Should
I try to force the issue? Should I back off? What do I do?*

Tory's mother lay in the hospital bed, pale, the
wrinkles on her face more prominent, but she was alive.
Tory walked to her mother with Mindy and Slade on
either side of her. Her mother's eyes fluttered open and
she smiled, a faint upturn of her mouth.

Tory cupped her mother's hand between hers.
"Mom—" The words choked in her throat.

"Grand-ma! You—kay?" Mindy leaned near Eleanor.

She licked her lips. "Now, I am." Her eyes closed
for a few seconds, then she looked again at Mindy.
"You've grown."

Mindy straightened to her full height. "Gus—says—
at least—an inch."

"Mom, can I get you anything? Bring you anything
from home?"

"No, just tired." Her eyes blinked closed. "Rest."

"I'll be back later, Mom."

Tory, Slade and Mindy started for the door when
Eleanor whispered, "Slade."

He turned and went back to the bed. "Yes?"

"Thank you."

His brow wrinkled. "For what?"

She swallowed hard and glanced at Tory. "For bringing my baby home." Then her eyes shut and her head sagged to the side.

He bent down and kissed her on the cheek. "You're welcome."

Tory's swirling emotions collided with her exhaustion. She made it outside the room before collapsing back against the wall and hanging her head so Mindy wouldn't see the tears gathering in her eyes.

"Mindy, why don't you go find Ashley and Jamie?"

Tory heard Mindy walk away, her foot dragging slightly on the linoleum floor. Then Slade laid his hand on her shoulders and lifted her chin so she looked him straight in the eye.

"I'm taking you to your sister's. No more sleeping at the hospital. You need to sleep in a bed and get some rest or you won't be any good for your mother."

She didn't even have the energy to argue with him. He was right. She knew it even though she hated leaving her mother.

Slade walked with his arm around her to the waiting room where he called to Mindy. Together they left the hospital. The trip to Judy's house was a blur. When she arrived at her sister's, Slade immediately escorted her to a bedroom where she saw their suitcase and sat her on the bed.

"Take a nap. When you wake up, you can eat something then go back to sleep. You have two days' worth to make up."

"Aye, aye, captain." She wanted to salute but couldn't lift her hand. Instead, she fell back and let Slade remove her shoes and place her legs on the mattress. Then he covered her, kissed her on the forehead and pulled the drapes before leaving the bedroom.

The warmth and softness of the bed cocooned Tory in a safe haven. Someone touched her shoulder and shook her. She burrowed deeper, not wanting to open her eyes to the real world.

"Tor-ee—Mom—are you—all—right?"

The frightened tone penetrated Tory's sleep-groggy mind. Her eyes bolted open to find Mindy standing next to her, her face crunched into a frown. "I'm fine, honey. Just tired."

"Mindy, you know you weren't supposed to bother Tory." Slade strode into the room.

Mindy hung her head. "I know. I was—wor-ried."

Tory reached up and cradled Mindy's face in her palm. "Don't be. I needed to catch up on some sleep." She looked toward the bedside clock and noticed it was nine o'clock. "Morning or night?"

Slade grinned. "Night. You haven't slept that long. Are you hungry?"

"Yes." She started to rise.

Slade motioned her back down. "I'll bring you a sandwich. You stay put and rest."

"But, Slade, I—"

He shook his head. "No arguments. You're still pale and you have dark circles under your eyes. A four-hour nap isn't nearly long enough to make up for two days without much sleep."

Her eyes drifted closed as the two left the room. Now that she was awake, her stomach was rumbling, and she realized she hadn't eaten much in the past two days, either. She'd mostly lived on caffeine to keep herself going. No food and lots of caffeine were not a good combination.

Ten minutes later she heard the door opening. She sat up as Slade came into the room with a tray. "You're spoiling me. I've never had dinner in bed. Actually, I've never had any meal in bed."

"Maybe the way I delivered it will help you to overlook the way I made the sandwich. I got carried away."

Tory laughed when she saw the layers of food between two pieces of bread. "You expect me to get that in my mouth?"

He lifted his shoulders, looking sheepishly at the plate with a three-inch-high sandwich on it. "You might want to remove some of the meat—or cheese—or lettuce—or—"

"I get the picture. You put everything on this except the kitchen sink."

"I wasn't sure what you wanted." He sat on the bed, facing her, the tray between them. "I probably should have cut it in half, too."

"Probably." Tory peeled back the top piece of bread

and took off some sweet pickles, a slice of tomato, a slab of cheddar cheese and one layer of meat. Then she cut the smaller sandwich into two sections. Her stomach rumbled in the silence.

Slade glanced at her and grinned. "You're not hurrying fast enough for your stomach."

Tory opened her mouth wide and bit into the smaller version of her dinner. After washing it down with some ice water, she ate some more. She gestured toward the remains on the plate. "Please help yourself."

Slade popped two slices of sweet pickle into his mouth, then rose. "I'm gonna put Mindy down to bed. I'll be back for the tray in a little bit."

By the time Tory finished eating her dinner, Slade re-entered the bedroom. "Where is everyone?"

"In bed."

"Already?"

"You have to admit it has been a long day. Even Ashley and Jamie have gone to bed."

"Good. Judy needs her sleep as much as I do." Tory covered her mouth and yawned.

Slade retrieved the tray, saying as he made his way to the door, "I'll be back."

Tory slipped out of the bed when he closed the door and rummaged around in her suitcase for her pajamas. She used the bathroom off the bedroom to scrub her face and brush her teeth. When she inspected herself in the mirror, she could understand Slade's concern. She combed her fingers through her messy hair and flipped it behind her shoulders before leaving.

Slade came back, dug his pajama bottoms out of the suitcase and went into the bathroom after her. Tory got into bed and pulled the sheet up, reminded of the Fourth of July weekend when Slade and she had shared a bedroom.

"I know this has been a difficult few days for you, Tory. If you want to talk, I'm here." Slade sat on his side of the bed.

"Is Mindy all right now that Mom will be okay?"

"I think so. She said a prayer for her tonight. Also for you."

"For me?"

"Because you were sad." Slade's gaze snared hers. "Tory, keeping things bottled up inside of you isn't good. I want to help you, but I figure there's a lot I don't know about what happened four years ago."

Tory grew rigid. "What do you mean?"

"The other day with Mrs. Johnston. The undertone of the conversation was tension-filled. Why?"

"Because she didn't think Brandon did anything wrong. She thought I had made up that story about the rape. After all, we were dating. Had been for over a month." Tory balled the sheet into her hands.

"Was she the only one?"

Tory stared at her fingers twisting the cotton material into a wad. "No. Several others voiced their opinions, too." The memories of the gossip that spread about her inundated her. Her throat closed, tears stinging her eyes. "Having a concussion and a few cracked ribs weren't enough for some people. I guess they wanted me battered, near death. In their eyes Brandon was a nice young man from a good Christian family. So it must have been my fault somehow." She lifted her tear-saturated gaze to his.

"Tory, I'm so sorry some people are narrow-minded." A nerve twitching in his jawline, he gathered her into his arms and pressed her against his T-shirt-clad chest.

For a few seconds Tory allowed herself to seek comfort in his embrace, his hand stroking the length of her back. Then their intimate situation engulfed her in sensations she wasn't ready to experience, not when she could replay all the hurtful things said about her. Panic surged to the foreground. She wedged her arms up between them and shoved away.

"No!" She scrambled from the bed and snatched up her robe. "Please, I'll sleep on the couch in the den. This won't work."

Tory fled the bedroom. Her heartbeat hammered against her rib cage while her breathing became shallow gasps. She escaped into the den, the silence of the house a balm that sought to soothe her tattered nerves. Thank goodness Slade hadn't followed her. She couldn't have handled a confrontation with all that had happened lately.

Using a throw pillow to cushion her head, she curled up on the couch and tried to sleep. But in her mind's eye all she could see was Mrs. Clayton the other day watching her with a narrowed gaze and an expression of contempt. Tory had done nothing wrong, so why did she feel so dirty and humiliated? But memories of Brandon's trial only confirmed those feelings. There had been times she felt she had been on trial instead of him.

Tory twisted on the couch, trying to get comfortable. In the dark she saw the digital clock tick off minutes— way too slowly. Around four she finally surrendered to sleep, exhaustion overcoming her racing mind.

Tory bolted straight up on the couch when she heard a knock at the den door. "Come in." Swinging her legs to the floor, she ran her fingers through her hair and straightened her pajamas and robe.

Slade stood framed in the doorway, no expression on his face. "I wanted to tell you that Mindy and I are leaving for Cimarron City in a few minutes. I can't keep acting like everything is all right between us when it isn't."

Chapter Thirteen

Tory chewed on her lower lip. Slade was right. Everything in their life wasn't okay. The threads of their marriage were fragile.

"I'm leaving my car for you. I've rented one to drive back to Cimarron City. It was delivered a few minutes ago. Mindy needs to be back home in her normal routine. You need time alone. Maybe talk to your sister. Heaven knows, I've tried to get you to talk to me, to let me into your life. I know this isn't the best timing, but I don't think there ever would be a good time." He turned to leave, then looked back over his shoulder at her. "Figure out what you want. I'll be at the ranch with Mindy. I have some figuring out to do myself."

Tory opened her mouth to stop him, but the closing of the door reverberated through her mind. So final.

She pushed to her feet, but her legs shook so much she sank back onto the couch. There was a part of her that wanted to stay in the den and hide. But the stronger part demanded she get up and at least say goodbye to Mindy. The child didn't need to be hurt by what was going on between her father and Tory.

Tory again rose, taking a moment to get her bearings. Then she strode from the room. She found Mindy and Slade in the entrance hall saying their goodbyes to Judy and Brad.

Mindy came over to Tory and took her hand. "I'll—take—real good—care—of Belle—for you."

Tory drew the child into her embrace. "I know you and your dad will. The ranch couldn't be in better hands." She kissed her on the forehead. "Remember I love you, Mindy."

"I—love—you."

Tory lifted her gaze to Slade's and the tormented look in his eyes nearly unraveled what composure she had. "I'll see you two soon."

Slade's raised eyebrows spoke of his doubts. "We'll call to let you know we've arrived safely." He grabbed his suitcase and turned toward the front door.

"Thanks," Tory murmured as she watched the two leave her sister's house.

The ache in her heart grew the farther away Slade and Mindy were. Her chest hurt when she drew in a deep breath. Why did she feel as though she would never see them again?

Panicked by that thought, she started forward. Slade pulled away from the curb. Her face pressed against the window, Mindy waved to Tory.

242   *A Family for Tory*

She returned her daughter's wave, tears flooding her eyes. *You're making a mistake letting him leave. He's the best thing that's happened to you.*

That was the problem. She did feel that way. But she didn't know if she was the best thing for Slade.

Her sister clamped her arm about Tory's shoulder. "Okay, you and I need to talk. Something is definitely wrong and I don't want to hear 'Everything's okay.'"

Tory cocked her head around to look at Judy. "Maybe I don't want to talk about it."

"I'm not accepting that. You need to talk about it. You keep too much inside, sis. Come on in and we'll have a couple of cups of coffee. Whatever it takes." With her arm still around Tory, Judy directed her toward the kitchen.

"Don't you think we should get to the hospital?"

"Nope. Not until you and I have that talk." Judy poured two mugs full of black coffee, then gave Tory hers. "Sit."

"All this bossing around reminds me of when we were kids."

Judy sat across from Tory. "And changing the subject will not work. What's going on with you and Slade? Why were you sleeping in the den?"

Tory took in the stubborn set to her sister's face and knew she wouldn't be allowed to leave until they had discussed at least some of what was happening in her marriage.

"I see those wheels turning, Tory. You're trying to figure out how much you can get away with not telling me. Let me help you get started. How much has coming back to Dallas affected you? I know you never wanted to return. And frankly, after the way some people treated you, I don't blame you." With her elbow on the table, Judy planted her chin on her fist and waited.

Tory raised the mug to her lips and took a long sip. "A lot. As long as I didn't see people like Mrs. Clayton and Mrs. Johnston, I could pretend I was fine, that I'd put everything behind me. But, Judy, I saw the contempt in their faces. I felt all over again the humiliation and condemnation I experienced back then. I felt dirty, as though I had been in the wrong, not Brandon. I know I shouldn't feel that way, but we had been dating. What if I le—"

Judy brought the flat of her hand down onto the wooden table. The sound echoed through the kitchen and caused Tory to flinch.

"Don't you dare start doubting yourself. You did nothing wrong."

Tory pointed to her head. "I know that in here." Then she laid her hand over her heart. "But I can't seem to grasp it in here."

"I have someone I want you to talk to." Judy went to the counter and grabbed a notepad and a pen. After scribbling on the paper, she tore it off and handed it to Tory. "We will continue this conversation after you see Susan Conway."

"Now?"

Judy checked her watch. "Yes, she should be home. She's a stay-at-home mom. I'll call her to tell her you're coming to see her."

"Why?"

"I want her to tell you. It isn't my place. Go talk to her."

"What about Mom?"

"Mom would be the first person to tell you to take care of this before anything else. You can see her later. This is too important to your future."

Future? Tory wasn't sure what kind of future she had. Slade had left with Mindy, disappointed and upset with her. And she couldn't really blame him.

Fifteen minutes later Tory rang Susan Conway's doorbell. A young, attractive woman answered the door with a smile.

"Come in. Judy called me. For some time I've wanted to meet you and thank you." Susan directed Tory into her living room and gestured for her to have a seat on the couch.

"Thank me? For what?"

"For doing something I couldn't. For being braver than I could be."

"Brave? Me?" Right now she didn't feel that way.

Susan sat across from Tory in a wingback chair. "Let me tell you a story. Maybe then you'll understand. Six years ago I was a freshman in college and ready to take the world by storm. I'd never been away from home, but I was confident I could handle anything. That was true until I dated Brandon Clayton."

Tory's breath caught in her throat, contracting it. She straightened, every muscle locked.

Susan's gaze fell away as she continued. "We'd been dating about three weeks. I thought I was so lucky because he was older and quite popular on campus. My roommate couldn't believe a senior was interested in me. I guess he thought I would do anything he wanted. When I wouldn't, he forced himself on me and left me battered and bruised physically as well as emotionally."

"But if he—"

Susan's tear-filled gaze reconnected with Tory's. "I didn't report the rape. I was too ashamed and just wanted to forget it ever happened."

Tory pushed her own feelings of shame aside and said, "But he hurt you!"

"At the time I thought maybe I'd done something wrong, something to provoke the assault. I dropped out of college and went home to lick my wounds." A tear rolled down her face. "But you didn't. You made him pay for what he did to you. I followed your trial closely and cheered when the verdict came in."

Tory slid her eyes shut, wishing she'd known about Susan four years ago.

"When I finally got up enough nerve to meet you and tell you about what happened to me, you were gone. It wasn't until later that I met your sister at church. Recently when I heard about your wedding, I told her about what happened to me and that I was glad you were able to move on with your life. She's the only other person who knew about my rape except my husband and now you."

"I wish I'd have known years ago. I thought I might have done something wrong."

"I know I've been a coward. I didn't realize until

recently that part of my healing was because of you. I knew I hadn't done something wrong, that he had because he did it to another woman."

Tory started to speak, couldn't and cleared her throat. "I wonder if there are others like us."

"I feel sure there are. Brandon Clayton is a sick man. He was handsome and charming on the surface, but that was as far as it went. You were the only brave one of us to come forward. And for that I thank you. May God bless you for many years to come."

Despite the heat outside the car, Tory switched off the air conditioner and rolled down all the windows. She wanted to feel the wind, to smell the fresh air. She wanted to remember she was alive and well with a husband and daughter waiting at home. She had a family whether she had any biological children or not.

Brandon Clayton hadn't taken away what she wanted more than anything in the world. God had brought to her doorstep a man who loved her even knowing her past. Why had she been so afraid to give herself totally to him? Yes, Brandon had taken her virginity away, something she'd wanted to give to her husband. But that was only a small part of her.

The wind felt warm against her skin, and Tory cherished the feeling as she headed her car toward Cimarron City and her ranch—their ranch. She'd spent another hour with Susan Conway, talking about their ordeals, emotionally washing themselves clean of Brandon's mark. They had prayed afterward, then hugged goodbye. When she had left Susan's house, she'd felt like a new woman, a free woman.

Suddenly the months with Slade took on a new meaning. He'd never once tried anything she hadn't wanted. He'd become her friend and confidant. He'd taken her house and turned it into a real home while she'd held on to her fear and shame. She'd let Brandon Clayton rule her life for the last time.

When she pulled into the lane that led to her house, her heart quickened its beating. Her mouth went dry. What if he and Mindy weren't there. What if he'd decided their marriage wasn't worth it? What if—? She shook the doubts from her mind. She was through doubting herself. She would fight for what she wanted most—to be Slade's wife and to have a family.

She parked in front of the house, hopped out of the car and hurried toward the porch. The sun's last rays were fading in the western sky. Dark shadows crept closer, but the lights on in the living room attested to someone being home. Her foot took the first step. The screen door flew open and Mindy came out.

"Mom, you're—home!" Mindy rushed at her, throwing herself into her arms. "I—missed—you."

Tory tousled the child's hair. "It was only a day. I had to make sure Mom would be all right before coming home." The word *home* rang in the warm summer air, loud and clear, a declaration of her feelings.

When Tory looked toward the door, Slade stood framed in the entrance to the house, his face hidden in the shadows of evening. "The doctor said Mom's operation was a complete success. She should be getting better each day. She sends her love."

"Mindy, it's been a long day and you have school tomorrow. You need to get ready for bed."

Mindy spun about, her hands on her waist. "But—Dad-dy."

Slade held the screen door open and moved to the side. "Scoot, young lady. Now. Tory and I will be in to say good-night in a few minutes."

When the screen door banged closed behind Mindy, Slade said, "I'm glad your mother is getting better. Judy called earlier to tell me you were on your way home."

"I asked her to let you know."

"Why didn't you call?"

Even though she'd sat in a car for the past four hours, she needed to sit down to stop the trembling in her legs. She eased onto the swing, leaving enough room for Slade. He took the chair across from her, his expression still obscured by the growing darkness.

Tory clasped her hands together. "What I have to say to you can't be done over the phone." She glanced out into the yard, barely making out the dark line of trees to the west. "No, that isn't the complete truth. I was scared."

"Why?"

There was no emotion in that one word and it sent a tremor down Tory's length. "Because I thought you might not be here. Because I didn't want to hear the anger in your voice. Because I've become a coward."

"Coward? You aren't a coward."

The incredulous tone to his voice prompted a smile.

"Oh, yes, I am. Four years ago I stood up for myself and it nearly destroyed me. I've been running ever since, hiding from the past, hiding from my feelings. Not anymore."

"What happened to change your mind?"

She saw the stiff set to his body, as though he were frozen. "You and Mindy. It took the threat of losing you two to force me to do some thinking. I had a long talk with a woman who helped me to see what I'd done. She thanked me for going to the police about Brandon Clayton. She hadn't been able to, but she was glad he was serving time for what he'd done."

Some of the tension drained from Slade. He leaned forward, resting his elbows on his knees, his face cast in the light streaming through the partially open drapes in the living room. "He'd raped another woman?"

"Yes."

Slade's hands curled into fists, then flexed. "Good thing he's in prison."

"She made me look at the whole ordeal of the rape and trial in a new light. I was wronged and I fought back. I have nothing to be ashamed of."

Slade surged to his feet and sat next to her on the swing, gripping her hand. "Ashamed? There is so much about you I admire. You have no reason to feel that way."

"That's easier said than done. I never shared everything with you. But that's gonna change starting now." She twisted so she faced him on the swing, their hands still linked. "I was saving myself for my husband. When I was a teenager, I'd made that decision. It had become very important to me as an expression of my love. Brandon took that away from me. He shattered a dream. He'd taken the decision out of my control."

Slade's fingers about hers tightened. "I know what it's like not to feel like you have any control over a situation."

"Then you understand?"

He nodded. "When I had that wreck, my life changed instantly. I learned firsthand how little control we really have over our lives."

"That's why faith in God is so important."

"I believe that now, but at the time I was angry and lashed out at myself, at God, at the Fates."

"My faith was the only thing that kept me going. I ran from my family. I wouldn't let them support me. I hid out here and licked my wounds, pretending everything was normal. It wasn't." Tory grasped Slade's other hand, too. "I wouldn't let a man touch me. I didn't like even getting near a man, and certainly being alone with one panicked me."

"You're alone with me. I'm touching you."

"That's just it. You don't threaten me. I let down my guard enough to really get to know you and what kind of man you are. I knew you would never hurt me. That's why I could agree to marry you and provide Mindy with a home."

He smiled. "I'm glad you realized that. I'd never hurt you."

Tory moved closer, their knees touching on the swing. "I wanted more and thought I was ready for it. Then we had to go to Dallas and all my memories of what happened slapped me in the face. Now I realize that if it hadn't been Dallas, something else would have triggered the buried feelings. I had to deal with them, not run from them."

"Have you stopped running?"

She leaned toward him. "Yes, definitely. I love you, Slade Donaldson, and I want us to be husband and wife in every sense."

His lips met hers in a gentle kiss. "I love you, Tory Donaldson."

"Let's go say good-night to Mindy before she wonders what happened to us."

Slade grasped Tory's hand as they walked into the house. The comfort of his touch melted any doubts she might still have. When they entered Mindy's bedroom, she was in her bed with the pillows propped up behind her back and a book in her lap.

"Dad-dy start-ed *Black—Beau-ty.*"

"I loved that book when I was a little girl."

Tory sat at the end of the bed while Slade scooted a chair close to Mindy. He began to read, his deep, baritone voice floating to Tory and enveloping her in its rich tones that she wanted to hear every day of the rest of her life.

When he finished the chapter, he snapped the book closed and put it on the nightstand. "Good night, sweetheart."

Mindy snuggled down into the covers while Tory arranged them around her and Belle. "I'm so glad to be home. After school tomorrow, you and I will go for a ride."

"Yes! Dad-dy, too?"

Tory slanted a look back at Slade. "Daddy, too. That is, if he can come home early from work."

"You two have a date," he said, lounging against the doorjamb.

Tory brushed a kiss across Mindy's forehead, then switched off the lamp on the nightstand. The light from the hallway illuminated her way toward Slade silhouetted in the doorway, relaxed as though he had not a care in the world.

In the hallway by her bedroom Slade drew her into his arms, his mouth claiming hers. When he pulled back, he whispered, "I love you, Tory," then gave her a quick kiss on the lips before releasing her and heading toward his bedroom.

Dazed, Tory watched him walk away. "But what about—"

He swung around, his hand on his doorknob. "As I told you before, you're in control. You're calling the shots. The next step is up to you."

The quiet click of his door as he closed it resounded in the hall. The silence of the house cloaked her in a feeling of safety. She glanced at her door then at his. Chewing on her bottom lip, she thought about her ride to the ranch, about her conversations earlier with Susan and Slade and knew what she wanted to do more than anything. She walked to his door and pushed it open.

He turned toward her, a smile of welcome on his face. She shut the door and flew into his embrace.

Epilogue

Mindy rushed into the spacious new kitchen decorated in palm trees and bamboo with red and green accents. She came to a halt beside Tory at the counter. "Laurie's here. She's the last one. Come on. I can't open my presents without you, Mom."

"Whoa. Slow down. I'm just about through with putting the punch together." Tory dumped the frozen lemonade into the large pitcher and stirred the liquid with a wooden spoon.

"Mom! We all want to ride."

Tory grinned and laid the spoon in the sink. "I know, but first the presents then the food. Is your dad ready with the video camera?"

Mindy cocked her head. "What do you think? Does he go anywhere without it?"

"Not lately," Tory said with a laugh. "You go back to your guests and I'll be right there."

"Promise?"

"Have I ever let you down?"

Mindy shook her head and hurried back into the den.

Tory swung around and scooped up Sean from the high chair. Banana bits were all over his mouth and the front of his shirt and even in his dark hair. "You are one messy eater, young man." She took a washcloth and wiped him clean. "We'd better get into the den. Your big sister is impatient. Maybe you can ride today, too. Of course, it will have to be with your daddy."

Sean grinned up at her and made babbling sounds as though he were telling her that would be fine by him.

The second Tory entered the den, Mindy tore into the first present in front of her. Sean played with one of Tory's buttons on her shirt while his sister opened one gift after another to the excitement of ten little girls from her class.

Slade moved to Tory's side, smiling at Sean. "Are you sure Gus is up to this? Eleven screaming girls may be too much for him."

"Are you kidding? He's gonna love every minute. He adores Mindy and anything she wants, she gets."

"Maybe I should rephrase the question. Are you and I gonna be up for eleven screaming girls trying to ride?"

"They're not screaming. They're just enthusiastic."

"Is that what you call this?" he shouted above the din. "I think they're all trying to talk at once."

Tory took a whiff. "I think our son needs to be changed."

"I'll trade you. You film this free-for-all while I change Sean."

"Oh, a man after my own heart." Tory patted her chest.

"Since you have mine, it's only fair I have yours." His mouth whispered across Tory's right before he plucked his son from her arms and gave her the video camera. "Don't aim directly at the windows. Too much light."

"Aye, aye, Captain."

She watched as Slade lifted his son high in the air and swung him back and forth. Sean's peals of laughter mingled with the chattering racket behind Tory. Her heart swelled as she took in the scene in the den. This was her family. It couldn't get any better than this.

* * * * *

Dear Reader,

A Family for Tory is centered around a therapeutic riding stable. I have had the good fortune to be involved with one and have seen the smiles on the children's faces when they ride. Children benefit so much from being around animals. I am continually amazed at how God has provided ways for us to heal from emotional scars as well as physical ones. I have tried to show some of them in this book.

Tory must learn to trust again and to let go of her fear. Slade must forgive himself for surviving a wreck while his wife didn't and his daughter ended up injured. Mindy must relearn some of the simplest things in life because of her surgery. The three of them with God's help become a family and help each other to heal.

I love hearing from readers. You can contact me at P.O. Box 2074, Tulsa, OK 74101, or Mdaley50@aol.com.

May God bless you,

Margaret Daley

Get 2 Books FREE!

Steeple Hill Books,
publisher of inspirational romance fiction, presents

Love Inspired

A series of contemporary love stories that will lift your spirits and reinforce important lessons about life, faith and love!

FREE BOOKS!
Get two free books by acclaimed, inspirational authors!

FREE GIFTS!
Get two exciting surprise gifts absolutely free!

Love Inspired

▲ To get your 2 free books and 2 free gifts, affix this peel-off sticker to the reply card and mail it today!

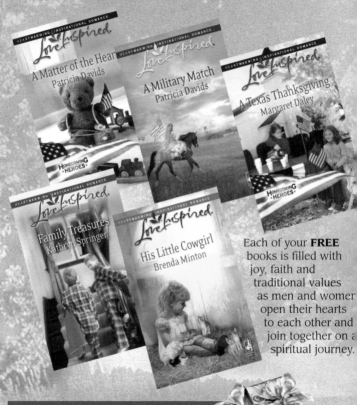

We'd like to send you two free books to introduce you to the Love Inspired® series. Your two books have a combined cover price of $11.00 in the U.S. and $13.00 in Canada, but they are yours free! We'll even send you two wonderful surprise gifts. You can't lose!

HEARTWARMING INSPIRATIONAL ROMANCE
Love Inspired
A Matter of the Heart
Patricia Davids
HOMECOMING HEROES

HEARTWARMING INSPIRATIONAL ROMANCE
Love Inspired
A Military Match
Patricia Davids

HEARTWARMING INSPIRATIONAL ROMANCE
Love Inspired
A Texas Thanksgiving
Margaret Daley
HOMECOMING HEROES

HEARTWARMING INSPIRATIONAL ROMANCE
Love Inspired
Family Treasures
Kathryn Springer

HEARTWARMING INSPIRATIONAL ROMANCE
Love Inspired
His Little Cowgirl
Brenda Minton

Each of your **FREE** books is filled with joy, faith and traditional values as men and women open their hearts to each other and join together on a spiritual journey.

FREE BONUS GIFTS!

We'll send you two wonderful surprise gifts, worth about $10, *absolutely FREE*, just for giving Love Inspired books a try! Don't miss out — **MAIL THE REPLY CARD TODAY!**

Order online at:
www.LoveInspiredBooks.com

GET 2 FREE BOOKS!

HURRY!
Return this card today to get **2 FREE Books** and **2 FREE Bonus Gifts!**

Love Inspired®

YES! *Please send me the 2 FREE Love Inspired® books and 2 FREE gifts for which I qualify. I understand that I am under no obligation to purchase anything further, as explained on the back of this card.*

affix
2 free
books
sticker
here

☐ I prefer the regular-print edition   ☐ I prefer the larger-print edition

113-IDL-EVML   313-IDL-EVP9   121-IDL-EVPW   321-IDL-EVDA

FIRST NAME   LAST NAME

ADDRESS

APT.#   CITY

STATE/PROV.   ZIP/POSTAL CODE

▼ DETACH AND MAIL CARD TODAY! ▼

® and ™ are trademarks owned and used by the trademark owner and/or its licensee. © 2008 STEEPLE HILL BOOKS

(LI-LA-09)

Steeple Hill®

Steeple Hill Reader Service — Here's How It Works:

Accepting your 2 free books and 2 free gifts places you under no obligation to buy anything. You may keep the books and gifts and return the shipping statement marked "cancel." If you do not cancel, about a month later we will send you 4 additional books and bill you just $4.24 each for the regular print edition or $4.49 each for the larger print edition in the U.S. or $4.74 each for the regular print edition or $4.99 each for the larger print edition in Canada. That is a savings of at least 20% off the cover price. It's quite a bargain! Shipping and handling is just 25¢ per book. You may cancel at any time, but if you choose to continue, every month we'll send you 4 more books, which you may either purchase at the discount price...or return to us and cancel your subscription. *Terms and prices subject to change without notice. Prices do not include applicable taxes. Sales tax applicable in N.Y. Canadian residents will be charged applicable provincial taxes and GST. Offer not valid in Quebec. Books received may not be as shown. Credit or debit balances in a customer's account(s) may be offset by any other outstanding balance owed by or to the customer.

If offer card is missing write to: Steeple Hill Reader Service, 3010 Walden Ave., P.O. Box 1867, Buffalo, NY 14240-1867

BUSINESS REPLY MAIL
FIRST-CLASS MAIL   PERMIT NO. 717   BUFFALO, NY

POSTAGE WILL BE PAID BY ADDRESSEE

STEEPLE HILL READER SERVICE
3010 WALDEN AVE
PO BOX 1867
BUFFALO NY 14240-9952

NO POSTAGE
NECESSARY
IF MAILED
IN THE
UNITED STATES

A MOTHER FOR CINDY

For I know the plans I have for you, declares the Lord, plans to prosper you and not to harm you, plans to give you hope and a future. Then you will call upon me and come and pray to me and I will listen to you. You will seek me and find me when you seek me with all your heart. I will be found by you, declares the Lord, and will bring you back from captivity.

—Jeremiah 29:11–14

To Judy Pelfrey.
Thank you for twenty-five years of friendship and
for your guidance and grace. May you reside in
God's loving arms always.

Chapter One

Peace at last.

With a deep sigh Jesse Bradshaw sank into the chair at her kitchen table. After the hectic past hour getting her son off to visit his friend Sean O'Brien, she now had time to read her daily verses from the Bible and collect herself before starting her day.

Dear Heavenly Father, please help me to make it through—

Honk! Honk!

Jesse bolted from her chair, nearly toppling it to the tile floor, and raced for the door. Not again. Stepping outside, she scanned her backyard and found that her geese had a large man who was holding a crying little girl, trapped by the edge of the lake. As Jesse hurried toward her pet geese, the one overriding impression was the anger carved into the stranger's face. He tried to shield the child from the irate birds that flapped their wings, hissing and honking their displeasure at their space being invaded.

"Step away from the nest," Jesse shouted across her yard that sloped to the lake behind her house.

"What do you think I've been trying to do?"

The man's anger was momentarily directed at her as she neared him. His dark gaze drilled into her while Fred darted at him and nipped his leg. The stranger winced and held the little girl up higher to keep the geese from attacking her.

"I'll get their attention. You run."

"My pleasure," he agreed between clenched teeth at the same time Ethel took her turn at his other leg.

"Daddy, Daddy, make them go away! I'm scared!" The child hugged her father tighter and curled her legs around him so they weren't a dangling target for the geese.

"Everything's okay, Cindy." He awkwardly patted the child's back while glaring at Jesse, clearly conveying his own displeasure.

"Fred! Ethel!" Jesse put herself between the geese and the man with the little girl. She waved her arms like a windmill and jumped up and down, yelling the pair's names in her sternest voice, hoping none of her neighbors saw this undignified display.

Thankfully Ethel calmed down and waddled toward her nest. Fred, however, would have nothing to do with her. He focused on the stranger, who was trying to back away. Flying around Jesse, Fred went for the man's leg again. Jesse threw herself in front of the goose. She got nipped on the thigh.

"Get out of here," she whispered loudly. Pain spread from the sore place on her leg as she continued to come between Fred and the intruders.

Carrying his daughter, the man hurried across the yard, a limp to his gait. At the edge of her property, he threw a glance over his shoulder, an ashen cast to his dark features. Jesse shivered in the warm spring air. This man was definitely not happy with her geese—or her.

Fred settled down as the two people moved farther away. After giving one final loud honk, he toddled back to Ethel and stood guard, his beady black eyes watching the pair disappear inside the house next door.

So those were her new neighbors, staying in the Millers' summer home.

Jesse headed for her back door, rubbing the reddened area on her thigh. Everyone in Sweetwater knew to stay away from her backyard while Ethel and Fred were guarding their nest. They could be so fierce when their home was invaded.

With all the activity at her own house, she'd forgotten about her new neighbors who'd moved in two days ago. She supposed she should bake them some cookies and welcome them to Sweetwater—oh, and warn them about her geese.

Shaking her head, she stepped into her bright kitchen and came to a stop just inside the door. Her grandfather sat at the table, his gray hair sticking up at odd angles, a scowl on his face.

"Those geese could wake the dead," he muttered into his cup of coffee while taking some sips.

"I'm sorry. I know you went to bed late last night. But someone was in our backyard. You know how they get with strangers."

Her grandfather's head snapped up, and he regarded her with a pinpoint gaze. "Not the Hawthorne boys trying to steal their eggs again?"

"Nope. Our new neighbors." Jesse eased onto the chair next to her grandfather. "And I have to say I don't think I made a very good first impression."

He peered at the clock over the stove. "It's barely eight. Awfully early to be paying us a visit."

"I don't think that's what they were doing."

His bushy dark brows shot up. "What kind of neighbors do we have?"

"Gramps, that's what I intend to find out later this morning."

Several hours later at her neighbor's house, Jesse pressed the bell and waited and waited. When the door finally swung open, she hoisted up the plate of chocolate chip cookies, as though it was a shield of armor, ready to give her welcoming spiel. The words died on her lips.

The man from earlier filled the entrance with his large frame. He wore a sleeveless T-shirt and shorts that revealed muscular legs and arms. Sweat coated his body and ran down his face as he brought a towel up to wipe it away. When her gaze traveled up his length, power came to mind. Her survey came to rest on his face. Her smile of greeting vanished along with any rational thought.

Earlier she hadn't really had time to assess the man who had been partially hidden by his daughter. The impression of anger and the need to get the man and his daughter to safety had been all she had focused on. Now her attention was riveted to him. His rugged features formed a pleasing picture and only confirmed his sense of power—and danger. When she looked into those incredibly dark-brown eyes, she felt lost in a world only occupied by them.

One of his brows arched. "Come to finish me off?"

His deep, raspy voice broke the silence, dragging Jesse away from her thoughts, all centered around him. "No." She swallowed several times. "No, I brought you and your family some cookies." She thrust the plate at his chest, nearly sending her offering toppling to the porch at his feet.

With a step back, he glanced down at the plate of cookies.

"They're chocolate chip," she added, conscious of the fact that he was now staring at her. Not one hint at what was going on in his mind was revealed in his expression. "I wanted to welcome you to Sweetwater—properly."

Finally he smiled, deep creases at the corners of his eyes that glinted. The gesture curled her toes and caused her heart to pound a shade faster. My, what a smile! His wife sure was a lucky woman.

"And earlier wasn't a proper welcome?"

"I'm sorry about not warning you concerning Fred and Ethel. Everyone knows to stay away from my backyard at this time of year. I meant to. But you know how it is. Time got away from me what with the order I needed to fill." Realizing she was babbling, she clamped her mouth closed, trying not to stare at his potent smile that transformed his face.

"Fred and Ethel are pets?"

"I raised Fred after a pack of wild dogs got his mother and father. A friend gave me Ethel for Fred. He really can be a dear."

"A dear? I don't think our definition of *a dear* is the same."

Despite his words, amusement sounded in his voice, and Jesse responded with a grin. "Well, not at this time when he's playing he-goose. You know males and their territory."

The man laughed. "I suppose I do." He took the plate and offered her his hand. "I'm Nick Blackburn and I'm sure my daughter and I will enjoy these cookies."

No wife? Jesse wondered, slipping her hand within his and immediately feeling a warmth flash up her arm from his brief touch. "I'm Jesse Bradshaw. Are you and your daughter going to be here long?"

"Two months."

She remembered the little girl's pale face and plea to her father. "Is your daughter okay?"

"Cindy is happy as a lark now that she's sitting in front of the television set watching her favorite show."

"How old is she? I have a son who just turned eight."

"She'll be seven later this summer." He stepped to the side. "Please come in."

When she'd come over to his house, she'd had no intention of staying. She still had that order to complete. "I'd better not. I can see I interrupted your exercises."

"Your interruption gave me a good reason to call it quits."

Again she looked him up and down, assessing those hard muscles that could only have come from a great deal of work. He had to exercise a lot or his body wouldn't be in such perfect shape. She began to imagine him pumping iron, sweat coating his skin. When she peered into his face, she found him staring at her, and she blushed. She didn't normally go around inspecting men.

"Well, uh," she stammered, searching her mind for something proper to say, "I'd like to say hello to your daughter and explain about Fred and Ethel." Jesse stepped through the threshold into his house. She felt like Daniel going into the lion's den, as though her life were about to change.

"Would you like a cup of coffee or iced tea? I think Boswell made some yesterday."

"I'll take a glass of iced tea if it's not too much trouble."

He gave her a self-mocking grin. "I'm not great in the kitchen, but I believe I can pour some tea."

"Is your wife home?" Boy, that was about as subtle as a Mack truck running someone over.

He turned and headed toward the back of the house, still limping slightly. "No, she died."

"Oh," Jesse murmured, feeling an immediate kinship with her new neighbor. Her husband had been deceased for the past four years and she still missed him.

She followed Nick into the kitchen and stood by the table. He took two glasses from the cabinets and retrieved a pitcher from the refrigerator. After pouring the tea, he handed her a glass and indicated she take a seat.

He tilted the glass to his mouth and drank deeply of the cold liquid. "This is just what I needed. It's unseasonably warm for the end of May."

"Are you from around here?"

"No, Chicago." He massaged his thigh.

"I noticed you're favoring your right leg. I hope Fred or Ethel didn't cause that."

"No. I just overextended myself while exercising. Sometimes I take my physical therapy a step too far." He shrugged. "I guess you can't rush Mother Nature."

Jesse chuckled. "I agree. Some forces have their own time frame."

"Like Fred and Ethel."

"Definitely forces to be reckoned with."

"Yes, I have a few bruises to prove that."

"I really am sorry. As I said earlier, I've been working hard to finish my latest order and before I realized it, two days had passed since you all moved in. I should have come over that first day and warned you."

"Well, consider us warned." Nick sipped some more tea, draining his glass. "Do you want any more?"

Jesse shook her head, realizing she hadn't drunk very much. She watched him go to the refrigerator and refill his glass. He still favored his right leg. "You said something about physical therapy. Did you have an accident?"

A shadow clouded his dark eyes, making them appear almost black. His jaw tightened into a hard line. "Yes."

A naturally curious person, Jesse wanted to pursue the topic, but his clipped answer forbade further discussion. "Are you here for a vacation?" she asked instead.

"Yes." Again a tight thread laced his voice.

"This is a nice place to take a summer vacation. Do you fish?"

"No, never had the time."

"Maybe Gramps can take you and your daughter out fishing one morning. He loves to show off his gear and favorite spots on the lake."

Nick didn't respond. He made his way back to the table and eased down onto the chair across from Jesse. "I'm afraid I've lived in the big city all my life. The great outdoors has never appealed to me."

"Then why did you come to Sweetwater?"

"The Millers are friends of mine. Since they weren't going to use the house this summer they offered it to me. It met my needs."

She opened her mouth to ask what needs but immediately pressed her lips together. Nick Blackburn was a private man who she suspected had opened up more in the past fifteen minutes than he usually did. Whereas anyone meeting her for the first time could glean her whole life history if he wanted. She wouldn't push her luck. Besides, he would be gone in two months.

"Daddy, I'm hungry. When's Boswell gonna be back?" Cindy asked, entering the kitchen. She came to a halt when she saw Jesse sitting at the table with her father. Her eyes widened, fear shining bright in them.

"Don't worry. I left Fred and Ethel at home." Jesse smiled, wanting to wipe the fear from the little girl's expression. "I came over to bring some cookies and to tell you how sorry I am about my geese this morning. When they're guarding their nest, they can be extra mean."

"I just wanted to pet them." Cindy's eyes filled with tears. She stayed by the door.

"They don't like strangers much, especially right now. Maybe later I can introduce you if you want."

Horror flittered across Cindy's face. "No." She backed up against the door.

"That's okay. Do you like animals?"

The little girl hesitated, then nodded.

"Do you have a pet?"

She shook her head.

An uncomfortable silence descended, charging the air as though an electrical storm was approaching. Jesse resisted the urge to hug her arms to her. "Maybe you can come over and meet my son and his dog, Bingo."

"He has a dog?" Cindy relaxed some.

"Yes, a mutt who found us a few summers ago."

"Found you?"

"Or, rather Fred and Ethel. You thought their racket was loud this morning. You should have heard it when Bingo came into the yard. I found him hiding under a bush, his paws covering his face. Of course, you would think that would teach him a lesson. Oh, no. Bingo still tries to play with them. They won't have anything to do with him."

"Not too smart. I've learned my lesson after only one encounter. Stay away from the geese," Nick said with a laugh.

"Actually, Bingo is pretty smart. Nate has taught him a lot of tricks. Maybe you can get Nate to show you, Cindy." Jesse felt drawn to the little girl who seemed lost, unsure of herself.

"Can I, Daddy?"

"Sure, princess."

"Great. Nate will be home later this afternoon. Come on over and I'll introduce you to my son and Bingo. I promise you Bingo is nothing like Fred and Ethel."

"Do you have any other pets?" Cindy took several steps closer.

"I'm afraid I could open my own zoo and charge admission which I probably should since it costs so much to feed them all. Nate has a fish aquarium and a python as well as three gerbils."

"He does!" Cindy's big brown eyes grew round. "He's lucky."

"I don't think he feels that way when he has to feed them. You should hear him complaining."

"I wouldn't mind doing that if I had a pet." Cindy's hopeful gaze skipped to her father.

"Princess, we've talked about this. We live in an apartment. Not the best place for an animal."

Cindy sidestepped to Jesse and whispered so loud anyone in the kitchen could hear, "Daddy's never had a pet. I think one would be good for him. Don't you?"

Nick looked as uncomfortable as the silence had felt

a moment before. He raked his hand through his dark straight hair that was cut moderately short. "I have enough on my plate without having to take care of a pet, too."

"But I'd do that, Daddy."

"Cindy, I don't think we should bore our guest with this."

The firmness in his voice brooked no argument. The little girl's mouth formed a pout, her shoulders sagging forward.

"Well, I'd better be going before Gramps wonders where I disappeared to. Come over after three, Cindy. Nate should be home by then." Jesse stood.

Nick rose, too. "Let me show you to the door."

"That's okay. I know this place well. I often visit when the Millers are here. I'm glad since they're going to be gone this summer that someone is going to be living here. I hate seeing this old house go to waste."

Nick smiled, the gesture reaching deep into his eyes. "Thanks for the cookies. I know I'll appreciate them."

His warm regard sent a shiver up her spine. She backed away. "Welcome to Sweetwater," was all she could suddenly think of to say. Her mind went blank of everything except the man's smile. Before she made a fool of herself, she rushed from the kitchen, relieved he would only be here for a short time.

"I'm sorry Nate couldn't be here this afternoon. He ended up staying at Sean's," Jesse said, running her palm over Bingo's wiry brown hair.

The medium-size dog rubbed himself up against Cindy, nudging her hand to keep her petting him. "That's okay. Bingo sure is nice."

"Yeah. We were lucky he found us. He has more loving in him than most dogs."

Cindy buried her face against Bingo's fur. "I wish Daddy would let me have a pet. I'd take good care of him."

"I bet you would." Jesse knew of a family down the road whose poodle had puppies a few weeks ago. They would soon be looking for homes for them. Maybe she could convince Nick that a dog would be good for Cindy. A poodle was a small enough dog to live in an apartment. "While you're here, you can play with Bingo any time you want."

"Nate won't mind?"

"Are you kidding? He loves to show off his animals. He wants to be a zookeeper one day."

Forehead creased, Cindy looked at her. "And you don't mind the snake?"

"I have to confess at first it bothered me. But now, I don't mind it. He usually keeps it in its cage. It's only gotten loose once."

"Mommy would have had a fit—" Suddenly the little girl stopped talking and stared down at the sidewalk.

"Snakes, especially big ones, can be scary." Jesse placed her hand on the child's shoulder, wishing she could take her pain away. She remembered having to deal with Nate's feelings after his father had died. She wouldn't have been able to help him as she did if it hadn't been for her faith in the Lord.

"Yes," Cindy mumbled and proceeded to pet Bingo some more, her face still averted.

"How long has your mother been gone?" Jesse asked, her voice roughened with sudden intense emotions.

Cindy lifted her tearful gaze to Jesse's, her lower lip trembling. "About a year. She died in a car wreck. Daddy was in the car, too. He was in the hospital a *long* time." Her voice wavered. "Daddy doesn't like to talk about it."

Jesse drew the child into her arms, stroking her hand down her back. "If you need to talk to someone, I'm a good listener." It had taken Nate a while to open up to her about his father's death, and after he had, he had been much better.

Sniffing, Cindy pulled away. "I'm okay. It's just that sometimes Daddy doesn't know what to do with me, being a girl and all." She swiped her hand across her cheeks and erased the evidence of her tears. "There's just times I wish I had a mommy, but I can't tell Daddy that."

Jesse's heart constricted, making her chest feel tight. There were times she was sure Nate wished he had a father, but she could never see herself married again. Mark had been a wonderful husband, her childhood sweetheart. She could never find another love like they had. She had been lucky once. She couldn't see settling for anything less than the kind of love she had with Mark.

Please, Lord, help me to be there for Cindy as I was

*for Nate. Guide me in the best way to help Cindy. She's
hurting and I want to help her.*

With her arm still loosely about Cindy's shoulder,
Jesse asked, "Does your father have any lady friends?"

The little girl shook her head. "He's always too busy
working when he should be resting." She glanced
toward her house. "That's what he's doing right now.
We're supposed to be on vacation, but he's been on the
phone for *hours*."

A plan began to materialize in Jesse's mind. "Maybe
we can do something about that."

Cindy's eyes brightened. "What?"

"I'll have a party and invite some friends to introduce
you all to Sweetwater."

"You will?"

"Yes. How does tomorrow night sound?"

"What about tomorrow night?"

Nick's question surprised Jesse. She hadn't heard
him approaching and to look up and see him standing
only a few feet from her was unnerving. Her heart
kicked into double time. She surged to her feet, smoothing down her jean shorts that suddenly seemed too
short.

"Cindy and I were planning a party to welcome you
to Sweetwater."

"You don't have to do that."

"I know, but I want to. So pencil me in."

His eyebrow quirked.

"It won't be a large gathering. Just a few people."
Jesse heard herself talking a mile a minute. She stopped

and took several deep breaths. "How about it? I'm a great cook."

"After tasting your cookies, you won't get an argument from me. They were delicious."

"Yeah, Daddy had half the plate eaten before I even had a chance to eat one."

Jesse laughed. "Then I'll make some more for dessert tomorrow night. My son loves chocolate chip cookies, too. They're a staple around our house."

"But not your husband?" Nick asked, a lazy smile accompanying the question.

"He loved them, too, but he died four years ago. A freak accident. He was struck by lightning." There she went, telling a person more than he asked.

"I'm sorry."

"Daddy, Bingo can do all kinds of tricks. Watch." Cindy stood. "Roll over." After the dog performed that task, she said, "Sit. Shake hands." The little girl took his paw in her hand. "Isn't he terrific? Dogs make good pets."

Nick tried to contain his grin, but it lifted the corners of his mouth. "I'm sure they do, princess."

"Then we can get one?" Cindy turned her hopeful expression on him.

"I'll think about it when we return to Chicago."

"You will?"

"That isn't a yes, young lady. Just a promise to consider it."

Cindy leaned close to Jesse and whispered loudly, "That means we'll get one when Daddy says that."

"I heard that, Cynthia Rebecca Blackburn."

"Oh, I'm in big trouble now. He's using my full name." The little girl giggled and began petting Bingo.

"Would you like to throw the ball for him? He loves to play catch." Jesse retrieved a red ball from the flower bed loaded with multicolored pansies along the front of her house.

"Yes." Cindy moved out into the yard and tossed Bingo's toy toward her yard. The dog chased it down.

"I didn't want to say anything in front of Cindy, but I know where you could get a poodle puppy."

His dark gaze fixed on her. "Thank you for not saying anything in front of Cindy."

"Then you aren't interested?" She heard her disappointment in her voice and grimaced. She never liked fostering her ideas onto another—well, maybe she did. Anyway, pets were good for children and clearly his daughter loved animals.

"I don't know. I—" He looked toward Cindy. "I've never had a dog before. Or any pet for that matter."

For just a few seconds she glimpsed a vulnerability in his expression before he veiled it. "If you decide to get one, I'll help."

"Until we go back to Chicago." A self-mocking grin graced his mouth. "Then, I'm on my own."

"It's not that difficult. Love is the most important ingredient."

"Isn't it always?"

"Yes, it is." She couldn't help wondering where his world-weary tone came from.

He took a deep breath. "I'll think about the puppy.

I'll have to consult Boswell, too, since he'll be taking care of the dog."

"Is that the older gentleman I've seen leaving your house?"

"Completely bald?"

"Yeah."

"That's Boswell. I don't know what I'd do without him. He takes care of the everyday details of my life as well as Cindy's."

"Cindy said something about you working this afternoon. What do you do?"

"I'm CEO of Blackburn Industries. We're into a little of everything it seems."

"And you live in an apartment?" she asked without really thinking. Her picture of his home obviously wasn't right.

A sheepish look fell over his features. "I guess it isn't your idea of an apartment. It takes up the top floor of the building I own on the lake in downtown Chicago."

She chuckled. "No. What pops into my mind is maybe four or five rooms at the most."

"Okay, maybe I have space for a pet. I just think dogs should have a yard. All I have is a terrace. Not the same thing."

"If you don't think a dog is a good idea, I know a lady in town who has some kittens she wants to find a home for."

"I get the distinct impression that if I want something, you're the lady to come to."

Jesse warmed under the smile directed at her. The

laugh lines at the corners of his eyes deepened and his stance relaxed completely. "I do know what's going on around Sweetwater. If it's to be had, I can probably get it for you."

"I'll keep that in mind."

"A kitten can be a totally indoor animal."

He threw up his hands. "Enough," he said, laughing. "You've convinced me, but I still need to talk with Boswell. Thank you for showing Bingo to Cindy. I haven't seen her smile like that in a while." He turned to leave, then glanced back at her. "You know, I could use a negotiator like you working for my company. If you ever think about moving to Chicago—"

Jesse shook her head, the idea of a big city sending a chill through her. "No, that will never happen. My home is here. I've lived here all my life and can't imagine being anywhere else."

"Oh, well, you can't blame a guy for trying." He started toward his daughter.

"I'll see you at six-thirty tomorrow night."

He stopped and swung back around, a question in his eyes.

"The dinner party. Casual attire. And Cindy is invited, too, as well as Boswell."

Cindy pulled on his arm. "Can we come, Daddy?"

"Sure, princess, if it's not too much trouble." He peered at Jesse.

"No problem. A piece of cake. I throw parties all the time."

Jesse watched the father and daughter walk away. If

he only knew about her famous little dinner parties, he might pack up and leave in the dead of night. Tara Cummings would be perfect for him. Cindy needed a mother and Nick needed—well, he seemed awfully lonely. He masked his vulnerability well, but she'd glimpsed it. Besides, any man who worked all the time needed to loosen up. There was more to life than work. Tara was definitely the person to match him with, especially after Clint broke off their engagement. Jesse hurried inside to call her friend.

Chapter Two

"Tara, you're early," Jesse exclaimed when she opened her front door to find her friend standing on the porch.

"I wanted all the juicy details before I meet this man. I heard the Millers weren't coming this summer to Sweetwater Lake. It's your new neighbor, isn't it?"

Jesse turned away from Tara. "I don't know what you're talking about."

"Jesse Bradshaw, we all know when you throw one of these little dinner parties it's to fix someone up. I'm single and recently out of a relationship. Perfect target for your matchmaking."

"I invited Susan Reed tonight, too. You won't be the only one single."

"If we exclude you, I'll be the only single woman here under the age of fifty. Right?"

Jesse slid her gaze away. "Cindy's coming."

"Who's Cindy?"

"My neighbor's almost-seven-year-old daughter."

"I knew it! You're up to your old tricks. Okay, tell me about your new neighbor. I've heard he is dynamite-looking, some kind of millionaire, and besides having a little girl, he has a manservant. He's from Chicago and is only here for a couple of months."

"Where did you hear all that?"

"The usual."

"Susan Reed?"

Tara nodded. "The best source of info in this town. Far better than our newspaper."

"There isn't much else I can add." For some reason she didn't feel right gossiping about Nick. Tara would have to discover for herself how vulnerable he was, how lonely he was, how attractive—*whoa, stop right there, Jesse Bradshaw!* A little inner voice yelled.

"Susan said something about you talking to him yesterday. Is he nice?"

"I wouldn't have invited you if he wasn't."

Tara brushed her long black hair behind her shoulders. "I knew that. I guess I'm a little nervous. Ever since Clint ran out on me, I'm a little gun-shy."

Jesse put an arm around her friend and began walking her toward the kitchen. "Perfectly understandable. Clint will regret his hasty decision one day."

"I just don't understand why he left."

Jesse patted Tara's arm. "Neither do I."

"Do you think he was overwhelmed with the wedding preparations? He kept asking me to elope with him and end the madness. I should have listened to him." Tears filled Tara's eyes.

"There, there. You'll forget about him in no time." Jesse continued to comfort her friend while she glanced up at the clock over her stove. Fifteen minutes and still so much to do. "You'll see, tonight will be the beginning of something magical."

Tara pulled back. "You think?"

"You know me. I have a sixth sense when it comes to matching people up."

Tara gave her a skeptical look. "*You're* the one who fixed me up with Clint last year."

The heat of embarrassment singed Jesse's cheeks. "We all fail every once in a while. Just a temporary setback." She waved her hand in the air. "Look at Maggie and Neil. They're getting married next month. It all started here one evening at one of my little dinner parties."

"Don't get me wrong, but they haven't gotten married yet. They had a *loud* argument today at the bank. I wouldn't be surprised if the wedding was called off."

"They did?"

"Yeah. He was angry about the money she was spending on the wedding."

The timer on her stove buzzed. Jesse jumped, startled by the sound, but glad for the interruption. She would check with Maggie tomorrow to see what was going on. Her reputation was obviously at stake here. "I'd better get these cookies before they burn."

"Chocolate chip?"

"What other kind is there?" Jesse reached into the oven at the same time the doorbell chimed. "Can you get that? I have one more batch to stick in, then I'll be in the living room. Just make Nick and his daughter feel at home."

"It could be Susan Reed."

"Nah. Gramps went to pick her up. You know he takes forever."

Tara halted at the entrance into the kitchen. "Is there something going on there that I should know about?"

Jesse laughed. "Could be. They've been friends for a long time and are now finally dating. It's about time that Gramps got involved with someone." *So he will stop meddling in my life,* she added silently.

"*Now* I know why you asked Susan here this evening. You're killing two birds with one stone, so to speak."

The doorbell rang again.

"Go, before my guests decide I'm not home."

"He sure is impatient," Tara grumbled and made her way toward the front door.

While spooning cookie dough onto the baking sheet, Jesse tried to listen to the people in the foyer. It was awfully quiet for a good minute, then she heard Tara's raised voice. Not a good sign. Jesse quickly finished her task and stuck the cookies into the oven.

When a man's voice answered Tara, Jesse knew something had gone wrong. That wasn't Nick speaking. She remembered his voice—how could she forget such a deep, raspy baritone that sent chills down her spine? Hurrying into the living room, Jesse came to an abrupt halt just inside the doorway. Standing toe-to-toe in her house, hands balled at their sides, were Tara and Clint, both furiously whispering to each other.

"Clint, what are you doing here?" Jesse asked, wiping her hands on her sunflower apron. *I didn't invite you,* she silently added, visions of all her hard work that day going up in smoke.

He shot Jesse a narrowed look. "Coming to stop *my* woman from making a mistake."

"I'm having dinner. How can that be a mistake?" Tara's voice rose again. "And I'm not *your* woman. Not since you sped away from my house after calling our wedding off so fast you probably got whiplash."

"We all know why Jesse has these little dinner parties."

The doorbell sounded. Dread trembled through Jesse. Oh great, her guest of honor had finally arrived and World War III was about to erupt in her living room. "Shh, Clint. If you behave yourself, you can stay," Jesse said as she scurried past the couple, smoothing her apron down over her white pants.

"And watch Tara flirt—"

"Clint Clayborne, you heard Jesse. Quiet."

The man thankfully closed his mouth, but the mutinous expression on his face spoke volumes. This wasn't going to be the fun-packed evening she'd envisioned, Jesse thought as she plastered a wide smile on her face and pulled open her front door.

"I'm sorry I'm late, but I got a last-minute call I had to take."

Nick returned her smile with a heartwarming one that quickened her pulse. "That's okay. Gramps isn't back with Susan Reed yet. Come in." Jesse stood to the side to allow Nick, Cindy and an older man, with a completely bald head, to enter. She offered her hand to him. "You must be Boswell."

"Yes. It is a pleasure to meet you, Mrs. Bradshaw."

"Please, Jesse."

She eyed the man dressed in an impeccable black suit, even though it was nearly summer and the dinner was a casual affair. Boswell fit the bill perfectly for a proper English butler with a rich accent, she thought, and she decided her grandfather would have competition for Susan's interest. That might shake things up a bit tonight—not to mention Clint sending her dagger looks every time she glanced his way.

"Mom. I can't find Bingo." Her son came to a screeching halt in the hallway.

"Everyone, I'd like you to meet my son. Nate, this is Cindy, her father, Mr. Blackburn, and Mr. Boswell."

"Just Boswell, madam."

Barking followed by honking permeated the sudden silence. "I think Bingo is out back."

"He knows to stay away from Fred and Ethel." Nate hurried toward the kitchen.

"Please have a seat in the living room. I'd better check on Bingo," Jesse murmured, following her son.

Before she took two steps into the kitchen, the dog shot through the doggie door and raced past her as if monsters were on his tail. She heard one of her geese's familiar honking and realized the dog had narrowly escaped—again.

"I thought he learned his lesson the last time," Jesse muttered as her son rushed after his pet.

"I only have to have one confrontation with those…geese to know not to get within a hundred yards of them."

Jesse jumped, surprised at the sound of Nick's voice behind her. He had come into the kitchen through the dining room and stood framed in the entrance, looking wonderfully handsome in denim jeans and a casual light-blue knit shirt.

"Then you're smarter than Bingo."

"What a relief." He folded his arms across his chest and leaned against the doorjamb, a crooked grin on his face. "Can I help you with anything?"

"With Boswell in your employ, I don't see you asking to help out in the kitchen much."

"I know my way around. I can fend for myself if the need ever arises. Remember, I served you tea yesterday." Nick threw a glance over his shoulder and lowered his voice, "Besides, things are heating up in the living room and I thought I would give—the man and woman some privacy."

"Oh, you must mean Tara and Clint." She'd almost forgotten about them as though Nick's appearance had wiped her mind blank. "Where's Boswell and Cindy?"

"Cindy ran after Bingo and Boswell ran after Cindy."

"They're probably all in Nate's room by now trying to coax the dog out from under the bed. That's where he goes to hide from Fred and Ethel."

"Not a bad idea. Smart dog."

"I've got everything under control."

Nick's brows shot upward.

"The dinner, I mean."

"Are you sure?" He gestured toward the stove.

Jesse whirled about, the scent of burning cookies mocking her words. If she hadn't been so preoccupied with her new neighbor, her senses totally focused on him, she might have remembered she'd had them in the oven or at least smelled something was wrong before it was too late. He had a way of dominating her thoughts. Scary. She was definitely glad he was only going to be here a few months.

Rushing forward, she yanked open the door, smoke billowing out into the kitchen. She coughed, the blast of heat hitting her. Grabbing the hot pads, she pulled out the baking sheet with fifteen toasty, dark-brown chocolate chip cookies on it.

She dumped them in the kitchen sink along with the baking sheet, then turned to find Nick not two feet behind her. Heat scored her cheeks, and she attributed it to the oven temperature bathing her face not seconds before, not to the fact he was so near that she actually could smell his clean, fresh scent with a hint of lime. It vied with the scent of scorched cookies and definitely was a much more pleasant aroma.

"Thankfully that's only one batch of the cookies. Dessert isn't completely ruined." She fought a strong urge to fan herself and instead flipped on the exhaust fan over the stove.

He scanned the kitchen which was neat and clean

with little evidence of any meal preparation having taken place. "What are we having tonight?"

"Aren't cookies enough? Granted, I don't have as many as I wanted, but I think each person will have at least three of them."

"A virtual feast. You'll get no protest from Cindy."

"And you?"

He shifted and leaned against the counter, taking his weight off his right leg. "I may need a bit more nourishment."

"Well, in that case, I have a potato salad, hamburgers and baked beans. I thought that would suit the children better. Now that the cookies are done, I'll put the beans in the oven and start the grill." She moved toward the refrigerator and took a casserole dish out.

"Grill them? Out back?"

Jesse peered at him as she placed the beans on the rack in the oven. "Yes."

"With those mon—geese?"

"The grill is on the deck. I thought we would eat out there, too. The evening is lovely. Fred and Ethel won't bother us."

"Weren't they just out on the deck chasing Bingo?"

"No, they always stop short of coming up the steps."

"You couldn't tell from the racket they were making."

"When night comes, they settle down."

"Night isn't for a few more hours."

She straightened, looking him directly in the eyes. "Trust me. You'll be fine."

"I'm not worried about myself, but Cindy was very upset yesterday morning."

"I know, but I want her to feel comfortable over here. Fred and Ethel will stay by the lake and their nest. I promise." She sensed the little girl needed a woman's influence right now in her life. She could never turn her back on a child in need. She intended to befriend Cindy while she was here. "If you want to help, you can bring the tray in the refrigerator out onto the deck while I check to make sure Tara and Clint are all right."

Nick pushed away from the counter. "I haven't heard any sounds from the living room in the past five minutes."

"No, and that has me worried. They were engaged and Clint called it off the other day, just weeks before they were to be married. Claimed he wasn't ready for marriage."

"Smart guy."

Jesse halted at the entrance into the dining room. She remembered Cindy's words about wishing she had a mother. "You don't believe in marriage?"

"It's fine for some people, but I'm not one of them."

The bitterness in his voice caused her heart to ache for the pain he must have endured. What had made him so against marriage? His late wife? Her death? She recalled her own anger after her husband had died. But she was definitely over that. She had been lucky to have one good marriage. The Lord had been good to her and she wanted to share the bounty. She wanted others to have what she'd had.

She escaped into the dining room, warily approaching the living room. She didn't hear any voices. Had they done bodily harm to each other? Clint had been furious that Tara was at one of her little dinner parties. When Jesse stepped into the room, she stopped at the doorway. Clint's arms were wrapped around Tara, his lips locked to hers, their bodies pressed together. The couple didn't even hear her come in nor sense her, so absorbed were they in each other. She was happy for her friend, but now, who was she going to find for Nick? The man needed a good woman to ease the pain in his heart. And Cindy needed a mother.

Deciding she had to rethink her strategy, Jesse started to back out of the living room when Clint and Tara came up for air. Her friend peered over at her and smiled.

"Clint ask me to run off and get married and I said yes." Tara's eyes were bright with happiness. "We're leaving tonight. Not a word to anyone until tomorrow, Jesse."

She held up her hands. "Not a peep out of me. Promise."

Clint threw her a perturbed look. "I should be really mad at you, Jesse, but I guess this dinner you planned knocked some sense into me, so for that reason you'll be welcome in our home." He drew Tara against him. "We need to get moving before Susan gets here."

Tara hurried to Jesse and hugged her. "You know just the right thing to do. What a matchmaker you are! I owe you."

The couple was gone before Jesse could blink. Okay,

this was a success. Not quite the one she had planned for the evening, but a match had been made. She would end this evening early and start over tomorrow. There had to be someone for Nick Blackburn, someone special who could change his mind about marriage and give Cindy what she wanted.

His leg ached. Sinking onto a chair on the deck, Nick rubbed it. The two geese were keeping a wary eye on him and he was keeping a wary eye on them out in the yard under a giant maple with a tree house in it and a large sign posted that read, No Girls Alowed. He chuckled at the sign on the ladder leading up to the tree house. What a cool place to escape to and play in. As a boy he would have liked it. But his childhood had been very different from Jesse's son's.

He couldn't believe he was even here this evening. He was doing it for his daughter who had taken a liking to Jesse. She needed a woman's influence in her life and most likely wasn't going to have one when they returned to Chicago in a few months.

Just this morning Cindy asked him about makeup. Six years old! His baby! He had told her she was years—and *years*—away from wearing any. She had wanted to know where her mother's was. That had stopped him cold. He had hated to tell her he'd thrown it out. The look on his daughter's face made him regret doing it in a fit of anger after he'd come home from the hospital that first time.

The throbbing in his leg reinforced his determination

to wipe his wife from his memory. The only good thing that had come of their marriage was Cindy, but what was he supposed to do with a little girl? He felt out of his element. He was at home in a boardroom, not playing dolls with his daughter.

He was determined to bond with Cindy one way or another these next couple of months. He owed her that after the past year with him in and out of the hospital having several surgeries on his leg or with him working long hours at his company because of all the time he had been injured. Now at least, he had a good team in place who could run the business while he kept in touch long distance. The only thing he needed to figure out was how he was going to accomplish bonding with his only child.

"I hope you're hungry. I think I prepared enough to feed half of Sweetwater."

Shoving away those memories he usually kept locked up, Nick turned his full attention to the petite woman hurrying across the deck toward him. She reminded him of a breath of fresh air. He liked her straightforward manner, something he wasn't used to in a woman. With his wife he'd never been sure what mood she would be in. Their last year of marriage, all they had done was argue.

"I can probably eat my fair share." He pushed to his feet, ignoring the dull throb that he hadn't managed to massage away.

Favoring his leg, he made his way to the propane grill, ready to assist Jesse. After she lit the grill, she slapped the hamburgers on the metal rack and stood back. He took a deep breath, inhaling her particular scent of jasmine. It teased his senses, reminding him he hadn't been around too many women socially this past year. He wanted to lean close and take another deep breath. He didn't.

Needing some space, he stepped to the railing, his back to her. He stared at the lake, its smooth, blue water having a calming effect on him. "It looks like you have everything under control."

"Yeah. Gramps accuses me of being a control freak. I'm not. Just very organized."

"So am I. I find it's easier to run a company that way."

"And a house." She came to stand next to him.

Her arm brushed against his. He tensed, the feel of her electric. He sidled a step away, a finely honed tension bolting through him. "Where's everyone? Still trying to coax Bingo out from under the bed?"

"I'm sure by now Nate is showing off his animal collection to Cindy and Boswell. Tara and Clint left. And I'm not sure where my grandfather is. He should have been home fifteen minutes—"

The sound of the back door opening interrupted Jesse. She turned at the same time Nick did and ended up touching him again. She shivered from the brief contact. The deck ran the whole length of the house, and they couldn't manage not to brush against each other?

"There you are, Gramps. We were just wondering where you were."

"Susan had something to show me. Lost track of time."

"I'm so glad you could come tonight, Susan." Jesse offered the older woman a bright smile she hoped would cover her sudden nervousness at the nearness of her neighbor. Stepping forward, she made the introductions.

"I wouldn't miss one of your little dinner parties for the world," Susan said as she checked out Nick. "It's so much better to get the latest firsthand."

Jesse blushed, aware that Nick was suddenly staring at her.

"Where's Tara?" Gramps asked, breaking the silence that had followed Susan's declaration.

"She had to leave—with Clint."

"Clint!" Susan exclaimed. "My, my, that does shake things up tonight. What are you going to do, my dear?"

Nick came up behind Jesse and said in a low voice, "Why do I get the feeling I'm missing something here?"

Jesse tried to ignore his question while she thought of an appropriate answer for Susan. "Not a thing. We're going to eat soon and enjoy each other's company. I'm tickled pink that Tara and Clint are back together." Jesse was sure her cheeks were past the pink stage. Cherry-red was more like it.

"You should be. You fixed them up in the first place." Gramps took Susan's hand and led her to the love seat where the tortilla chips and guacamole dip were on a glass table in front of them. He began to munch.

If her grandfather kept his mouth full, maybe she would make it through this evening without Nick realizing she'd planned for him to meet and hopefully date

Tara. Of course, there was always Susan, who was a fountain of information and loved spewing it. Jesse was positive that Nick wouldn't appreciate knowing he was part of one of her matchmaking schemes, especially after his earlier comment concerning marriage.

Why was he so against marriage?

"Jesse, dear, I think you should turn the hamburgers." Susan scooped up some dip on a chip and popped it into her mouth.

Caught off guard, Jesse spun about and hurried toward the grill. She flipped the patties over, grimacing when she noticed the slightly charred side. "I really can cook, Nick. I've been distracted this evening. Normally one of my parties goes over without a hitch."

"How often do you entertain?" Nick asked, amusement dancing in his eyes.

"Oh, whenever the urge strikes me." She waved her hand in the air as though to dismiss the subject as unimportant and hoped no one commented.

"I have to admit, this is a beautiful setting for a dinner. I had my doubts about eating outside with those two so near." Nick tossed his head in the direction of the geese now waddling toward the lake. "But you were right. They're staying away."

Fred flapped his wings as though he knew he was being discussed. Jesse chuckled. "You probably shouldn't take a tour of my backyard any time soon."

"You'll have no argument from me."

The back door burst open again, and the children, followed by Boswell, came out onto the deck. Cindy and Nate raced toward them, skidding to a halt a foot in front of them.

Cindy grinned, showing her missing front tooth. "Daddy, you should see Nate's room. He has so many pets. I got to hold Julia, Rita and Sadie. They're gerbils. Julia went to the bathroom on Boswell."

Jesse swallowed her laugh and tried her best to keep a straight face. Looking at Boswell, she noticed a wet spot on his black suit coat. "I'm sorry. She does that sometimes when she's picked up. Nate should have warned you."

"It must have slipped his mind." Boswell sent a censured look toward Nate.

"It did, Mom. Promise."

"I just came out here to tell you, Mr. Blackburn, that I'm going back to the house to change."

"Sure." Nick, too, was having a hard time keeping his mirth to himself if the gleam glittering in his eyes was any indication.

"Please, begin eating without me. I know the children are hungry."

When Boswell disappeared, Jesse and Nick couldn't contain their laughter any longer. "I wish I could have seen his expression when that happened," Jesse said, wiping the tears from her eyes.

"His face turned real red." Nate grabbed a handful of chips and stuffed them into his mouth.

"I never saw Boswell move so fast." Cindy giggled. "I wanted to play with the animals longer, but Boswell thought we should join the adults."

"Is Boswell a nanny?" Susan asked.

Cindy pulled her father over to the other love seat. "Oh, no. Boswell is a *manservant*," she answered in a serious tone as though she had been corrected before about Boswell's role and wouldn't make that mistake again.

While Nick and Cindy got to know her family, Jesse finished the dinner preparations and put the food on the long picnic table she'd already set earlier. She removed Tara's place setting, genuinely happy for her friend. Tara wouldn't have been right for Nick, Jesse decided, now that she knew him better. Tara was flighty and so absentminded that she would have driven Nick crazy after the first date. No, she would have to find someone more disciplined and in control, more organized.

God, please help me to find someone for Nick, someone to be a good mother for Cindy.

As she called the others to the table, the perfect match came to Jesse's mind. Felicia Winters, the lady with the kittens, and Jesse knew how she could get them together without raising Nick's suspicion with another dinner party. She smiled as she sat between Gramps and Nate and across from Nick. She looked right into his dark eyes and shivered. He was staring at her with an intense, probing gaze as though he were trying to read what was going on in her mind. Heavens, she couldn't have that!

"Do you think Boswell will come back?" Nate asked after Jesse said the prayer. He bit down on his hamburger, managing to stuff a third of it into his mouth.

"Young man, this isn't a race to see who finishes first." Jesse passed the baked beans to Gramps.

Her son stopped chewing for a few seconds, then swallowed his food, making a gulping sound. Jesse rolled her eyes and hoped she didn't run out of patience.

Nate slurped some of his milk, leaving a white mustache on his face. "Sorry, Mom."

She unfolded his napkin and gave it to him. "Please wipe your mouth."

"Jesse, he's doing fine. He's just being a boy."

Jesse resisted the urge to nudge her grandfather in the side to keep him quiet. Instead, she sent him a narrowed look. She loved Gramps, but he wasn't the best role model for her son. Thankfully he wasn't cussing like he used to. When he'd first come to live with them three years before, she remembered having to cover her son's ears on more than one occasion.

"Mr. Blackburn, do you think Boswell will be coming back?" Nate asked again after wiping the napkin across his mouth. Her son took a smaller bite of his hamburger this time.

"He rarely passes up a meal he doesn't have to cook."

"Boswell cooks?" Nate screwed his face into an expression of disbelief. "Gramps wouldn't be caught dead in the kitchen."

"He does more than cook. He takes care of Cindy and me."

A frown creased Nate's forehead. "He's a maid?"

Nick leaned forward. "I wouldn't say that too loud. He doesn't like to be referred to as a maid."

"But that's what he is," Gramps cut in between bites of his baked beans.

This time Jesse did nudge her grandfather in the side.

He grunted. "Well, child, if he cleans up the house, he's doing the work of a maid. If he ain't proud of his job, then he shouldn't do it."

"I'm very proud of my vocation," Boswell said from the steps that led up onto the deck.

Gramps shot him a suspicious glance. "I wouldn't be hanging around down there too long. No telling when Fred will—"

"Gramps! You know Fred isn't that bad. Don't scare Cindy."

Her grandfather mumbled something under his breath and resumed eating.

"I'm not scared," Cindy announced to the silent table of people.

Boswell sat next to Susan Reed and smiled at her as he placed his napkin in his lap. "I must say the aroma coming from here would entice anyone to crash this party."

"I love your British accent. How long have you been in this country?" Susan asked, her whole face lit with a smile.

Gramps muttered something else, just low enough that no one else could hear. Jesse was thinking about stomping on his foot to keep him quiet, but decided nothing would keep her grandfather quiet if he chose otherwise.

"Twenty years."

"Then you're practically an American."

Boswell looked shocked at even the thought of not

being considered English. He tightened his mouth while his hand clutched his fork, his knuckles white.

"This is the best—" her grandfather paused, groping for the right words to say with children listening "—country in the world," he interjected in the conversation between Boswell and Susan.

Boswell's face turned beet-red. His knuckles whitened even more around the fork still clenched in his hand.

Jesse knew the Revolutionary War was about to be fought again on her deck. She shot to her feet, her napkin floating to the bench. "Gramps, will you help me with the dessert?"

"I'm not through yet. Besides, what can be so hard about carrying a tray of cookies?"

"I—" She couldn't think of anything to say.

"I'll help you." Nick stood, walked by Boswell and leaned down to whisper something in the man's ear.

Jesse followed Nick into the kitchen. "I don't know if it's wise to leave my grandfather and Boswell out there together. When Gramps gets going—" She let the implied threat trail off into silence.

Nick's chuckle was low. "I believe Boswell can hold his own. I reminded him that Cindy and Nate were listening."

"I wish that would work with my grandfather. He told me when he turned seventy a few years back that he had earned the privilege of speaking his mind whenever he wanted. I've gotten him to tone down his language, but even that was a battle. I love my grandfather, but he isn't always the best male example for my son." She peered out the window at the group left on the deck. "Well, I guess what you said worked. The two men are still seated and I don't hear any shouting."

"That's a good sign."

"I really don't need your help. I was just trying to get Gramps away from the table."

"Really?" One of his dark eyebrows quirked.

"And as usual, it didn't work." Jesse walked to the refrigerator to retrieve the gallon of homemade peach ice cream she and Nate had made earlier that day. "If you want, you can get the bowls from the cabinet and some spoons from that drawer." She gestured toward the one next to the dishwasher.

She slid a glance toward him as he opened the cabinet. They were alone. This was her chance to see about the kitten for Cindy and set her plan in motion for him to meet Felicia. She noticed the sure way he executed his task as though he was very familiar with her kitchen. This man seemed at home anywhere— even when Fred was attacking him yesterday morning. His well-built body—whoa! That wasn't what she was supposed to be doing, ogling her guest, a guest she was planning to fix up with Felicia.

Jesse tore her gaze away from him and asked, "Have you made up your mind about the kitten for Cindy?" There she was back on track with her plan—Felicia and Nick.

Chapter Three

"I don't think I have much choice." Nick placed the bowls and spoons on the counter.

"You always have a choice. I've got a feeling you're never backed into a corner that you don't want to be in." Jesse cradled the ice-cream container against her chest while retrieving the tray of chocolate chip cookies. The cold felt good against her. It seemed to be unusually hot in the kitchen.

"True, especially in business. But this is personal and it involves my daughter. She wants a pet bad. I suppose a kitten is better than a dog, snake or gerbil, and Boswell agreed with me."

"Then you'll get Cindy a kitten?"

"Yes. You said you knew where I could get one."

She nodded. "We can go tomorrow afternoon. I'll call Felicia and arrange it."

Nick opened the back door and let Jesse go first.

"Don't say anything yet to Cindy. I want it to be a surprise. I don't think she would get a wink of sleep if she knew she was going to pick out a kitten tomorrow."

"My lips are sealed." Jesse pressed them together to emphasize her point, but it was hard for her to contain her happiness. Her plan was back on track. Tomorrow he would meet Felicia and be impressed with her knack for organization. Her home was spotless.

Okay, so maybe Felicia was just a little bit too organized and obsessed with having a clean house, Jesse thought. The sound of the sofa cover crunching beneath her when she sat on Felicia's couch punctuated the silence with that declaration. The plastic stuck to the backs of Jesse's legs and made her conscious of her every move.

The simple act of crossing her ankles and smoothing her shorts down drew Nick's attention. One corner of his mouth lifted. For a few seconds his gaze ensnared hers, and she felt as though they were the only two people in the room. His way of drawing a person's focus to him must be a valuable tool in the business world. In her world, it was disconcerting, Jesse decided.

"I'm so tickled you want to give one of my babies a home." Felicia straightened a stack of magazines on the coffee table. The top one sat at a slight angle from the others. Definitely out of place. "I won't give my babies away to just anyone. Thankfully Jesse can vouch for you."

Somehow Felicia managed to cross her legs, the silence from her action indicating a certain degree of grace that Jesse obviously didn't possess or the fact this woman had had a lot of practice sitting on her plastic covers. Jesse wanted to believe it was the latter.

"Have you ever had a pet before?" Felicia asked, cutting into Jesse's musing.

"No, but I'm sure we'll be able to manage," he answered with all the confidence of a man who was used to running a large company.

"You have to do more than just manage. You have to love your pet." One of Felicia's cats curled herself around the woman's leg, purring. She picked up her pet and buried her face in its fur.

"I can do that," Cindy chimed in, bouncing several times in her enthusiasm.

The sound reverberating through the room drew Felicia's look. The "look" would have made anyone freeze, Jesse thought, and she began to reassess her friend's candidacy for Cindy's mother. Glancing about, Jesse wondered if Felicia spent every wakened moment cleaning her house. The thought sent a shiver through Jesse. She hated cleaning her house and avoided it whenever possible.

Maybe she was being too harsh in her judgment of Felicia. After all, the woman loved cats and anyone who was an animal lover must have room in her heart for children. Jesse stood. "Why don't Cindy and I go pick out a kitten while you and Nick work out the details?" Jesse took the little girl's hand and quickly left the living room. Nick and Felicia needed time alone to get to know each other.

The four kittens were out in the sunroom. One was sleeping on the white ceramic tiled floor, two were prowling and the last one was playing with a piece of gold ribbon. The black kitten with a white mark on its forehead batted the ribbon, chasing it around. Cindy laughed and went over to it. It stopped to check the little girl's lacy socks, licking her leg. She laughed again and picked up the kitten. Jesse noticed the cat was a male.

"I want this one. What do you think?" Cindy cuddled him to her face. "Oh, she's so cute."

"It's a male."

"How can you tell?"

Jesse wasn't prepared to go into the facts of life with Cindy. For a second, nothing came to mind. "He's made differently," she blurted out, sweat beading on her upper lip.

"Oh." Cindy seemed to accept that lame reason, hugging the kitten to her. "Let's go show Daddy."

So much for giving Nick and Felicia time to get to know each other. Jesse searched her mind for a delay tactic. "Don't you want to check out the other kittens to make sure he's the one?"

Cindy shook her head. "I know."

Jesse stood for another minute in the middle of the sunroom, before saying, "Then I guess we should show your dad." Hopefully five minutes was long enough for them to strike up a…friendship. Suddenly the idea of a relationship between Nick and Felicia didn't seem right and that thought bothered Jesse.

When she and Cindy entered the living room, silence

hung in the air, Nick's expression neutral. Felicia looked as though she were sitting in a dentist's chair waiting for the drill. Jesse plastered a smile on her face, intending to get the conversation going.

Nick shot to his feet. "We'll take good care of the kitten. Are you sure you don't want any money, Miss Winters?"

Miss Winters? Not a good sign.

Felicia straightened, bristling at his suggestion. "No. A good home is all I request, as I told you a few minutes ago, Mr. Blackburn."

Mr. Blackburn? *Definitely* not a good sign.

"I'll take real good care of Oreo," Cindy said, nuzzling the kitten.

At the door Nick stooped to slip on his shoes while Jesse put hers on then held Oreo so Cindy could buckle her sandals. When Felicia had asked them to take off their shoes before coming into her house, Jesse should have realized the meeting would go downhill from that moment. Nick had started to say something but snapped his jaws closed. That hadn't stopped Cindy from blurting out the question they had all wanted to know, "Why?"

"Goodness me. You might get some dirt on my carpet," Felicia had answered.

Well, one good thing came of this visit, Jesse decided as the door closed behind them. Cindy had her kitten. That had to be worth something.

"An interesting woman," Nick commented as they walked to Jesse's car. "I'm surprised she has cats in her house. Won't they track in dirt?"

"Her cats never go out."

"I see."

Jesse doubted it. She really needed to try one more time. "Felicia's very nice and good with animals…well, cats at least."

"I'm sure she is."

"She's the town librarian. Every Saturday she has a story hour for the children. She's quite good at reading to them. Nate loves to go. Maybe Cindy could go with him next Saturday."

"I'll see," he said as though he wasn't certain he wanted his daughter within a hundred yards of the neat freak whose house they were standing in front of, not a blade of grass out of place.

Nick finished his last leg lift and pushed to his feet. Sweat drenched him. Taking a towel and wiping his face and neck, he stared out the picture window that faced Jesse's house. He saw her climb the steps to the deck and enter her kitchen, her movement a graceful extension of her lithe body. With her brown hair cut short and feathered about her face, her large green eyes and ready smile emphasized her pixie look.

He remembered the time he'd seen Jesse right after he'd finished his physical therapy exercises. He couldn't believe it had only been five days ago. She was all Cindy talked about—besides her kitten and her new friend, Nate. Suddenly he seemed surrounded by Jesse and her family. And the last thing he needed or wanted was another woman in his life. He was still piecing his life back together after his accident and his unhappy marriage to Brenda.

He turned away from the picture window and limped toward the door, determined to accomplish two things this summer: get to know his daughter better and get back to being one hundred percent after the last operation on his leg. For two months he'd promised to devote himself to those two tasks. He could run Blackburn Industries from here for that short amount of time. He would have to leave the everyday affairs of his company to his capable staff, but he already had been doing that since the accident. Cindy needed this. He needed this.

"Daddy! Daddy!" Cindy slid to a halt, tears streaming down her face.

He knelt in front of her, the action intensifying the pain in his leg. He ignored it and clasped his daughter's arms. "What's wrong, princess?"

"Oreo's gone!"

Jesse kneaded the dough, flipped it over and started all over again, shoving her palms into it. She pounded her frustration out on the soon-to-be loaf of bread. Still no one came to mind as a possible candidate for Nick and time was running out. He would only be here seven more weeks. Courting a potential wife didn't happen overnight. Of course, it would help if he left his house more often. Then she might have a better chance of fixing him up with someone.

Who? That was the problem. She had been so

wrong about Tara and Felicia. The third one was the charm. But who?

She placed the dough in a blue ceramic mixing bowl and covered it with a damp cloth. The doorbell chimed. She quickly washed her hands, then hurried to answer it.

The worry on Nick's face prompted her to ask, "Is something wrong with Cindy?"

"Yes—I mean, no, not her exactly. Oreo. He's gone. We can't find him and she's beside herself. You haven't seen him, have you?"

"No." She stepped out onto the porch and automatically scanned the area as though that would produce the errant kitten.

"I thought so, but I had to ask. I'm desperate. I promised Cindy I wouldn't come home until I found Oreo. I've been up and down the street, along the lakeshore. Nothing."

"What happened?"

"Oreo darted out the front door when Cindy came back from playing with Nate this morning."

"I'll get Gramps and Nate. We'll come over and make some posters to put up around town. Cindy can help with them. It'll make her feel better if she's doing something."

"When I left, she was in her room crying. She didn't want to talk or do anything."

"I'll get the supplies we need and be right over."

"What should I do in the meantime?"

"Hold Cindy."

"I tried. She cried even louder."

"That's okay. Hold her anyway." Jesse rushed back into her house to gather some poster board, markers and her family.

When they arrived at Nick's house, Boswell immediately opened the door before Jesse had a chance to ring the bell. Silence greeted her as she entered. She hoped that meant that Cindy had calmed down.

As Boswell closed the door, the little girl, with Nick following, rushed into the foyer, her eyes bright with unshed tears. "You think we'll be able to find Oreo? Daddy said you're gonna help."

The eager hopefulness in the child's voice touched Jesse. She hated making promises she couldn't keep, but it was hard not to say what Cindy wanted to hear. "If Oreo is in Sweetwater, we'll find him."

Heavenly Father, please help me find Oreo. Cindy has already lost a lot in her short life. I know I just made a promise I might not be able to keep. Please help me to keep this one promise.

"What if—"

Jesse laid her hand on the child's shoulder. "No what-ifs. That's wasted energy. We need to make some posters to put up around town and then form search teams to scour the area."

"Then let's get going." Cindy took Jesse's hand and dragged her toward the kitchen.

Jesse threw a glance over her shoulder at the rest of the group who remained standing in the foyer. "You heard her. Hop to it."

The children sat on the floor in the kitchen and made posters while the adults used the counter and table. Cindy copied off Nate and drew a kitten that looked more like a dog.

Nick leaned close to Jesse and whispered, "Do you think this will help?"

Jesse got a whiff of his clean, fresh scent with that hint of lime. Her pulse rate kicked up a notch. This was a rescue mission, nothing more, she reminded herself and said, "I wouldn't be doing it if I didn't. The people in this town are wonderful. When they hear that Oreo is missing, they'll help look, too. This is the best way to get the news out. That and talk to whomever we see while we're putting the posters up."

Doubt reflected in his gaze, Nick went back to work, absently massaging his thigh.

"Is your leg bothering you?"

"Nothing I can't handle."

Jesse wondered about that as she studied the tired lines on his face and the pinched look he wore. He'd already been out looking for the kitten.

"I think it might rain later. I have more trouble when the weather is about to change."

"Then we'd better hurry and get these posters up. We can probably put them in some storefront windows so if it rains it won't matter."

When the group was finished, Cindy wanted to go with Nate and Gramps while Boswell was going to check out the lake area again. Jesse and Nick decided to go in the opposite direction from the children and

Gramps. They were all to meet at Harry's Café on Main Street when they were through.

As they started to go their different ways, Cindy said, "Boswell, please don't go near Fred and Ethel."

The older man smiled. "I wouldn't think of it, Miss Cindy."

"Oh." The little girl brought her hand up to cover her mouth, her eyes growing round. "What if Oreo went close to Fred and Ethel? Shouldn't someone check?"

Jesse bent down in front of Cindy. "Believe me. We would have heard a ruckus if Oreo had. But if it will make you feel better, I can check."

The tears returned to Cindy's eyes. "Please."

"Then that's my first stop." She started to stand up.

Cindy tugged on Jesse's arm, stopping her, and whispered in her ear, "Please don't let Daddy get too close. I don't want him hurt again."

A lump jammed in Jesse's throat. "I'll take good care of your father."

"He might not be able to walk very far. His leg's hurting him. It always does after he does his exercises. He'll need to rest, but he'll act like he doesn't."

Surprised at the child's keen observation and assessment of her father, Jesse gave her a reassuring look. "I'll make it seem like it's my idea."

Satisfied that her father would be taken care of, Cindy hurried to Gramps and Nate at the end of the driveway. Boswell took off toward the lake.

Nick came up beside Jesse. "What was that all about?"

"Nothing. Just girl talk."

"Girl talk?" He shook his head. "In the middle of all of this?"

"Let's go. I told Cindy I would check the area by Fred and Ethel's nest first, but you have to stay back."

"Believe me, I didn't have any intentions of going near those two."

Nick followed Jesse around back of her house and waited by the deck while she approached the two geese. They never took their eyes off her, but they remained quiet while she surveyed the area for she wasn't sure what. Everyone would have heard if Oreo had come near Fred and Ethel. But a promise was a promise.

As Jesse made her way back to Nick, his gaze fixed on her and her pulse rate responded as it had earlier. For a few seconds she felt as though they were the only two people in the world. He had a way of stripping away the rest of mankind with merely a look. The intensity in his eyes unnerved her. She wasn't even sure he was aware of it. It cut through defensive layers that protected her heart and was very confounding. When she'd lost Mark she vowed she would never put herself in that position again. The pain of losing her husband had been too much. Sticking to that promise had kept her safe for the past four years.

"All clear," she said, eager to get their search started. There were lots of people in town and suddenly she needed to be around a lot of people. She might even be able to come up with a third candidate for Nick while they looked for Oreo.

As Nick nailed up the posters, Jesse stopped various townspeople to let them know they were looking for a lost kitten, all black except for a patch of white above his eyes. She assessed the women they encountered as possible candidates, but none were suitable.

"Do you know everyone in town?" Nick asked as he hammered another poster to a telephone pole.

"Practically, but then I've lived all my thirty-two years here."

"I've lived all my thirty-five years in Chicago, and I don't know everyone there."

Jesse chuckled. "Not the same thing. A few million more in population can make a difference."

He eyed her. "I'm beginning to wonder with you if it would. Have you ever met a stranger?"

"Sure. You."

Nick favored his right leg more than usual as he walked beside her down the street. He tried not to act as if it were bothering him, but Jesse noticed, had for the past three blocks. That was why she had taken a shortcut to the café. She'd promised Cindy she would look after Nick—whether the man wanted her to or not. And she suspected he would be appalled if he knew what she was thinking.

She stopped in front of Harry's Café. "Let's take a break. The rest of the group should be here soon."

Nick hesitated, surveying the street as if he were checking to make sure every pole had a poster on it.

"It's been a long day. I was up unusually early this morning. I need to refuel. I could use a cup of coffee."

She realized six wasn't unusually early in some people's book, but she normally slept until six-thirty so it wasn't a lie. Actually she'd tossed and turned a good part of the night, trying to get her neighbor and his problem out of her brain. She hadn't been very successful so she could use a shot of caffeine to keep going.

Nick opened the door for her and trailed her into the café to a booth along the front window. He slid in across from Jesse, the pinched look about his mouth easing some as he sat. For a few seconds Jesse found herself wanting to soothe away the tired lines about his eyes. She quickly flipped open the menu she knew by heart and studied it.

"I'm starved. I think I'll get a piece of pecan pie, too. They have the best pecan pie in the state here. Goes great with coffee." Jesse was beginning to wonder if Millie, one of the people they had met while passing out posters, had rubbed off on her. First, she was avoiding eye contact with Nick and now she was chattering away nonstop. Next, she would start giggling.

She needed to find a woman for him. Then maybe she wouldn't think about him all the time!

The waitress came over and took their orders. Jesse studied the young woman who was the café owner Rose's niece from Louisville and immediately dismissed her as a candidate. She was too young and, according to her aunt Rose, wild. She wouldn't be a good influence on Cindy.

As the waitress brought them their cups of coffee, the door opened and in walked Beth Coleman. Jesse caught her friend's eye and motioned her to their booth. Beth was quiet, direct and sensible. She was also a very attractive woman with shoulder-length blond hair and sky-blue eyes. She might be just right for Nick. Why hadn't Jesse thought of her before now?

"Beth, it's so good to see you," Jesse said with more enthusiasm than usual.

"We just saw each other yesterday at the grocery store."

Jesse cleared her throat. "I'd like you to meet Nick Blackburn. He's staying in the Millers' house for the summer. Why don't you join us?" She scooted over to give Beth some room to sit.

Her friend hesitated for a few seconds, then took a seat next to Jesse. "I'll join you until Darcy arrives. I needed to talk to you anyway about making one of your dolls for the Fourth of July charity auction at the church. Will you contribute again this year?"

"Of course. I've already started on the doll. I should have it done in a week or so." Jesse looked across at Nick. "Beth's a great organizer. Every year she almost single-handedly puts together a charity auction to benefit the needy families in our area. She also teaches high school English. On the side she teaches art to the young children in the summer. She's quite talented. Beth's so good with children any age." Had she left anything out? Had she made her sound too good to be true? Was she losing her touch as a matchmaker?

Beth blushed a deep scarlet.

"It's nice to meet you. I think I've met half the town

today." Nick took a sip of his coffee, a thoughtful expression on his face.

"Jesse's a great one to introduce you around town. I think she knows more about me than I do. Maybe I should take you along on my next job interview."

Panicked her friend might be leaving town, Jesse said, "Nate has a few years to go before he gets to high school. He's got to have you for English. You aren't looking for another job, are you?"

Beth laughed. "You never know."

Jesse studied her friend for a moment, wondering what she meant by that answer. "Nick has a six-year-old daughter. It might be nice if she joined one of your classes this summer. Nate's taking the art class. It starts next week. What's nice is that the parents can participate with the children."

"I'm a firm believer that parents and children should do a lot of activities together. I have a few openings still in the art class if you're interested, Mr. Blackburn."

"That really will have to be Cindy's choice. I'll talk to her about it."

His gaze narrowed onto Jesse. She tried not to squirm under its intensity, but it was difficult to sit still.

"Just let Jesse know. She can tell you how to sign up your daughter." Beth rose, waving toward someone entering the café. "I see Darcy. I'd better go. We still have a lot of planning to do for the auction. It's only a month away." She hurried toward Darcy Markham.

Jesse ignored Nick—or rather his glare—and watched her best friend from high school fix her gaze on her and Nick in the booth. She could see a surprised expression descend on Darcy's face. Bypassing the table Beth had snagged for them, Darcy headed straight toward Jesse.

"Okay, Jesse Bradshaw, what's going on here?" Nick asked, his deep, raspy voice compelling her to look away from her friend and toward him.

Chapter Four

Jesse wanted to say, "Quick. Hide me," before Darcy reached the table, but instead she found her voice snatched away at the intensity in Nick's dark eyes. She wished she didn't blush so easily because she felt the effects burned into her cheeks as Nick stared at her and Darcy who would never let it go that she was having coffee with a man. Just because Darcy was deliriously happy now that she was married to Joshua didn't mean everyone else had to be. Where her best friend got that idea was beyond Jesse—well, maybe she did know since she usually felt that way, except for herself.

Darcy stopped at the table. "Jesse, I'm so glad to see you today. I had a brainstorm last night and was going to call you after I talked with Beth about it. I—"

Darcy's voice faded into the silence. Jesse tore her gaze from Nick's and looked at her friend who swung her attention from Jesse to Nick then back. "Have I interrupted something?"

Jesse saw the gleam sparkle in Darcy's eyes and immediately said, "No, we were just waiting for Cindy, Nate, Boswell and Gramps to show up."

"I know who Nate and Gramps are. Who are Cindy and Boswell?"

"Cindy is my daughter and Boswell works for me." Nick held out his hand. "I'm Nick Blackburn, Jesse's neighbor."

"Oh," Darcy said, drawing that one simple word out and putting more meaning into it than she normally would. "I'm Darcy Markham. I've known Jesse for years. We went to school together."

While Nick wrapped his hand around Darcy's and shook it, Jesse asked, "What did you want to tell me?" hoping that would take her friend's mind off what was obviously dancing about inside Darcy's head. Jesse had been a matchmaker too long not to see the signs in another, and she was not going to be a party to anyone trying to fix her up.

Darcy dragged her attention from Nick and regarded Jesse. "We can talk later. I wouldn't want to interrupt anything." She started to leave.

Jesse caught her arm and held her in place. "No way, Darcy Markham."

Her friend grinned. "Say that again."

"What? *No way?* Or *Darcy Markham?*"

"Darcy Markham." A dreamy look glazed Darcy's eyes.

"Darcy just got married a few months ago—

actually Valentine's Day, so you have to forgive her getting sidetracked when you say her new name. Now, back to my original question, what did you need to tell me?"

"I thought we would form a group, maybe meet Saturday afternoons to talk."

"Who, you and me? We talk all the time."

"I thought maybe you, me, Beth, Zoey and Tanya. Zoey and I just moved back to Sweetwater and Tanya— well, she could use some—" Darcy glanced away then back "—some support. I'd better go. I'll talk with Beth about it and get back to you later. Nice to meet you, Mr. Blackburn." Darcy hurried toward Beth seated at a table near the door.

Jesse watched her friend for a few seconds longer. There was more to this group than Darcy was willing to say in front of Nick.

"I'm beginning to think you really *do* know everyone in Sweetwater." Nick's voice cut into her thoughts and pulled her attention away from Darcy and toward him. "Of course, I haven't met Zoey or Tanya yet, but I do think I met everyone else today while hanging up posters."

Jesse shifted in her seat in the booth. "We had to get the word out about Oreo. I wonder where everyone else is."

Nick stared out the large plate glass window that ran the length of the front of the café. "I see Nate, Cindy and your grandfather coming now. Do you think your grandfather is okay?"

Jesse spied the group on the sidewalk across the street.

Gramps leaned against the post waiting for the stoplight to turn green while the two children danced about him, barely containing their energy. "Gramps keeps telling me he's too mean to get sick. My son has him wrapped around his finger. He'd do anything for Nate."

"That must be nice."

The hard edge to Nick's voice piqued her interest. "Do you have any grandparents alive?"

He shrugged. "I don't know."

"You don't?" she said before she could stop the words.

"I left home—such as it was—when I was sixteen."

"You were a runaway?"

Nick picked up his glass, his hand clenched so tightly about it that Jesse wondered if he would break it. "You have to have a home in the first place to be able to run away from one."

"You were living on the streets?" Sweetwater was small enough that the people who lived there took care of anyone in need, so the concept was new to Jesse even though she had read about it happening in other places.

Nick's tensed expression eased as he looked beyond Jesse. He smiled. "How did it go, princess?"

Cindy slid into the booth next to her father. "Everyone said they would look for Oreo. We stopped at the church and said a prayer for him. Nate said it would help."

Nate sat next to Jesse. "Yeah, Mom always says a prayer can work miracles."

"Daddy, I hope God listened to me."

Nick put his arm about his daughter. "I'm sure He did."

Jesse didn't think Cindy heard the doubt in her father's voice, but she had. Nick's gaze caught hers and held it for a few seconds. There was more than doubt in Nick's eyes—there was a bleakness that ripped through Jesse's defenses. Cindy needed a mother, but Nick needed much more than that. He needed to believe in the power of the Lord. He needed to believe in life again. He might think their conversation was over because of the arrival of the children, but she had every intention of continuing it later.

"Are you sure about ordering pizza?" Nick asked as he came up behind Jesse on the deck of her house.

She surveyed the darkening sky to the west, a large bank of ominous-looking clouds rolling in. A surge of panic zipped up her spine, and she determinedly shoved it into the background. "Yes. Boswell deserves a night off after finding Oreo today." *And I don't want to be alone,* she added silently, the wind picking up, the temperature dropping rapidly.

"This is one father who is happy Boswell found Oreo by the lake. After going all over town today, I was sure the kitten was long gone or—"

"Or what?"

"Some animal's dinner." He looked toward the water.

"If you mean Fred and Ethel, they wouldn't do that."

He shook his head. "I was thinking about the owl I hear every morning when I drink my coffee on the deck.

I've heard owls prey sometimes on animals like skunks. You have to admit Oreo could be mistaken for one."

"I hadn't thought of that." Jesse shivered, hugging her arms to her, more from the cooling breeze than from what he had said.

"I may be a city guy, but I do know a few things about the country. One I just learned recently. Not to go near geese."

Jesse laughed, focusing on the man near her rather than the storm brewing. "I'm so glad you're a quick learner. Now if you would only rub off on Gramps."

"I heard him leaving not long after Boswell arrived."

"Probably for the best. He said he was going to Susan Reed's for dinner, but frankly I think he feels threatened by Boswell."

Nick's chuckle spiced the air. "Boswell can have that effect on a person. When he first came to work for me, I wasn't sure if we would last a week. But he was wonderful with Cindy and that counted a lot in my book. I must admit now that I don't think I could make it without him."

The dark cloud completely obliterated what light there had been from the setting sun. The only illumination on the deck came from the kitchen and den. Jesse felt the need to go inside, but she didn't want to break the mood by suggesting a change. She suspected that Nick didn't open up much about himself.

Instead, she leaned back against the railing, gripping its wood, and asked, "How long has Boswell worked for you?"

"Over three years."

"What made you hire a manservant? Isn't that a bit unusual?"

"Actually I had advertised for a nanny-housekeeper."

"And Boswell applied?"

"Sort of. A friend suggested him and after meeting him I decided he was the best person qualified for the job. I always hire the best."

"What did your wife have to say about it?" The second she had spoken the question Jesse wished she could have taken it back. A cloud as dark as the one in the sky dropped over his features and the temperature seemed to fall even more.

"Brenda didn't care."

There was a wealth of unspoken emotions in those simple words that struck a chord with Jesse. His pain wrapped about her heart and squeezed. She reached out to touch his arm and he took a step back. The rejection hurt.

"I'm sorry."

"What's there to be sorry about? My wife didn't want to be involved with the mundane household chores like cleaning, shopping, cooking. That's why I hired Boswell."

So much more wasn't being said, Jesse realized as she watched Nick shut down his emotions, not one shred of evidence of what he was feeling visible on his expression. She needed to watch what she said. She was way too curious for her own good. It was obvious he didn't want to talk about the past and all the prodding on her part wasn't going to change that.

She shoved herself away from the railing, noticing a piece of paper swirling on the wind and racing across the deck. She snatched it from the crevice it was lodged in and balled it into her fist. "I'd better order that pizza now. I don't know about you, but I'm starved."

Silence greeted her announcement and heightened her unease.

She entered the kitchen while Nick stayed out on the deck. After calling in the order, she started for the back door and stopped herself. He needed time alone or he would have come inside when she had. She always wanted to fix everyone's problems when some people didn't want her to. She needed to learn to back off when the message was loud and clear.

Jesse began setting out the plates and napkins for the pizza. The back door opened and closed. The atmosphere in the kitchen sharpened as though someone was taking a knife and honing it to a razor's edge.

"I'm sorry if I opened old wounds. I didn't mean to," Jesse said, not facing Nick as she shut the cabinet. She didn't want to see no emotions on his face; she didn't want to see that bleak look, either. Both bothered her.

The sound of his footsteps cut through the silence that hung in the air. She felt him near, could smell his particular lime-scented aftershave. She licked her dry lips, pushed herself off from the counter and whirled around to face him. He was only a foot away, so close she could touch the hard planes of his face, smooth his frown away—if she chose to. She kept her arms at her sides as though frozen. In that moment she felt as though she would shatter into a thousand icy particles.

"No, I'm the one who is sorry. I'm not used to having…a friend. You were only trying to find out about me."

The word *friend* came out stiff sounding, as though he had never said it before. If truth be told, she wasn't used to having a male friend. She had many females as friends but not a man. She forced a smile to her mouth. "Yes, friend. I figured you needed someone to show you around Sweetwater. After all, you're going to be here for two months."

"And you've decided you're that person?"

"We're neighbors. That's what neighbors do for each other."

"Not in Chicago."

"Well, in Sweetwater they do and since you're in Sweetwater, you're stuck with me." Again the second she had said the sentence, she wanted to take it back. What was it about this evening that was making her say things she shouldn't? Must be the storm brewing. She hated bad weather. She acted irrationally with no forethought to what she was going to say.

One corner of his mouth lifted. "You make it sound like a sentence."

"You might feel that way before it's over," she said in a flippant tone, wanting to lighten the mood before she began to confess all her deep, dark secrets—or worse, he did. Then she would have to do something about them.

"Can I help you with anything? Set the table? Wash your windows?"

"If I thought you were serious about the window washing, I'd take you up on the offer another day. Haven't you noticed there's a storm brewing?"

"Kinda hard to miss. It was spitting rain when I came in."

"Then just in case we'd better get a few flashlights out."

"Does the electricity go off a lot when it storms here?"

"No, but I like to be prepared." Then she might feel she had some control over the bad weather. "How is Cindy when it storms?"

He thought a moment. "She's usually okay. Our apartment is well insulated. It has to be a really bad storm for us to hear it."

"I wish I could say that. This house is old and I think we can hear a pin drop outside."

"How is Nate?"

"Fine. He's like his father. He loved a good thunderstorm." *Better than me,* she wanted to add, but hoped no one discovered her weakness. She tried to put up a brave front for the family, but it was getting more difficult. She had never done well in a storm before Mark was struck by lightning. Now she came apart inside with each sound of thunder and flash of lightning. On one level she knew her actions were way out of proportion to what was going on, but on a deeper level it didn't make any difference.

"Where are your flashlights?"

"I have several in the drawer by the refrigerator and a couple in the drawer in the coffee table in the den."

"You *are* prepared." Nick retrieved the two flashlights from the kitchen drawer, then headed toward the den.

While he was gone, Jesse stared out the window over the sink, listening to the wind brush the limbs of the oak tree against the house and the raindrops pelt the panes as though they were fingernails trying to claw their way inside. Her hands clutched the counter so hard they ached. It had begun and from the looks of the clouds earlier it would be a doozy. She shouldn't have invited Nick, Cindy and Boswell to dinner—to watch her fall apart. If she hadn't, she could have closeted herself in her bedroom and huddled under the covers until it was over.

"I've got two more flashlights. Anything else you want me to do?"

Jesse caught herself before she gasped. She hadn't heard him returning, so lost in thoughts of the storm. *Focus on the man,* she told herself and turned toward Nick. "No, I think all we need now are the pizzas and we'll be set."

Not a minute later the doorbell chimed. "Want me to get it while you get Boswell and the children?" Nick asked, already walking toward the front door.

Jesse spotted her money on the counter and started to go after Nick. She stopped herself, realizing he had intentionally ignored it because he had decided he would pay for the pizzas, had stated that very thing when she had suggested ordering out. In that second she realized Nick Blackburn was a force to be reckoned with—like the storm.

She made her way to Nate's room and found Cindy and her son on the floor playing with Bingo and Oreo. Boswell sat on Nate's bed watching the two children, not one expression crossing his face—not even boredom. She could see where Nick would think that Boswell was perfect for him. They both didn't show much of what they were thinking. *Two of a kind,* she thought with a laugh.

"The pizzas are here. Wash up and come to the kitchen."

Nate hopped up. "You ordered pepperoni, didn't you?"

"Of course."

"Yes!" He pumped his arm in the air. "Mama Mia makes the best pepperoni pizza." He raced past Jesse with Cindy following on his heels.

Boswell pushed himself off the bed. "If what young Master Nate has been telling us is true, then we are in for a delightful treat."

"If you like pizza, then, yes, you are. You can't beat Mama Mia's."

"Is she Italian?" Boswell motioned for her to leave before him.

"Mama Mia is a man named Charlie and about as American as apple pie and baseball."

"I see."

"You do? I'm not sure I do. I went to school with Charlie and all of us knew any restaurant he opened would be successful. He was a great cook as a teenager.

He just thought the name Mama Mia would help him
when he first opened his restaurant ten years ago. We
tried to tell Charlie *his* name would go further than a
made-up one."

"Some people don't believe enough in themselves
and put on a facade for others."

Jesse glanced at Boswell and wondered whom he
was talking about. Himself? Nick? Someone else? Was
the man lonely? Did he have a girlfriend in Chicago?
Maybe she should try to fix him up as well as his
employer. "Well, Charlie has plenty of confidence now.
He's opened a chain of these pizza parlors all over
Kentucky. Quite successful but still lives here and is
very involved in the original restaurant. We're lucky in
Sweetwater."

When Jesse entered the kitchen, the children had
finished washing their hands and were drying them
with paper towels. Nick had placed the boxes of pizzas
on the table and the aroma peppered the air with smells
of cheese, bread, meat and spices. Jesse's mouth
watered. Fear always made her hungry.

As she sat at the table, the first rumble of thunder
followed by a flash of lightning made her stiffen,
gripping the edge of her chair. She glanced around,
hoping no one noticed the fear she imagined etched
into her features about now. Again she wondered why
she had invited her neighbors to witness her falling
apart. She generally avoided even Darcy and Beth who
knew so many of her secrets while growing up.

Nate started to reach for a piece of pizza. Jesse gave

him a stern look. He snatched his hand back and bowed his head. Cindy followed suit while Nick frowned and Boswell stared.

"Remember we say a prayer before eating," Jesse said and folded her hands in front of her. "Dear Heavenly Father, bless this food that we are about to enjoy. Watch over those less fortunate then us and provide us with the means to help them when we can. Amen." Silently she added, *And help me to get through this evening without making a fool of myself.*

When she brought her head up, she found Nick lifting his and she was relieved that he had gone along with the prayer. She got the impression that he hadn't stepped foot in a church in a long time, if ever. Maybe that was why they had moved next door for the summer. Maybe she was supposed to show him the power of the Lord in a person's life. Nick was hurting deep inside. She wanted to help. And in the process maybe help Cindy find a mother.

"Isn't this great?" her son said while his mouth was stuffed with pepperoni pizza.

"Nate! Please wait until you finish eating your food before you talk."

Her son gulped down a mouthful of food, then washed it down with some milk. "Sorry." He turned to Cindy who was next to him. "What do ya think?"

The young girl bit off a more delicate bite than her son and chewed it thoroughly before answering, "Great! You were right."

Nate puffed out his chest. "Of course. I know the best places in town for food."

"My son, the connoisseur."

"What's that?" Nate took another big bite of his pizza.

"An expert, in this case of food." Boswell used his fork to cut off some of his slice and brought it to his mouth.

"Yep, that's me. I know the best place to get a fudge sundae, a hamburger, fries. You name it. I can tell you where to go."

Another crack of thunder sounded with lightning striking close by. Jesse jumped, nearly choking on her food. She began to cough. Nick patted her back while tears filled her eyes. A long moment later she breathed normally again and took a large swallow of her water.

"Mom, you okay?"

She waved her hand. "Just went down the wrong way."

"Mom doesn't like storms," her traitorous son announced to the whole table.

Everyone regarded her. She could feel the heat burning her cheeks. "I—I—" What could she say to that?

"When it storms really bad, she usually hides out in her room."

"Nate, I don't think my habits need to be discussed at the table." Jesse clenched her hands in her lap and pinched her lips together.

"Sorry, Mom. I just wanted them to know why you jumped."

Her jaw ached from gritting her teeth. Her nails dug into her palms. When more thunder rumbled the walls and lightning scorched a path through the air not far from the window, Jesse managed only to flinch, but her fists tightened even more. She nearly came unglued when she felt Nick's hand cover hers. She slanted a look at him and saw him wink. Something inside her relaxed a bit even though the wind and rain slashed at the house.

"I saw, Master Nate, that you had the game Trouble. Anyone up for a rousing game of Trouble?"

"I am," Cindy said, leaping to her feet with a piece of pizza in her hand.

"Me, too." Nate stood, finishing his last bite. "Can we take our food to the den and play a game, Mom?"

"Fine."

"I'll make sure they don't get any food on the furniture." Boswell scooted his chair back and rose, while the children grabbed up a piece of pizza and raced from the room.

"I will supervise the children while you finish eating."

When Boswell left, the silence lasted for a few seconds then thunder filled it, reminding her that a storm raged outside—not that she had ever forgotten except for a few seconds when Nick had touched her hands and winked at her. "We'd better clean up this mess."

"That's something I can handle."

Jesse began taking the plates over to the sink. "I don't get the impression you do too many dishes."

"I have in the past."

"You did?"

"Distant past. When I was working my way through college, I had a variety of jobs. One was being a dishwasher at a fancy restaurant. I took pride in the fact that I didn't break one piece of china or crystal."

"I am impressed. How long did you wash dishes?"

"Two days."

Jesse laughed. "What happened?"

"I convinced the owner I would be better suited as a busboy."

"How long did that last?"

"Three days. I became a waiter at the restaurant when one didn't show up and stayed for two years. The pay wasn't great, but the tips were. Funded my last two years of college."

"So you're the kind of guy who seizes the moment."

"Definitely." Nick opened the dishwasher and took the first plate that Jesse rinsed off. "That job taught me a few lessons."

"What?"

"Hard work pays off. And how to grit my teeth when someone was being condescending. That it's better to be rich than poor. After working there, I decided I wanted to be one of the people who was waited *on,* not the waiter."

"There's more than one way to be rich in life than having money."

"When you grow up poor, scrambling for something decent to eat, it doesn't seem that way. I have a feeling we came from two very different backgrounds. You grew up here in Sweetwater, right?"

"Yes."

"You probably never wanted for a thing."

She turned so she could face him, not one expression visible on his features. "I had a good childhood. My father made a nice income. My mother didn't work outside the home. We went to church every week. I was a cheerleader, class secretary in high school and on the girl's softball team. A pretty normal childhood for Sweetwater."

"But not for me on the streets of Chicago. My father left my mom when I was two so I never really knew my father's family. Mom worked two jobs to try to put some food on the table and keep a roof over our heads. Sometimes she was successful, other times not. I can remember days going without much food except peanut butter sandwiches. We didn't even have money for the jelly. To this day I can't eat peanut butter."

She reached toward him. "I'm sorry."

He took a step back, staring at her outstretched hand. "What for? It wasn't your fault." He pivoted toward the table and strode to it to pick up the last of the dirty dishes.

His stiff back drew her toward him. She started to move forward but stopped herself. She knew by his earlier actions that he would reject any offer of comfort. Swinging back toward the sink, she grabbed a glass.

Thunder and lightning, close and deafening, shook the house.

Taken off guard, she jerked back and the glass slipped from her nerveless fingers. In slow motion she watched it crash to the floor, shattering into hundreds of shards at her feet.

Another round of thunder and lightning sent her back against a solid wall of human flesh. Arms held her and turned her around. The comfort she had wanted to offer Nick was evident in the softened expression on his face. His arms wound about her and drew her to him.

For a few seconds she forgot the storm. She felt as though she'd come home.

Chapter Five

The jasmine scent that he'd come to associate with Jesse inundated Nick. For a few seconds it felt so right to hold this woman to him and give her the comfort she needed. Then his memories flooded him like her scent, and he realized the danger in getting too close to Jesse Bradshaw. She could make him wish he were different, that he had never known the heartache of being married to Brenda.

From an early age he had learned to be a survivor and the only way he knew to survive was to distance himself from anything or anyone who might hurt him. He hadn't with Brenda and he had paid dearly for that mistake. The dull pain in his leg when he did too much was a reminder if he ever dared to forget.

He continued to hold Jesse who trembled in his arms. The warmth from her body threatened to melt his defenses. He fought to keep them intact, desperation vying with his needs as a man that he'd kept buried for over a year.

Finally he stepped back, his hands clasping her upper arms. "Are you all right?" He heard the slight quaver to his words and winced at the vulnerability he was exhibiting. Never show your weakness to another, he had been taught through the years when he had struggled to take care of himself after his mother's death. And Brenda certainly had reinforced that when their marriage had begun to fall apart.

Jesse's green eyes glistened with unshed tears. "No—yes." She shook her head. "I don't know. Nate was right about me not handling storms very well."

"We all have things we are afraid of."

"What is yours?"

Being asked that question, he wanted to say. Instead, he shrugged and decided to tell her the partial truth. "Going hungry." He'd told Jesse more of his past than he had anyone else except Brenda. And in the end his deceased wife had used that knowledge to hurt him. He couldn't believe he had disclosed so much to Jesse. He hadn't known her long, and yet she was so easy to talk to— to make him want to forget his past. That realization sent panic through him. He hardened his heart, determined not to give in to the weakness of wanting to be needed.

"Thankfully that's not likely going to happen to you."

"Whereas storms will always be around?"

"Yes." She shoved her hand through her short brown hair. "I never liked thunderstorms as a child, but when I lost Mark to a lightning strike, my fear multiplied. I'm the reason—" She bit her bottom lip to keep it from trembling. A tear leaked from her eye and ran down her cheek. Turning away, she swiped at her face. "I can finish cleaning up later."

"I can stay as long as you need me." The only person who had really needed him was Cindy, and he felt as if he had let her down on more than one occasion.

"You don't have to baby-sit me. I've lived with this irrational fear for over thirty years. I'll manage."

The quavering in her voice belied her tough words. He clasped her shoulder. "Why don't we join Cindy and Nate and play a game of Trouble?"

Looking back at him, she smiled but the edges of her mouth quivered. "You just want to take advantage of my weakened resolve."

"You've discovered my strategy."

"I must warn you I am very competitive—" she cocked her head and listened "—and I think the storm is moving away from here."

"What a nice challenge. You at your peak."

Her laughter saturated the air, all traces of the tension of the past hour gone. "I could say the same thing about you."

He swept his arm across his body and indicated the door that led to the den. "I thrive on a good challenge."

"Let me pick up the broken glass first, then I'll gladly thrash you at a game of Trouble." She bent down to begin the task.

"I'll help." He knelt next to her, his arm brushing against hers.

The casual touch was like a bolt of lightning streaking up his arm. He felt the electricity zip through his body and nearly dropped the piece of glass he had picked up. He steadied himself, drawing in a deep, composing breath. His senses were imbued with her scent of jasmine, and he was right back where he was a few minutes ago—needing and wanting something that would be no good for him.

When the glass was cleaned up, he put several feet between them. "On second thought, I'd better call it an evening. I forgot I still have some calls to make overseas. Now that the storm is abating we should be able to get home without getting too drenched."

Disappointment fretted across her features. "I can loan you a couple of umbrellas. You can bring them back tomorrow."

"Sure. I'd better go get Cindy and Boswell." He backed away, his gaze caught in hers. He felt like a coward, tossing down a challenge then reneging. That wasn't his usual method of operation. But he was a survivor and he needed his space before he did something foolish. Jesse Bradshaw was the marrying kind, and he would never marry again because he was a survivor.

Nick leaned close to Jesse and whispered, "I can't believe you talked me into this class."

"Don't tell me you're one of those people who doesn't like to get his hands dirty."

"I think we're past that."

Spying Nick's hands covered with paste used in making his papier-mâché animal, Jesse laughed. "I think you're right. What is that, by the way?"

"I'm crushed. You can't tell it's a cat?"

She tried to contain her laughter but wasn't very successful. "Sorry. Where's its tail?"

"It's a tailless cat." He looked offended, but merriment frolicked in his eyes. He nodded toward her papier-mâché animal. "What's that?"

"A dog and this is his tail." Jesse pointed to a stub at one end of a blob of paper pulp.

"If you say so."

"Daddy, what do you think?"

"Sweetie, you've done a great job with your, er—" he studied his daughter's art project "—rabbit."

"It's not a rabbit. I decided to do a bird." Cindy slapped on some more wet paper.

"Oh, great bird. Now that I look at it closer I can see its wings." He pointed toward the area sticking out of the side.

"That's his beak and that's his tail."

"Yes. Yes. Tail and beak."

Jesse pressed her lips together, but her laughter continued to bubble up inside her. She bent toward Nick and whispered, "You need to learn to let your child tell you first what they did before committing yourself."

"Committing myself is the optimum phrase here. I'm definitely not projecting an image of an industry leader."

"No, but you are projecting an image of a wonderful, devoted father."

"I am? Well, in that case, it's all worth it." He studied Cindy's papier-mâché animal, his brow wrinkled in a thoughtful look. "She told me earlier she was doing a rabbit."

"Sometimes they change their minds. Be vague and let them talk about their artwork."

"Mom, I'm finished. Do you like it?"

"Nate, I love your animal. What a neat choice of colors."

"I know horses aren't blue, but it's my favorite color."

After properly admiring her son's work, she mouthed the word, "see," to Nick. He inclined his head.

Beth Coleman stood at the front of the room. "Class, when you're through making your animals, we're going to let them dry and you can take them home next Saturday. If you haven't finished painting your project, we'll have some time next week to complete it. It's time to clean up."

"Painting! I haven't finished making my animal." Nick picked up his project and one of the legs fell off. "This is why I didn't put a tail on my cat. I'm having a hard enough time with the four legs."

"Daddy, your cat looks funny."

"You think?"

Cindy giggled. "I'll help you next week."

"I think I'm a lost cause." He took his three-legged cat to the shelf to store it.

Jesse hung back, letting him talk to Beth who was supervising the storing of the projects. They spoke a brief moment—not nearly long enough to make a proper connection—then he headed back to the table.

As Cindy and Nate left to put their projects on the shelf, Jesse said, "Don't you think Beth is wonderful with the children?"

Nick stopped cleaning up the mess he'd made and looked at Jesse. "Sure."

"She has the patience of Job."

"I'm sure she does."

"I'm surprised she isn't married with a horde of children of her own. She would make a great mother."

Nick's eyes narrowed. "Why are you telling me this?"

"I don't want you to worry about Cindy if you can't come. She'll be in good hands."

"You mean I don't have to come and do the art projects each week?"

This conversation wasn't going the way she wanted, Jesse thought. In fact, the whole class hadn't gone as she had wanted. Beth had hardly paid much attention to Nick. Of course, with Jimmy throwing up at the beginning of class then Cal trying to eat the paste she hadn't had much time to pay attention to anyone. "Beth encourages the parents to participate, but you don't have to."

"That's a relief." He wiped his hand across his forehead before he realized it was still covered with partially wet papier-mâché paste.

Jesse knew the second he remembered his hands weren't clean. His eyes widened as he rolled them skyward as though he could see the white trail he'd left on his forehead.

"I'm definitely more comfortable in a boardroom than a classroom." He snatched up a paper towel and cleaned his forehead. Then he looked down at his jeans and T-shirt and grimaced. "Boswell won't be too happy with me. I think I have more paste on my clothes than the project."

"Believe me, it washes out."

"I suppose with kids it would have to."

"Definitely." Jesse saw Beth hurrying by and said, "Beth, can I help with anything?"

Her friend stopped, took a deep breath and pushed her hair back behind her ear. "Class usually isn't this hectic."

"You remember Nick Blackburn from the other day at the café."

Beth started to offer her hand, then remembered it was covered with paint and just smiled instead. "Yes. You have an adorable little girl."

"Yes, isn't Cindy cute?" Jesse shifted to allow another parent by, which caused Nick to have to move closer to Beth. Things were looking up. Maybe she would be able to stop searching for someone for Nick.

"Thank you. I think she'll enjoy this class, but I may not always be able to come. Will it be okay if someone else brings her?"

"Sure, whatever works best for you. The important thing is that Cindy enjoys herself. I've got to go and catch Cal's mother before she leaves. I'm glad Cindy will be joining the class."

As soon as Beth left, Nick busied himself cleaning up his work area, then washing his hands, his glance not once straying toward Beth. Disappointment sagged Jesse's shoulders as she stood back and tried to decide what had gone wrong. Why couldn't she find someone for Nick? Beth would be perfect. Why couldn't either one of them see that?

Another plan popped into her mind as the members of the class began to leave. Slowly Jesse straightened her area, cleaned the table off and washed her hands, too. Cindy and Nate danced about, trying to contain their energy but not doing a very good job. Even Nick finished and watched Jesse with a furrowed brow.

"Do you need help?" he asked, picking up her art project to take over to the shelf.

There was only one more student in the class. Jesse purposefully moved in slow motion as she gathered up her purse. Beth said goodbye to Cheryl and her mother.

Jesse checked her watch. "It's nearly lunchtime. Why don't we get something to eat at the hamburger joint across the street?"

As she knew they would, both Cindy and Nate said, "Yes!"

"How can I say no?"

"You can't. Let's see if Beth would like to join us." Before Nick could reply, Jesse rushed toward her friend. "We're going to get some hamburgers at Joe's Diner. Want to come?"

"Sorry, Jesse. I've got to meet with Reverend Collins

about the Fourth of July auction before I meet you at Darcy's. Some other time."

Beth grabbed her purse and headed toward the door to the classroom before Jesse could form a reply. *Lord, are You telling me to pass on this one? Nothing seems to work with Nick. I need some help here. I'm not doing a very good job with this man.*

"Our teacher has other plans?"

Nick's deep husky voice sent a shiver down her spine. She wheeled around. "Yes." Her voice came out breathless as though she had run in a marathon. Her chest barely seemed able to contain the beating of her heart.

"Then can we leave now?"

"Sure."

With Nate and Cindy leading the way, Jesse and Nick walked from the school building and across the street to Joe's Diner. The aromas of grilled meat and French fries drew Jesse like a magnet. She loved all the wrong foods for a woman who should watch her weight.

Nick paused at the door. "Do you think I look okay to eat out in public?" He gestured toward his less than clean clothes.

"No better than I." Jesse waved her hand down the length of her attire of knee-length blue shorts and white T-shirt with splashes of paste and paint. "I don't think Joe will mind." Glancing through the picture window, Jesse added, "Besides, I see several other class participants inside so we won't be the only ones."

"Thank goodness none of my acquaintances in Chicago can see me now. They would be shocked."

"Because of your clothes or because of the place you are eating lunch at?" Jesse entered the diner in front of Nick and weaved her way toward the table in the back where the children had already camped out. Joe's Diner had simple fare and was plainly decorated with wooden tables and chairs that had seen many years of customers, and few objects adorning the white walls.

"Both. I actually had to go buy some more casual clothes after being here for several days and realizing my wardrobe wasn't small-town America."

"I suppose three-piece suits are a little out of place in Sweetwater. Mind you, we do occasionally wear our good clothes but mostly overalls and jeans are the mainstay of our wardrobe," Jesse said with a straight face.

Nick stared at her for a long moment, then chuckled. "I deserved that. And for the record, I don't wear three-piece suits. Too stuffy for me." He slid a chair out for Jesse and waited until she sat before he took the seat next to her.

"Daddy, can I order anything I want?" Cindy opened the menu and tilted her head to the side as though she was enthralled with what was written on the paper before her.

"Maybe."

Peering around the side of her menu, Cindy screwed up her face into a frown. "Maybe?"

"I'm not saying yes until I hear what it is you want. The last time I said yes without knowing the terms I was stuck with a set of books you haven't even looked at since you got them."

"What are you having, Nate?" Cindy asked, going back to studying her menu.

"The hamburgers are the best in town and you can't beat Joe's French fries. But I also like the onion rings, too."

"I want all that, Daddy."

"French fries *and* onion rings?" One of Nick's eyebrows rose.

Cindy nodded. "And a hamburger with chocolate milk."

"That's an awful lot to eat."

Cindy closed her menu and straightened in her chair. "I'm mighty hungry after all that work this morning."

Nate slapped his menu down. "I'll have the same, too."

"Are you gonna eat it this time? The last time you didn't finish half your burger." Jesse collected the menus and waved to Lila to let her know they were ready to order.

"I'm hungry, too. Gramps says I'm a growing boy who needs fuel to grow."

"That's an interesting way to put it," Nick said, unwrapping his silverware and placing his paper napkin in his lap.

"So you're gonna eat every bit of it this time?"

Nate bobbed his head up and down.

When Lila came to take their orders, Nick told her what they wanted—hamburgers and French fries for everyone with two extra side dishes of onion rings.

After she left, Jesse took a drink of her water. "I hope Dr. Wilson doesn't see us eating this. This goes against every diet I've heard of."

"Don't tell me you watch your weight?" Nick said with a laugh.

"Yes. If I don't, who will?"

His gaze roamed down the length of her. "I can think of a few who might."

Heat flamed her cheeks at the amused look—with a hint of something she didn't dare put a name to—in his eyes. She needed to champion Beth before she forgot her mission to find Nick a suitable wife. "What did you think of the art class today?"

"Do I have to go back?"

"Daddy, I want to go next Saturday."

Nick turned his attention to his daughter. "*You* can, princess. It's me we're talking about."

"You don't wanna go?" Cindy squirmed in her chair, a pout forming.

"Yes, Nick, you don't want to go?"

Nick threw Jesse a narrowed look before addressing his daughter. "I'm not very good at creating art."

"Daddy, you don't have to be." She dropped her head and stared at the table.

"Cindy, if you want to go, I'll take you, but I'm not promising you that I'll participate."

"That's okay, Daddy. Jesse will be there to help me if I need it. Maybe she can help you."

"Sure, Nick. I'd be glad to." Jesse contained her laughter that threatened. Nick probably wouldn't appreciate it. She doubted he was put in the hot seat much, and the man definitely looked as though he wanted to squirm in his chair.

"I think I can manage but thanks for the offer," Nick said, relief on his face as the waitress placed the plates of food in front of everyone, effectively ending the conversation.

Jesse leaned toward Nick and whispered, "Beth is a wonderful teacher. Cindy and *you* will learn a lot."

"I'm sure Beth is, but papier-mâché isn't my idea of art."

"Beauty is in the eye of the beholder."

Nick took a bite of his hamburger. "Mmm. This is delicious."

Jesse noted the surprise in his voice and couldn't help responding, "There's nothing fancy about Joe's food, but it is great tasting."

"I can appreciate a hamburger with the best of them." Nick bit down again and chewed slowly as though savoring it.

"Daddy, can I go to church with Nate tomorrow?"

Lifting his hamburger toward his mouth, Nick stopped in mid motion. He peered at Jesse.

"It's okay with me. I would love for Cindy to come with us. You can, too, if you want."

Nick shifted in his chair, putting his hamburger down on his plate. "Sweetie, if you want to go that's fine with me."

"Will you come?" Cindy picked up her milk and took a long drink.

"I can't, princess."

"Why can't you come?"

"I have some business that I need to take care of."

Cindy cocked her head and stared at him. "On Sunday?"

"Some overseas calls. Maybe some other time." Nick shifted again in his chair.

Jesse wondered about the uncomfortable expression on Nick's face. Did he believe in God? He was allowing Cindy to go to church and yet he wouldn't go himself. She had the feeling there was more to the story than overseas calls.

"Don't forget later on this afternoon Boswell said we could finish that Trouble game we started the other night. I'll bring it over to your house." Nate wiped his mouth then wadded his paper napkin and put it by his empty plate.

"Ah, I seem to remember a challenge about a game. But then someone had to leave before making good on his challenge." Jesse popped an onion ring into her mouth, relishing the taste of the batter that Joe used.

"I'll play you a game of Trouble any place, any time," Nick said, tossing down his napkin in a dramatic display.

Jesse's gaze locked onto Nick's. "Fine. I'll come over after I go to Darcy's this afternoon." Beth always went to church and this would be a great opportunity to throw them together again. And just maybe Nick would see the power of the Lord at work. Maybe while playing a game of Trouble she could find a way to persuade Nick to accompany his daughter to church.

"You're on," he said, his gaze boring into her with an intensity that rocked her.

When Jesse glanced away, she caught her son and Cindy staring at them. For a few minutes she had forgotten the children were sitting at the table with them. And she suspected Nick had, too, if his ashened features were any indication when he looked toward Nate and Cindy.

"Every time I see this beautiful bookcase, I want one in my house. If Joshua ever decides to start a side business on his days off, I'll be the first to order a built-in bookcase." Jesse stood in front of the beautifully carved piece of furniture being discussed, running her hand along its oak surface.

"What days off? If he's not investigating a fire, my dad has him at the farm, learning the business right along-side me." Darcy went to answer the doorbell that rang.

"How do you feel about that?"

As her friend put her hand on the knob, she said, "I'm fine with it. Dad and I have come to terms with me feeling as if he only wanted a son. I want both Sean and Joshua to learn the business. Joshua and I plan on having a large family. I'll need the backup." She opened the door and greeted Beth and Tanya.

As the ladies came into the living room and sat, Jesse asked, "Any news, Darcy?"

"I'm not pregnant…yet." She smiled. "But it's fun trying."

Beth blushed. Tanya laughed. And Jesse remembered.

"Does anyone want anything to drink while we wait for Zoey to arrive?"

Tanya and Beth shook their heads while Jesse said, "No."

"Wasn't she always late for everything?" Beth asked, smoothing her long jean skirt.

"You know, I think you're right. I'm glad she's come back home from Dallas but not under the circumstances." Darcy sat in one of the chairs with matching ottoman.

"It must be awful not knowing if your husband is dead or alive." Jesse took the other chair.

"I think the government has given up searching and has declared him dead." Beth put her sensible beige purse on the floor next to the couch.

"But still she will always wonder," Jesse murmured, realizing she didn't have to wonder about that at least. Finding her husband outside in the backyard after the horrendous sound of the lightning strike was still permanently etched into her mind. For a year she'd had nightmares reliving that.

"I went to see Tom a few days ago in prison." A frown marred Tanya's beautiful dark features. She clasped her hand to her mouth. "Oh, I'm sorry, Darcy. I shouldn't talk about him with you."

"It's okay, Tanya. I've forgiven Tom long ago. Pain can drive a person to do a lot of bad things."

That was one of the things she loved about Darcy, Jesse thought. Her friend had such a generous heart. Tom had almost accidentally killed Darcy when he had set fire to the barn she was in, and yet she could forgive the man. Darcy had embraced the true meaning of forgiveness when she had turned back to the Lord.

"We didn't talk long. He didn't have much to say. He looked thinner and pale. I can't help him."

"Who drove you to see him?" Jesse asked, remembering why Darcy had wanted to start this weekly group: to help Tanya who suffered from a manic depressive disorder and whose husband was in prison for arson. Jesse had to agree that Tanya needed a circle of friends and with Zoey's return home she suspected she did, too.

"Reverend Collins. He's been so good to me. I don't want him to retire at the end of this year."

Beth leaned forward. "I've tried to talk him out of it. In fact, I tried just this afternoon, but he feels it is his time."

"How did your meeting go with the reverend? I wish you could have come to lunch with us."

"My meeting with the reverend was fine. What I want to know, Jesse Bradshaw, is why are you constantly trying to throw me and Nick Blackburn together? Are you trying to matchmake?"

The silence in the house was deafening as everyone waited for Jesse to answer. She cleared her throat, aware all eyes were on her. "I simply asked you to lunch. Can't a friend do that without having an ulterior motive?"

"You're evading my question which means you are matchmaking. Jesse, I am *not* looking for a husband. After my youngest brother leaves for college next year, I'm traveling and seeing some of this world. I won't have time to be married then." Beth pinned her with her sharp gaze. "Nick seems like a nice man. Why don't you fix *yourself* up with him?"

Now it was Jesse's turn to squirm under the scrutiny of her friends. "Because I'm not looking for a husband, either. I had one."

"I'm too old and set in my ways to have one now."

Darcy chuckled. "Too old! Beth, you're only a few years older than us."

"But all of you have been married. I haven't ever."

"You can't put an age on marriage," Jesse said, rising, needing to move about.

Beth stood, too. "Right. You can't. So why aren't you looking for a husband? You were happily married for a long time. Why don't you want that again?"

The doorbell chiming drew everyone's attention toward Zoey's arrival. Jesse hung back, fighting the pressure building in her chest as though a band were around it, squeezing tight. In her mind's eye she could see Mark on the ground not moving, not breathing. When he had died, he had taken a part of her with him. She couldn't ever risk losing any more of herself. If so, there would be nothing left.

Chapter Six

Jesse started to ring Nick's doorbell, but stopped before pressing it. She turned away, the question Beth had asked her still plaguing her.

What is it about your new neighbor that threatens your peace of mind? Frankly, after seeing you two together, I think you're scared of the feeling he generates in you. Is that why you're trying to match him up with every female in town?

She had denied Beth's observation and hadn't answered her friend. She didn't have an answer. And that did frighten her.

Why was she trying to find him a wife? Yes, Cindy wanted a mother. What girl her age didn't? But why had she taken the job on? She was sure a man like Nick was capable of finding his own wife—if he was looking for one, which he kept telling her he wasn't. Like her. She wasn't looking for a spouse, either. So she needed to quit trying to fix him up with any woman who was breathing and walking around. He wasn't a threat to her peace of mind because neither one of them wanted a partner. She was safe.

With that thought she wheeled about and rang the bell. She would help Cindy as much as possible while she was in Sweetwater. That was the least she could do for the young girl. And if she could be a friend to Nick, that was fine, too.

Nick opened the door. When he saw her, he smiled and something inside her melted. Her resolve?

"Come in and save me from those two children."

Save him? How about herself? She felt her resolve slipping and fought to shore it up. He did have the greatest smile with a dimple in the left cheek. It lit his face and shone deep in his eyes with creases at their corners. That was it. She'd always liked the way a person smiled. Her husband had had a great smile, too.

"You're the adult. What could those two darlings possibly be doing?"

"Cheating. Ganging up on me to make sure none of my game pieces ever sees the light of day."

"Not Nate and Cindy. You must be imagining things."

"It's two against one. That's not playing fair."

"But that's life and life isn't always fair."

"Humph. No wonder Boswell gladly gave up playing so he could fix dinner." Nick gestured toward the den at the back of the house. "I think it's your turn to be their victim."

Jesse led the way, glancing back over her shoulder at Nick. "I thought you and I had a game to play."

"How did your meeting go with the ladies?"

"It wasn't exactly a meeting. It's just a few friends getting together."

"I've met Darcy and Beth. Who else was there?" Nick asked as they entered the den.

"Zoey and Tanya. If you go to church with us tomorrow, you can meet them. I'll introduce you to them."

"I haven't agreed to go to church."

"You will."

"I will?" One brow arched.

"The Lord is on my side. I mean to get you to church."

For a few seconds there was a panicked look in his eyes before he veiled it. "Are you trying to save my soul?"

"I'm trying to show you that you aren't alone in this world."

"It won't work. I've been alone for most of my life," he whispered close to her ear.

His breath tickled her neck. His words froze her heart for a beat. "That can always change if you want."

"Maybe I like my life the way it is. I answer to no one and I control my own destiny."

She turned slightly to face him. "That's sad."

Surprise flickered into his gaze. He took a step back, stunned for a moment. He started to say something when Cindy and Nate spotted them by the door.

"Daddy, ready for another game?"

"Mom, you can play, too."

Nick fixed his gaze onto his daughter. "I think it's Jesse's turn to play you all."

"But you can play, Daddy. There are four colors so there's enough for everyone."

"I need to help Boswell with dinner. Do you want to join us for dinner, Jesse and Nate?"

Jesse started to say no when her son piped in, "Yeah, what are you having?"

"Tacos."

"Great. I love tacos."

"Boswell knows how to make tacos?" Jesse asked, having a hard time picturing Boswell preparing anything less than English or French cuisine.

"He's lived in this country for a long time. He's picked up a few American habits. He loves Mexican food."

Cindy hopped to her feet. "Nate and me can help him. He's let me before. You and Jesse have a game to play. Remember, Daddy?"

Nick grinned with none of the warmth of earlier. "How can I forget? Fine. We'll play our match while you two help Boswell."

Cindy and Nate raced from the room, leaving Jesse with Nick by the door. Trouble was set up on the game table in front of the picture window that looked out over Sweetwater Lake. Ducks and geese swam on its surface, smooth as glass. Peace reigned outside while inside trouble was brewing.

Nick swept his arm across his body. "After you. I'll even let you pick which color you want to be and go first."

Jesse sat at the table, toying with a yellow and a red

piece. "I can't decide which of these colors I want. I like both of them."

"Yellow suits you more. You're always so upbeat." Nick took the blue pieces and put them in the game board.

"Is there a reason you picked blue?"

"It's my favorite color. I have no trouble picking what piece I will use."

"Decisive. Sure."

"Yep."

"I don't have a favorite color. The color I like will depend on my mood. Some days it is yellow. Others red or orange. Sometimes even green or blue."

"Indecisive? Unsure?"

"Nope. I don't like to lock myself down to only one favorite color. God made so many beautiful colors that I like them all. I don't like to limit myself. I like to keep myself open for all the possibilities life has to offer." Jesse selected the yellow pieces to use.

"How did we get into a philosophical discussion when all we were doing was picking our game pieces?"

She shrugged, tossing the die in her palm. "Just getting to know my neighbor."

"I can get impatient when things are going too slow. Throw the die."

"My, my. You are testy this evening." She rolled the die and it came up a three.

Snatching it up, he smiled, this time the deep, warm, toe-curling one. "Just thought I would speed your getting to know me along faster."

When the die came up four, he passed it to her.

"That's so sweet, Nick, but what I love about getting to know someone new is delving into what makes the person tick."

"Did you make that last statement to rattle me?"

"Why, no. I would never resort to using tricks to win." She grinned, enjoying the dismay that appeared on his face.

"What's happening?" Cindy whispered to Nate.

"I think my mom just put one of your dad's pieces back at the start."

Cindy tried to peer around Nate who was at the door to the den, peeping into the room, most of him hidden so the two adults couldn't see him. "Who's winning?"

"My mom is, but your dad is catching up."

Cindy stood on tiptoes and nearly toppled over. She clutched Nate to steady herself. "I hope your mom wins."

"Why are you two standing here spying?"

·Boswell's whispered question caused Cindy to jump. She whirled around and put her finger to her mouth to quiet him. "We don't want them to know we're watching."

Boswell nodded toward the two adults. "I think they know."

Both Nate and Cindy glanced over their shoulders and saw Jesse and Nick watching them with amused looks on their faces.

"Come on in. I'm about to win. All I need is a three." Nick rolled the die and a three came up. He moved his piece the necessary places, then leaped to his feet, high-fiving both Cindy and Nate's hands. "I won. I won."

Frowning, Jesse stared at the board game as though that could change the outcome.

Nick paused in his celebration with the children, sighed and said, "What time do I have to be ready for church? That's the least I can do since I trounced you at Trouble."

Jesse's frown transformed into a full-fledged smile. "Sunday school starts at nine-thirty and church at eleven."

"Church only!" Nick said, a tinge of panic in his voice. He started putting up the game.

"But, Daddy, I want to go to Sunday school with Nate and meet some of his friends. Can't you come to both?"

Jesse thought Cindy had the pout and big eyes routine down pat. She loved the child's slightly bowed head as an added touch. How could Nick say no to that?

"Princess." He looked at his daughter's sad expression and shook his head. "Okay, just this one time."

Cindy threw her arms around his neck and kissed him on the cheek. His smile returned and Jesse felt its full effect. Maybe she should take lessons from the child. She certainly knew how to get to her father.

"Dinner is served, sir," Boswell announced from the doorway.

"Just in time. I've worked up quite an appetite." Jesse put the lid on the Trouble game. "I need my strength for our rematch."

"What rematch? I've had all the Trouble I care to have for the day."

"Do you mean the game or something else?"

"Both. They come in the form of two females."

"Daddy, I'm no trouble." Cindy took his hand and led him toward the kitchen.

"Sweetie, all females are trouble."

"Yeah!" Nate chimed in as he followed them into the kitchen with Jesse next to him.

"I object. We are not." Jesse noticed that Boswell had the food lined up on the counter, buffet-style. The kitchen smelled of cooked ground beef. She loved that aroma. The table was set for five, everything color coordinated and matching. She suspected anything Boswell did was done that way. Even the flower arrangement of yellow roses went with the yellow place mats and napkins.

After everyone filled their plates and sat at the table, Jesse said the prayer, making sure she thanked God for getting Nick to agree to come to church, and then they dug into the food. It was a good five minutes before anyone said anything.

"Can I ride with you all tomorrow?" Cindy asked, finishing up her second taco.

"Sure, and your dad can, too. That is, if he wants."

"I think I'd better drive my own car."

He said it so quickly that Jesse couldn't resist teasing him with, "Afraid you'll get trapped at church?"

His hard gaze bore into her for a long moment. "No. Tell you what. I'll drive everyone to church tomorrow. That way we all go together and I'll get to drive my own car."

Jesse started to protest, took a look at the challenge deep in his eyes and swallowed her words. "That's fine with me. We'll need to leave by eight-thirty."

"I thought Sunday school started at nine-thirty. Isn't it only about a ten-minute drive to the church?" Nick picked up his third taco.

"I have to make coffee for the adult class."

"What are the kids gonna do while you're making coffee? Is there an early service going on at that time?"

"Until a little after nine. But Nate can give you a grand tour of the place or you can always help me make coffee and get all the supplies out."

Cindy downed the last of her chocolate milk and wiped her mouth with her hand. "Can Nate and me go play with Oreo now?"

"Sure, if it's okay with Jesse."

Jesse scanned the kitchen. "Where is Oreo?"

"He's in my bedroom. We have to keep him in there when we're eating. He likes to jump up on the table."

After the children left the kitchen, Boswell began to clean up.

Being the one who always cleaned up at her house, Jesse felt guilty. "Can I help?"

Boswell stopped stacking the dishes and looked at her, his expression neutral. "Madam, this is my job. Thank you for asking, however."

Nick scooted back his chair. "That's our cue to get lost. We can wait for the children in the den."

When Jesse was out of earshot of Boswell, she said, "I don't think I would ever adjust to having a servant full-time. There are too many things I like to do around my house my own way."

"For me it was get help or drown. My wife didn't like to do anything around the house. If I wanted any kind of order in my home, I had to get someone else to do it. Boswell was a lifesaver."

"Did your wife work?"

Nick snorted. "Work! No, not unless you wanted to say she worked at playing hard."

Jesse sat at one end of the brown leather couch while Nick took the other end. She twisted around so she faced him with one cushion between them. "She did a good job with Cindy. She is a precious, polite young lady."

"That wasn't my wife. I can't even say it was me. That was Boswell's doing."

"Is that why you want to spend some time with Cindy this summer? To get to know her?"

"Yes." Nick looked away, his features unreadable. "She's almost seven and I should know my own daughter, but I don't. I was always working, trying to make my company as successful as possible."

"What does success mean to you?"

"Having enough to provide for my family."

"How well do you have to provide before you're satisfied?"

Nick shot to his feet, stiff, his hands curling and uncurling at his sides. "Cindy is never going to know what it's like to want for something to eat or something warm to wear. Never. Not as long as I have a breath in my body."

"But that doesn't seem likely, does it? From what I understand your company is doing very well."

He whirled around, the lines of his face hardening. "But things can change with the snap of a finger. One day I'm healthy, not a care in the world. The next I'm fighting to stay alive and walk again."

"So for you there will never be enough?"

Pacing, Nick prowled his fingers through his hair. "I don't know. I suppose one day there will. Maybe when Cindy is grown-up and making her own way in the world, when I don't have to worry about her."

"As a parent you don't stop worrying just because your child has grown up and moved out. Are you sure you'll be satisfied then?"

He came to a halt in front of her. "I can't answer that. I don't know what the future holds for me. That's my whole point."

"You're right. Life isn't something we can always control. But that can be a wonderful thing, too. If we always know what's going to happen, we can get bored, complacent. This way those little surprises can keep life exciting, keep us on our toes."

"I grew up with no control over my life."

"As a child I didn't have a lot of control over my life, either."

"Maybe a better word is *stability*. You've lived in Sweetwater all your life in a nice house with a whole bunch of people who cared what happened to you."

"Sweetwater takes care of their own."

"No one goes hungry?"

"Not if we know about them."

"I wasn't lucky enough to know a place like Sweet-water."

Jesse's gaze riveted to his. "You do now."

"Why is it important that I attend church with you all tomorrow?"

"I think giving God a chance would help you. Have you ever gone to church?"

He opened and closed his hands. "Yes, when I was growing up. I can remember praying to God for something to eat some nights. It didn't help."

"Are you so sure about that? You're here. You have more than enough now. You didn't die from starvation. Have you ever considered what you went through made you a stronger person? Just because we pray for something doesn't mean we'll get it."

"I wasn't asking for a new toy. I was asking for food or warm clothing. For—" He swallowed hard and turned away.

"For what?"

He stiffened. "Nothing. It doesn't matter now."

"I think it does or you wouldn't have stopped."

Jesse hadn't thought it possible but Nick grew even tenser. She rose and covered the distance between them, placing her hand on his shoulder. Beneath her palm she felt the bunched muscles.

"I'll come to church with you tomorrow because I agreed to it, but that is all. There's nothing there for me anymore."

Jesse's heart broke at the words he uttered. How

could someone turn away from God? From the sacrifice that Jesus made for mankind? "Can Cindy come with us whenever she wants?"

He drew in a deep breath and released it slowly. "If she wants."

"What happens when you return to Chicago? What if she wants to continue attending church?"

He shook his head. "I don't have an answer for you."

The broken pieces of her heart shattered even more until there didn't seem to be anything left. His childhood had been so different from hers. He'd wanted for so much while she had lived a safe, protected life. He blamed God.

Lord, help me to show him the way back to You. How do I help him to see that loving You doesn't guarantee a person an easy life? It only guarantees a person an eternal life in Your kingdom.

"Daddy, come on! We're gonna be late. Jesse needs to get to church to make the coffee."

Nick winced at the loud shouting from his daughter who stood at the bottom of the stairs, probably with her hands on her waist and tapping her foot against the tiled floor. Shoeless, he went to the top step and said, "I'll be down in a minute."

"Hurry. I don't wanna be late for church." Clothed in a pink dress, Cindy danced from foot to foot.

Nick walked back into his bedroom and searched for his brown loafers. *Church.* His memories of church when he was a young boy were vague. His mother would take him each week, spend some extra time praying after everyone left, then come home and cry herself to sleep later that night. Her prayers hadn't helped them. *His* prayers hadn't, either. He'd used to listen to his mother's cries, then get on his knees and offer his own prayer until one day he'd given up trying. What was the use? No one cared. After that he had made a promise to himself. He would only depend on himself. No one else—not even God.

A chill burrowed deep into his bones as he found his shoes and slipped them on his feet. Glancing at himself in the mirror, he noted his casual attire of tan slacks and navy-blue button-down shirt. He was as ready as he would ever be.

Ten minutes later Nick sat behind the steering wheel of his SUV with Jesse next to him and the two children in the back, chatting in lowered voices as though they were telling secrets they didn't want the adults to hear.

Nick tossed his head toward the children. "Should we be worried?"

"Nah. They're just being children."

Tension grew the closer Nick got to the Sweetwater Community Church. His stomach muscles knotted and his palms were sweaty about the steering wheel. The thump of his heart against his chest increased as his breathing quickened.

When he turned into the parking lot at the side of the church, he had begun to force deep breaths into his lungs to slow his bodily functions down. The second he switched off the ignition, Cindy and Nate pushed open the back doors and leaped from the car. He watched them race for the building that must house the Sunday school classes.

Silence reigned in the car, heavy with tension and suppressed emotions.

His white-knuckle grip on the steering wheel underscored for Jesse the tension that held Nick. She wanted to wipe it away; she wanted to smooth the deep worry lines that carved his features. "You don't have to come in until nine-thirty. I can get the coffee started." She reached out and lay her hand on his arm. The muscles beneath her palm bunched.

"No, I'll help you. I *need* to keep busy."

What had happened to him as a young boy? Jesse wondered when she heard the desperate emphasis on the word *need.* "Sure. I could always use the help. There never seems to be enough time. And speaking of time, we'd better get moving or there'll be no coffee when the first service is over."

As Jesse approached the church with Nick beside her, sounds of the organ and voices singing drifted to them. She angled closer to Nick and took his hand. His cold fingers sent a chill through her that not even the eighty-plus temperature could warm.

He halted by the double doors into the lobby. "I shouldn't have come. This was a mistake."

She could have reminded him of their deal, but she didn't think it would have made any difference. Something from the past gripped him so hard that it governed his actions even today. She pointed toward a garden on the side of the building. "Why don't you sit out there? I can get everything ready. I shouldn't be long."

He stared a long moment at the pine trees in the garden from past Christmases, then focused his attention on her. "You don't mind if I don't help?"

"That wasn't part of the deal. And frankly, you have fulfilled your part of the wager. You have come to church. There wasn't a time allocation of how long you would stay once you came."

Some of the tension in his expression dissolved. Without a word, he wheeled around and headed toward the garden. Jesse slipped inside the building and hurried to the kitchen. Fifteen minutes later she had the coffee made and the supplies laid out on the table. She heard the last hymn being sung as she walked through the lobby and out the double doors.

God would forgive her if she didn't make it to church this morning. She had a more important mission: to discover what had driven Nick away from the Lord.

When she followed the stone path that led to the heart of the garden, she found Nick seated on a bench, his shoulders hunched over, his hands loosely clasped together between spread legs. He stared at the ground at his feet. The tightness around her chest constricted. His body language projected hurt, but she knew when he saw her, his expression would be neutral.

She moved forward. He caught sight of her and lifted his head, his features unreadable. He straightened, even his body conveying nothing of what he was feeling inside.

He glanced at his watch and for a few seconds puzzlement graced his expression.

"I only have to make the coffee. I don't have to serve it. I figured I would keep you company for a while—if that's okay."

He shrugged.

She sat on a bench across from him under the shade of a maple tree, relishing the few degrees of coolness it offered. "Do you want to talk about it?"

"What?"

The defensive tone in his voice cautioned her to move slowly. He wouldn't open up easily if at all. "Your feelings toward the church, God."

He grimaced, looked away.

"Something happened to you. I thought talking about it might help."

"I doubt that."

"When I have a problem, talking about it helps me to work through it."

"That's you."

She inhaled a deep, composing breath. "Has keeping it bottled up inside of you helped?"

His eyes widened for a brief moment then grew narrow as he pinned her with a sharp look. "You deal with your problems one way. I deal with mine another."

"My question still stands. Has it helped to keep everything bottled up inside of you?"

"There isn't much to tell. The church isn't for me. I tried it once. It doesn't meet my needs."

"When? As a child or an adult?"

"Does it matter?" He shot to his feet, his arms stiff at his sides.

"Yes, it matters. How we perceive things as a child is different than we do as an adult."

"If you must know, God let me down." He pivoted away from her, staring through the pine trees toward the parking lot.

"He doesn't promise us a perfect life where everything works out the way we want."

"For years I'd heard about the power of prayer. Well, let me tell you it doesn't work. He doesn't listen."

"He listens. He just doesn't always do what we want. When Mark died, I prayed to Him. I wanted my husband back, but that wasn't going to happen. I did ask Him to help me get through my grief. The Lord was there for me. If it wasn't for Him, I'm not sure what I would have done, especially during the long hours at night when I wanted Mark by my side in bed."

Nick faced her again, his gaze drilling into her. "How do you know the Lord was there for you? You can't see Him."

Chapter Seven

"I know," Jesse whispered, feeling Nick's anguish as though it twisted her insides. "I can't see the wind, either, but I see its effect and know of its existence."

"I've learned to be practical. I don't just take someone's word for something. I need to see it."

She spread her arms wide. "Look around you. Everything you see is God's work. In school I studied photosynthesis and knew God existed. Nothing that complex could randomly exist. Put simply, plants give off oxygen and take in carbon dioxide while we give off carbon dioxide and take in oxygen. What a neat interdependence. Like a marriage, we need each other. That happens a lot in nature. It's the best testimony to the existence of God."

"I wish I had your faith, but it's not that easy."

She held out her hand. "All you have to do is take the first step. Come to church. See for yourself through an adult's eyes. Your perspective might change."

He shook his head. "If anything, I'm much more jaded than I was as a child."

"Perhaps, but you still look at things differently."

He stared at her hand stretched toward him for a long moment, then fit his within her grasp. "I told you I would come to church and I don't back off from a promise even though you were going to graciously let me."

She wasn't going to argue with his reasoning. It was important to her to get him inside to the service. A first step, she hoped, of many more to come.

In the lobby she found Nate with Cindy, talking with Sean and a few of his Sunday school friends. They all surrounded Crystal Bolton in her wheelchair, discussing something the young girl said.

Nate saw her and waved her over. "Mom, Crystal wants to join our basketball team this fall."

"I think that would be a good idea. What does your mom say about it?"

"She said I could try. I saw a special on TV about people in wheelchairs doing all kinds of different sports. Some people with only one leg ski. Others ride horses. Mom would flip out if I wanted to ride a horse. That's why I thought playing basketball would be better. I love to watch the Kentucky Wildcats play."

"What's this about basketball?" Tanya Bolton asked, joining the group.

"I need to get active, Mom. I thought I would play basketball and get a wheelchair that is light and made to do things like that."

Tanya gripped the handles on the back of Crystal's wheelchair. "We'll talk about it later. Church is about to start."

Jesse saw the shadow of doubt in her friend's eyes. Tanya had just started working after her husband had gone to jail for arson. Money was tight for her, and a new wheelchair would cost a lot of money. She doubted Crystal would get one unless she came up with a way to raise the money. "We'd better get inside, too, Cindy and Nate. Ready?"

The children hurried in front of her and Nick, taking a seat next to Tanya and Crystal, who sat in the aisle in her wheelchair. Tension emanated from Nick as the service started. His actions were stiff as though at any moment he would break into a hundred pieces.

When Reverend Collins began his sermon on the bounty of God's love, Jesse laid her hand over his on the pew between them and smiled. The tight lines about his mouth eased, and he linked his fingers through hers. Through the sermon she noticed that Nick listened to the reverend's words, and after it, he relaxed his tensed muscles and even attempted to sing the last song.

When the congregation began to file out of church, Jesse said, "You have a beautiful voice. Do you sing much?"

"Never," Nick said quickly, as though the mere thought was ridiculous.

"I love to sing, but as you could hear, I wasn't gifted with a beautiful voice."

His gaze trapped hers. "I like your voice."

She blushed. "Are you deaf? Did you not hear me singing right beside you a moment before?"

He chuckled. "You aren't exactly on key, but your speaking voice has a pleasant sound to it."

The color in her cheeks must have flamed even more because she was hot as though the air-conditioning didn't work in the church. "Thank you. I haven't had that compliment before."

"Mom, we're gonna go outside and play. We'll be at the playground."

"Most of the kids go outside after the service while we adults visit inside where it's cool." Jesse watched Cindy and Nate disappear with several other children, Nick's daughter pushing Crystal in her wheelchair. "Cindy has made some friends."

"Usually she's shy."

"Nate won't let her be shy. He doesn't have a shy bone in his body."

"I've noticed. He takes after his mother. I think he knows everyone in town."

"Probably. He's even introduced some people to me."

"No. I don't believe that," Nick said with a laugh, falling into the line of people waiting to say something to the reverend.

"Really." When Jesse reached the front of the line, she said, "Reverend Collins, this is my new neighbor, Nick Blackburn. He and his daughter are here for two months."

The reverend took Nick's hand and shook it. "I'm glad you could visit our church. I met your daughter earlier with Nate. She was telling me how God helped find her little kitten last week."

Surprise flitted into Nick's eyes. "She was hiding in a bush by the lake, and Boswell found her right before he was heading back to the house."

"I enjoyed your sermon today, Reverend Collins."

"The heart of our faith is God's love for his children. It's not that different from the love we have for our own children. Sometimes we have to let them stumble to make them stronger, but that doesn't mean we don't love them."

Nick frowned, his eyebrows slashing downward. "Is that why there is so much suffering in the world?" he asked Jesse as they walked away from the reverend.

"There is evil in this world, Nick. You know that. God is in a constant battle with that evil. People have free will."

"Hey, you two. Jesse, I looked for you before the service. Where did you disappear to?" Darcy asked, joining them in the lobby.

"I wanted to show Nick the garden we planted last year. Even in the heat it's a beautiful place to spend some time."

"It's our meditation garden. I find when things get a little hectic around here it's a good place to escape to for a few minutes."

"This place get hectic? Never!" Jesse saw Joshua weaving his way through the crowd toward his wife. "Nick, this is Darcy's husband, Joshua Markham. They're the ones who teach the summer Sunday school class for the elementary school children. We don't have a regular schedule during the summer."

"I met your daughter this morning," Joshua said after shaking Nick's hand. "She joined the class with Nate and had a lot of good questions. She was very interested in the story of Moses. I hope she comes back again."

Even though Nick was good at hiding his emotions, Jesse could sense his stress. So much was being thrown at him that his system was overloading. "Cindy has an open invitation to come to church with me and Nate. I hate to cut this short but we have to head out."

When Jesse stepped outside, she heard Nick release a long breath. The tension in his expression slipped away. She suspected he was at home in a business environment but a social one was alien to him, especially because this past year he had been recuperating from a series of operations and learning to walk again.

"Thank you," he murmured on the sidewalk in front of the church.

"For what?"

"For understanding. Now where's that playground?" He searched the area.

Perplexed at his half answer, Jesse pointed at the back of the building. "Around on the other side." Mark had always been so easy to read. She had been able to tell what he had been thinking almost before he had. With Nick she was constantly wondering what was going through his head.

As they walked toward the playground, Jesse said, "Darcy and Joshua just got married a few months back. I'm so happy both of them discovered each other. It was touch-and-go there for a while. Joshua had sworn off ever marrying and Darcy was only here for a few months helping her father run his breeding farm while he was recovering from a heart attack."

"Marriage is fine for some people. I'm just not one of them. Once was enough for me to find that out. I don't make the same mistake a second time. That's one of the reasons I've been so successful in the business world."

"Business and personal lives are two different things."

"Not to me." Nick saw Cindy and waved her over to him.

The young girl ran up to her father, a big smile on her face. "Can I come next week?"

He glanced at Jesse, then placed his hand on Cindy's shoulder. "Sure. Jesse said you could come with her."

"But I want you to come, too. Daddy, you said we would do things together."

His chest expanded with a deep breath that he held for a few seconds before exhaling. "We'll see, sweetie, next week."

"In the meantime, how about you two going fishing with Nate and me? I thought we could have a picnic later," Jesse suggested.

"Yes!" Cindy shouted, jumping up and down and clapping her hands.

"I guess we'll be going fishing," Nick said.

Cindy whirled around and raced toward Nate to tell him.

"I'm sorry. I should have said something before mentioning it in front of Cindy. If you don't want—"

Nick placed his finger over her mouth to stop her flow of words. "I want. It was nice of you to ask us to go with you."

"Nice? Ha! I hate fooling with the bait. I was hoping you would volunteer for the job."

"What do you use?"

"Worms."

"This should be fun."

"I know a sarcastic tone when I hear one. It will be fun."

"If you say so." A smile leaked out, making his eyes glitter with merriment.

"I do."

"I think I'll go with you all and show you the best places to fish." Gramps came into the kitchen while Jesse finished up packing the picnic basket.

She looked up. "I thought you were going over to Susan's house for dinner. Lately you've been going over to see her on Sunday evenings."

"I guess I shouldn't assume anything. She told me she had other plans this evening when I mentioned I would stop by."

"Oh, what's she doing?"

Gramps lifted his shoulders in a shrug, but a frown remained on his face. "Beats me. She didn't say and I asked her straight out. She avoided the question. Most unusual."

"Well, it's not like you two are going steady or anything."

"Yeah, but for the past six weeks we have been doing

something together on Sunday *night*. I just thought we would tonight."

"Did you say anything to her before today?"

"No, I didn't think I had to."

Jesse went to the refrigerator and removed some ham and cheese to make her grandfather a sandwich. "You probably should from now on."

"So you think she doesn't have anything to do but is trying to teach me a lesson?"

Removing the bread from the cabinet, Jesse began to put the sandwich together. "Susan doesn't lie. She must have something going on."

He rubbed his chin. "But what? Maybe I should stay here after all and take a long walk this evening."

"Gramps, don't you dare spy on Susan. That wouldn't set well with her if she found out and you know very little is kept a secret for long in Sweetwater."

His shoulders slumped forward. "Fine. I'll tag along with you all."

Jesse wrapped the sandwich in aluminum foil. "Ask her again tomorrow if it bothers you that much."

"I might not see her tomorrow. Two can play hard to get."

Jesse rolled her eyes toward the ceiling, wondering at the games people played, trying to manipulate a situation to their favor. *You're just as guilty, Jesse Bradshaw,* a tiny voice in her mind interjected. She thought about the times she had tried to fix Nick up when he hadn't wanted to be fixed up with a woman. *He doesn't want* to get married again. He made that very plain this morning at church.

So why am I trying to get him married? The answer to that question was one she was afraid to acknowledge. There was something about Nick that threatened the neat little world she'd created after Mark's death. She had control over this world. She had friends and family whom she loved and who loved her. She had a job she enjoyed. Her emotions were safely wrapped up in her life in Sweetwater. She didn't want to shake up that world.

She was overreacting to the few little stomach flutters and racing heartbeats. Nick and she could be friends. No more trying to fix him up with any female between the age of twenty-five and forty. She could help Cindy while the little girl was in Sweetwater and perhaps even be able to guide Nick back to the Lord.

"Where are you thinking of going?"

Her grandfather's question cut into her musing and pulled her back to the project at hand. "I thought we could fish near where Joe's Creek empties into the lake. That's not too far from here. We can walk there. Hopefully we'll catch some fish."

"I'll let you walk there. I think I'll bring the skiff. Maybe the children will want to fish on the lake."

And leave her and Nick alone. That thought flittered across her mind, along with a sense of panic. She immediately shut down the thought before it took hold. She and Nick were friends. That was all. Even if she had wanted more, he had made it very clear he didn't want a long-term relationship with any woman.

"Fine. We'll meet you over at Joe's Creek." Jesse closed the basket and grabbed the wooden handles to lift.

"I'll take that for you."

The husky sound of Nick's voice caused the back of her neck to tingle. She sucked in a deep breath and almost forgot to breathe. Finally when her lungs screamed for oxygen, she exhaled, then inhaled and released it immediately.

Nick brushed his fingers over the back of her hand holding the basket as he took it from her. "What do you have in here? Your whole kitchen?"

"Just a few things to eat for dinner. Fishing can make a person mighty hungry."

"I agree. Lifting those fishing rods can be taxing."

"You just wait. You'll be glad I brought this food. Where's Cindy?"

"Nate let us in and he wanted to show her something in his room."

"Is Boswell coming?"

"No, he had something to do."

"He shouldn't stay cooped up in the house. It's a beautiful day."

Nick cocked his head and scrunched his mouth into a thoughtful expression. "You know, I don't think he's staying home. I got the impression he was going somewhere."

"We're ready." Nate appeared in the doorway with Cindy and Bingo beside him.

Gramps headed for the back door. "I'll take the fishing equipment in the skiff."

"Can we go with you, Gramps?" Nate hurried across the room with Cindy and Bingo trailing behind him.

Her grandfather paused and peered back at Jesse. "Is that okay with you two? I can even take that basket."

"Only if the children wear a life jacket."

"Ah, Mom, I can swim."

"You know my rule. When you're in the boat, you have to wear a life jacket."

"Fiiinne."

Nick and she followed her grandfather and the children down to the pier, skirting the area where Fred and Ethel were with their baby geese. Nick helped Cindy put on her life jacket then he deposited the basket in the bottom of the skiff. By the time the fishing equipment and the three passengers were in the small boat, there was no more room for anything or anyone else.

After Nick untied the ropes, Gramps started the motor and the skiff slowly left the dock. "See you two at Joe's Creek. Don't get lost in the woods."

Jesse could hear Cindy say, "The woods? I don't want Daddy to get lost."

Her grandfather's booming laugh sounded in the quiet afternoon air. Then Nate explained to Cindy how small the woods around Joe's Creek was.

"Do you think they'll be all right?" Nick asked, frowning as he watched the skiff head toward the shoreline to the east.

"Yes. I'd never have let Nate go if I thought otherwise. Don't worry."

"Easier said than done. I used to not worry about

Cindy. Now I do all the time. After my accident I realized how precarious life can be, how quickly it can change."

"Life is a series of changes. Nothing stays the same for long." Jesse heard her own words and realized how much she had been trying to keep her life the same, too.

"So how long is this walk to Joe's Creek?"

"Oh, about a mile. Not too far."

"Speak for yourself."

Even though his tone was teasing, Jesse remembered Nick's bad leg and said, "There's a road that is about three or four hundred yards away from where we're gonna fish. We can drive if you want."

Nick massaged the top of his right thigh. "I'll be fine. I need to walk more. When I return to Chicago, I want this leg one hundred percent."

Jesse moved down the pier. "You miss being in Chicago?"

"I miss working. I conduct some of it from here, but I promised Cindy and myself I would take some time off so I'm trying to minimize the amount of time I work while in Sweetwater. But for so many years work is what has defined who I am. That's not easy to walk away from."

"But you aren't walking away from it. You still have your work. It'll be there when you go back." Jesse noticed that Fred kept a wary eye on them as they avoided the area where the flock of geese grazed in the tall grass by the lake.

"I've done such a good job of hiring capable managers that the company is practically running itself."

"And that bothers you?"

"The last few years of my marriage to Brenda, I knew she didn't need me. But my company did. Or so I thought. Now I know I was kidding myself."

"So what are you going to do when you get back?"

"I'll get Cindy settled in school, then…" He paused. "I don't know. I haven't decided. I do know I need to spend more time with Cindy when we get back."

"You have a wonderful daughter."

"Each day I am discovering just how wonderful. This afternoon she asked me if we could help get Crystal a new wheelchair so she could play basketball. She offered the money she had been saving."

"That's so sweet, but I'm not sure Tanya wants Crystal doing that."

"If she decides to, I would be glad to buy the wheelchair."

"You would?"

"I have plenty of money. I give a certain amount every year to different causes. It would be nice knowing who will benefit."

"Then some good things are coming out of your visit to Sweetwater."

He didn't say anything about her comment concerning Sweetwater, and she wondered if he regretted coming to spend a couple of months in the house next to hers. Her community wasn't like Chicago at all.

Jesse, my girl, what did you want him to say? That Sweetwater was the perfect place to live? That he couldn't think of any place better to be? She shook her head as if that could rid herself of that little voice in the back of her mind.

When Bingo ran ahead of them yelping, she realized they were near Joe's Creek and the others. She could hear Nate and Cindy laughing while Gramps grumbled, his words too low to make out what he was saying.

She and Nick stepped out of the shadow of the trees that ran along the creek and found Gramps trudging toward shore, pulling the rope attached to the skiff.

Nate saw them. He began to laugh even more, pointing to his great-grandfather. "He didn't tie the boat up good enough. It started drifting away. He had to run after it before it ended up in the middle of the lake."

"He was funny splashing in the water." Cindy continued to laugh beside Nate.

With water dripping off him, Gramps grumbled some more, bent down and tied the skiff again, checking to make sure the rope wouldn't slip free. "You two distracted me."

"Welcome to a Bradshaw picnic," Jesse whispered to Nate. "Sure you want to stay?"

"Isn't laughter supposed to be the best medicine?" he asked, chuckling at the loud sloshing sound Gramps made with his wet tennis shoes as he headed back to the boat to retrieve the last of the fishing equipment.

Nick leaned back against an oak tree, resting his arm on a knee. "Are there any more cookies left?"

"Nope. Cindy and Nate finished off the last two before leaving with Gramps to head back home."

"That's what I thought, but I was hoping a couple or three slipped down inside the basket." The back of his head touched the rough bark of the tree as his eyes slid closed, and he relished the quiet of the moment. A bird chirped above him. A person more used to the woods would probably know what kind of bird. He had to admit he had rarely spent time in the country and this was certainly an experience.

"Did you enjoy fishing even though you didn't catch anything?"

Jesse's question brought a smile to his lips. "Seeing you try to bait your hook was well worth the time spent trying to fish."

"*You* were supposed to bait my hook for me."

"But your grandfather insisted you do it yourself. I was taught never to go against my elders."

Jesse snorted. "At least I caught a fish. And Nate. And Gramps. And Cindy."

"Yeah, did you see her big smile when she pulled in that fish?"

Jesse finished putting the trash and leftover food into the basket. "It's called a crappie. She enjoyed herself."

"And so did I." Pushing to his feet, Nick took the blanket he had been sitting on and began folding it. "Anytime you want to ask Cindy and I to come fishing please feel free to."

"I can loan you a couple of rods and reels so you and Cindy can go anytime you want."

"I'll see what she says, but I think she liked the skiff the most."

"Has she ever been in a boat?"

"She went on a friend's yacht on Lake Michigan once. Not quite the same experience. I'm not even sure she realized she was on the water. She stayed in the cabin and watched TV the whole time." Nick took the basket and started toward the trail they'd used earlier.

The "woods" were no more than twenty or thirty trees of various kinds that flanked one side of the creek. In less than three minutes he and Jesse emerged from the woods and saw their houses in the distance. Gramps docked the skiff at the pier behind Jesse's home. The children ran ahead of the old man toward Jesse's deck.

Nick looked toward the lake, glass smooth. The sun had sunk below the tree line to the west, and the sky was ribboned with oranges and reds. He drew in a deep breath saturated with the scent of forest and earth. "It's a gorgeous day," he murmured, surprised by the feeling of contentment that held him.

Stepping over a log, Jesse slipped and nearly fell. Nick quickly dropped the basket and grabbed for her. Steadying her, he brought her up against him. Her jasmine scent chased away all others. He filled his nostrils with it, closing his eyes for a few seconds as he savored having a beautiful woman in his arms.

Then the fact he was holding Jesse registered, and he quickly let her go, moving back a few paces while he picked up the basket.

But the rapid rise and fall of her chest attested to the effect their encounter had on her. Something more than friendship could develop between them if he allowed it. It wasn't fair of him to take this any further. He would be gone in a month's time and Jesse deserved more than that. She deserved a husband like her first one, who would love her totally and be committed to a relationship that would last a lifetime. He had learned the hard way he wasn't that kind of man. He wouldn't make that mistake again.

"That's funny." Jesse frowned. "Where's Gramps going?"

Nick followed the direction Jesse pointed and saw the older man hurrying toward the house he rented. Jesse's grandfather still clutched the cooler with the fish they had caught. The way he held himself suggested one angry man. "My house? Why?"

"Oh, no. Look."

Boswell brought two tall glasses outside and handed one to a woman. "Who is that?"

"I think it's Susan Reed and Gramps isn't a happy camper. We'd better hurry and intercede." She hastened her steps.

"Unless we can fly we won't make it in time."

Nick watched Jesse's grandfather come to halt in front of Boswell who sat next to Susan on the deck. The old man's shouts could probably be heard in town or across the lake.

"Oh, my." Jesse began to jog.

As Nick and Jesse approached the trio, Nate and Cindy stood between Gramps and Boswell with Susan off to the side wringing her hands and shaking her head.

"So this was why you didn't come with us fishing. Trying to horn in on my gal."

"Gerard Daniels, I am not your gal."

"Yes, you are." Gramps flicked a glance toward Susan before returning his steely look to Boswell, almost toe to toe with him.

"No, I am not. I invited Boswell to experience a good American dinner at my house."

This time Jesse's grandfather turned his full attention to Susan. "*You* invited him? On *our* night?"

Jesse stepped forward before a war erupted on Nick's deck. "Nate, why don't you show Cindy your snake?"

"She's seen it," Nate replied as though there wasn't anything that could possibly drag him away from the action.

"Nate!"

Except the warning tone in his mother's voice, Nick thought with amusement.

"Oh, all right." Nate huffed. "I don't see why I have to show her something she's already seen."

"Daddy?" His daughter whined, clearly not wanting to leave either if her eager expression was any indication.

"Go on, Cindy. We'll be over in a minute."

Nate and Cindy stomped off, whispering between themselves, while Jesse's grandfather pressed his lips together and glared at Susan.

When the children were inside Jesse's house, her grandfather said, "Well, what do you have to say for yourself, Susan Reed?"

Susan returned his glare, folding her arms across her chest. "Absolutely nothing. I'm going home, Gerard Daniels. Alone." She swung to Boswell, smiled at him and said, "Thank you for a lovely evening. I'll see your stamp collection another time."

"I'll walk you to your car."

Susan shook her head. "I can find my own way. But thanks, anyway."

When she was gone, Jesse's grandfather moved to block Boswell's path into the house. "Stamp collection? When trying to lure a woman home, couldn't you come up with something better than that?"

Boswell straightened his shoulders and looked down his nose at Jesse's grandfather. "I would put my stamp collection up against anyone else's around here. I have some rare stamps."

"I just bet you do. Is that what you told Susan to get her to come back here after dinner?"

Boswell puffed out his chest. "What I say to Susan is none of your business. Now if you will kindly move, I am retiring for the evening." He didn't wait for Jesse's grandfather to step aside. He pushed past him and was inside the sliding glass doors before Gramps could recover and say anything.

He stood staring at Boswell's retreating back, clenching and unclenching his hands. "Well, I never," he muttered.

Jesse lay her hand on Gramps's shoulder. "You'd better clean the fish before they spoil."

Gramps frowned. "I don't understand Susan anymore. Why would she go out with him?" He flicked his wrist toward the sliding glass door.

"Gramps, have you ever talked to Susan about how you feel?"

He stared at her as though she had suddenly sprouted a second head. "Why would I do that? I'm not good with words. She should know how I feel."

"A woman likes to hear a man tell her. Don't expect her to read your mind."

He whirled about and stalked toward Jesse's house. "I've got fish to clean. The rods and reels are still on the pier. I don't have time to tell a woman how I feel."

Jesse's posture seemed to deflate.

"Are you all right, Jesse?" Nick touched her arm.

She jerked away as though surprised to find him there. For a few seconds her weariness lined her face then gradually a smile transformed it into a picture of serenity. "Yes. Gramps sometimes takes an extra dose of my patience, but I love him."

He held out his hand to her. "Come on. I'll help you get the fishing equipment. I want to get my half of the fish, too."

"Half! I don't recall you catching half."

The fit of her hand within his comforted him. He began walking toward the pier. "But I was hoping you would take pity on a novice and give me more than my share."

"Tell you what. I'll do one better. We'll have a fish fry tomorrow night and you, Boswell and Cindy are invited."

"Are you sure about Boswell and Gramps being together?"

"They're two grown men and they'll have to learn to behave around each other."

"Just because you declare it doesn't mean it will happen."

"I'll have a talk with Gramps and point out the fact young ears will be listening. That usually works."

The growing darkness cloaked him in a sense of well-being. Even though his leg ached and he found himself limping more profoundly, being next to Jesse made the pain insignificant. The sound of the water lapping against the pier calmed him. The fresh scent of nature soothed his senses. But most of all, Jesse's presence pacified the restlessness within.

At the end of the pier where the rods and reels lay, Nick paused, turning toward Jesse. The shadows of dusk didn't hide her smile. The gleam in her eyes drew him a step closer. Linking both hands with hers, he laced their fingers and brought them up between them.

The pounding of his heart drove all rational sense from his mind as he leaned toward her.

Chapter Eight

Nick paused. A whisper separated Jesse from him. If she moved even an inch, their lips would touch. Her heartbeat kicked up a notch, thumping against her rib cage so loudly she wondered if he could hear it.

Releasing her hands, he brought his up to cup her face, so lovingly she wanted to melt against him. His gaze linked to hers as their fingers had been only seconds before, a tangible connection.

"You are so beautiful."

His softly spoken compliment robbed her of coherent thought. She stood before him mesmerized by his eyes, dark pools that reflected a painful past, an inner struggle. He fought to mask his expression but she saw his anguish, hidden from most.

"Today was fun."

She latched on to his comment as though it were a lifeline. "Yes, it was." Her mouth dry, she licked her lips. "Nate got a kick out of showing you how to fish."

He grinned, tiny lines fanning out from his eyes. "I noticed your grandfather laughing a few times at my poor attempt to cast a line."

"That's why they tolerate me. I'm great at untangling lines."

"I noticed."

The space between them shrunk. Their breaths tangled. His hands combed through her short hair and pressed her closer. His mouth settled over hers, and she thought the world had stopped spinning. She clung to him and savored the feel of his lips as they moved over hers.

When he pulled back, she realized she was losing her battle to remain detached. She cared about Cindy, but she also cared about Nick—too much. They lived in different worlds. His revolved around his work in Chicago. Hers revolved around her faith and Sweetwater and that wasn't going to change. She didn't see any way for their two worlds to mesh together.

Quickly before she lost her nerve, she stepped back. "Why did you do that?" *Why did you make me care about you?*

His brows slashed downward. "I don't know why. It seemed the right thing to do at the time." Moving away even farther, Nick bent and picked up the rods and reels, cradling them in his arms.

"I consider you a friend."

"I feel the same way."

"But that is all. There is no future in anything else."

A frown carved his features with harsh lines. "It was just a kiss, Jesse. I agree there is no future for us. You're the marrying kind and I don't want to get married."

His words hurt. "I don't, either. Besides, you live in Chicago and I live here. I won't leave Sweetwater. My life is here." Her voice rose a level.

"My life is in Chicago," Nick said in a near shout.

She placed her fists on her waist and glared at him. "I like a quiet, simpler life."

He started to say something, stopped and snapped his mouth closed. Then he chuckled. "Actually I'm beginning to value quiet and simple," he whispered, scanning the area.

The tension siphoned from Jesse. She didn't normally blow up at a person for no reason and a kiss wasn't really a good reason. "Sorry. I think I overreacted. You took me by surprise."

"I took myself by surprise. It was a nice kiss, though."

Something inside of her melted as she thought back to the kiss. "Yes, it was."

"Still friends?"

She nodded.

"Good." He released a long sigh. "Because Cindy adores you."

"And Nate adores you."

"I'm thinking about seeing if the Millers will sell this house. I'd like to buy it and use it as a summer home."

His declaration shocked her. Her mouth parted but no words came out. He would return each summer! The mere thought sent her mind whirling, her pulse rate speeding.

"I haven't said anything to Cindy yet so I would appreciate it if you wouldn't. I'm not sure if I will, but this is a good place for her. We both could use some down time where it is quiet and we can regroup as a family."

Jesse heard his explanation, but the words didn't really register. She was still trying to work through the fact she would see him every summer—just long enough to begin to care—whoa! She wasn't going to go there. If he did buy the house, she would deal with it when it occurred.

"What do you think?"

"I think Sweetwater is a good place for Cindy. She has already made some friends, and Nate will be excited if you come back every summer."

"And you?"

Oh, dear, why did he have to ask that question? "Of course," she finally answered, her throat thick with emotions she was trying to deny.

"It's important to get along with your neighbors. There isn't anyone on the left and with you on the right I know this would be a good place."

"You can say that after what we witnessed earlier between Gramps and Boswell?"

"I guess I'd better get Boswell's opinion. He's invaluable and I wouldn't want to lose him."

"Gramps can have that effect on people. I really don't blame Susan for looking elsewhere. She and Gramps have been dating on and off for several years. She's wanted to take the relationship to the next level and my grandfather has been dragging his feet. Commitment shy."

"I can understand that."

"Here, let me help you with those rods."

"Nah, I've got them." He glanced about. "I guess we'd better head to the house. It's almost completely dark."

She hadn't noticed how dark it had become. The light at the end of the pier that automatically came on gave off enough illumination that she could see Nick's face. But the surrounding landscape was obscured as though someone had thrown a dark blanket over them, shielding them in their own world.

"I'm surprised that Nate and Cindy haven't come out to see where we are." Jesse began walking toward the end of the pier.

Nick fell into step next to her. "They're probably quizzing your grandfather about what happened."

"I hadn't thought about that. We'd better hurry. No telling what he will tell them." She quickened her pace.

Nick placed the rods and reels down by the back door. When Jesse entered the kitchen, she found Nate, Cindy and Gramps sitting at the table, drinking sodas and eating some oatmeal cookies. She thought of the caffeine in the sodas and groaned.

"Gramps, Nate isn't supposed to have a soda this late."

"So upset, it must have slipped my mind."

Nate quickly downed the rest of his can. "I'll go to bed on time."

"But will you go to sleep on time?"

"Sure." Her son flashed her a grin, popped the last bit of cookie into his mouth and leaped to his feet. "Come on, Cindy. I'm going to feed my animals. Wanna help?"

"Yes." Cindy grabbed her last cookie and stuffed it into her mouth as they raced from the room.

"I guess I'll be leaving, too." Gramps pushed himself to his feet and scooped up the remaining cookies to take with him.

Jesse stared at the mess left on the kitchen table, crumbs, empty pop cans. "What just happened here?"

"I think it's called fleeing the scene of the crime."

"We'll be lucky if they go to sleep before three in the morning. They have enough sugar and caffeine in them for ten kids." Jesse retrieved a dishcloth from the sink and wiped off the table.

Nick tossed the cans into the recycling bin. "When Cindy doesn't sleep, I don't sleep."

"That's being a full-fledged parent. Never rest unless your child is resting. I've worked on many a doll in the middle of the night. Not a bad time to read, either."

"I'll keep that in mind when I'm up tonight. Better yet, I'll call you and you can keep me company."

"Sure," she said, not really thinking he would.

But six hours later Jesse answered the phone on the first ring, nearly jumping out of the chair she sat in. "Hello," she said breathlessly.

"Hi. I thought you'd be up, and when I saw your light on in the den, I figured I would take you up on keeping me company."

"Nick?" she asked, knowing full well it was him.

"Who else would be calling you this late?"

Jesse glanced at the clock. "It's three!" She had been so busy on her latest doll for the Fourth of July auction at church that she had lost track of time.

"Very good."

"Cindy's still up?"

"No, she went to bed hours ago."

"Then why are you up?"

"Couldn't sleep. I guess all that talk about not sleeping put the suggestion in my brain. Is Nate still up?"

She listened for any sound coming from upstairs. His room was right above the den. "No, I guess he's finally gone to sleep. You know, I could have been Gramps. He doesn't always sleep well."

"I saw you through the window."

Jesse lifted her head and stared at the darkness outside. She often forgot to draw the drapes. Rising, she walked to the window and looked toward Nick's house. With a phone to his ear, he watched her. She waved. He waved back.

"You really should pull your curtains."

"This isn't Chicago."

"I know. Every day I am reminded of how different Sweetwater is from Chicago." He moved away from the window. "What are you doing? You look so intense working at that table."

"Making a doll for the church benefit."

"When is it? I might have to buy it. I know Cindy would want an original doll by Jesse."

"It's for an auction and it's on the Fourth of July. The money goes toward our outreach program so I hope you will come and force the bidding up high." She missed seeing him in the window. Reluctantly Jesse pulled the drapes, then returned to her chair at the card table.

"You've got yourself a date," Nick's deep raspy voice came through the receiver.

The word *date* sent a shiver down her spine. She clutched the phone tighter to her ear and squeezed her eyes shut for a few seconds, reliving the *kiss*. Her mouth tingled. "Maybe Cindy would like to help me make a doll she can donate to the auction."

"I'll ask her. And while you keep my daughter entertained, I'll take your son fishing. I went online when I couldn't sleep and got some information about fishing that should help me. I'm determined to catch one this time."

"Sure. We can add them to the fish fry."

"Sounds good to me."

She heard him yawn and yawned herself. "We'd better get some sleep or we won't be much good tomorrow."

"Sweet dreams, Jesse."

She sat for a long moment, her hand lingering on the receiver, visualizing Nick in his house, dressed comfortably, with a lazy smile on his face and a dancing gleam in his eyes, his feet propped up on an ottoman. At home. In Sweetwater.

She sighed and wiped the picture from her mind. Too dangerous.

* * *

Jesse sat at the kitchen table with her hand cupping her chin and her elbow on the wooden surface. Her eyelids began to slide closed even though Nate and Gramps were talking—had been nonstop for the past fifteen minutes. The drone of their voices lulled her to sleep—sleep she should have gotten the night before. Even when she went to bed, she'd tossed about on her mattress as though she were a small boat on an ocean caught in a big storm. And at the center of the storm was Nick Blackburn!

"Mom!"

Nate shook her shoulder, rousing her from her dreamlike state. She straightened, blinking. "What?"

"You weren't listening to what I said."

"I'm afraid I didn't get enough sleep last night. A little boy was up way too late and kept me up, too."

Nate dropped his head. "Sorry, Mom."

"That's okay, sweetheart."

His head shot back up, and he grinned from ear to ear. "Did you hear? Nick's taking me fishing this morning. Isn't that great?"

"Wonderful, darling." Jesse took a large swallow of her lukewarm coffee, hoping the caffeine would kick in real soon before she laid her head on the table and started snoring.

"He wants me to give him some more pointers on how to fish. Me, Mom," Nate pointed to himself. "Can you believe it?"

She ruffled her son's hair. "Yes. You're a good fisherman."

"You need to take the skiff to O'Reilly's Cove," Gramps advised as he stood and shuffled toward the coffeepot to pour himself some more of the brew. "Should be some fish there. All he should have to do is put his line in the water to catch anything." He lifted the glass pot toward Jesse.

"Yes, please." She slid her mug with painted lady-bugs on it across the table, then slid it back when her grandfather refilled it to the brim. Steam wafted to the ceiling, the rich dark color reminding Jesse of Nick's eyes. Why was it everywhere she turned she thought of Nick? "I think Gramps is right. O'Reilly's Cove has some of the best fishing on the lake."

"Gramps, it's okay if we take the skiff then?"

"Sure, son. I've got some powerful thinking to do today so I won't be using it." Gramps eased back into his chair, cradling his mug between his hands.

"Thinking?" both Nate and Jesse said at the same time.

"Every once and a while a man's got to do some thinking about his life. Take stock of the direction it's heading. You'll learn that as you grow up."

Jesse wasn't sure one hundred percent her grandfather was just talking to Nate. There was a look in his eyes that said his comments were also aimed at her. She didn't see any need to change the direction her life was heading. She was content with it the way it was. And everything will be back to normal when Nick and Cindy leave in a month, she declared silently.

She repositioned herself in her chair, trying to get

comfortable. Again she found herself staring at the coffee in the mug and thinking about the man next door. He should be here soon. How did she look? She'd been so tired when she had gotten up that she hadn't even looked in the mirror when she'd combed her hair.

A knock at the back door sent Nate leaping from his chair and hurrying to answer it. The man who had plagued her thoughts appeared in the entrance with a smile on his face but tired lines about his eyes. Good, he hadn't gotten any more sleep than she had, and it was affecting him, too.

"Ready to go after Moby Dick?" Nick stepped into the house with Cindy right behind him, eating a piece of toast with strawberry jam.

"Moby Dick?" Nate asked, his face screwing up into a confused expression.

"A whale in a story I once read."

"There aren't any whales in the lake." Nate whirled toward his great-grandfather. "Are there, Gramps?"

"No, son. He was just kidding."

"Oh." Nate turned back to Nick and said in a serious tone, "There is an old catfish that Gramps keeps trying to catch. He's pretty slippery. He lives in O'Reilly's Cove. Maybe you can get him."

"Or maybe you can." Nick saw the coffeepot still half full. "May I have a cup before we hit the water?"

"Yes." Jesse rose and went to the counter to pour Nick a mug. "Are you ready to help me make a doll, Cindy?"

Still chewing the last of her toast, the little girl nodded. Nick leaned against the counter and sipped his coffee. "The second she heard about the plans for today, she grabbed the last piece of toast on her plate and dragged me out the door. I didn't even get to finish my coffee. So this is a welcomed relief." He raised his mug.

"Did you get anything to eat? I could fix you something."

Nick shook his head. "I'm fine. Coffee is all I need right now. How far is this O'Reilly's Cove? Do we walk or drive?"

"You can use the skiff. Much easier." Gramps stood and brought his cup to the sink, then headed toward the door.

"Why don't you come with us, sir?"

Before disappearing out the back door, Gramps glanced over his shoulder. "Thanks, but I've got plans."

When her grandfather closed the door, Nick asked, "He isn't going over to my house to see Boswell, is he?"

Jesse walked to the window to watch her grandfather head away from Nick's house. "No, I don't think so. He likes to walk when he has some thinking to do. I wouldn't be surprised if he turns up at O'Reilly's Cove later."

Nate tried to whistle but didn't quite make the correct sound. "That's far."

"Are you ready to leave?" Nick finished the last of his coffee and placed the mug on the counter by the sink. "I saw the fishing equipment on the deck by the door."

"Gramps checked to make sure we had everything."

"You'd better get your ball cap. It's gonna be hot in a few hours." As Nate and Cindy left the kitchen in search of his hat, Jesse said, "Make sure he puts on sunscreen every hour. He tends to burn easily if he doesn't. And he will have to wear a life jacket. He'll complain."

Nick's gaze captured hers. "I'll take good care of him. Like he was my own." After he said the last sentence, Nick's eyes widened for a few seconds, then he turned away so Jesse couldn't see his expression.

But his words stuck in her mind and played through her thoughts as she watched her son and neighbor walk down to the pier and get into the skiff. Even when working with Cindy to make a small baby doll for the auction, she couldn't keep from thinking about Nick. What were he and Nate doing right that moment? Had they caught a fish yet? Were they having a good time?

"Jesse. Jesse." Cindy's voice pulled her from her thoughts. She shook the image of Nick seated in the skiff steering it toward the calmer water of the cove. "Sorry, I was thinking about a…friend."

"Is this enough stuffing for the arms?"

"I'd use a little more." Jesse rose from her worktable in the den and walked toward the window.

The sparkling blue water gleamed in the sunlight. She looked toward the direction of O'Reilly's Cove, wondering what Nate and Nick were doing. Maybe Cindy and she should drive around to the cove and try to spot them. She could use a break and she was sure Cindy could, too.

"Want to check out what your dad and Nate are

doing?" Jesse rolled her shoulders to work the stiffness out of them.

"Daddy didn't eat any breakfast. Maybe we could bring them something to eat."

"What a wonderful idea." Jesse walked to Cindy and hugged the child. "Your father is lucky to have you as a daughter."

"Boswell says he needs me."

"And I agree with Boswell. What do you think we should bring them to eat?"

Cindy laid the arms to her doll on the table and stood. "Daddy likes ham or turkey sandwiches."

"Great. I've got some turkey and I'll fix a peanut butter and jelly one for Nate. Do you want one, too?"

"Yes."

In the kitchen with Cindy's help Jesse had the sandwiches prepared in ten minutes. She took several sodas from the refrigerator and a bag of cookies from the pantry and placed the food and drinks in a big paper sack.

"Ready." Jesse grabbed her set of keys and started for the back door.

Fifteen minutes later she and Cindy stood on the shore at O'Reilly's Cove and waved at Nick and Nate in the skiff out in the middle about thirty yards away. When her son saw them, he got to his feet, waving back at them. The skiff rocked in the water. Nick gripped Nate's hand and yanked him back down on the seat.

The sound of the motor echoed through the tree-lined cove. Nick directed the skiff toward them and shore. The second he landed the boat on the small sandy beach, Nate jumped from it and splashed through the shallow water toward them.

"I'm sure glad Gramps didn't see you standing up in the boat. Now you see why I have you wear a life jacket."

"Don't tell Gramps I forgot."

"No more complaining about wearing a life jacket."

"Promise."

"Finished the doll already?" Nick asked Cindy, appearing at Nate's side.

"Almost, Daddy. I've got all the parts done. We just have to put it together."

"We thought we would take a break and bring you guys something to eat. Hungry?"

"Yep. What you got?" Nate peered into the sack that Jesse held.

She gave him the bag. "Sandwiches, sodas and cookies. Nothing fancy."

"I'm starved. My kind of lunch—food." Nick said, checking out the sack's contents, too.

Jesse chuckled. "You wouldn't be so hungry if you didn't skip breakfast. It's the most important meal of the day."

"Have you been talking to Boswell? That's what he says."

"Nope. Know that fact all on my own."

Nate took the sack to an outcrop of rocks and put it down on a flat one that resembled a stone table. Both her son and Nick delved inside and withdrew the contents, Nate licking his lips while Nick's eyes gleamed in appreciation.

"Fishing is hard work. I could eat double this." Nick unwrapped his sandwich and took a big bite.

"All you've done is sit around waiting for a fish to take the bait. That isn't hard work in my book. By the way, do you have any?"

Nick shook his head while chewing his second bite. After washing his food down with a swallow of pop, he said, "Worrying is hard work."

"What in the world are you worrying about?"

"When or even *if* I'm gonna catch a fish."

Jesse stepped away from the children who sat on the rocks, eating peanut butter and jelly sandwiches. "You're really getting into this fishing."

"I've got a reputation to uphold."

"What reputation?"

"Whatever I set my mind to, I do well."

"Then I've got confidence you will conquer fishing…one day."

"I hear doubt in your voice that it won't be today."

"There's more to fishing than just putting your line in the water and getting a fish."

"I know that."

"You can't conquer it in one day. Gramps has been doing it for years, and he's still amazed at some of the things that have happened."

"Like the old catfish that has evaded him?"

"I personally hope he never catches it. It gives him something to look forward to each time he goes out."

"And we need something to look forward to when we wake up each morning."

"Yes. I thank God every day I get out of bed."

"Why? He took the one person you loved the most away from you."

The harsh tone of Nick's voice took her by surprise. His words snatched her breath. She couldn't think of anything to say for a long moment. Then an answer came into her mind as though God spoke to her. "Mark is with the Lord now. One day I will join him so he's not lost to me. My memories of my husband will sustain me until then." She tilted her head. "Why are you angry with God?"

"If He loves us so much, why do we suffer?"

"He's never denied us free will. We have choices. Sometimes they lead to heartache. As a parent, do you not find there are times you must discipline your child? That is the way children learn."

"Gramps!"

Nate's shout drew Jesse's attention. Her grandfather strode across the beach toward them.

"I was nearby and thought I would see how you two were doing. Caught any fish yet?"

"No," both Nick and Nate answered at the same time.

"Nick got a nibble and I think I lost the old catfish. He snapped my line. I had to show Nick how to fix it."

"I half expected you to be here when I showed up. What took you so long, Gramps?" Jesse asked, seeing the intensity in Nick's features smooth into a neutral expression.

"I made a little stop on the way." Her grandfather stared at the ground, toeing the sand at his feet.

"Did Susan see you?"

His head shot up. "No. I know she was home. Her car was in the driveway, but she wouldn't open the door to me."

"Do you blame her after your antics last night?"

"That's okay. I'll catch her when we're setting up for the Fourth of July celebration. She won't miss that. She'll have to talk to me then."

"Daddy, can we help set up, too? Jesse told me they could always use extra people." Cindy hopped down from her rock to come stand by her father. "They spend all day the day before getting everything ready."

When Nick didn't answer immediately, Jesse said, "If you have something to do, Cindy can go with us. Her doll will be on display on a table until the auction."

"No, I'm pretty free until the end of July. What time?"

"We have breakfast together at seven, then there's an early morning worship service for the helpers, then we start setting up. The service is at eight. We will probably be putting things out by nine. You can always meet us there at nine."

"Daddy, Jesse needs me to help with breakfast. She's in charge of it. Can we go at seven?"

Chapter Nine

Nick looked from his daughter to Jesse, feeling trapped. He couldn't deny Cindy her request but that meant they would stay for the service at eight. Ever since the one he had attended with Jesse, he hadn't been able to get the reverend's words out of his mind. They haunted him with memories of his past, attending church with his mother every week until she was too ill to go. She died a broken woman, her hard life dragging her down until she couldn't get up anymore.

"Daddy, can we?"

"Sure, sweetie. We can help."

Cindy clapped and hurried back to Nate on the rocks. She grabbed a cookie and stuffed it into her mouth, then finished her soda. Gramps joined them, taking a cookie from the bag.

"Will you be all right with going at seven?"

"You mean can I deal with attending a church service? Yes. It's important to Cindy."

"You know Cindy is right. I could use a few extra pair of hands to help with breakfast."

"What time do you need us there?"

"Six or six-thirty, whenever you can make it."

"The day is getting longer and longer. When do you usually finish getting everything ready?"

"Oh, about five or so. It depends on how many times we stop to chat."

"I'm thinking the setup is one big social event."

"Almost more than the actual Fourth of July celebration."

Nick turned to Nate. "Are you ready to fish some more?"

"Yep. Gramps is gonna ride back with us in the skiff."

"We might be a while. I'm determined to catch a fish." Nick began walking toward the boat, his leg aching.

Gramps put an arm about his shoulder. "Son, fishing happens in its own time frame. Just because you want it doesn't mean it will happen today. But I can give you some pointers to help your cause."

Nick pushed the skiff out into the water, took his seat and started the motor. He waved goodbye to Jesse and Cindy. He'd been pleased to see them earlier and hated seeing them leave. But he and Nate had some serious fishing to do. Despite what Gramps said, he intended to catch himself a fish today.

"You want me to be in charge of the bacon? Have you gone daft?" Nick asked standing in the middle of the church kitchen. "You remember what I nearly did to the fish at the fish fry the other night. Charred is not one of my favorite ways to eat fish or bacon."

With wooden spoon in hand, Jesse placed her fists on her waist. "Darcy called and told me she's running late. She was supposed to help me cook."

"How about one of the other ladies?"

"Beth's taking care of the biscuits, Zoey the gravy and I'm doing the eggs. You can trade places with any of us." When he didn't say anything, she continued, "Here let me show you how, using the microwave. It's about a minute for each piece of bacon." Using a paper plate and paper towels, Jesse stacked six pieces, then punched in the time. "All you have to do is get it out, check to make sure they're done enough, then repeat the process."

"I can do that." Relieved, Nick moved in front of the microwave, his gaze fixed upon the clock ticking down the seconds.

"Of course you can. Weren't you the man who finally caught the old catfish at O'Reilly's Cove?"

He tossed her a look with a smile deep in his eyes.

"The same man who threw the catfish back in the water?"

"He'd been around too long for me to be the one to end his life."

"You're a softie, Nick Blackburn. Gramps couldn't believe after hours sitting in the skiff waiting for a fish to take your bait that you managed to bring in the catfish and then you decide to let him go."

"I know. He lectured me the whole way back to the pier that if I'm going to go fishing I should eat what I catch."

"Maybe fishing isn't for you."

"I enjoyed spending time with Nate."

Jesse cracked several more eggs, added milk, salt and pepper, then whipped the contents of the bowl before pouring it into a skillet. "He had a good time. He's never had a chance to show an adult how to do something. He felt very important, especially when his pupil outfished most people who have been trying for that catfish for years. He's been telling everyone he taught you everything you know."

"Is that why Sean wanted my autograph?"

"Yep, you've become a local hero. How did you manage to keep the fish on the line?"

Nick appeared sheepish. "Don't tell anyone I don't know. I guess you can chalk it up to beginner's luck."

"Mom, Cindy and I have set the tables. Anything else you want us to do?"

Jesse began mixing some more scrambled eggs for the second skillet. "Can you two put the pitchers of orange juice out on each table?"

The beep of the microwave sounded and Nick went to work removing the paper plate and sticking another one inside. "How many people are coming for breakfast?"

"About twenty. If we get too many it becomes confusing when we're trying to put everything together later. A few parishioners will stop by this afternoon, but most of the work is done by the committee." Jesse stirred the eggs in the first skillet. "Beth is the organizer of this event every year and it always goes like clockwork. She's very good at organizing."

Nick glanced at the woman taking a batch of biscuits out of the oven. "She does a lot around here."

"I don't know what we would do without her. She's quite remarkable."

"I could use someone like her at my company."

A seed of jealousy took hold and surprised Jesse. Not but a few weeks before, she had been trying to fix Nick up with Beth and now she didn't want— She had no right to be jealous. Nick deserved someone to love him unconditionally. She'd had that once in her life and knew how important that was. She suspected Nick hadn't.

Jesse untied her white apron and hung it up on a hook by the door. "The last pan of biscuits is in the oven. They should come out in about fifteen minutes. I'm going to greet everyone as they arrive and have them start eating. We have a lot to do today."

Nate rushed into the kitchen with Cindy right behind him. "Can we eat now? I'm starved."

"Me, too."

"Sure. Save us a seat. We'll be through in a few minutes."

The microwave beeped again and Nick handled it as though he cooked all the time. "This is much easier than frying bacon in a pan."

"Not as messy, either. Next I have to teach you something more complicated."

"And threaten Boswell? I can't do that to the man."

"I don't think anyone can threaten Boswell. Have you seen Gramps and Boswell when they run into each other out in the yard?"

"They're like rams squaring off."

"And Susan has gone into hiding, which is so unusual for her."

"Can you blame her? Both of them walk by her house several times a day. I've never seen Boswell like this."

"I've never seen Gramps like this, either." Jesse removed the first skillet of scrambled eggs then the second one. She ladled the contents on a large platter.

Zoey breezed by and whisked the platter from her hand to take to the first round table in the rec hall. Jesse made some more for the second table which would be filling up quickly as people arrived.

Fifteen minutes later Jesse and Nick sat down at the third table with Cindy, Nate, Zoey, Beth, Darcy, Joshua and Reverend Collins. Jesse took Nick's and Nate's hands, then bowed her head as the reverend said the blessing. She noticed Nick followed suit after a few seconds of hesitation. Cindy's amen sounded above all the others and brought Nick's head up, a surprised expression on his face.

Jesse began passing the platters around. As she spooned some scrambled eggs onto her plate, she glanced across the table and saw Darcy pass up most of the food, which was unusual for her friend. Darcy's features were pasty.

"Are you all right, Darcy?" Jesse asked while pouring some orange juice into her glass.

Her friend peered at Joshua for a long moment, then said, "My stomach's upset. That's why I was late."

"If you aren't feeling well, you should go home. We can do it without you." Beth drowned her two biscuits in white gravy.

"I'll be fine in a while." Darcy took a deep breath. "I have an announcement. I'm pregnant and have a touch of morning sickness that usually goes away about ten. Then I'll be ravenous."

"That's great news! Congratulations, you two." Jesse lifted her orange juice glass. "Here's to the happy, soon-to-be parents."

"I've got months and months to go. I'm not due until February."

"This is wonderful. I'll get to plan a baby shower," Zoey said, breaking her bacon into pieces to mix with her eggs. "And I have lots of baby clothes you can use if you have a little girl. Tara is growing so fast she hasn't used half of what she has."

The heavy thickness in Zoey's voice caused the people at the table to grow quiet. Jesse's own throat constricted. Her childhood friend had recently returned to Sweetwater, a widow with three children, one born after her husband disappeared, now presumed dead by the government agency he worked for. At least she had known when Mark had died. She had been able to have some closure at the funeral, but Zoey hadn't.

"Mom, can I have some orange juice?" Nate's voice broke into the silence.

Someone at one of the other tables laughed. Another person said something about children having bottomless pits when it came to food. Relief flowed around the group. Zoey blinked back tears and smiled, her eyes shimmering.

"This is the reason I came back to Sweetwater. It's nice coming home to people who care." Zoey brushed a lone tear from her cheek and picked up her fork to eat her eggs.

Nick leaned close to Jesse and whispered, "I'm beginning to see why you said you take care of your own. I heard about her husband's plane going down in the Amazon. It must be hard not knowing one hundred percent if he's dead or alive. But she seems to be doing okay because of you all." He indicated the people at the table.

"Remember Darcy mentioning us meeting on Saturdays when we were at Harry's Café? We started the group of ladies because of Tanya and Zoey. They need our support."

"That was the meeting you had last week?"

She nodded. "We solved the problems of the world."

How different would his life had been if he had grown up in a town where the people cared what happened to their neighbors? Nick wondered, taking in each adult sitting at the table. They had been friends a long time, had grown up together. He didn't have that. Work had consumed him and that had left little to no time to form friendships. He hadn't even done a good job with his marriage. He and his wife had been strangers living in the same house. Even his relationship with his daughter was much like that. But he was doing something to change that. He would be the kind of father Cindy deserved.

"Who's cleaning up?" Nick asked when he finished the last of his breakfast.

"Everyone." Jesse rose with her plate and utensils.

Nick looked up at her. "Won't that be a bit crowded in the kitchen?"

"Some will clear and throw away the paper plates and cups, plastic utensils, some will wash and put the dishes in the dishwasher and some will stack the chairs and fold up the tables. Shouldn't take too long."

If he hadn't seen it himself, he would have doubted it could be done so quickly and efficiently. No one barked orders or told anyone what to do. People did what had to be done and the rec hall and kitchen were cleaned up in fifteen minutes. Again he felt as though these people worked as a well-coordinated group who had been together a long time and knew each other well. Jesse made sure he was included, but he still felt as though he were that little boy looking through the toy store window at the electric train set that never appeared under his Christmas tree.

After cleanup, the workers began filing into the sanctuary for the short service. Nick hung back to the last, hesitant to go inside. He didn't belong. The strong urge to escape descended, but his feet wouldn't move toward the outside doors. Sweat broke out on his upper lip. Two sets of doors called to him—one offered the escape in his head he knew he should take, the other offered a place in a town that cared. Torn with indecision, he rubbed his hand across his mouth.

Nick took a step toward the double glass doors that led to the outside. Then another. He stopped and glanced back at the doors that led into the sanctuary.

Jesse stood in the entrance into the sanctuary, waiting for him. Her face shone with a radiance and calm acceptance of whatever he chose for himself. She didn't say a word.

You don't belong in there.

God has forsaken you.

There is nothing you can give to these people but money.

Doubt after doubt inundated him. His gaze riveted to Jesse's. She smiled and held out her hand to him.

What if I gave God a second chance? What if He gave me a second chance?

His heartbeat accelerated. He spun on his heel and covered the distance between them. Taking her hand, he squeezed it, the beat of his heart continuing to pound against his chest.

"Are you all right?"

The concern in Jesse's voice and expression touched him, thawing the ice his emotions were encased in— had been for a long time. Why couldn't he have met her years ago—before Brenda, before life had happened? Now it was too late. "I'm fine. I'm a survivor, Jesse, so nothing gets me down for long."

"That's good. I thought for a minute you were leaving."

He peered into the sanctuary and noticed Reverend Collins was about to start the service, but he wanted to ask Jesse something before he lost his nerve. "How do you do it?"

"Do what?"

"Know what a person needs and supply it."

"I'm not sure there's a big secret involved. We pray a lot. We just know usually what needs to be done."

"Are you telling me God tells you?"

"Yes, our faith in the Lord is part of it. We're attuned to each other's needs."

"So when someone's hurting, you're there for him, helping him pick up the pieces."

"I hope so. That's what friends do for each other."

Not from his experience, he thought, the emptiness in him growing, consuming him, refreezing the wall around his heart.

Despairing, he moved into the sanctuary, his fingers linked with Jesse's. That connection made him feel human, almost a part of the town, the church. He grasped on to the bond she offered, and even as they slid into a pew, he didn't release her hand. For a short time he could pretend he belonged.

He finally let go when Reverend Collins said a prayer, asking God to watch over each person before him, to forgive their sins, and to guide them in the ways of Christ. Nick listened to the words and wondered if it was possible for God to forgive his sins—especially the one of turning away from Him, of denying His power.

"Cindy, you can place your doll next to mine." Jesse gestured toward the center table set up for items to be auctioned off the next day.

The child laid the baby girl down next to Jesse's,

her hand lingering on its brown curly hair. "Can I bid on an item?"

"Sure you can."

"Can I bid on the item I gave?"

Jesse knelt down and clasped Cindy's arms, turning the little girl to look at her. "Just because you donated it, doesn't mean you can't bid on it. How much money do you have saved?"

Cindy tilted her head and tapped her finger against her chin. "I think I've got twelve dollars after giving Daddy some money for Crystal's wheelchair." She paused, thought about it and said, "No, I have ten dollars and fifty cents. I bought an ice-cream cone the other day."

"Do you want to give the baby to the auction? It's your decision because you made it."

Frowning, Cindy continued to tap her finger against her chin, taking another moment to think. "I want to give it to the auction. I want to help feed the hungry children."

Her throat tight, Jesse swallowed hard. "Then we will keep the baby in."

Cindy ran her hand over Jesse's doll, a Victorian lady dressed in white lace, black buttoned-up boots, a hat with feathers and a parasol. "I like your doll, too. Do I have enough money for both of them?"

Remembering how much her doll always went for, Jesse smiled and said, "Don't worry. You concentrate on bidding for your doll." She had just decided what she could get Cindy for her birthday.

"Cindy, come on. I need help putting up the streamers." Standing in the doorway to the rec hall, Nate motioned for Cindy.

The little girl whirled around and rushed toward Nate, her pigtails bouncing as she ran. Jesse watched the two children disappear, remembering the sweet gesture Cindy had made. She wanted more children, Jesse thought, sliding her eyes closed, taking a deep, composing breath that still left her chest constricted.

"She certainly is an adorable child."

Jesse gasped, her eyes snapping open. "Beth Coleman, you aren't allowed to sneak up on someone. I think my heart stopped beating."

Beth laughed. "Then quit daydreaming when you should be working."

"You are a hard taskmaster."

"I've raised three siblings. I've had great experience."

"Isn't next semester Daniel's last one?"

Beth's face brightened. "Yes, and then I can do what *I* want."

"Which is?"

"To travel. See the world."

"You're really thinking of leaving Sweetwater?"

"Not permanently but I do want to see what's out there." She leaned close to Jesse. "That's why I wasn't interested in your little matchmaking attempt with your neighbor."

Zoey joined them. "Matchmaking? Jesse? Mom used to write me about your little dinner parties. When I came back, she warned me never to accept an invitation unless I was looking for a man."

Jesse clasped her chest. "I'm shocked. I have friends over for dinner. That is all."

"Where do you want this, Beth?" Joshua asked, carrying a long table with the help of Clint.

"Right next to this one." Beth pointed to the end of the row of tables. "Hey, Clint, didn't I hear that you had to rescue Tara from one of Jesse's dinner parties?"

Clint set the table on the floor, then approached them, sweat beading his brow. "Sure did. If I hadn't, my woman could have been dating Nick Blackburn as we speak." Clint waved his hand toward Jesse. "At least that was *her* plan."

"Clint, my scheme knocked some sense into you." Jesse planted her hands on her hips. "It took my neighbor's interest to spur you into doing what you wanted to do all along."

The man's face blanched. He wiped the sweat from his brow with the back of his hand. Jesse started to kid him about being married when she noticed that several others in the group were looking beyond her shoulder, their expressions troubled. She peered back and found Nick standing a few feet to her left. She gulped and sent up a silent prayer for help. The angry look on Nick's face stole her breath, her thoughts.

Slowly she turned toward him while everyone fled to the four corners, leaving her alone with the man. "How much did you hear?"

"Enough."

"It isn't what it seems."

"And what does it seem?"

The lethal quiet in his voice should have warned her to run while she had the chance. Instead, she stood her ground and said, "That I set—that I used you—" There was no way to explain what she had done except straight out. "I tried to fix you up with various women in town because I thought Cindy needed a mother." She didn't breathe until she finished the last word, then she took in such a deep one that her head swam. She grasped the table's edge to steady herself.

"So when you were dragging me around town introducing me to all these women, you were really trying to fix me up?"

She nodded, not daring to say another word. The fury in his eyes cut through her.

"Even after I told you I didn't want to get married?"

Another nod.

He took a step toward her. "Why?"

She hadn't thought his voice could get any quieter and she'd still hear him, but it did. And it still held a deadly edge to it. She shuddered. "Because Cindy wants a mother." *And because you're dangerous to my peace of mind.*

"I don't have a say in it? You didn't bother to make sure it was something I wanted? What makes you think you know what is best for me and Cindy?" He snapped his fingers. "Ah, I know the answer to that. It's that ability you have of knowing what a person needs before he even knows it."

Sarcasm drenched his words and stung Jesse. She noticed they were the only ones in the rec room. She backed up against the table, wanting to escape as all the others had. "I only wanted to help."

"Did I ask you for your help?"

She shook her head, the thundering of her heartbeat a roar in her ears.

He thrust his face to within inches of hers. "I will not be controlled. I lived in a marriage where my wife tried to control my every move with her behavior. I will not be trapped into a marriage to someone who wants to mold me into someone I'm not."

Trapped between the table and Nick, Jesse had nowhere to go. She could smell the minty flavor of his toothpaste, the lime scent of his aftershave. She could see every harsh line on his face, the hard gleam in his gaze directed totally at her.

"I was wrong. I knew that after Beth, and I stopped. I'm sorry."

He stepped back, giving her some breathing room. Her apology seemed to take the steam out his anger— at least she thought so until he pivoted and headed for the door, saying, "I've got to get out of here."

The rigid way he held his body spoke volumes. He was still furious at her, and she didn't think he would listen to a second apology. She'd never fixed anyone up without his knowledge so why had she with Nick? Because he stirred feelings in her that she thought had died with Mark. She had acted out of desperation to protect her heart. She couldn't risk getting hurt again so she tried to make him unavailable. The only thing was, he was unavailable…but for a different reason.

The auctioneer held up Jesse's doll to get the bidding started. She chewed on her thumbnail, every muscle taut with stress. The day had started out a disaster and gone downhill from there. She usually had a great time at the Fourth of July celebration, but Nick kept his distance. Cindy sensed the tension between them and asked a zillion questions which she didn't have an answer for.

"One hundred. Do I have 110?"

Jesse blinked, realizing she'd better bid on her doll before someone else got it. She wanted to give it to Cindy as a birthday present. She waved her hand and the auctioneer saw her bid.

"We've got 110. How about 120, folks? This is a genuine Jesse doll. We all know how much work goes into it."

Nick held up his hand.

"One-twenty. Do I hear 130?"

Jesse pressed her lips together and nodded.

"One-forty?"

"One thousand," Nick said, folding his arms across his chest.

The audience gasped. Jesse glared at Nick, but he kept his gaze trained on the auctioneer. The man turned to her. She shook her head.

"I have one thousand. Once. Twice." The auctioneer paused and scanned the audience in the rec hall. "Sold to Mr. Blackburn for one thousand dollars."

As Beth brought the next item up for bidding, the people around Jesse began to whisper among themselves. Nick strode toward the table where he could pick up the doll and pay for it. Several parishioners stared at her, watching her reaction to his taking her doll. She knew everyone knew about their little fight the day before. Two patches of heat scored her cheeks. The walls seemed to be closing in on her.

She spun around and hurried toward the door. As she escaped, she heard Cindy bid five dollars on her doll. She should stay, but she'd had enough of being the object of people's gossiping. She sought the quiet of the garden and the stone bench in the middle.

Shutting her eyes, she listened to the silence that was occasionally broken by a bird's chirping or a car passing on the road in front. She wanted her life to return to normal. She didn't want Nick angry at her.

She heard footsteps approaching. She opened her eyes and saw Nick come to an abrupt stop when he spied her sitting on the bench. He started to turn to leave.

"Don't go."

He froze, his back to her.

"Did Cindy get her doll?"

Slowly he faced her, a cold expression in his eyes. "Yes."

She sighed. "Oh, good. I wasn't sure if ten dollars would be enough."

"What do you mean ten dollars? I paid another thousand for it."

"Do you think money is the answer to all problems?"

The only sign of his own feelings were in the clenching and unclenching of his hands. "It sure can help, especially when you are hungry and need a place to sleep."

"Throwing money at a problem isn't a lasting solution."

"As I understand the object of the auction is to raise money for your outreach projects. So why are you upset? Is it because I outbid you for your doll?"

She shot to her feet, feeling at a disadvantage looking up at him from the bench. "No, that is not it. Cindy was excited about bidding on her doll. She wanted to win it. You took that away from her."

"She wanted her doll that she made. I got it for her. Simple."

"Life isn't always that simple."

"You've got that right—at least not here in Sweetwater. But in Chicago I know the rules. Cindy and I will be leaving early to return home."

"We are?" Cindy asked, hugging her baby doll to her chest.

Chapter Ten

Nick closed his eyes for a few seconds, then turned toward his daughter. "I think it's time for us to go home."

Cindy's bottom lip quivered. Her teeth dug into it. "But we aren't supposed to leave until the end of July."

"Something's come up."

"What?" She clutched her doll tighter to her.

"I need to get back to work."

"But, Daddy, you promised." Tears welled in the child's eyes.

"I'm sorry, princess."

Jesse heard the desperate ring in Nick's voice and wanted to ease the strain between father and daughter. She took a step toward the child.

"You broke your promise." Cindy whirled around and ran from the garden.

The rigid set to his shoulders sagged forward. He

dropped his head for a long moment, and if he believed in the power of prayer, Jesse would have thought he was offering up one to the Lord. The fact that he wasn't saddened her. God could help in times of trouble.

"I can talk with Cindy if you want."

He stiffened. "I should never have left Chicago. I know what to expect there."

"But would that have been the best thing for Cindy? Obviously you thought at one time it would be good for you two to get away to really get to know each other. Has that happened? Have you become closer to Cindy?"

He waved his hand toward the area where his daughter had stood a few minutes before. "I would have said yes five minutes ago. Now I don't know."

"I'm sorry. I can't say it any plainer than that. I was wrong to try to fix you up without your knowledge."

Combing his hand through his dark hair, he released a long breath. "What you did made me realize I don't belong here."

"How?"

"Sweetwater is different from Chicago, and I don't mean small town versus big city. It's more than that."

"We care."

"There are people in Chicago who care." Again he ran his hand through his hair, frustration in every line of his body. "I don't know if I can put it into words." He scanned the area as if looking for a way to escape. "I need to find Cindy."

He disappeared quickly, and Jesse collapsed down

on the stone bench, wanting to continue their conversation, to explore what was troubling him. She suspected he felt out of his element, therefore not in complete control. And that bothered him—more than he probably would even admit to himself.

The next morning Nate glanced around, then climbed the ladder to the tree house in the large maple tree in the corner of his yard. He scrambled inside, past the sign that read No Girls Alowed, with a big pink X through it. He remembered the day last week when he'd let Cindy change the sign. She'd been laughing as she made the big pink X with a marker. She wasn't laughing now. She was huddled in the corner with her knees drawn up against her chest and her arms clasped about her legs.

"I got your note." Nate sat cross-legged on the wooden planks in front of Cindy.

"I don't wanna leave. Help me."

Nate hated seeing the tears streaming down Cindy's cheeks. They made him sad. "Maybe your dad would let you stay with us. We have an extra bedroom."

She shook her head. "I want him and Boswell to stay, too."

Tilting his head to the side, Nate pulled on his left ear and thought. "You know I saw a movie once where the little boy ran away to keep his parents from getting a divorce and his dad leaving. You could do that."

Cindy's eyes grew wide. "By myself?"

He rubbed the back of his neck and looked out the big hole that served as a window in the tree house.

"Well…well, I guess I could come with you and protect you."

"You would!"

He nodded.

"When? Daddy is talking about leaving soon— maybe even tomorrow."

Nate shifted, rolling his shoulders. "I guess we could today. Right now. I know a place we can hide."

Cindy unclasped her legs and stretched them out in front of her. "I'm kinda hungry. What will we do about food?"

"Go home and get whatever you think you'll need. I'll get some food and meet you back here in half an hour."

Cindy scooted toward the opening that led to the ladder. "Do you think we'll be gone long?"

"Nah. In the movie when the father and mother searched for the little boy, they realized they didn't want a divorce."

"How long did it take?"

"Half a day. So everything will work out and we'll be home by dark."

Cindy went down the ladder first. "Bring a lot of food. I'm really getting hungry."

Jesse put the finishing touches to a doll that depicted a young Colonial girl. She held it up, pleased at how it had turned out. Her curly dark hair reminded Jesse a lot of Cindy. Where were Nate and Cindy? Nate had run in here a while ago and was gone before she had completed dressing the new doll.

The doorbell rang.

Jesse pushed back her chair and went to answer the front door. Surprised to find Nick standing on her porch, she stepped aside to allow him into her house. He stayed where he was, a scowl emphasizing how displeased he must still be with her.

"May I help you?" she asked, leaning against the door, her hand tightly clasped about the knob.

"Have you seen Cindy?"

"Not lately."

"How about Nate?"

"About half an hour ago. Why?"

"I can't find them." He drew in a deep breath, the hard lines of his face deepening even more. "And Cindy's new dolls are gone as well as Oreo."

"Have you checked the tree house? They were up there earlier."

"Yes. No sign of them."

"I'm sure they're around here some place. Let me see if Gramps knows where they went. Come in."

He hesitated, scanning the area before making his way inside.

Jesse closed the door, aware of the level of tension in the small entry hall skyrocketing. She quickly went in search of her grandfather, feeling the scorch of Nick's gaze on her back as though she had done something to cause the kids to disappear.

Jesse found Gramps in the kitchen, rummaging in the refrigerator for something to eat. "Have you seen Nate or Cindy?"

"Nope. Not lately. Where is the ham you had and the sodas? In fact, there were some grapes here a while ago. Where are they?"

Jesse walked to the refrigerator while Gramps moved to the side to allow her to look inside. "That's strange. They were there after breakfast when I put the food up. I was going to make ham sandwiches for lunch." She checked her watch. "In another hour."

"Well, someone took them. And I suspect that someone is Nate." Gramps stepped in front and began searching for something else to eat. "Did he say anything about going on a hike or a picnic with Cindy?"

Jesse shook her head, then because her grandfather was still peering into the refrigerator said, "No. And if he was, he knows he has to get an okay from me."

"Well, there's quite a bit of food missing. Half a loaf of bread is gone, too."

Jesse spun around and headed back to the entry hall, not happy with what she was beginning to think happened. "Gramps doesn't know where the kids are. Was Cindy still upset about leaving earlier than you'd planned?"

He looked away. "I said something about leaving soon at breakfast. She ran off. That's why I was trying to find her to talk to her."

Her stomach muscles twisted into a huge knot. She had a bad feeling about this. "I think maybe our children have decided to run away."

"Why do you think that?"

"She took her favorite things. Nate took some food. I bet if I look in his room some of his favorite objects will be gone, too."

"Why would they do that?"

"Because Cindy doesn't want to leave Sweetwater."

"We're just leaving a few weeks earlier than we would have. She knew we were only going to be here for a short time."

"Cindy has found a home here." *Even if you haven't,* Jesse silently added.

"Chicago is our home."

Nick said the sentence with such force that Jesse stepped back. "I'm only stating what I see. I know she was looking forward to celebrating her birthday here. She said something to me about it. She has met some children at church she wanted to invite to a party."

"We can have a party in Chicago."

Jesse was beginning to hate the word *Chicago,* especially when Nick said it. "Does she have a lot of friends there?"

"I—" He raked both hands through his hair. "I don't know. Surely she does."

"You don't know?"

"With the wreck everything has been turned upside down. I've been in and out of the hospital. Nothing has been normal. I'm sure she does from school."

"Did she ever bring any friends home?"

He shook his head. "Not for a long time."

"I know you're mad at me, but that doesn't mean you can't stay until the end of July."

His mouth hardened into a grim line. "Let's just find the children."

"You're afraid, aren't you?"

He closed the distance between them, invading her personal space. "Yes, I'm afraid something might happen to Cindy. I would never forgive myself."

"That's not what I meant."

"I know. But I don't want to get into what you were talking about. My focus is on Cindy."

"Nate knows the area and wouldn't let anything happen to her." She finally moved away from him before she tried to smooth away the frown lines on his face. She was sure the children weren't far—they were just hiding, waiting for them to come after them. "I'll tell Gramps. He can help look as well as Boswell. There are a few places we should start with. Some of Nate's favorite hangouts."

Nick watched Jesse leave the entry hall, his body taut, his breathing shallow. He'd come so close to telling her yes he was afraid. Afraid of the feelings he was experiencing toward her. Afraid of what the town of Sweetwater was doing to him, to his family. Afraid of believing again—of giving control of his life over to God.

He'd fought so hard to maintain some kind of control in his life only to have it snatched away in a blink of his eye. One moment he and Brenda had been on the highway, the next they were heading for a large oak tree. In one second his whole life had changed. He'd almost died, nearly lost the use of his leg. Most of all the years he'd thought he had some control over his life had been wiped away with the wreck.

And now his daughter had run away. He couldn't lose Cindy, too. He hadn't yet made up for all the years he'd been too busy working to be the kind of father she deserved.

Lord, if You're listening, please watch over Cindy and help me to find her safe. I know I haven't prayed in years but Cindy is an innocent. She doesn't deserve something bad happening to her. She's already lost her mother. Please protect her and bring her home safe.

The words of his prayer filled his mind and heart with hope. He would find Cindy and she would be all right.

The sun started its descent toward the line of trees to the west. Sweat drenched Jesse's clothes and cloaked her face. She wiped her brow then her neck and looked toward the sun beginning to set.

"It'll be dark in an hour or so," she said, stopping by a tree and leaning against it while she removed her sneaker to dislodge a pebble.

Nick walked a few paces, then stopped when he saw she had. "And we haven't found the children. We should have by now." His cell phone rang and he answered it. When he flipped it closed, he said, "That was Boswell. Nothing."

Jesse's phone went off not a minute later. "Yes?"

"Sorry, Susan and I haven't found them yet. We'll keep looking around the downtown area. I saw Darcy and Joshua and they are searching the eastern part of the lake as well as Zoey and Beth and some others from church. We'll find them, honey."

When Jesse hung up, she didn't look toward Nick for a long moment while she tried to compose herself. She'd been so sure they would find the children in the first hour of searching. They hadn't and now it had been almost eight hours. A tightness in her chest was expanding to encompass her whole body. She felt as though she would shatter any second.

Finally she peered at Nick. "That was Gramps. They've found nothing, but everyone is still looking. We'll find them before dark."

"What if they are hurt? What if—"

"Nick, don't go there. Please, I can't deal—"

She couldn't finish her sentence. Emotions swelled into her throat, closing it. She tried to draw air into her lungs but couldn't seem to get a decent breath. She grasped the tree to steady herself, but the land tilted and spun before her eyes. Squeezing them shut, she continued to inhale until she had forced some fresh air into her lungs.

Nick wound his arms about her and brought her flat against his chest. The rapid beat of his heart mirrored hers. She clung to him. With a light touch he stroked the length of her back over and over.

"We're going to find them, Jesse. I promise you."

She leaned back to stare up into his face. A smile flirted about the corners of her mouth but she couldn't maintain it. "I think we've traded roles."

His mouth lifted in a grin that instantly vanished.

"Your optimistic outlook has finally rubbed off on me. Come on. Let's go back to the house and get some flashlights so we can keep going when it gets dark. I won't stop until we find them."

"Knowing the people of Sweetwater, they won't, either. We'll find them. You're right."

He put his arm around Jesse and started back along the lake toward their houses. "That's one of the appealing things about Sweetwater. You aren't alone."

"I can't believe I'm hearing you say that."

"I can respect certain things, but that doesn't mean it is for me. I'm a loner. Have been most of my life."

"Doesn't mean you have to be *all* your life. I can't imagine not having people around me who care what happens to me. I know if I have a problem I have a lot of people I can go to for help. That's comforting."

"The only person I can depend on is myself."

"How about Boswell?"

Nick frowned. "Boswell is an employee. I have good employees who do their job well."

"So if you stopped paying Boswell, he wouldn't care about you or Cindy?"

He was silent for a long moment. "That's a question for Boswell."

"You're ducking the question."

"I don't know the answer."

"I've seen you two interact and you're friends as well as employer and employee." Jesse stepped over a log as they neared her property. She saw her house through the trees. "I have some energy bars. We

should get something to eat and drink. It may be a
long night."

"While we're here, let's check around. No one has
in a few hours."

"Good idea," Jesse said as they emerged from the
trees on the west side of her house. She glanced toward
the tall maple where Nate had his tree house. In the
opening she spied Oreo trying to climb down. She
grabbed Nick's arm. "Look."

At a jog he headed toward the ladder and scrambled up it with Jesse right behind him. "Cynthia
Blackburn!"

"Is Nate there? Are they all right?" Jesse asked,
blocked from seeing inside by Nick's large body.

Nate stuck his head out the window. "I'm here,
Mom. We're fine."

Those were the sweetest words she could have
heard. As she clung to a rung of the ladder, she sent
a silent prayer of thanks to the Lord, then said,
"Young man, you get down here right now. I have a
few words to say to you and I prefer looking you in
the eye when I say them." Jesse hopped to the ground,
then backed away from the maple so the rest of them
could come down.

Nick stood beside her as both children climbed down
the ladder, Cindy holding her two dolls while Nate had
Oreo. Jesse had a strong urge to hug her son while she
yelled at him. Relief and anger mingled to form a ball
of conflicting emotions inside her.

"What do you two have to say for yourselves?" Nick

asked, such a quietness to his words that the children's eyes grew round.

Cindy sidled up to Nate and clutched her dolls even tighter. "I don't want to leave early. You promised me." Her bottom lip stuck out while her eyes glistened with unshed tears.

"Do you two have any idea how much trouble you caused everyone in Sweetwater? Half the town is looking for you." Narrowing her gaze on the pair belonging to her son, Jesse put her hands on her waist.

"They are?" Nate asked, his voice cracking.

"Yes, young man. You have a lot of explaining to do. The first thing you're going to do is write a letter of apology to the people who have given up their time to search for you."

"That's a very good idea, Jesse. Cindy, you can do the same thing."

Cindy and Nate dropped their gazes to the ground, their chins resting on their chests.

"After that you can donate some of your time cleaning up around the church. There are weeds to be pulled, gardens to be tended. I'm sure that Reverend Collins can come up with a list of chores for you to do, Nate."

"Cindy will help him."

"For how long?" Nate brought his head up to look at Jesse.

"I'm so mad at you right now that I'd better not say. I think I might ground you for the rest of your life. So don't push it. Right now you march yourself inside and go straight to your room."

Nate gave Cindy the kitten, then trudged toward the back door. When he reached the deck, Boswell appeared between the two houses. His face lit when he saw Cindy.

"Daddy, are you mad at me?"

"I can't believe you would pull something like running away. I was so worried about you. What if you had gotten hurt?"

"Nate was with me."

Boswell stopped at Nick's side. "Everything okay? Where were they?"

His normal composure was gone. His clothes were dirty and wrinkled as though he had traveled over rough terrain searching for the children. Jesse had never seen Boswell like that. "They were in the tree house."

"But didn't you look there?"

"Yes, but not for a few hours."

"I'm tired. I want to go home." Cindy tried holding both her kitten and dolls, but Oreo slipped from her grasp and darted across the yard. She started after her pet.

"I'll take care of her, sir. You'd better let the authorities and everyone know you've found the children." Boswell hurried after Cindy and the kitten, rounding them up and taking them into the house next door.

With both children safe and inside their homes, Jesse turned to Nick, suddenly aware they were alone. She stared into the liquid darkness of his eyes and remembered how he had held her when she had started to fall apart. If she wasn't careful, she could become used to his particular brand of comfort.

"I don't know how to—" Her cell phone blared, interrupting her thankfully because she wasn't sure what to say to Nick. Instead, she answered her call.

"Just checking in. Find them yet?"

Gramps's gruff question pulled her back to the situation at hand. "Yes, Nick and I did a few minutes ago. They were in the tree house out back."

"But you looked there."

"I think because it was getting dark they decided to come closer to home."

"Have you called the police yet?"

"No. I haven't had time."

"I'll take care of it. I'll also let everyone else know. Then I'm coming home to have a few words with that great-grandson of mine."

When she finished talking with her grandfather, she said, "Gramps will take care of letting people know we found them."

Nick smiled. "I wonder what Boswell thinks of Susan and Gramps together."

"Do you think Boswell really liked Susan?"

Nick lifted his shoulders in a shrug. "It's hard to tell. Boswell is a very private person."

"Like his employer?"

"Yes." Nick's gaze caught hers and held it for a long moment.

A light breeze stirred the summer heat about Jesse. She brushed the damp tendrils away from her face and drew in a deep breath of the rose-scented air. The glittering blue of the lake drew her attention. Its smooth surface reflected the colors of the setting sun—red, orange, pink. Vibrant colors. Ones that reminded a person she was alive, that her son was safe, that the man she had come to care about was only a foot away. She could reach out and grasp his hand, hold on to it and possibly convince him not to leave.

She could. She wouldn't. As the hours had passed and they hadn't found the children, all the pain of losing Mark had come back to haunt her. She had to protect her heart. She couldn't go through losing someone close to her again. It was bad enough that Gramps was getting older and his health was declining.

"We'll stay until the end of July."

Nick's proclamation both frightened and thrilled her. She wanted Cindy—and him—to stay, and yet the more she was around them, the more she wished they were living in Sweetwater permanently. He had made that very clear that wasn't possible. Only heartache laid ahead if she fell in love with Nick Blackburn.

"But I don't want to tell Cindy right away."

"Aren't you risking her doing something like today again?"

"No, because I'm going to make it very clear if she doesn't behave we are leaving immediately. That I will pack up and be gone in an hour's time."

The idea of how quick his presence could be erased from her life gripped her as though a vise held her tight. "I would like to throw her a birthday party. Is that all right?"

"No."

With her emotions swirling in all different directions, Jesse suddenly felt deflated and tried not to show her disappointment. "Why not?"

"Because I am. But I'll accept your help. How about it?" he asked with a smile.

"You've got yourself a partner."

His eyes widened for a few seconds before he said, "Great. I'll have to depend on you to invite all the friends she has made."

"You'd better be careful. Depending on someone? Tsk. Tsk. What will people think?"

"That I have good taste. Who better than you—the woman who knows everyone in town—to tell me whom to invite to my daughter's birthday party?"

Jesse began walking toward her deck. "I'm going to take that as a compliment."

"It was a compliment. I probably know maybe three of the other people who live in my building and that's from seeing them in the lobby."

"Not the elevator?"

"I have a private elevator that goes only to my floor."

"So you don't have to mingle with your neighbors."

"Truthfully, even if I had neighbors next door, I wouldn't have had the time to get to know them. I was always working."

"How are you surviving not working so much?"

He smiled. "At first I thought I would go crazy. Lately I have had a lot of things to keep me occupied."

"Like today."

"That and picnics, fishing trips, dinners."

"So it is possible for you to find things to do besides work and you don't fall apart."

Chuckling, he said, "I would rather not spend another day like this one."

"I agree. I'm exhausted both mentally and physically. After I have a little talk with Nate, I'm heading to bed."

"Without dinner?"

"I don't even have the energy to fix myself something to eat."

He arched a brow. "You've got it bad."

"There you two are," Gramps called out as he and Susan came out of the house and stood on the deck.

"I'll see you tomorrow and we'll coordinate the chores the kids need to do." Nick took her hand and squeezed it before strolling toward his house.

Jesse stared at him for a few seconds, then mounted the stairs to the deck. She noticed her grandfather's arm around Susan's shoulder. The older woman had a huge smile on her face that took years off her age. Her blue eyes twinkled as she edged even closer to Gramps.

"Does everyone know the children are safe?"

"Yes, so you don't have to worry about that. Why did they run away?"

"Because Cindy didn't want to leave and Nate wanted to help her."

"That's my boy, coming to a female's rescue."

"Gramps, I would hardly call what Nate did rescuing Cindy. She wasn't in jeopardy."

"It's all in how you look at it. Just think if Cindy had

gone off by herself what kind of trouble the child might have gotten herself in."

Jesse shuddered at the thought. "So you think I should reward my son?"

Gramps shook his head. "Just remember this day could have ended a lot worse. Besides, if Nate and Cindy hadn't run away, I might not be holding Susan right now."

"Gerard," Susan said, playfully punching him in the arm while her cheeks flamed red.

"You know I'm right. You've been avoiding me, but you couldn't ignore a plea to help look for the children."

Jesse narrowed her eyes. "If I didn't know better, I'd think you put the children up to running away."

Susan pulled away. "Gerard, you didn't?"

"No, I would never do that to Nick and Jesse." He grinned. "I was banking on charming my way back into your life. I wasn't going to let an Englishman break us up."

"Us as in a couple?"

Gramps turned fully to face Susan and cupped her face. "Us as in a couple. I love you, Susan Reed, and I want to marry you."

Susan's eyes brimmed with tears. One fell on Gramps's hand. He pulled her against him. "Will you, Susan?"

"Yes. Yes, I will, Gerard Daniels."

Jesse backed away from the pair, wanting to give them some private time. But her heart expanded in her chest, her breath caught in her throat. Her own tears of happiness welled to the surface. What a beautiful way to end a horrible day.

Chapter Eleven

"Is this a weed?" Cindy asked, kneeling in the grass with a bucket half full next to her.

Nate stared at the green plant. "I think anything taller than the grass is a weed."

Cindy yanked on the plant, leaving most of the roots in the ground. She tossed it into the bucket. "When is your mom coming back?"

"She had something to do in the church, then she's going to bring us some sodas to drink."

Cindy dragged the back of her hand across her forehead. "It sure is hot."

"Yep. Let's work over by that tree where it's shady." Nate gestured toward a tall oak.

"Good idea." Cindy hopped to her feet and carried her bucket to a spot under the tree. "I wish I wasn't leaving at the end of next week. Why can't we live here?"

Nate put his bucket next to hers. "You know if my

mom and your dad got married, you could live here in our house. Then you wouldn't have to worry about leaving."

Cindy's eyes brightened. "Yes! That's it. I would love to have Jesse as my mom."

"And your dad is cool."

Cindy's bright expression dimmed. "But how do we get them together?"

"I saw a movie once where two girls got their mom and dad alone on a date and everything worked out."

"Yeah, that could work. We're usually around when they're together." Cindy thought for a moment. "But how are we gonna do that?"

Grinning, Nate explained, "We'll plan a picnic at O'Reilly's Cove and not show up."

"I thought Gramps and the kids were going to be here. Where are they?" Jesse looked around O'Reilly's Cove and only saw a sandy beach and a large rock slide jutting out into the calm blue water. No skiff. No people other than she and Nick.

"Look." He pointed toward a picnic basket with a blanket spread out under an elm tree. "They must be around here somewhere. They've left the food. I'm hungry. Let's see what they fixed for lunch."

On top of the basket there was a note weighted down with a rock keeping it from blowing away. Jesse recognized her grandfather's handwriting and picked it up and read it aloud. "'Enjoy. Decided to take the kids with me to look for a ring for Susan. We'll be back when we are through.'" She crunched the paper into a ball. "I thought I was going with Gramps to help with the ring."

"I can't believe the kids agreed to go—" Nick rubbed his chin. "Unless they're up to something."

"What?"

"Take a look around. Secluded cove. Basket full of food. A blanket. What does that bring to mind?"

"A date?"

Nick nodded.

"You know, I've heard those two whispering a lot lately. Yesterday at church when I brought them their sodas while they were weeding, they were giggling and giving me strange looks. I should have figured they were up to something. We should just leave and meet them in town—if they are really going to look for a ring, that is."

"And give up all this food? Let's eat first, then surprise them at the jewelry store."

"I guess. I am hungry." Jesse lifted the lid on the basket. She began laying out the cartons of food.

"I can tell Boswell wasn't in on their scheme. This all looks like it came from a fast-food chicken place."

"This no doubt is Gramps's contribution to the plan. He thinks all food should be fried, even vegetables."

Sitting on the blanket near Jesse, Nick took a piece of fried chicken and bit into it. "Not bad."

"Mine's better. I have a secret batter recipe that was passed down in my family." Jesse went straight to the coleslaw, loving this particular place's recipe. "Do you want any of this?" she asked in a generous mood as she held up the container.

"Nah. I think I'll stuff myself on chicken. I don't get fried food often. Boswell's on a health kick."

"Since you're a meat-and-potato kind of guy, I'll let you have the mashed potatoes while I eat the biscuits." She bent closer to whisper, "But don't tell anyone that our lunch isn't what you would call well balanced."

He inhaled a deep breath. "You smell good."

His smile curved his full mouth and centered her attention on it. For a second she allowed herself to respond to his compliment, a warmth flowing through her. Then her panic took hold and she said, "That's because we didn't walk here but drove instead." She leaned away, reminding herself not to get too close to Nick. That was when she started thinking things that weren't possible.

His chuckle mingled with the sounds of water lapping against the shore, a bird up in the elm tree above them, the rustle of the leaves from the gentle breeze. "True."

The warm feeling returned and chased away the panic. She raised her gaze to his, the mischievous gleam pulling her even closer to him. His mouth that looked so good with a smile on it was a whisper away from hers. So much for putting distance between them, she thought, her eyes sliding closed.

His thumb touched her lips first, caressing her with a lightness that shivered down her. Then his mouth claimed hers and she could taste the spicy chicken he'd been eating as well as the mint of his toothpaste. Those sensations heightened the intimacy of the moment as his arms went about her and drew her against him.

The sound of a flock of geese flying overhead broke them apart. Jesse scooted away, needing to put that space between them before her emotions were totally involved. Who was she kidding? They were totally involved and she was going to end up getting hurt. More than ever she needed to back off.

She propped herself up against the tree trunk and ate her coleslaw while Nick silently finished off two more pieces of chicken, then started in on the mashed potatoes. A frown descended over his features the longer he sat across from her as though he didn't like the direction his thoughts were going in.

"When you go back to Chicago, what are you going to do?"

He continued eating, his gaze trained on a spot between them. "Work. That's all I know how to do. I've neglected my company long enough."

"How about Cindy?" Her original assessment that the child needed a mother hadn't changed.

"I'll adjust my schedule to accommodate Cindy."

"Are you listening to yourself? You make her sound like she's part of your work to be squeezed in accordingly."

His head jerked up and his regard sharpened, cutting through her. "Cindy will be my number one priority."

"She isn't a job. She's your daughter."

This time he surged to his feet. "I know she's my daughter. I don't need you to tell me that. Nor do I need you to tell me how to raise her."

"She told me she wants to take dance lessons. Did you know that?" Jesse rose, squaring off in front of

Nick, ready to do battle for the little girl she had come to love like her own.

"No."

"She wants to get to know a girl on the third floor in your building, invite her over to play. She wants you to read bedtime stories to her like you are now. She wants to go to her mother's grave site and put flowers on it. You haven't taken her and she doesn't understand why."

With each sentence Nick winced until pain crumbled his defenses and shone through. "Because I can't bring myself to go to Brenda's grave. She nearly killed me and sometimes I think it was intentional. I think she was willing to die as long as she could take me with her."

Jesse sucked in a breath and held it until her lungs burned. She didn't know what to say to that assertion. She blinked, trying to assimilate what he had told her about his deceased wife. "I thought it was an accident."

"That's what the police report says, but you didn't see her face right before we went off the road and toward the tree. It was full of hatred, all directed at me." He shuddered, hugging his arms to his chest as if to ward off a chill even though the temperature was over ninety degrees.

"I'm sorry." She wanted to go to him but something in his stance forbade it.

"Do you know what my first coherent thought was when I woke up in the hospital?"

She shook her head, her heart bleeding for him.

"I was glad she was dead," he said, his voice weak, his breath ragged, his expression full of self-hatred. "I wished for someone to be dead. How can your God forgive that?"

"He can be your God, too. You can start by asking Him for forgiveness and then forgiving yourself."

"I didn't think I could hate someone so much, but Brenda made my life at home unbearable to the point I never wanted to be there. So I did what I had been doing for years. I worked fourteen-, fifteen-hour days. I missed the first six years of Cindy's life. I'm just beginning to really know my daughter."

She couldn't stay away from him another second. Jesse took him into her embrace and held him tight against her. She felt him shudder again and again as though he were reliving the wreck and his feelings all over. "Turn to the Lord. If you truly want forgiveness, He will. But you should also forgive Brenda. Until you do, you won't be totally free of the past. It will always be there to drag you down."

When Nick backed away, he scanned the area, his composure falling into place as though he hadn't opened up to her and let her glimpse the pain he felt. "I've had enough of communing with nature. Let's go find the children."

"It shouldn't be too hard to find Gramps's old truck in town," she said, picking up on his need to lighten the mood. "I have a couple of ideas where they might be."

"Not the jewelry store?"

"I doubt it. If they went, Gramps wouldn't stay long. He'd pick the first ring he saw that he could afford. Gramps and shopping do not go together."

Nick helped Jesse put the food into the basket, then

he folded the blanket and they headed for his SUV. The drive into town was done in silence. Jesse watched out the side window. The lake and woods disappeared as Nick turned onto the road that led to the downtown area of Sweetwater. She said nothing further about the torment eating at Nick, but it was there between them, making the quiet tension-packed.

On Main Street Jesse straightened and pointed toward Gramps's old red pickup. "Just as I suspected. They're at Harry's, probably having lunch."

"If I know Cindy, she's having more than lunch. She has developed a fondness for Harry's vanilla milk-shakes." Nick parked two doors down from the front of the café. "I'm glad it's past lunchtime or we'd never have gotten a parking spot so close."

Coming around the front of his car, Jesse shaded her eyes and studied Nick for a moment. "You're getting to know Sweetwater quite well. Be careful or someone might mistake you for a native."

"Never. I have *big city* written all over me."

She gestured at him. "Take another look at yourself. Jean shorts, T-shirt and tennis shoes. You don't appear very big city to me."

He frowned at her as he opened the door to Harry's.

Jesse spotted the children and Gramps at the back in a booth. The waitress was clearing off the table, leaving only the milkshakes that each one of them had ordered as a dessert.

Cindy sucked on her straw so hard her cheeks went in. "Daddy," she said when she saw him negotiating his way toward the booth. "You weren't on your picnic very long."

"We were dying to see what ring you all picked out." Nick slid in next to Cindy and Nate.

Jesse took the seat across from Nick next to Gramps. "Yeah, where is it?"

Her grandfather stirred his chocolate milkshake with his straw, seemingly fascinated by the swirling motion he had created.

"Gramps, the ring."

He looked up. "We haven't gone yet. We all decided we needed nourishment before making the big decision so we stopped in here first."

Jesse propped her folded arms on the table. "That's great! Then Nick and I can give our two cents' worth."

Gramps scowled. "Don't need a whole army going into the small jewelry store. You two go find something else to do."

She leaned toward his ear and whispered, "You're not being very subtle."

"I'm never subtle. You're a young, attractive woman who should be dating instead of trying to fix every Tom, Dick and Harry up with a date."

"Who's Tom?" Cindy asked.

"And Dick?" Nate asked, then turned to Cindy and added, "Harry must be the owner of the café. But I thought he was married to Rose."

"Figure of speech, kids." Gramps waved his hand over the table. "Your mother is concerned about everybody else's love life but her own."

Red-hot flames had to be licking at her face because Jesse felt on fire. "Gramps!"

"Well, it's the truth, young lady. You have so much to offer a man. You know how to cook and keep a house. You're a terrific mother and you were a great wife to Mark."

Jesse rose on shaky legs, gripping the edge of the table to keep herself upright. She wanted to throttle her grandfather. She'd never been so embarrassed in her whole life. "I need some fresh air." She spun on her heel and fled the café, aware of the stares from the other patrons.

She heard Nick say something to the group then him following her. Her feet couldn't carry her fast enough— away from her family, away from Nick. All she wanted to do was hide. Nick clasped her shoulder halfway down Main Street and halted her progress toward the park.

"Hold up. My mending leg can't keep up with you. I'm not up to jogging yet."

He could have said a lot of things that wouldn't have stopped her, but that did. She glanced back at him, seeing the grimace around his mouth that indicated he had overused his leg. "Sorry about that."

"You know, your grandfather has a point. One of the things I like about you is your caring and concern for others."

His words cooled the heat of embarrassment blanketing her face. She turned completely around. "Are you still angry with me for trying to fix you up without your knowledge?"

"I have discovered fixing people up is part of who

you are. I do recommend in the future making sure all parties are aware of what you're doing." Linking his hand with hers, he started walking toward the park. "I am curious why you haven't tried your skills on yourself."

"I've been married. As I've told you before, I'm not interested in getting married again. It's someone else's turn at happiness." Even to Jesse's own ears her words lacked her usual conviction.

"I've been married, too. That didn't stop you from trying with me."

"But you weren't happy, and besides, Cindy wants a mother."

"And Nate doesn't want a father?"

His question brought a halt to her step. She'd known Nate needed a man's influence and had hoped that Gramps would be it. She loved her grandfather, but Nate needed more than Gramps could give him. "I've never asked him."

"You have a wonderful child who would make any man proud to call son."

"I know."

"Then what's the problem?"

I'm the problem, she thought. *How can I risk that kind of hurt again? How do I deserve happiness when—* She shrugged as though she didn't have an answer.

"You've never been tempted with all those men you've fixed up?"

"Never once." *Until you,* she added silently.

"That's hard for me to believe with all your warmth and kindness."

"Well, it's true. It's easier not to get involved."

He moved in front of her and blocked her path. "Why? I know why I say that. But your marriage was a good one. Why wouldn't you want to experience that again?"

"I've had my chance."

"Where's it written down that everyone only gets one chance at a happy marriage?"

"I didn't say that."

"You've implied it. Didn't you tell me Darcy had a good marriage the first time around and now the second time, too?"

She chewed on her bottom lip, trying to figure out how to stop the direction the conversation was going. "We need to discuss Cindy's party. What can I do to help?"

"You aren't going to get out of discussing this by asking a question. I may not be as good a listener as you are, but something isn't right here. You're avoiding my questions, giving partial answers, not the complete truth. Why?"

She moved around him and headed for a wooden bench by the fountain in the center of the park. Again she heard him right behind her, not allowing her to get away. When she sat, he eased down next to her, his thigh touching hers, his presence trapping her.

"I'm not going anywhere. What's troubling you?"

"Is this how you made your millions? Dog someone until they do what you want?"

"Yep. That particular skill has come in handy on a number of occasions and you aren't going to change the subject."

She stared at the cars that passed the park on Main Street. She would never forget the evening her husband had died. The memory trembled through her with such a force she shook. Folding her arms to her, she said, "You might not think so highly of me if you knew the truth."

"What truth?" he asked in such a low voice that it barely sounded.

"I'm the reason my husband is dead. Not quite the paragon of virtue, am I?"

"Why don't you tell me what happened?"

Again that quiet voice that forced her to listen carefully to him. Her teeth dug into her lip, the words stuck in her throat. She hadn't shared her private, innermost thoughts on her husband's death with anyone.

He took her hand and laced his fingers through hers.

She peered at their hands linked together and said, "I had taken his hammer outside to fix some outdoor furniture we had in the yard. It started to rain and he didn't want it left out there. He was very particular about his tools. When he ran out to get the hammer, lightning struck him."

"So you blame yourself for his death because you left the hammer outside in the rain? Do I have it right?"

She nodded, her throat clogged with emotions long buried.

"It was a freak accident. He didn't have to go get it. He chose to. Remember, free will."

"But I knew how he was about his tools. He was especially particular about that hammer because it had been his dad's. I shouldn't have used it. Or at the very least, I should have put it back when I was through."

"Why didn't you?"

"Nate fell and hurt his knee. I took him inside to clean him up and then forgot about the hammer until it started to rain."

"Why did your husband go out and not you?" He shifted on the bench so he could face her.

"Because I have always been afraid of thunderstorms and he knew that. He went because he knew how upset I was getting. The weather was starting to get bad."

"It wasn't your fault. None of it. You can't keep beating yourself up over an accident, an act of nature."

"One minute Mark was here, the next he was gone. I can't go through that again. It hurt too much."

Nick slipped his arm about her shoulder and pulled her against him. "I'm finding out the hard way we can't control our lives like we wish we could."

"But if I had just—"

He laid his finger over her mouth to still her words. "Weren't you the one who told me I had to forgive myself if I wanted to move on with my life? You need to practice what you preach."

"I'm trying."

"Do you think God blames you for Mark's death? Or does anyone else?"

"No."

"Then you need to quit blaming yourself. We can't completely control life. I am slowly discovering that truth. I've tried for years and haven't really succeeded. We are quite a pair. Full of guilt," he said with a laugh that held no humor.

"So what are we going to do about it?"

"Half the battle is knowing what the problem is." He rose and extended his hand. "Let's go back and get a milkshake. I happen to share a fondness for one, like my daughter has."

Jesse placed her hand in his. Was she using her guilt over Mark's death to keep her rooted in the past? The past was a known entity—the future wasn't.

Chapter Twelve

Nate pushed Cindy higher in the swing on the church playground. "Let me know if you want me to stop."

She giggled, the wind blowing her long hair behind her and cooling her face. "I love to swing and try to see over the trees."

"Me, too."

When Cindy finally came to a stop and got off to let Nate use the swing, she said, "We're leaving the day after my birthday party."

"That's in three days." Nate plopped down on the wooden seat and gripped the ropes.

Cindy positioned herself behind him and gave him a push. "Do you have any more ideas? I don't want to leave." She belonged in Sweetwater. Why couldn't her daddy see that? She had friends and her daddy laughed now. He never had before.

"I don't know what else to do. We've tried to leave

our parents alone, but it hasn't done anything. Why don't you tell your father you want to stay? He might decide to. He came to church today when you asked him to."

"Maybe…if I tell him how bad I want it." She pushed Nate again. "Then if we stay, he can marry your mom." *That's a perfect plan,* Cindy thought and smiled.

Nick wandered along the path in the garden beside the church, drawn to the pond with goldfish and a small waterfall, its sound soothing to the soul. Was he using his anger like a shield to keep himself isolated from people? He couldn't deny that for a good part of his life, his anger toward the Lord had consumed him. And look where it had led him—alone, struggling to get to know his daughter.

He sat on the large rock beside the pond and stared at the clear water with orange goldfish swimming about the green plants. But where did he go now? He needed to get back to something familiar. He felt so lost. Too many things had changed in his life lately.

Lord, show me the way. What should I do?

The plea came from his heart, battered and bruised. The minute evolved into ten and still nothing stood out as a clear path for him to follow. He rose, berating himself for thinking an answer would come just because he'd finally asked. He shook his head, turning from the pond. He wasn't good at asking for help. He started back toward the church parking lot to find Cindy and leave.

His daughter stood next to Jesse and Nate. When she saw him, she ran toward him, a huge grin on her face. She skidded to a stop and began to pull him toward Jesse.

"We're invited to another fish fry tonight. Gramps caught a whole bunch yesterday."

Gramps? When had his daughter begun calling Gerard Daniels Gramps? Alarm bells rang in his mind. The feeling of being trapped closed in on him.

"Honey, we have a lot to do in the next few days before we leave. Don't you—"

Cindy stopped, a pout replacing her grin. "I want to live in Sweetwater, Daddy, all the time. I don't want to leave in a few days. I hate Chicago."

He stooped in front of her and clasped her arms. His leg ached from pushing himself too much that morning when he'd exercised, but he needed to make it clear to Cindy their home was in Chicago. "Hon, we have to leave. My work is there. Maybe we'll come back for a holiday next summer."

"You run the company. Why can't you run it here? You have been."

He hadn't allowed himself to think of that possibility because it opened up too many unknowns. He already had little control over his life. How could he give up all of it? Sweetwater was a nice place to visit. But to live here? He slowly rose, the pain in his leg sharpening. He focused on it, pulling his thoughts away from the prospects of settling down in a small town.

Jesse waved him to her. "Did Cindy ask you about the fish fry? Gramps got some tasty catfish. You know, that secret batter I use for chicken I also use for catfish."

The urge to say no was strong, but one look at Cindy's eager expression and he found himself saying, "Sure. Can I bring anything?"

"Nope. I've got things covered. Boswell's welcome to come, too."

"Are Gramps and Susan going to be there?"

"Yes. Gramps is giving her a ring this afternoon when he picks her up so she'll be showing it off."

"Do you think it's wise then to have Boswell there?"

"We can't leave him out of our family plans." The second Jesse said *our family* her eyes widened and her mouth snapped close. She swallowed hard. "I mean, Gramps will be fine. He and Susan are engaged."

Nick took Cindy's hand, needing some space. Suddenly his chest felt tight, and it was difficult to draw in a good decent breath. "I'll ask Boswell. What time?" He stepped back.

"Six. Nate wants to play croquet after dinner. Up for a game?"

"Sure." Nick backed away some more, pulling Cindy with him. "See you then." He turned and started for his SUV.

"But, Daddy, I wanted to stay and—"

"I need to get home and make some calls. You can see Nate later."

He would call his top executives and set a meeting for first thing Friday morning. Then he wouldn't be tempted to stay another weekend that might evolve into more.

***

Jesse stared out the window over the sink toward Nick's house. "Cindy, you did say your father would be coming shortly?"

"Yes, he's been on the phone most of the afternoon, but he told me he would be along soon." The little girl stirred the secret batter.

"Where's Nate?"

"Getting the croquet set out."

"If you want to help him, I can finish dinner by myself."

Cindy hopped down from the stool. "Okay. But I want to help fry the fish. Will you call me when you need me?"

"Yeah." Jesse put the batter mixture into the refrigerator to keep until she cooked the fish.

When the little girl left, Jesse checked the stove clock. Six-thirty. It wasn't like Nick to be late. She heard the front door open and close and Gramps call out to her.

"I'm in here."

Gramps and Susan came into the kitchen. Jesse dried her hands on her apron as she moved toward the couple.

"Let me see the ring."

Susan displayed the half carat, emerald-cut diamond in a gold setting.

"It looks wonderful on your hand. Welcome to the family, Susan." Jesse hugged the older woman, a sudden well of tears filling her eyes. She was so glad Gramps had found someone after being a widower for twenty years.

"Who else is coming to dinner? Is this one of your

little dinner parties to fix someone up?" Susan asked, splaying her fingers to look at her own engagement ring as though she didn't believe it was on her hand.

"I'm retiring."

"Why?" Gramps asked, walking to the stove to check what was cooking. He lifted a lid and took a deep breath. "I love green beans and new potatoes. And, Susan, this is why I go fishing so much. For the fish Jesse fries up for us."

"I'm through meddling in other people's lives," Jesse finally answered her grandfather as he finished peeking into the pots on the stove.

"You weren't meddling. You were trying to help." Gramps put his arm around Susan's shoulder. "If I'm not mistaken, you fixed us up."

"I was meddling." Jesse went back to the counter, as surprised as Gramps and Susan at her declaration. She hadn't thought about the decision; it had just come out. Now that she thought about it, however, it was for the best. "Look what almost happened with you two. You and Boswell almost got into a physical fight."

"But that wasn't your doing. That was me. I set out to make Gerard jealous and it worked a little too well."

"You did!" Gramps stared at Susan.

"Yes. If I hadn't, you might have continued to be content with just dating. I wanted something more."

Gramps beamed. "You never said anything."

"I'm so glad everything worked out for you two." Jesse walked to the stove to turn down the temperature on the food since Nick hadn't arrived yet.

"How about you and a certain young man?" Susan snuggled closer to Gramps.

"By the way, where is Nick?"

"I don't know. He hasn't come yet." Jesse latched on to her grandfather's question, hoping that Susan wouldn't pursue hers.

"You two sure have been seeing a lot of each other. Anything you want to tell us?"

Jesse should have known that Susan wouldn't let the topic go. She was the town gossip, after all. "He's a good friend."

"There's something to say about being good friends. Sometimes it leads to a relationship beyond friendship," Susan said.

"Not in this case. He's leaving on Thursday."

"Someone should shake some sense into you two," Gramps said, starting for the back door. "Are Nate and Cindy outside?"

"Yes," Jesse said as her grandfather and Susan went in search of the children, leaving her alone with her thoughts.

She went back to the sink and looked out the window toward Nick's house. What if he decided to stay in Sweetwater? What would she do? She thought about him being her permanent neighbor and a warm glow suffused her. Something beyond friendship? Was that possible considering their problems? A picture of two households blending into one began to take root in her mind until she put a halt to the dream. That was all it was. A dream. Something just out of reach.

A movement out the window caught her attention. Nick strode toward her backyard. Her heart increased its beating as she anticipated him knocking on the kitchen door. When the sound came, she hurried to answer it.

The first thing she noticed when she opened the door were the tired lines about his eyes. She stepped to the side to allow him to enter, shoving the dream to the dark recesses of her mind.

"Is everything okay?"

He kneaded the cords of his neck. "Yeah. Just had some business to take care of. So much to do when I return to Chicago."

The image of them as a couple vanished completely at those words. At every turn possible he made it clear he was going back to Chicago after Cindy's birthday. "I thought your company was running smoothly."

"It is. I have a good staff, but still I have let things slide this past year. I'm thinking of expanding into a different market. I want to get moving on those plans once I return."

It didn't appear as though this past year had really changed anything with Nick. His life would continue to revolve around his work with his family—Cindy— coming in second place. Her heart twisted with that thought.

"Where does Cindy fit into your plans?"

"I won't neglect her."

"What about attending church? She has shown such an interest in God and Jesus."

"If she wants to continue attending, I can take her."

"I'm glad." Some of her worries eased as she headed back to the stove to finish preparing the fish to fry.

"I saw Susan and Gerard on the deck. Susan is sporting quite a rock."

So now they had progressed—or rather regressed—to small talk. "Yeah. I'm so happy for them. Where's Boswell? Isn't he coming?"

"He'll be along in a little while. He was packing some boxes for the move and wanted to finish what he'd started."

Again a reference to his leaving. Jesse sighed, trying to keep a rein on her emotions, at least glad that he was open to going to church with Cindy. But she hadn't thought she would be so affected by her neighbor's departure. She had come to care about Cindy—and Nick. She would miss them, and so would Nate.

"Can I help you with anything?" Nick asked, standing in the middle of her kitchen, surprisingly looking at home there.

She removed the bowl of batter for the fish from the refrigerator. "Cindy wanted to help me fry these. Can you tell her I'm ready?"

"Sure. Anything else?"

"Nope. That should about do it. We'll eat in about twenty or thirty minutes."

When Nick left, Jesse sagged against the counter, drained emotionally. This was a celebration of Gramps and Susan's engagement, but for the life of her she didn't feel like celebrating. Sadness encased her in a cold blanket.

* * *

"I'll get it," Cindy yelled when the doorbell rang.

She ran to it and tugged the door open. Nate stood on the porch with a red-orange-and-yellow wrapped present in his hands.

"Come in." Cindy grabbed his arm and dragged him inside. "You're the first to arrive. I need to talk to you."

"What's wrong?"

"Everything." She placed the present on the table in the entry hall, pulled him toward the den and shut the door. "We're going for sure. I've tried talking to Daddy, but no matter what I say he isn't changing his mind. My things are packed. What do I do now?" The question ended on a sob.

"I don't know. Let me think." Nate paced about the room, his features pinched into a frown. Suddenly he stopped and faced Cindy. "I've got it. Whenever Mom has a problem, she prays about it. She tells me it always helps. Why don't you pray about staying in Sweetwater?"

"Yes. God will listen." Cindy threw her arms about Nate and hugged him tight. When she pulled away, his cheeks were flaming red. "You are the best friend I ever had." His face grew even redder.

The door to the den opened and Nick stepped inside. "Cindy, you've got friends arriving. You should be greeting them."

"I wanted to say goodbye to Nate." Cindy hurried past her father.

"We're not leaving yet," Nick said, but Cindy was halfway down the hall.

Nate started after Cindy.

"Is Cindy all right?" Nick asked, his words stopping the boy.

"She wants to stay here."

"I know. I wish we could but—" Nick couldn't explain to the child his need to return to his normal life. This time in Sweetwater was a summer holiday, never meant to extend beyond July.

Nate smiled. "Everything will work out. You'll see."

The boy's optimism panicked Nick. "You two aren't planning on running away again, are you?"

"Oh, no. We learned our lesson. Mom was so upset with me, and I don't want to worry her like that again."

Relief slumped Nick's shoulders. "Good. I don't want to worry like that again, either." The sound of children's voices floated to Nick. "We'd better see who has arrived."

Cindy tore into the wrapping paper on the gift that Nate had given her. Inside was a male doll made by Jesse that complemented the one her father had won at the auction. A grin lit the little girl's face. "I love it. Thank you, Nate." She looked toward Jesse. "And you."

"You're welcome. I have another present for you." Jesse moved through the children sitting around Cindy watching her open her gifts.

"You do?"

Jesse handed her the present she had specially picked out for the child.

Cindy took the paper off more carefully this time,

and when she revealed the gift, a look of awe graced her features. "A Bible."

"I thought you should have your own."

"Thank you." Cindy stared at the book for a long moment, her fingers tracing the gold lettering of her name, engraved on the black leather.

"I hope everyone is hungry. The pizzas are here," Boswell announced from the doorway. "We are eating out on the deck."

Ten children hopped to their feet and raced toward the back of the house. The room was emptied in less than a minute except for Nick, Jesse and Cindy.

Cindy rose more slowly and walked to Jesse. The child hugged her. "Your gifts were perfect. I love you."

Jesse smoothed Cindy's hair back from her face. Her throat swelled with emotions. Swallowing several times, she said, "I love you, too. You're a special little girl."

She tugged Jesse down closer so she could whisper in her ear, "I have a plan. The Bible will help me with it." She kissed Jesse on the cheek, then hurried from the room.

Stunned, Jesse straightened, her gaze locked with Nick's equally surprised expression. "It was Cindy's birthday, but I think I got the best gift of all."

Gone was Nick's shock to be replaced with a frown. He stalked past Jesse, leaving her alone in the living room. Nick's reaction to Cindy's statement dashed any hope that he was considering staying in Sweetwater. Why had she clung to the hope that he might have wanted to? She hadn't wanted to get involved with anyone.

Then why does it hurt so much to see his frown?

She wanted to escape to the safety of her home, away from Nick, away from the dream she was beginning to have—Nick, her, Nate and Cindy as a family. But she wouldn't. This was Cindy's special day and she was determined to stay no matter how much her heart was breaking. When they were gone tomorrow, she would put her life back together. She had done it once after Mark's death, and she had known her husband for years. This shouldn't hurt as badly. But it did.

Jesse headed into the kitchen to see if she could help Boswell. He came through the back door with an empty platter. "Need any help?"

"Yes, out there corralling eleven children." He motioned toward the deck with his head.

"Are you sure you don't want me to help get the food ready?"

"There's nothing else to do but take the cake out and dish up the ice cream."

"I can do that."

Boswell stopped reaching for the cartons of ice cream from the freezer and stared at her. "What's the problem?"

"I prefer working behind the scenes."

He studied her for a moment. "Fine. I'll take the cake out. Why don't you put some ice cream in each bowl? I'll be back in a minute to get them."

"Thank you," she said, realizing she sounded almost desperate. She was glad Boswell hadn't commented on her tone of voice.

Jesse busied herself dishing up the chocolate ice cream into red plastic bowls, then sticking red plastic spoons in each one. She had finished with the last bowl when the back door opened. She spun about with a smile, thinking it was Boswell returning for the ice creams. Instead, it was Nick.

She stiffened, her smile vanishing.

Boswell hurried around Nick and placed the bowls on the large platter, then he was gone. Nick continued to stare at her with a penetrating gaze that caused her muscles to grew tighter.

When Nick finally spoke his tone was low, void of any emotion. "Thank you for getting the clown. The children really enjoyed him, especially the animals he made out of balloons."

"No problem. Ken loves to perform."

"I also appreciate your arranging for the children from the Sunday school class to come to the party. Cindy's having a great time."

Such polite strangers, Jesse thought. Is this what it is going to come down to? To part as though they never knew each other? For close to two months Nick and Cindy had consumed her every thought and awakened moments. How was she supposed to say goodbye tomorrow and not be affected?

Because his gaze had narrowed on her face as though he were trying to read her innermost thoughts, Jesse turned away and cleaned up the mess she had made spooning the ice cream into the bowls. Her hand shook as she wiped the counter. "I'm glad the party is a success."

"Only because of you."

A wealth of emotion sounded in his voice so close

that she jumped, startled by his nearness. She whirled about. Nick stood not a foot from her and she hadn't even heard him moving toward her. For a few seconds his vulnerability that he had occasionally allowed her to see flashed into his eyes, making them dark. Automatically she started to reach for him. He saw and backed up, an arm's length away.

"I wish things could have been different between us, Jesse, but I'm no good at marriage. It's best I leave and, frankly, coming next summer wouldn't be a good option for either one of us."

With her heart cracking into pieces, she nodded. "Of course, you're right. Why subject each other to our presence? And Cindy doesn't need false hope. She's been through enough without having her think there could be more between us." She was amazed at how calm her voice was while inside she was coming apart atom by atom.

"It's not you, Jesse. It's me. I did a lousy job with my first marriage. I don't repeat mistakes."

"I see you still haven't forgiven yourself, have you?"

"I'm working on it. I'm learning to pray again." He released a heavy sigh. "My life has been so mixed up this past year. I need to get back to what is familiar. Nothing has been and I feel so lost at times."

Jesse began to gather the pieces of her heart to her; she began to erect a barrier between herself and Nick. She had to if she was going to get through his departure. "I imagine when you get back to Chicago, Sweetwater will seem like a nice but brief interlude in your life. I'm glad you're exploring your relationship with God. He will help you when you need it. Now I'd better get out there before Cindy wonders where I am." She started past him.

He grasped her arm and halted her step. "Jesse, I wish it could—"

"Hey, I enjoyed your company and friendship, but it is time to move on. I told you at the beginning I wasn't looking for anything more than friendship." She didn't tell him that had changed somewhere over the weeks she had gotten to know him. She didn't want him to feel any worse than he already did about leaving Sweet-water.

"Sure." He released his grip on her arm and watched her walk to the door.

The drill of his gaze into her back propelled Jesse to move fast before her facade crumpled and she wept for what wouldn't be…in front of him.

Out on the deck the warm July sun heated her body but didn't completely rid her of the chill that was embedded deep in her bones. She rubbed her hands up and down her arms to chase the cold away. Focusing on the eleven children sitting at the long table eating cake and ice cream, she forced herself to live for the moment—not in the past and certainly not in the future.

But as she approached Cindy, she thought that in twenty-four hours she would be gone from her life— Nick would be gone—for good. She offered the child a false smile while inside a part of her froze.

* * *

Dressed and ready to leave Sweetwater, Cindy knelt by the bed and clasped her hands. "God, I need Your help. I want Daddy to stay here. I want Daddy to marry Jesse. Please help me find a mother."

"Cindy, are you ready to go?" Nick peered around the partially opened door. "What are you doing, princess?"

Cindy rose. "Praying to God about staying here."

Nick felt as though his daughter had reached into his chest and squeezed his heart in her fist. He wished he could give her what she wanted; he just couldn't make that commitment. He was trying to put his life back together after this past difficult year. How could he uproot that life and live in Sweetwater—pursue Jesse?

He moved into the room and sat on the bed, patting the area next to him. When Cindy eased down beside him, he wrapped his arm about her shoulders and said, "Sweetheart, God does not grant every wish a person asks for."

"I know. Jesse told me He knows what is best and sometimes things happen differently than we want for a reason we may not know at the time. But I have to tell Him what I want. How important it is to me."

The hand about his heart tightened. He struggled to bring air into his lungs. He couldn't even tell Cindy they would be back next summer. After his discussion with Jesse yesterday, he knew that wouldn't be a good idea. She had so much to offer a man. What if she had found a husband by next summer? How could he live next door to her and want—

He shook that thought from his mind and stood. "Cindy, we need to get on the road. I want to be in Chicago by dark. Do you have everything in the car?"

With eyes glistening, she nodded.

Nick drew her to him and held her tightly against him for a long moment. "I love you, honey. We'll get back into our life in Chicago and everything will be fine."

Cindy pulled away, a tear rolling down her cheek. "No, it won't." She ran from the bedroom, pounding down the stairs.

Nick listened to her open the front door and slam it shut. The quiet in her bedroom taunted him, eroding his composure he had so carefully erected over the past twenty-four hours. He released a deep breath out through pursed lips and headed for his SUV.

Jesse stood in the middle of her kitchen, unsure of what to do. Through the window over the sink she glimpsed Nick's car in the driveway, packed and ready to go. She had to say goodbye to Cindy, but her legs wouldn't move toward the door. If she saw Cindy, she would see Nick and she didn't know if she could handle that encounter.

Nick and Cindy were leaving today. For good. She knew he wouldn't return next summer and that decision was for the best. How could she live next door to him and not dream of more? And the longer she was around him the more she would want that dream.

The doorbell chimed.

"I'll get it," Nate yelled and clamored down the stairs, the sound echoing through the house.

It would be Cindy coming to say goodbye. Jesse willed her legs to walk toward the entry hall. If she saw the little girl now, maybe she could avoid Nick. That thought prodded her to move faster.

"I prayed, too," her son said as Jesse came into the entry hall.

"It didn't work. Daddy and I are leaving in a few minutes." Cindy hung her head, her shoulders hunched.

"What didn't work?" Jesse asked, wanting to make sure the children weren't up to something else.

"Praying for Cindy to stay here."

"Oh," was all Jesse could think of to say. The pain in the children's eyes reflected her own hurt.

"Cindy. Cindy!" Nick shouted from his front yard.

"You'd better go. It sounds like your dad is getting worried." Hugging the child, Jesse kissed the top of her head. "I hope you'll write to us."

Cindy nodded. "I've got your e-mail address." Instead of leaving, she threw her arms around Jesse again and clung to her.

"Cindy, we need to go now." Nick appeared in the open door, a neutral expression on his face.

He was a master at hiding behind an expressionless facade, Jesse thought, wishing she could disappear. Now she must say goodbye to him as well.

"But, Daddy—"

"*Now,* young lady."

Cindy let Jesse go and stumped to the door, a frown firmly in place as she passed her father and headed down the steps. Nate went after her.

Jesse wanted to shout to her son not to leave her alone with Nick, but the words clogged in her throat. She cleared it and said, "Have a safe trip." Moving toward the door, she grasped the handle, ready to shut it as soon as possible.

Nick opened his mouth to say something but pressed it closed. For a second an emotion—regret?—flickered in his eyes, but quickly that bland expression descended. "Goodbye, Jesse." He pivoted and hurried toward his SUV.

Jesse watched for a couple of seconds too long, then finally closed the front door. Collapsing back against the wood, she squeezed her eyes shut to keep the tears inside. She would not cry over him. This was for the best. A relationship wouldn't have worked out between them because...

For the life of her she couldn't think of one reason it wouldn't. She knew there were reasons but her mind went blank. Her heart ruled and it bled.

Chapter Thirteen

"Anyone want any more iced tea?" Jesse asked, holding up the glass pitcher.

"No, I'll float home if I have a refill. As it is I spend half my time in the bathroom." Darcy set her tall glass down on the coaster.

Zoey laughed. "That's what being pregnant does to a woman. Reduces her to checking out every rest room everywhere she goes. I should know. I've got three kids."

"That, or standing on the scales moaning about all the pounds she is gaining." Tanya took the pitcher and poured some more tea.

"True. I'm already gaining faster than I should, and I'm only three and a half months pregnant. What in the world am I going to look like in a few more months? The Goodyear blimp?"

"I got to raise three children without the wonders of being pregnant. I think I lucked out after listening to you all." Beth grabbed a chocolate chip cookie from the platter on Jesse's coffee table.

"Yeah, in a few months you won't know what to do with all your free time," Zoey said.

"I can't believe Daniel's finally graduating from high school. It's been a long battle to get to this place, but after he goes off to college in January, I'm a free woman."

Jesse sank down onto a lounge chair, tired, her heart not really into this weekly Saturday afternoon gabfest even if the four other women were her good friends. She listened to them talk about school starting, raising children and dieting, all subjects she usually commented on. But not this time.

Darcy had started this circle of friends because of Tanya's and Zoey's needs a few months back. Now Jesse found she needed their support, but wasn't sure how to ask. She'd never been good at asking for help.

Darcy cocked her head and looked at Jesse. "You're awfully quiet. What's up? Nick?"

Leave it to her best friend from high school to home in on what was eating at her, Jesse thought and said, "Yes. They've been gone a month and I still think about him every day. I'm even dreaming about him." She gestured toward her face. "Hence the tired lines."

"Did you tell him how you felt about him?"

"What do you mean?"

"Did you tell him you loved him?"

"I don't—I mean, I love Cindy and care for Nick. I—"

Darcy held up her hand. "Hold it right there. You love

him, Jesse." She motioned toward her face. "Hence the tired lines."

"Tell him. How can he make a good decision about the future without all the information?" Beth picked up her glass, running her finger along its edge.

"I can't call him. I don't have his number. It's unlisted."

"You looked it up?" Tanya asked, snatching up a cookie and taking a bite.

Jesse nodded. "One night right after he left. I wanted to make sure he got home okay." That was the feeblest excuse because Cindy had e-mailed them when she had arrived.

"There are other ways of contacting him. You know where he lives. You have his e-mail address. You could call him at work. Why haven't you tried harder?" Beth took a sip of her drink, then replaced her glass on the coaster.

If her friends had said this to her two weeks ago, Jesse would have broken down and cried. But she didn't have any tears left in her. Her emotions were dried up. Where her heart beat there was emptiness. "I don't want to be hurt anymore. I made it through Mark's death. I thought I had protected myself against that kind of pain. I was wrong. Nick made me relive it all over again when he left. I only knew him for two months and I fell hard for him. Those feelings scare me."

"It means you are alive. Haven't you heard love is what makes the world go around?"

"That coming from the only married woman in the group," Jesse said, a headache beginning to form behind her eyes.

"Hey, Zoey and Tanya are still married." The instant Darcy said those words, she clamped her hand over her mouth, her eyes wide. "I'm so sorry, Zoey and Tanya."

Zoey smiled but there was a sadness in her eyes. "I am married. That is a fact. Ignoring it won't change it. Just because my husband has disappeared, is probably dead, doesn't mean you all have to watch what you say around me. It's been a year."

Tanya finished chewing her cookie. "Even though my husband is in prison, I'll stand behind him. I made a vow to God that I would."

"We're quite a group, aren't we?" Beth shifted, uncrossing her legs.

"We are. I appreciate your advice and I will think about trying to call him. I don't think it will make any difference that I love him. We live too far apart."

"That can be changed. He could live here. You could live there." Zoey brushed her long hair behind her shoulders.

"I'm not talking about mere miles. He hasn't been able to forgive himself or his wife and without that I don't think we could ever be truly happy. His past would come between us."

"Let's pray." Beth held out her hands.

Everyone joined hands and bowed their heads.

"Dear Heavenly Father, bless this group with Your wisdom. We give You thanks for all You have done for us. Please guide us in what needs to be done and especially help Jesse through this difficult time. Amen."

Beth looked up at Jesse. "Talk to Nick. Let him know how you feel."

As Jesse cleaned up after her friends left, she thought back over their advice. E-mailing was out of the question—too impersonal. Should she call Nick at work? Or, should she go to see him? Her hands trembled as she put the dishes in the sink. If she did anything, she should do it in person. But could she see Nick again? What if he had moved on, didn't care? How could she face his indifference?

"That will be all. Go home, folks." Nick closed the file on his desk and waited until his three vice presidents filed out of his office before he allowed the exhaustion he felt to show.

His shoulders hunched, he collapsed back in his chair and spun around to view the lights of Chicago. Nighttime. He should have been home an hour ago, but the meeting had gone over and now he wouldn't arrive before Cindy was in bed. He liked reading to her before she went to sleep, but Boswell would in his place. That thought didn't settle the restlessness he experienced more and more since coming home to Chicago.

Nothing satisfied him—not even work. The only time he felt remotely at peace was when he attended church with Cindy. When he stepped through the sanctuary's doors, he felt as though he wasn't alone in this world—that God was truly with him. The first Sunday had surprised him. Now he looked forward to going to church and experiencing the peace in his soul.

Nick gathered up some papers to review and stuck them in his briefcase. Quickly he headed for the elevator and the car that would be waiting for him downstairs in front of his office building.

On the short drive home he laid his head on the cushion and closed his eyes, trying to remember a night when he had gotten enough sleep. Not since Sweetwater. Not since his dreams were haunted by Jesse—by the promise her laugh brought to him. She had shown him the way back to the Lord. She had given him his life back with his daughter. What was he doing in Chicago?

When the driver stopped in front of his apartment building, Nick climbed out and hurried to the penthouse elevator. Maybe Cindy was still awake. He needed to hold his daughter. To see her smile. To chase away the demons that plagued him.

Inside his apartment that took up the whole top floor of the building, he saw the skyline of Chicago lit up with lights, the lake beyond. He didn't stop to admire the view but tossed his briefcase on the large round table in the middle of the foyer. He strode through the elegant living room with its drapes open, down the hall toward Cindy's room.

Boswell met him as he came out of his daughter's room. "I just read her a story. Even though she was fighting sleep, I believe she is still up."

"Good." Nick stepped around Boswell and peered into Cindy's room.

His daughter had slipped from between the sheets and knelt beside the bed. She folded her hands and said,

"God, I almost forgot to pray to You. Please bless Daddy, Boswell, Jesse—"

Nick didn't want to interrupt his daughter while praying. He was glad she had added praying into her nightly routine. He even found himself ending his day with a prayer to the Lord. He remembered his first few awkward attempts. But Jesse had once said to him that praying was like having a conversation with the Lord. It didn't have to be fancy—just plain and simple and from the heart. After recalling that advice it had been easy for him.

"—and God, don't forget my request for a new mother. Please make sure Mommy doesn't mind. I still love her, but I want someone to make my daddy happy because he's the best daddy in the world and he deserves it. I want Jesse."

His throat constricted. He wanted Jesse, too. Why hadn't he seen what she had done for him and Cindy? Why had he run away from the best thing that had happened to him? Because he was afraid he couldn't make Jesse happy as she deserved. Because he hadn't been a good husband in his first marriage.

"Daddy, you're home!"

Nick forced his attention on his daughter, smiling and walking into her bedroom. "I couldn't let you go to sleep without saying good-night to me."

When he bent down to give her a kiss, Cindy threw her arms around his neck. "I've already had a story, but you can read me another one."

"I can, can I? Which one?"

Cindy grabbed the book that Boswell had obviously been reading from her nightstand. "This one. He read chapter five."

"So I should read the next chapter." Nick sat on the bed and let Cindy snuggle against him.

He opened the book to chapter six and began to read. Halfway through the second page he noticed that Cindy was asleep. He slipped his arm from around her shoulders and stood. After tucking her in, he grabbed Cindy's Bible and left her bedroom, glancing back at his precious daughter as he switched off the overhead light, something she liked left on until she fell asleep.

Wearily he walked into the living room and sat in a chair near the bank of floor-to-ceiling windows. He stared out into the dark night, lit with thousands of lights from the many buildings. He had some thinking to do. He could continue with his life the way it was— only half full—or he could make a change, a drastic change.

He opened the Bible and read through the story of Christ. The words of hope took root in his heart and grew as the Lord's message to His people flowed through his mind, stirring his faith that had laid dormant for so long. When he finished reading Luke's account of Jesus's life on Earth, Nick closed the book and absorbed the peace he felt. He knew what he had to do. What if Jesse rejected him? What if she had gone on with her life never giving him another thought? How could he face her disinterest?

He sighed, staring unseeing at the darkness beyond

his windows. Exhaustion clung to him like a wet blanket. His eyelids grew heavy. He closed them and leaned back, relaxing in the lounge chair. Sleep whisked him into the land of dreams….

Someone shook his arm. He heard a child's voice through the fog and tried to focus on it.

"Daddy, wake up. What are you doing out here?"

Slowly Nick opened his eyes and looked at his daughter standing at his side with her forehead creased, her eyes dark with concern.

"Are you all right?" Cindy held her Bible clasped to her chest.

He straightened in the lounge chair, blinking at the bright light streaming through the windows. "What time is it?"

"Eight."

"Eight!" He started to rise, stopped himself and settled back into the chair. He remembered the dream he'd had the night before. It was Jesse and his wedding and his daughter stood at Jesse's left while Nate stood at his right. The sense of well-being still encased him with satisfaction. The dream had confirmed what he must do if he was ever going to be happy.

He patted his lap and Cindy leaped up into it. "Honey, would you mind if I went away for a few days?"

She frowned. "Where?"

"To Sweetwater."

"I want to go."

"If all goes well, you'll be going back to Sweetwater permanently. I'm going to ask Jesse if she will marry me."

Cindy didn't say anything for a good minute, then she let out a holler that Nick was sure they heard on the street below. This was the right decision. He knew it in his heart.

"I'm sorry, Mr. Blackburn is out of the office for the next few days. May I take a message?"

Jesse sank down onto the chair by the phone. "Yes, tell him—no, I'll call back later." She hung up, disappointed and relieved at the same time.

Wiping the perspiration from her brow, she thought about the wisdom of telling him how she felt over the phone. Maybe she should go to Chicago and see him in person? It had taken her several days since meeting with her friends on Saturday even to get the courage up to make the call to his office.

Lord, help me. I don't know what to do.

She heard the front door opening and closing. Nate yelled he was home and then the sound of him charging up the stairs floated to her. Still she couldn't decide how to proceed with Nick. She chewed on her bottom lip and stared at the floor as though the tiles had an answer written on them.

Someone cleared his throat. Jesse looked up, her heart hammering against her rib cage. Nick.

Frozen, she stared at him as hard as she had the floor. Was he a mirage?

Then he moved farther into the kitchen, a smile deep in his eyes. "Hello, Jesse."

His words came to her as though they were spoken

to her from afar. Still she couldn't move. What was happening didn't seem real.

"Jesse?" Concern darkened his gaze.

She blinked, breaking the trancelike state she was in. She surged to her feet, words tumbling through her mind. "Nick, what are you doing here? I just called your office and they said you were gone for a few days."

"I am gone. I'm here." His mouth lifted in a lopsided grin, humor lighting his eyes.

"I mean—I—" The words were gone as she peered at his handsome face—a face she had seen many times over the past month in her dreams.

"You called my office? Why?"

With three strides he was only a foot from her, so close she could reach out and touch him. Feeling weak, she backed up against the desk, clutching its edge to keep her from collapsing. "Why are you here?"

"I couldn't stay away any longer."

"Why?" Her heart increased its beat, so rapidly that she kept her grip on the desk. She still couldn't believe he was here in her house in Sweetwater.

"It's simple. I love you, Jesse Bradshaw. I have for quite some time, but have been too much of a fool to do something about it."

She collapsed back on the desk, her legs trembling. "You love me?"

He clasped her arms. "Yes. I love you. Now will you tell me why you were calling my office? Is something wrong?"

She reached up to touch his face, to trace his mouth.

"I didn't have your private home number and I needed to talk to you so I tried your office."

"Why did you need to talk with me?" Nick cuddled closer, bringing her flat against him.

She drew in a deep breath of his distinctive scent of lime and relished it. "I felt I should tell you how I felt about you."

He brushed his lips across hers and whispered, "And how do you feel about me?"

She framed his face and looked deep into his eyes. "I love you, Nick Blackburn, with all my heart. I didn't make that clear to you before you left. I should have. You need all the facts to make the best decision."

"I agree." He laid his forehead against hers, love shining in his eyes. "I'm a little slow when it comes to my emotions, but I finally figured out that just because I wasn't a success at my first marriage, I shouldn't doom myself to loneliness, especially when I have a wonderful woman like you to love and who loves me."

"Have you forgiven yourself and Brenda?"

"Last night I listened to my daughter pray to God asking for a new mother. But she also told God how much she loved her mother and to make sure she didn't mind she wanted a new one. That made me start thinking. Even though Brenda wasn't the right wife for me, she gave me a beautiful daughter and she loved Cindy. She was a good mother at least. So how can I hate someone who gave me Cindy?"

"And yourself?"

"If God can forgive me, then I can forgive myself."

"Oh, Nick." Jesse wound her arms around him and pulled him toward her.

His mouth claimed hers in a deep kiss that rocked her to her soul. Sensations she had thought she would never experience again after Mark's death flooded her.

"Do you two have to do that?"

Nick jerked back. Jesse looked toward the doorway to find her son standing there with a toy sailboat in his arms.

"Nate Bradshaw, were you eavesdropping?"

"I waited and waited. Finally I decided to come see if you two had made up. I want to show Nick the new sailboat I made. I thought we could sail it on the lake."

"Sure. Can you give me a minute with your mom?"

"Are you moving back here?" Nate asked as he headed for the back door.

"I hope so."

"You are?" Jesse asked, her surprise slipping out, suddenly remembering that barrier to their relationship.

Nick glanced at Nate who was still in the kitchen, then turned toward Jesse. "Yes, if you'll agree to marry me. I can run Blackburn Industries from here. Besides, I have decided to cut back on working so much." He took her into his arms again. "I want to devote my time to my new family."

"Mom, tell him yes so we can go to the lake and sail my boat."

Jesse laughed. "Yes, I'll marry you."

Her son's shout of joy filled the kitchen as Nick kissed her so thoroughly that her toes curled.

Epilogue

"Do I look all right?"

Jesse fixed the pink satin bow in Cindy's hair, then stepped back to appraise her maid of honor. "You look perfect, honey."

The child took her bouquet of pink roses and clasped them in front of her. "You're so beautiful, Jesse."

Her throat tight, Jesse said, "Thank you."

In the mirror she saw herself as Cindy did, wearing a pale pink silk suit with pink pearl buttons on the jacket and a straight skirt that fell to just below her knees. She picked up her bouquet of white orchids tied together with a pink bow.

"Are you ready?" Jesse asked, stepping into her two-inch high heels that had been dyed to match her suit.

With a nod Cindy led the way to the sanctuary where Nick and Gramps would be standing with Reverend Collins. From the back of the church Jesse surveyed the small gathering of friends and family. Nate, dressed in a black suit with a gray tie, offered her his arm to walk her down the aisle. A few stray strands of his hair stuck out and Jesse took a moment to brush them into place.

He squirmed. "Mom, Nick's waiting!"

"I know. A few extra seconds won't make a difference. He isn't going anywhere."

When Nate's hair was tamed, Jesse nodded to the organist to begin the wedding march and she and her son started down the aisle following Cindy. Jesse smiled at her circle of friends in the front pew. Darcy sat between Joshua and Sean while Zoey was holding baby Tara between her two other children, Mandy and Blake. Beth took up one end of the pew with Tanya at the other end. Crystal was in her wheelchair next to Tanya. Everyone's expressions reflected the joy Jesse was feeling as she walked toward the man she loved, toward her new life with Nick.

The sunlight streamed through the round window above the altar and shone on the cross that hung from the ceiling. Jesse looked heavenward. *Thank you, God, for bringing me Nick and Cindy. Thank You for giving me a second chance at love.*

Jesse stopped next to Nick and took his hand as they faced the reverend. Together, a couple, a family.

Reverend Collins spoke of love and marriage, but all Jesse could see or hear were Nick's face and his words as he repeated his vows. Her world centered around him and her family.

When the wedding ceremony was over, instead of

leaving the sanctuary, Jesse and Nick greeted their friends who surrounded them with their well wishes.

In the midst of people Cindy tugged on Jesse's arm to get her attention.

"What's wrong, sweetie?"

"Can I call you Mom now?"

Jesse hugged Cindy to her, a sudden well of tears misting her eyes. "I would be honored to be your mother."

* * * * *

Dear Reader,

The story of Jesse and Nick in *A Mother for Cindy* came easily to me. It seemed to flow from my thoughts to the written page. The story is about a lonely man who finds his way back to God. There are times in people's lives when they doubt the Lord, often when something difficult has happened to test them. Sadly some turn away and never find their way back to the Lord. Others are lucky and have a special person to show them the importance of God's love and power. They come back to God a richer person, for their journey strengthens them.

I love hearing from my readers. You can contact me at P.O. Box 2074, Tulsa, OK 74101, or MDaley50@aol.com.

May God bless you,

Margaret Daley

Love Inspired

Maya Logan has always thought of her boss, Greg Garrison, as a hard-nosed type of guy. But when a tornado strikes their small Kansas town, Greg is quick to help however he can, including rebuilding her home. Maya soon discovers that he's building a home for them to share.

HEARTWARMING INSPIRATIONAL ROMANCE

Love Inspired

Healing the Boss's Heart

Valerie Hansen

AFTER the STORM

Look for

Healing the Boss's Heart

by

Valerie Hansen

AFTER the STORM

Steeple Hill®

Available July wherever books are sold.

www.SteepleHill.com

LI87536

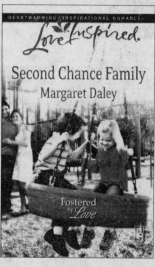

REQUEST YOUR FREE BOOKS!

2 FREE INSPIRATIONAL NOVELS
PLUS 2
FREE
MYSTERY GIFTS

YES! Please send me 2 FREE Love Inspired® novels and my 2 FREE mystery gifts (gifts are worth about $10). After receiving them, if I don't wish to receive any more books, I can return the shipping statement marked "cancel". If I don't cancel, I will receive 4 brand-new novels every month and be billed just $4.24 per book in the U.S. or $4.74 per book in Canada. That's a savings of over 20% off the cover price. It's quite a bargain! Shipping and handling is just 50¢ per book.* I understand that accepting the 2 free books and gifts places me under no obligation to buy anything. I can always return a shipment and cancel at any time. Even if I never buy another book, the two free books and gifts are mine to keep forever.

113 IDN EYK2 313 IDN EYLE

Name   (PLEASE PRINT)

Address   Apt. #

City   State/Prov.   Zip/Postal Code

Signature (if under 18, a parent or guardian must sign)

Mail to Steeple Hill Reader Service:
IN U.S.A.: P.O. Box 1867, Buffalo, NY 14240-1867
IN CANADA: P.O. Box 609, Fort Erie, Ontario L2A 5X3

Not valid to current subscribers of Love Inspired books.

Want to try two free books from another series?
Call 1-800-873-8635 or visit www.morefreebooks.com

* Terms and prices subject to change without notice. Prices do not include applicable taxes. Sales tax applicable in N.Y. Canadian residents will be charged applicable provincial taxes and GST. Offer not valid in Quebec. This offer is limited to one order per household. All orders subject to approval. Credit or debit balances in a customer's account(s) may be offset by any other outstanding balance owed by or to the customer. Please allow 4 to 6 weeks for delivery. Offer available while quantities last.

Your Privacy: Steeple Hill Books is committed to protecting your privacy. Our Privacy Policy is available online at www.SteepleHill.com or upon request from the Reader Service. From time to time we make our lists of customers available to reputable third parties who may have a product or service of interest to you. If you would prefer we not share your name and address, please check here. ☐

LIREG09

Love Inspired
HISTORICAL
INSPIRATIONAL HISTORICAL ROMANCE

Actress Hannah Southerland's work is unseemly, but her loyalties are strong. When her sister Rachel foolishly elopes, Hannah is determined to bring her home—even joining forces with Reverend Beau O'Toole, brother of Rachel's paramour. Beau wants a traditional wife, which Hannah is not. But this unconventional woman could be his ideal partner—in life and in faith.

Look for
Hannah's Beau
by
RENEE RYAN

Available July wherever books are sold.

Steeple
Hill®

www.SteepleHill.com

LIH82816

HEARTWARMING INSPIRATIONAL ROMANCE

Experience stories
centered on love and faith
with a variety of romances
just for you,
with 10 books every month!

Love Inspired®:
Enjoy four contemporary,
heartwarming romances every month.

Love Inspired® Historical:
Travel to a different time with two powerful
and engaging stories of romance, adventure
and faith every month.

Love Inspired® Suspense:
Enjoy four contemporary tales of intrigue
and romance every month.